"Ha[w]...

"Fast, ...
a ...

—Bestselling author Christina Dodd

PRAISE FOR THE DUCHESS DIARIES SERIES

How to Capture a Countess

"A delightful, sprightly romp is what Hawkins does best, and when she sets her witty tale in Scotland and adds a charming castle and an engaging cast of characters, readers have the beginning of an appealing new series."

—*RT Book Reviews* (4 stars)

"Hawkins delivers a fast-paced, robust historical novel filled with wit and romance!"

—*Night Owl Reviews*

"Readers will enjoy this jocular tale as Rose and Sin fight, fuss, and fall in love!"

—*Genre Go Round Reviews*

"A beautifully written romance filled with passion, zest, and humor."

—*Addicted to Romance*

"The wildly unconventional courtship of Sin and Rose is spiced by a chemistry that practically leaps off the pages. Readers will be thrilled to every witty repartee between these reluctant lovers."

—*Coffee Time Romance & More*

A Most Dangerous Profession

"Spellbinding . . . one thrilling adventure after another."

—*Single Titles*

"Complex characters and plot, a parallel story line, a quest, two star-crossed lovers, and fast pacing make this a most delightful read."

—*RT Book Reviews* (4 stars)

Scandal in Scotland

"A humorous, fast-paced dramatic story that's filled with sensual tension. Hawkins's passionate, intelligent characters make it impossible to put down."

—*RT Book Reviews* (4½ stars, Top Pick)

"Rollicking good fun from beginning to end! Pure, vintage Hawkins!"

—*Romance and More*

One Night in Scotland

"Hawkins begins the Hurst Amulet series with a keeper. Readers will be delighted by the perfect pacing, the humorous dialogue, and the sizzling sensual romance."

—*RT Book Reviews* (4½ stars, Top Pick)

"A lively romp, the perfect beginning to [Hawkins's] new series."

—*Booklist*

"Hawkins is one of the most talented historical romance writers out there."

—*Romance Junkies* (5 stars)

"Charming and witty."

—*Publishers Weekly*

"An adventurous romance filled with laughter, passion, and emotion . . . mystery, threats, and plenty of sexual tension, plus an engaging premise which will keep you thoroughly entertained during each highly captivating scene. . . . *One Night in Scotland* holds your attention from beginning to end."

—*Single Titles*

"With its creative writing, interesting characters, and well-crafted situations and dialogue, *One Night in Scotland* is an excellent read. Be assured it lives up to all the virtues one has learned to expect from this talented writer."

—*Romance Reviews Today*

Also by Karen Hawkins

Available from Pocket Books

KAREN HAWKINS

How to Pursue a Princess

Pocket Books

New York   London   Toronto   Sydney   New Delhi

Pocket Books
A Division of Simon & Schuster, Inc.
1230 Avenue of the Americas
New York, NY 10020

This book is a work of fiction. Any references to historical events, real people, or real places are used fictitiously. Other names, characters, places, and events are products of the author's imagination, and any resemblance to actual events or places or persons, living or dead, is entirely coincidental.

First Pocket Books paperback edition June 2013

POCKET and colophon are registered trademarks of Simon & Schuster, Inc.

For information about special discounts for bulk purchases, please contact Simon & Schuster Special Sales at 1-866-506-1949 or business@simonandschuster.com.

The Simon & Schuster Speakers Bureau can bring authors to your live event. For more information or to book an event, contact the Simon & Schuster Speakers Bureau at 1-866-248-3049 or visit our website at www.simonspeakers.com.

Manufactured in the United States of America

10 9 8 7 6 5 4 3 2 1

ISBN 978-1-4516-8520-6
ISBN 978-1-4516-8521-3 (ebook)

To Hot Cop:

Thank you for being such a terrific Writer's Husband and listening to me discuss (at length) my characters' lives as if they were real people, and for accepting without too much question that, for the moment, they are.

Acknowledgments

A huge acknowledgment to Sheridan Stancliff of SheridanInk.com for her invaluable help in doing that most impossible of all tasks for a writer: getting organized. Also, thank you for finding so many wonderful and creative ways for me to connect with my amazing readers. You rawk, sister.

One

From the Diary of the Duchess of Roxburghe

Since, while under my roof, my goddaughter Miss Rose Balfour met and married my great-nephew the Earl of Sinclair, people have been whispering that I am the first word in matchmaking—the Perfectress of Romance, the Grand Curator of Courtship, and (my favorite) the Duchess of Hearts. Naturally, I'm well aware that these titles are ridiculous, for I had little to do with Rose and Sin's romance; it happened on its own with very little assistance from me.

Except when needed, of course.

Those who know me best realize that I never interfere in the lives of others. Not unless they need it and are crying out for help in such a way that one cannot ignore their desperate pleas.

For example, take Rose's sister, the lovely Miss Lily Balfour. If ever a young woman was in need of a husband, it is she, and I'm certain she's begging for help, but is just too proud to do it aloud. Fortunately, I am not deaf to her silent pleas and am determined that she will accept one of the many invitations I've sent to her. So far, though, all of them have been politely refused.

However, I shall not despair, for I'm sure there must be a way to help the poor, desperate lass.

Caith Manor, Scotland
May 2, 1813

Lily Balfour blinked, but the words on the paper still swam before her eyes, numbers and words merging into a befuddled mess. "I don't understand. How did this happen?"

Pacing before the fire, Papa shook his head, his white hair standing on end where he'd run his hands through it. "Och, I don't know. I just don't know." He was showing his age more than usual this evening, worry etching deep lines on his face. "I didn't realize the terms were so dire. Lord Kirk said—"

"What?" Dahlia, who'd been sitting quietly to one side of the fireplace, stared at their Papa. "You borrowed funds from Lord Kirk?"

Lord Kirk was their neighbor, a wealthy, grumpy, taciturn widower who'd been horribly scarred across one side of his face by an accident of some sort—Lily wasn't sure how, for he never spoke of it. In fact, he rarely spoke about anything or to anyone . . . except to her sister Dahlia.

Some months ago, Lily had discovered that somehow Dahlia had been lured into speaking with Lord

Kirk, even visiting his library and talking for hours about books they'd read. Neither Lily nor her oldest sister, Rose, had been happy about the relationship; warm, friendly, lovely Dahlia could do far, far better than such a grumpy, taciturn man. Fortunately, before many weeks had passed, Lord Kirk had said something insulting about Papa, and the always-loyal Dahlia had broken off all contact with the man, which had relieved everyone.

"How *could* you?" Dahlia demanded now, her eyes blazing.

Papa winced. "Now don't look like that. I planned on paying back the funds. If things had gone well, you'd never even have known that I'd borrowed them."

Lily waved the loan papers. "Apparently 'things' didn't go as planned, and now you owe the funds *and* the interest, *and* a penalty, and—oh, Papa!"

He rubbed a hand over his face. "What have I done? I should have paid more attention, but—Lily, I don't know how it is, but I could have sworn the percent was far less than what it is."

"You didn't read the terms?"

He flushed. "Of course I did. I just don't remember them."

Lily dropped the papers on the table and exchanged a worried glance with her sister, who looked as bemused as Lily felt.

Dahlia, always the pragmatist, folded her hands in her lap, her brow furrowed. "Papa, why did you take out this note? However did you spend three thousand pounds?"

He wrung his hands. "Oh, that. Well. I—I wanted you both to have a season in London, as your sister once had."

Lily shook her head. "Nonsense. We've never asked for such a thing."

"Besides," Dahlia added, "Rose promised to take us into society when she returns from her honeymoon in three months."

"Yes, but that's so far away," he said, looking a bit desperate. "You both should have your season now, so I borrowed some funds and invested them, knowing that if all turned out well, then I could surprise you."

"Humph," Lily said.

Dahlia lifted her brows in disbelief. "What did you invest in?"

He gulped, but said in a defiant tone, "Flowers." A known horticulturalist, his undying passion was his pursuit of the perfect rose—one he intended on calling the Balfour Rich Red.

"You didn't!" Lily said.

Dahlia's brows snapped down. "This loan had nothing to do with paying for us to have a season, did it? You just wanted the funds for your flowers."

Papa didn't reply.

Lily took a steadying breath. "How did you convince Lord Kirk to loan you such an amount for something as far-fetched as rose development?"

"I told Kirk it was for a personal matter. Being a gentleman, he didn't ask for more."

"So he made you this large loan for an unknown reason?" Dahlia asked, suspicion still bright on her face.

"Well . . . yes." Papa raked a hand through his hair. "It was a gentleman's agreement, so I thought that if I couldn't pay, he'd simply renegotiate the note. But instead . . . ."

Dahlia's eyes sparkled with anger as she turned to Lily. "I think less of Lord Kirk for agreeing to such a ludicrous arrangement. He had to know Papa'd never be able to repay such a sum."

"One would think," Lily agreed. "Papa, you've said time and again that the man's the devil."

Papa held out his hands in a supplicating manner. "He's the only wealthy man I know."

"And so you knowingly entered a devil's arrangement." Dahlia's voice shook. "All to order yet more flowers."

"And build a new hothouse and repair the others." When his daughters continued to glower at him, he added rather lamely, "Which I only did so that I could send both of you to London for a season, of course."

"Balderdash!" Dahlia said.

Lily pinched the bridge of her nose. "I cannot believe this."

His shoulders slumped. "I know, it was madness. But I had good intentions."

"Good intentions won't repay a loan," Lily returned sharply. "If you owed those funds to anyone else, I'd say we should throw ourselves on their mercy and ask for more time, but since it's Lord Kirk—" She shook her head.

"He'd refuse," Dahlia finished in a stiff tone.

"It's all my fault." Papa clasped his hands behind his back and dipped his head, his pacing feverish. "I've made such a mull of things. Now that I've read the papers, I can see that the terms of the loan weren't what I'd hoped, but—"

"Not what you'd hoped?" Lily said, unable to help herself. "Papa, I don't know how you planned to repay the *interest*, much less the principal. The terms are outrageous. In order to meet this loan, we have to find three thousand pounds in one month!"

"Lily, please, you must understand; I thought that with a new greenhouse, and more funds to invest in buds, I could finally afford to have the exotics shipped from China that I need to develop the Balfour Rich Red. Once that was done, we'd be able to sell the roses for a phenomenal profit. Why, just look at how well the Balfour rose has been selling."

"Well?" Lily almost choked. "Over the last three years, you've made a total of"—she picked up the ledger and flipped to the last ink-spattered page—"three hundred pounds and six shillings."

Papa looked startled. "Is that all? Good God. That's—" Papa raked a hand through his white hair, mussing it even more. "Oh dear."

Lily closed the ledger. "Perhaps if we gave some of the funds back, then Lord Kirk would find it in his heart to—"

"It's gone," Papa said sadly.

"All three thousand pounds?"

He nodded miserably. "It seemed so much at first, but then one of the greenhouses sprang a leak, which cost much more than I expected, and then there were issues with the water pipes we had installed for the mister, which cost—" He shuddered. "And all of that meant weeks of delay. By that time, your sister Rose had gotten engaged and then married, and that took yet more time from my work and—" He spread his hands helplessly. "Time passed and then . . ."

"The note came due," Dahlia finished.

"It's past due." Lily tapped her finger on the paper. "Two months ago."

Dahlia blinked. "Then why are we just now finding out about this?"

Papa sighed. "I was hoping Lord Kirk would forget about it."

"You hoped he'd forget a loan for three thousand pounds?"

"Well, yes," Papa said defensively. "Since I accepted the loan, he's never said a word. Not once. But then—" Papa sighed. "This morning, he visited after breakfast."

"Kirk was here?" Dahlia's voice cracked on the last word.

"Yes, while you were still abed. I had just finished

breakfast and had come out into the foyer, and he arrived as I was gathering my coat and hat. He was very polite in his request—uneasy, even, as if he didn't wish to ask for the funds at all."

"He must need the money," Dahlia said. "Odd, because he certainly seems well-heeled. His house is of the first stare, and he has so many horses and carriages."

"I wondered that myself."

"So Kirk asked for repayment," Lily said impatiently. "What did you tell him?"

"That I could pay it, of course, just not right away. He said that so long as I repaid him within the next month or so, all would be well. He actually seemed a bit embarrassed about the whole thing."

"He should be," Dahlia said sharply. "Especially after charging such an exorbitant amount of interest."

"But it's worse than mere interest." Lily tapped the note again with one finger. "Not only has Papa made a loan he can't repay, but he used Caith Manor as collateral."

"*What?*" Eyes wide, Dahlia turned to Papa. "It's not yours! There's an entail on the house and land."

Papa brightened. "Then the note won't stand?"

Lily grimaced. "Papa, it means that not only do you owe the funds, but if Lord Kirk sets forth a complaint, you could end up in gaol for using something that's not yours as collateral."

"Prison?" Papa looked as if someone had just hit him in the stomach. "Good God."

Dahlia pressed a hand to her temple. "Oh no!"

Silence filled the room, broken only by the crackling fire. Lily wished Rose were home; as the oldest sister, she had always been the one to solve their problems. But now that Rose was on the Continent with her new husband, Lily was left to handle the problems that beset their little family—a task she wasn't certain she was ready for, especially now that Papa had thrown them into such a fix.

Lily's gaze flickered to her sewing basket at her feet, and she had to curl her fingers into her palms to keep from reaching for it. Just this morning she'd taken the bodice from an old gown made of pink jaconet and, turning it inside out so that it could serve as a lining, was fitting it inside a shell of brown kerseymere. Once she'd added long sleeves and trimmings, it would be a fashionable spencer.

Nothing gave Lily more pleasure—or peace—than sewing. She was good at it, too; her sisters were forever telling her that she was better than any Edinburgh modiste.

It was a pity she couldn't just set up a modiste's shop and earn the funds to pay Papa's loans. Sadly, though she'd enjoy it very, very much, it would take years to gain enough clientele to pay back such a huge amount.

Papa sighed. "I'd thought to ask Rose's new husband for enough money to cover the loan, but they left for their honeymoon before I could think of a way to do so."

"I'm glad you didn't," Lily said sharply. "Lord Sinclair and Rose are deeply in love. It would have been awkward if you'd asked for money the second she wed him."

"I know, I know." A hint of wistfulness colored Papa's voice. "Although I doubt Sinclair would have thought it so much. Three thousand pounds is but a pittance to a man like him."

"But not to Rose."

"Yes, yes. You're right, of course." Papa sank into a chair across from them, his shoulders sagging. "I wish I'd never borrowed those funds."

Dahlia took a deep breath. "As do we all. I suppose . . . I suppose I could talk to Lord Kirk."

"*No*," Lily said.

"Now wait a moment." Papa eyed Dahlia thoughtfully. "Kirk is fond of Dahlia. Perhaps she can—"

"He *was* fond of her," Lily corrected. "They had a falling out."

Dahlia's face was bright pink. "I don't mind speaking to him again if I must."

"There!" Papa interjected, looking hopeful.

"No, no, and *no*." Lily sent Papa a stern look. "I won't have it."

Papa read her meaning in her gaze. "Yes," he said abruptly. "You're right. I was just thinking— But it's best if we find another way." He looked at his daughters regretfully. "I should have never involved the two of you; this is my fault. I must find the answer somehow. And if it comes to prison, then that's where I'll go and—"

"No," Dahlia said. "I will talk to Lord Kirk. It's the only way." When Lily started to speak, Dahlia added, "It won't be a sacrifice. He's a little gruff, but he has a surprising sense of humor and"—Dahlia fidgeted with a button on her pocket—"he wishes to marry me."

Lily's heart sank. *Oh no.* "You never said a word."

"Because I refused him, so there was no need. Perhaps if I agree, then he will see his way to forgive the note and—"

"No," Papa said. "Good God, Dahlia, he's twice your age!"

"No, he's not. He's only eight years older."

"Eight?" Lily couldn't keep the disbelief from her voice. "I find that hard to believe. But whatever his age, he's too old for you. Besides, if anyone is to get us out of this predicament through an advantageous marriage, it should be me."

"You?" Papa looked surprised. "But you've always said you'd never marry."

"Because I've never met anyone who has sparked my interest, nor has anyone shown any interest in me, which is a perfect set of happenstances. But now that Rose is gone, I'm the oldest, so it's up to me to resolve this issue."

Dahlia looked troubled. "Lily, you can't."

"Why not?" Lily forced a smile. *It's not as if I would*

*have ever opened a modiste's shop, anyway. That is a
mere dream.* "I've been thinking lately that I'd like
to taste a more fanciful way of life. Just think of the
parties and gowns, amusements and luxurious apart-
ments. And once I'm wed to a wealthy gentleman,
Dahlia can come and stay with me." The more Lily
thought about it, the more certain she was that this
was the way to proceed.

Besides, what other options were there?

Dahlia clasped her hands in her lap. "No, Lily.
That sounds lovely, but who would you marry? There
are no single gentlemen except Lord Kirk for miles
and miles."

"Our godmother is forever inviting me to her social
events—she invited me to a house party which begins
quite soon, in fact—so the means of meeting an eligible *parti* is readily available. I should respond to her
invitation as soon as I can." She frowned. "Where
is it? I tucked it away somewhere." Lily stood and
crossed to the small tray that sat upon a side table.
She pulled out a stack of correspondence and looked
though it. "Here it is!" She waved a thick missive written on heavy pink paper.

"I don't know about this." Dahlia's voice was
tinged with concern. "While it sounds like a simple
matter to find and marry a wealthy man, especially
with the help of our godmother, I wonder if the thing
can be accomplished in such a short time. We only
have a month or so."

"Which means that I cannot dawdle."

"But, Lily, what if you don't meet anyone worth falling in love with at the duchess's house party? What then?"

"I shall leave the quality of available suitors to our godmother. She always promises a bevy of what she terms"—Lily opened the letter and read—"'eligible and handsome young men of good fortune and family.' When she puts it that way, how could I fail to fall in love with at least one of them?"

Papa was looking more hopeful by the minute. "Och, it's a capital idea, Lily. It just might work."

"Of course it will." Lily resumed her seat and placed the letter into Dahlia's waiting hand.

Her sister read through the missive. "The duchess is certainly bald in her purpose. I dislike that."

Up until now, Lily hadn't liked it either, which was why she hadn't accepted any of her godmother's invitations. But now, a growing sense of determination filled her. "She's merely being kind. She knows our marriage prospects are quite dim here at Caith Manor."

"I suppose so."

"So it's settled. I'll go to the duchess's house party, where I'll meet a lovely, wealthy man and solve all of our problems."

Papa brightened. "I daresay a house party will be quite fun, too. According to Rose, the duchess plans many amusements for her guests."

"Exactly," Lily said with a bravado she didn't feel. "And I just made some new gowns for the coming year and was wondering where I'd ever find events formal enough to wear them."

"Your gowns are without compare," Dahlia complimented, obviously still troubled but trying to smile.

Lily pursed her lips, her mind moving rapidly over the items in her wardrobe. "I shall need some new shoes, and two pairs of long gloves, for mine are quite worn, but that should be enough for now."

"You may borrow my gloves, which are like new, for I've used them only once. You may also borrow my blue half boots and both pairs of my ballroom slippers. Oh, and you must take the new red cape that you made me. It's still chilly in the evenings."

"Thank you, Dahlia. That should set me quite well." She caught her father's look, noting the sad turn of his mouth, and her irritation at him disappeared. He was a dear man, but scientific of mind, which left very little in the way of common sense. But despite his faults, she loved him dearly. "Papa, don't look like that." She went to stoop beside his chair, where she hugged him tightly. "We'll find a way out of this mess. But you must promise that in the future you won't take any more silly chances and put so much at risk."

He hugged her back, smelling as he always did of mint, lavender, and potting dirt. "I will never again be so foolish. But"—he tilted her chin up so that her eyes met his—"are you certain you wish to do this? I won't have you making an unnecessary sacrifice."

Lily thought of Dahlia's hesitant offer to talk to Kirk and, aware that her sister watched, forced a merry smile. "Yes, yes, a thousand yeses! I'll enjoy the parties and rides while the duchess finds me a wealthy, handsome, generous husband whom I shall love forever."

Lily planted a kiss on Papa's forehead and then stood. "Come, Dahlia! You must help me pack. I've men to impress, and a future husband to find!"

Two

From the Diary of the Duchess of Roxburghe

I sent out a lure to Lily Balfour, and it seems that she has finally—to use one of Roxburghe's horrid fishing terms—"taken the bait." Now I've but to plan a house party and cajole certain eligible young men to exchange the entertainments of London for a few weeks of amusements at my country estate here in Scotland.

Such a feat might be difficult for other hostesses, but I have the ultimate enticement to lure handsome bachelors from the madness of the London season—fields teeming with foxes and pheasant, and a stable filled with the finest hunters imaginable.

Bless Roxburghe. He is an excellent husband.

Floors Castle
May 7, 1813

A young footman ran lightly down the back steps into the servants' quarters, hurried around the corner, then knocked on the washroom door. A muffled voice bade him enter, and he hurried inside, only to stop in astonishment. Three tubs of warm water had been placed in a line, where six housemaids—working two together—scrubbed roly-poly pugs. More maids and the housekeeper, Mrs. Cairness, worked at another table, where they dried additional balls of fur with large towels.

One of the pugs barked and then attacked the towel as the housekeeper tried to dry him. She chuckled and played tug-of-war with him for a moment before she wrapped the other side of the towel about his round body and rubbed him dry. Finished, she kissed the pug's head before she handed him to a waiting footman, who carried him to the next table.

There, two maids and the butler, Mr. MacDougal, stood in wait. The maids held a pug between them as the butler carefully combed its hair, trimmed its nails, then tied a kerchief about its thick neck.

The footman, belatedly remembering his purpose, stepped forward. "Mr. MacDougal, I—"

The butler held up a gloved hand.

The footman gulped back his words.

MacDougal squinted at the dog in front of him, then picked up a silver-backed comb and carefully ran it over the dog's left ear. It was an older dog, his muzzle well grayed as he sat panting, his tongue hanging to one side of his wide mouth as he stared at the footman through milky eyes.

The footman shifted from foot to foot, waiting.

Finally, the butler tilted the little pug's face up and said with a note of approval, "There's a guid lad, Randolph. Now ye look quite the gentleman. I believe her grace will approve."

The pug's little tail twirled as he barked in agreement.

The butler placed the silver comb back on the table and said to the maid, "Take Randolph to the kitchen fer his dinner. Cook was preparing their dishes when I left a half hour ago. Once ye've finished, return here. Her grace will be home soon and they must all be bathed by the time she arrives."

"Yes, Mr. MacDougal." The maid curtsied, then carefully gathered Randolph and hurried from the room, careful to close the door behind her.

The butler turned to the footman. "Now, John. What did ye need?"

John blinked. Lord, but he'd almost forgotten why he'd come in search of the butler. It wouldn't do to be so slack in his duties before Mr. MacDougal. The butler was a fixture at magnificent Floors Castle, having served her grace since he'd been a young lad of seventeen, the only servant who could claim such longevity. As such, MacDougal had unprecedented power. "Yes, sir. I came to tell ye that—"

"Here, Moira." Mrs. Cairness was toweling dry another of the pugs. "Take puir wee Teenie to Mr. MacDougal to comb. He's as dry as we can make him."

The housemaid bundled the dog in his towel and

carried him to MacDougal, who eyed the damp hair with a critical eye. As the butler began to comb the dog, he asked, "Well, John? Out wit' it."

"Yes, sir! I'm sorry, I was distracted by the dogs. Her grace just returned from the vicar's and wishes to—"

"Her grace has returned? Why dinna ye say so?" MacDougal put down the comb and peeled off his gloves. "She wasna due back fer two more hours! Mrs. Cairness, would ye finish here?"

The housekeeper handed a towel to a waiting chambermaid and then crossed to the butler's side. "O' course. Ye go ahead and welcome her grace. I'll have the dogs brought to her once't they are all dried, combed, and fed."

"Thank ye, Mrs. Cairness." The butler picked up a stiff brush from a shelf beside the door and brushed his clothes. "Well, John, where is her grace?"

"She went to her bedchamber to change, but she asked tha' ye meet her in the sitting room as she's a grand project fer ye."

MacDougal swallowed a sigh. *Wha' are ye a'doin' now, yer grace?* He replaced the brush on the shelf and then made certain his cuffs were in order. "John, tell Cook that her grace will wish fer dinner after all, fer she dinna stay at the vicar's as planned."

The footman bowed smartly. "Yes, sir!" He dashed off.

Several minutes later, MacDougal arrived in the sitting room just as her ladyship settled into a chair opposite Lady Charlotte, who was tucked into the corner of the gold silk settee. Both ladies appeared agitated, their faces flushed, their chins lifted.

While it wasn't unusual to see her grace in a taking—her being a woman of passion, as it were—it was odd to see her companion so overcome. The youngest daughter of the late Earl of Argyll, Lady Charlotte was a spinster who'd made her home with her grace and was now an indispensable part of the household. She was the duchess's constant companion and was known for her calm, soothing presence.

Now, though, Lady Charlotte's cheeks were stained with color. "Of all the *nerve!*" she said, her button-bow mouth pressed into a disapproving line. "I've never been so insulted!"

"Nor I! I'd like to—" The duchess snapped her mouth closed, her brilliant blue eyes flashing over her prominent nose.

MacDougal bowed before the duchess. "Ye're home early, yer grace. I've asked Cook to prepare ye and Lady Charlotte a nice light supper."

"Thank you," her grace said impatiently. "As you've guessed, we didn't stay at the vicar's."

"No," said Lady Charlotte, her lace mobcap askew. "Not after *that woman* arrived."

MacDougal waited, but Lady Charlotte and her grace merely sat stewing in silence, apparently reliving some horrible memory. He gently cleared his throat. "I dinna suppose tha' Lady MacInnis was at the vicar's?"

Her grace's newest rival, Countess MacInnis, had

recently moved into a large estate only a short distance from Floors Castle. The duchess and the much younger countess had rapidly begun competing for guests for their many social events, so MacDougal was surprised when the duchess shook her head. "It has nothing to do with Lady MacInnis. Not this time, anyway."

Lady Charlotte blew out her cheeks in exasperation. "Lady MacInnis is a *saint* compared to the Grand Duchess Natasha Nikolaevna."

"Ye met a grand duchess?" MacDougal couldn't keep the surprise from his voice. "At the vicar's?"

"She's visiting with her grandson." Her grace shoved her red wig back into place from where it had slipped to one side.

"He's a prince." Lady Charlotte picked up her knitting, her movements agitated. "What was his name again?"

"Piotr Romanovin, the Prince Wulfinski," the duchess said with a dismissive sniff. "They are royalty from some tiny country near Prussia, where I've no doubt they wear atrocious full red skirts made of coarse material, dance like whirligigs, and embroider every tablecloth and napkin with horrid red-and-green borders."

"I believe Oxenburg is quite beautiful." Lady Charlotte put her cap back into order. "The Duke of Richmond has been there and said it was breathtaking, but dreadfully cold."

"Richmond thinks the Pavilion at Brighton is quite

the thing, too. The man has no taste whatsoever. And neither did that prince. His boots were dull, his cravat merely knotted, and his coat fit far too loosely. He looked disheveled."

"But despite his lack of fashion, he was very handsome." Lady Charlotte pulled her knitting basket toward her and settled her newest project into her lap.

"He might have been handsome," her grace said grudgingly.

"He was polite, too," Lady Charlotte added. "But *she* wasn't."

"*She* was a *harridan*." The duchess's blue eyes blazed.

"I was never more insulted!" Lady Charlotte's knitting needles clacked with every word as she turned to MacDougal. "The vicar introduced us—"

"Obviously not realizing how rude she could be," the duchess interjected, "or he'd have never put us in such an awkward situation."

MacDougal nodded sympathetically. "She sounds horrid, yer grace, grand duchess or no'."

The duchess pressed her mouth into a flat line. "She acted as if she thought we were *nobodies*."

Lady Charlotte nodded, her needles clacking faster. "The woman *ignored* her grace!"

MacDougal couldn't contain his shock.

Lady Charlotte looked vindicated. "Exactly. The grand duchess refused to even look at us until the vicar insisted she at least greet us. He was astonished at her rudeness as well."

The duchess sniffed. "He might have been surprised, but I was not. I expect such things of foreigners. It's a wonder we allow any of them into the country, for they ruin everything."

"Yes," Lady Charlotte agreed, completely ignoring the fact that her own mother had been an Italian woman of genteel birth. "Her grandson, the prince, tried to apologize—"

"—which is the *only* reason I invited them to our coming house party."

MacDougal blinked. "Pardon me, yer grace, but did ye say 'house party'?"

"Yes, yes. We're to have a house party. I decided just this morning only an hour before I met the prince and *that* woman."

Lady Charlotte eyed the duchess with appreciation. "Margaret, it was very generous of you to invite them."

"Yes, it was, although we do need more men and, as you say, he was quite handsome. Even if he attends, we're still short three." The duchess leaned back in her seat. "Which reminds me why I sent for you, MacDougal. We're having a house party in a week's time and I need you to add the grand duchess and her grandson, the prince, to the invitation list."

"There's already a list?"

"Of course there's already a list. How else would I know we're short three men?"

"Aye, yer grace. I'm sorry I wasna thinkin' properly."

"You'll need that list, too, so you know who to send invitations to."

He bowed, trying to stifle a sigh as he thought of the work that needed to be done.

Lady Charlotte nodded to the small rosewood secretary that sat nearby. "You'll find the list on the left-hand corner. The invitations are to go out in tomorrow's post."

"Yes, me lady." He went to fetch the list written in Lady Charlotte's delicate handwriting. Some fifty or so guests were listed on the neatly written sheet. Beside each man's name were a series of marks. After looking at it for some moments, he carried it to Lady Charlotte. "I beg yer pardon, me lady, but these marks here . . ." He pointed to them.

"Oh, that! Ignore it. It's just our code."

"Code?"

"Yes. We place a tick beside each bachelor. Then we give each man with a title a small circle. If they have a fortune, then we draw a pound symbol."

"And what's this symbol, me lady?" He pointed to what appeared to be a drawing of a sprout of grass springing from the ground.

"That's what I drew if the bachelor in question had all of his own hair." Lady Charlotte glanced at the duchess. Satisfied her grace was busy murmuring endearments to Randolph, her ladyship leaned toward MacDougal and said in a low tone, "Her grace didn't deem it important, but I do like a man with a full head of hair."

"Yes, me lady, although this symbol looks a bit like a sprout o' grass than a head o' hair."

"I suppose it does." She shook her head sadly. "It's quite disappointing how many gentlemen did not earn that mark. It is perhaps the most important of all."

Unable to think of anything more to say, MacDougal merely nodded. "Aye, me lady."

The duchess gave Randolph a hug and placed him back on the floor, where he waddled to the fire and plopped onto the rug. "MacDougal, her ladyship and I shall be planning some activities to amuse our guests. We want them to mingle, of course."

The duchess was indeed up to her old tricks, so he'd best ready the castle. As he folded the list, his mind was already racing ahead to which footmen would need to be pressed into service in the front hall and during dinners, and the outcry Mrs. Cairness would make on discovering that bedchambers must be prepared, and quickly.

"It's a simple three-week affair. My goddaughter Miss Lily Balfour will be attending."

Lady Charlotte beamed before saying in a confidential tone, "It's because of Miss Balfour that we're having the house party at all, although she thinks we've had it planned for months."

MacDougal remembered Miss Lily Balfour's sister Rose quite well, and how determined the duchess had been to match the young lady to Lord Sinclair. "I take it there are to be several outings fer the guests?"

"Small ones. A picnic, a visit to the folly, perhaps a boat ride on the lake . . ." The duchess waved her hands. "Those sorts of things."

"But no archery," Lady Charlotte said, shuddering. "Not after our last house party."

"Och, no!" MacDougal said, remembering the mayhem from their last attempt.

Both ladies stared at him and MacDougal hurried to add, "The weather is so chancy in the spring."

"Very true," her grace said. "Although it is appealing to think of an arrow accidentally hitting the grand duchess."

Lady Charlotte instantly agreed, telling MacDougal, "That woman had the temerity to suggest that our king was too fat to serve as the head of state."

"Actually, I must agree with that comment," her grace stated. "It was the only thing she said that made any sense. If the king gets any fatter, they'll have to exchange his steed for a draft horse similar to those used in the fields."

"That wouldn't be very kingly," Lady Charlotte said.

The two continued to discuss the king's weight as MacDougal considered the planning that needed to be done. The floors and silver must be polished, bedchambers cleaned and readied, and the grand ballroom opened and prepared, the furnishings uncovered and dusted. It would take every servant available, as well as some hired from the village, to get the house ready. He looked at the list once again and noted a small scribble in one corner.

As soon as there was a slight pause in the conversation, he asked, "Yer grace? I beg yer pardon, but ye wrote somethin' upon the bottom o' yer list." He squinted. "It says 'Butterfly Ball.'"

"Oh yes! I almost forgot. We're to have a ball, too. A small one, but a ball nonetheless."

Lady Charlotte added eagerly, "It will be quite a feat for her grace if she can entice enough people from the London season to attend a ball in the middle of the country." Her knitting needles ticked along. "Everyone will want to come, for her grace will offer the gentlemen something they will be longing for— hunting!"

MacDougal managed to look sufficiently impressed, though he secretly thought that Lord Roxburghe wouldn't be pleased to hear that his carefully selected stables were about to be invaded by a pack of potential suitors. Sadly, his grace was in London, attending to business, and was not to return until a week after the scheduled party.

The duchess looked like the cat who'd swallowed the cream. "No man will be able to resist the lure of my invitation, especially after weeks of being forced to toe the line of society. We shall have plenty of eligible bachelors for Miss Lily to choose from."

Well, there was no more to be said. Every moment he stood here was a moment wasted. With a graceful bow, he said, "Yes, yer grace. I'll see to it that the invitations are sent and the house readied immediately." At her pleased nod, he left the sitting room, pulling the door closed behind him.

Out in the hallway he called to the young footman who hovered in the hallway, "Come, John. It's time to batten down the hatches. Her grace is on the warpath again, and it's all men to stations!"

Three

From the Diary of the Duchess of Roxburghe

The entire castle is being readied for our guests. So far, over one hundred and ten have confirmed their attendance at our little Butterfly Ball, with forty-two staying the entire three weeks for the preceding house party. Charlotte says that Countess MacInnis is beside herself with envy, but I never pay attention to what other people think. I simply plan excellent entertainments and let the world do what they may.

Meanwhile, my goddaughter Miss Lily Balfour arrived yesterday. She's quite lovely, with gray eyes and bright red-gold hair. We had a lovely talk, and I could tell from what she did not say that funds are tight at Caith Manor and she is, indeed, in dire need of a well-placed husband. I have found the perfect candidate: the wealthy Earl of Huntley, who's been widowed for over two years and is now in the market for a tractable, wellborn wife, though he's had lamentable luck in that area—until now.

Judging from the sparkle in her eyes, I don't believe Miss Balfour is tractable, but she is both lovely and wellborn. In addition, she is not a society miss, like so many others who've set their caps at the poor earl. I think Huntley will find her innocence and honesty refreshing.

I must say that if they happen to enter into a marriage, my reputation as a matchmaker extraordinaire will be established once and for all. Not, of course, that I intend to meddle. Such is not my style. I merely present the opportunity, and stand back and allow nature to have its way. . . .

Lily turned her horse down the wide path that led toward the woods. Behind her, Floors Castle sat amid well-manicured lawns filled with flowers. The castle was luxurious and beautifully appointed, but Lily felt nothing but relief as the trees obscured it from view.

For the last two days she'd been a perfectly behaved guest, smiling and nodding, greeting people she didn't know with the appearance of pleasure. Every minute had been torture. The days had been filled with nonstop introductions, and if she had to remember one more name, she feared her head might explode.

The shade under the trees cooled the air, and she pulled Dahlia's red cloak tighter. Lily allowed the horse its head, the peacefulness of the forest calming her frayed nerves. She'd had no idea how uncomfortable and lonely it would be, coming to a castle where she knew no one. The duchess had been lovely, although she and Lady Charlotte had quizzed Lily mercilessly when she'd first arrived. She'd let them know in as delicate a manner as possible that she was quite ready to form a suitable marriage, but she'd offered no more than that. No one needed to know about the Balfours' distressed financial situation, but she had the uncomfortable impression that the duchess's shrewd blue eyes had seen far more than Lily intended.

The horse's hooves were muffled on the packed dirt, the trees moving overhead in the breeze. Birds sang, leaves danced, and the scent of pine tickled her nose. Peace settled over Lily as the quiet wood settled about her.

It was so good to get away from the pressing crowd at the castle. This morning the duchess had mentioned that the Earl of Huntley would be arriving tomorrow, and it was obvious from her arch glance that she favored Huntley as a potential suitor for Lily. Apparently the earl was wellborn, fabulously wealthy, handsome, and a perfect gentleman.

Lily should have been excited—here was her chance for a more-than-favorable marriage, one with a carefully selected candidate. Instead, all she felt was deeply and irrevocably sad.

She sighed and tilted her face to the dappled sun streaming through the leaves overhead. If she wished to save her family, she had to come to terms with a marriage of convenience. It wasn't unusual; in fact, women were judged on the quality of husband they managed to snare. Women groomed themselves and learned genteel arts such as embroidery and watercolors, a smattering of foreign languages, and just a touch of classical history, in order to attract men of wealth and breeding. *They learn everything but the art of making a well-cut riding habit.* She sniffed derisively. *That's a true art.*

She smoothed the navy-blue skirt of her habit with satisfaction. Just this morning, as she was waiting for her mount to be brought around, two of the duchess's august guests—both ladies dressed in the highest fashion—had stopped to ask which modiste had made her habit. She smiled with pride. *If I can't find a satisfactory husband, I can always support the family. If only my skill with a needle could also save Papa—and Caith Manor—from his folly.*

She sighed. *It has to be marriage, then. Why, oh why, am I finding this so difficult to accept?* She firmed her chin and said aloud, "This is how the world operates." Men looked for women who would grace their table and manage their homes and present them with heirs, while women looked for men who would provide for them and the ensuing family. It had been this way for centuries. So why did she feel so . . . bereft?

"I'm being silly," she told her horse.

His ears flickered, but he offered no further comment.

She sighed and patted his neck, glad that no one was about to hear her. Really, it was a simple—

A fox jumped out of the shrubbery and dashed across the path, a streak of red near the horse's hooves.

The horse reared, whinnying madly as he pawed the air.

Lily hung on for dear life, clutching at the horse's mane, at the saddle, trying to hold on to anything that might stop her fall. But being perched upon a sidesaddle and weighted with the heavy skirts of her riding habit, she was no match for the frightened horse.

The horse threw itself upon its back legs and, with a scream, Lily tumbled to the ground.

Twenty minutes earlier, on the other side of the river, a carriage had creaked to a stop beneath a towering oak. An old woman pushed back the curtains with a hand heavy with jewels and looked out the window, disbelief on her deeply wrinkled face. "This is it?"

"What? You do not like it?" Piotr Romanovin, Prince Wulfinski of Oxenburg, threw open the carriage door and called to the coachman to tie off the horses. "It is charming, *nyet?*" Flashing a smile, the prince reached up to help his grandmother to the ground.

His Tata Natasha, a grand duchess more aware of her title than any king or queen he knew, gathered her velvet cloak as if it were a shield and stared at the cottage that sat in a small clearing. In silence, she noted the broken shutters, the half-missing thatch roof, the front door hanging from one hinge, and a profusion of flowering vines growing across the windows. "*Nyet,*" she said bluntly. "This is not charming. Come." She turned back to the carriage. "We will go back to the big house, where we belong, and leave this foolishness to the wilds."

"It's not a big house, but a manor. And *this*"—he gestured to the cottage—"is to be my home. It is here I shall live."

"You are a prince of Oxenburg. You cannot live in a hovel."

"I'm a grown man who will live where and how he wishes."

Tata Natasha scowled. "This is all your father's fault. You are the youngest and he could never tell you *nyet.*"

"Oh, he's said it quite often."

"Pah! You are spoiled and don't even know it."

He arched a brow. "Do you or do you not wish to see my new home?"

She scowled at the cottage. "Just look at this place! The roof—"

"Can be fixed. As can the shutters and the door and the chimney."

"What's wrong with the chimney?"

"It needs to be cleaned, but the craftsmanship is superb. It just needs some care."

She eyed her grandson sourly. The prince was larger than all of his brothers, and they were not small men. At almost six feet five, he towered over her and all nine of their guards.

But large as Wulf was, he was her youngest grandson and the most difficult to understand, given to fits and starts that were incomprehensible to all and left his parents in agonies.

Take the simple matter of marriage. His brothers seemed to understand their responsibilities and were scouring the courts of Europe for suitable brides. But not Wulf. He'd refused every princess that came his way, be they short or tall, thin or fat, fair or not—it didn't matter. With only the most cursory of glances, he'd refused them one by one.

Tata Natasha shook her head. "Wulf, your cousin Nikki, he was right; you have gone mad. You purchased a beautiful house—" At Wulf's lifted brows, she sighed. "Fine, a manor, then. One with twenty-six bedrooms, thirty-five fireplaces, a salon, a dining room, a great hall, and a ballroom. It is beautiful and fitting for a prince of your stature. This"—she waved a hand—"is a hovel."

"It will be my home. At least until I've found a bride who will love me for this, and not because I can afford a manor with more chimneys than there are days in a month." He tucked his grandmother's hand in the crook of his arm and pulled her to the cottage door. "Come and see my new home."

"But—"

He stopped. "Tata, it was your idea for me to meet the world without the trappings of wealth."

"No, it was *your* idea, not mine." When his gaze narrowed, her wrinkled cheeks heated. "I *might* have suggested that it would do you good to discover what it was like to be a normal man and not one wrapped in privilege, but I never suggested *this*." She waved at the cottage.

"But you were right; I must find out for myself. Now come. See my new home." He pushed the crooked door to one side.

"Such a waste of time." She tugged her arm free so that she could hold her skirts out of the dirt. "Why not marry a princess?"

He shrugged. "I didn't see one that I liked."

Tata Natasha turned to face him, her chin pushed forward. "What *do* you like, Wulf? What sort of a woman do you wish to meet?"

He raked a hand through his black hair, his gaze distant. "I want one who will treat me as a man and not as a bag of gold. One with passion and fire. One who will marry me because of me—not my title or wealth."

"You cannot deny your birthright. Your father would have an apoplexy if he found out, and his health is not good."

"I know." Wulf's jaw tightened. "For that reason, I will not hide that I am a prince. But I will not admit to my wealth."

Tata sighed. "I wish your father had never passed that ill-thought law allowing his children to marry as they wished."

"He married for love and he wished us all to have the same luxury."

"He married my daughter, a crown princess!"

"Of the Romani."

Tata's black eyes flashed. "The Romani blood is purer and older than any other royal bloodline!"

"I know," the prince said simply. "But it was against the laws of Oxenburg, which only recognized traditional kingdoms—"

"Foolishness!"

"—so he changed those laws. Thus he was able to marry his bride and make her the queen he always thought her."

"Humph. He could have just written a law acknowledging the Romani."

Wulf wisely refrained from pointing out the political imbroglio that would have caused and said in a soothing tone, "Father did what he thought best. He married Mother because he loved her and she loved him. He knew he was fortunate in that, and he wishes for all of us to have the same."

Tata threw up a hand. "Love, love, love! That is all you and your father talk of! What about duty? Responsibility? What about that?"

Wulf smiled indulgently as he pushed open one of the shutters, letting light stream into the cottage, illuminating a stream of golden dust motes that danced in the air. "Rest assured that I will marry a strong woman, one who will give me many brave and intelligent sons. Surely that is responsible of me?"

Tata wished she could smack her son-in-law. What had he been thinking to free his sons to marry commoners? It was ridiculous. And look what it had led to. Here was her favorite grandson, looking for a wife among the heathens that populated this wild and desolate land. "If you will not believe in the purity of bloodlines, then how will you know which woman is right for you?"

"I'll know her when I see her."

Tata ground her teeth. "Why did we have to come to this godforsaken part of the world to find your bride? Scotland isn't even civilized."

He sent her a humorous glance. "You sound like Papa."

"He's right, for once." She scowled.

"Tata, everyone knows me in Europe. But here . . . here I can be unnoticed." He took her hand and led her to the center of the cottage. "My little house is more spacious than you thought, *nyet?*" He could even stand upright, provided he didn't walk toward the fireplace. There the roof swooped down to meet it and he'd have to bend almost in half to sit before it.

Still, he looked about with satisfaction. The front room held a broken table and two chairs without legs. A wide plank set upon two barrels had served as a bench before a huge fire, where iron hooks made him imagine fragrant, bubbling stew.

Tata walked toward the fireplace, coughing as her feet stirred up dust. "Where will you sleep?"

"Here." He went to the back of the room, where a tattered curtain hung over a small alcove. A bed frame remained, leather straps crisscrossed to provide support for a long-gone straw mattress. "I will have a feather mattress brought down from the manor. This frame is well made and I will sleep like a baby." He placed a hand upon the low bedpost and gave it a shake. The structure barely moved.

Tata grunted her reluctant approval and looked around. "I suppose it will make a good hunting lodge once this madness of yours is gone."

"So it will. I'll have some of my men begin work on it at once. I need it cleaned, fixed, and well stocked with firewood."

She shot him a reluctantly amused glance. "A poor man of no wealth does not have men to help with such things."

"I am not playing this part because I wish to, Tata. I am playing it because I must."

"Humph."

"I will help as I can, but I've no experience with thatching. I'd be foolish to try now when the rainy season is about to begin."

"At least you are keeping some of your good sense about you."

"I'm keeping all of it." He smiled at her fondly and held out his arm. "Thank you for coming to see my new home. Come, I'll take you back for tea."

She took his arm, wishing he weren't so blasted charming. It was hard to argue with a grandson who smiled at her as if she were the best grandmother in the world. "Not the English kind of tea. It's so weak it tastes like hot water."

He gave her a look of mock horror. "Of course not! I will get you good tea from our homeland. We brought enough for a year, though we will only be a month or so."

Tata paused before she walked out of the doorway. "Do you not think a month is too little time to persuade a woman to marry you? One who thinks that a title and this cottage is all you possess?"

He looked surprised. "Do you think we should stay longer?"

Ah, the certainty of this one is as endearing as it is surprising. She reached up to pat his cheek. "Wulf, think a bit. I know that the women have always come to you, but what you propose to do now will change that. You wish to win a woman's heart and not just her interest. You must get to know her, and reveal yourself so that she falls in love with you. Even then, it may not be enough. Love cannot be commanded to appear merely because you have decided it."

He cast her a glinting smile. "You have so little faith in me. I should be insulted."

She shook her head, wondering what the next few weeks held for her grandson. Life had always smiled upon this one. He was a handsome man—handsomer than any she knew—and he was a wealthy prince, as well. "You do not yet know the world, and so your plan is as arrogant as it is foolish. You expect to meet a woman and *POOF!*—both of you will fall madly in love, but it does not happen that way."

His smile faded, his green eyes darkening. "Tata, I told you of my dream. That is why we are here."

"Yes, yes. Your dream of Scotland, of a woman with hair of red—"

"Not red. Red and gold, with eyes the color of a summer rain. And don't tell me you don't believe in dreams, for I know you and the Romani too well."

She scowled. "The dreams of our family have always had meaning, but it is rare that they are as clear in meaning as the one you claim to have had."

"I've had this exact dream four times now, Tata. And every time, it is the same woman who—"

A woman's scream tore the air.

Wulf spun toward the door.

Tata grabbed his sleeve. "Let the guards—"

"No. Stay here."

Then he was gone, shouting to his men to protect his grandmother as he ran from the cottage.

Four

From the Diary of the Duchess of Roxburghe

Huntley arrived early and I spoke to him at length, delicately suggesting that it was time for him to wed again. He nodded thoughtfully, and I believe he has already come to this conclusion himself. I'm sure that all it will take is one look, and the deal will be done. All I have to do is find Lily.

We seem to have somehow misplaced her.

Lily slowly awoke, her mind creeping back to consciousness. She shifted and then moaned as every bone in her body groaned in protest.

A warm hand cupped her face. "Easy" came a deep, heavily accented voice.

Lily opened her eyes to find herself staring into the deep green eyes of the most handsome man she'd ever seen.

The man was huge, with broad shoulders that blocked the light and hands so large that the one cupping her face practically covered one side of it. His face was perfectly formed, his cheekbones high above a scruff of a beard that her fingers itched to touch.

"The brush broke your fall, but you will still be bruised."

He looked almost too perfect to be real. She placed her hand on his where it rested on her cheek, his warmth stealing into her cold fingers. *He's not a dream.*

She gulped a bit and tried to sit up, but was instantly pressed back to the ground.

"*Nyet,*" the giant said, his voice rumbling over her like waves over a rocky beach. "You will not rise."

She blinked. "*Nyet?*"

He grimaced. "I should not say '*nyet*' but 'no.'"

"I understood you perfectly. I am just astonished that you are telling me what to do." His expression darkened and she had the distinct impression that he wasn't used to being told no. "Who are you?"

"It matters not. What matters is that you are injured and wish to stand. That is foolish."

She pushed herself up on one elbow. As she did so, her hat, which had been pinned upon her neatly braided hair, came loose and fell to the ground.

The man's gaze locked on her hair, his eyes widening as he muttered something under his breath in a foreign tongue.

"What's wrong?"

"Your hair. It is red and gold."

"My hair's not red. It's blond and when the sun—" She frowned. "Why am I even talking to you about this? I don't even know your name."

"You haven't told me yours, either," he said in a reasonable tone.

She hadn't, and for some reason she was loath to do so. She reached for her hat, wincing as she moved.

Instantly he pressed her back to the ground. "Do not move. I shall call for my men and—"

"No, I don't need any help."

"You should have had a groom with you," he said, disapproval in his rich voice. "Beautiful women should not wander the woods alone."

Beautiful? Me? She flushed. It was odd, but the thought pleased her far more than it should have. Perhaps because she thought he was beautiful as well.

"In my country you would not be riding about the woods without protection."

"A groom wouldn't have kept my horse from becoming startled."

"No, but it would have kept you from being importuned by a stranger."

She had to smile at the irony of his words. "A stranger like you?"

The stranger's brows rose. "Ah. You think I am being—what is the word? Forward?"

"Yes."

"But you are injured—"

"No, I'm not."

"You were thrown from a horse and are upon the ground. I call that 'injured.'" His brows locked together. "Am I using the word 'injured' correctly?"

"Yes, but—"

"Then do not argue. You are injured and I will help you."

Do not argue? Goodness, he was high-handed. She sat upright, even though it brought her closer to this huge boulder of a man. "I don't suppose you have a name?"

"I am Piotr Romanovin of Oxenburg. It is a small country beside Prussia."

The country's name seemed familiar. "There was a mention of Oxenburg in *The Morning Post* just a few days ago."

"My cousin Nikki, he is in London. Perhaps he is in the papers." The stranger rubbed a hand over his bearded chin, the golden light filtering from the trees dancing over his black hair. "You can sit up, but not stand. Not until we know you are not broken."

"I'm not broken," she said sharply. "I'm just embarrassed that I fell off my horse."

A glimmer of humor shone in the green eyes. "You fell asleep, eh?"

She fought the urge to return the smile. "No, I did not fall asleep. A fox frightened my horse, which caused it to rear. And then it ran off."

His gaze flickered to her boots and he frowned. "No wonder you fell. Those are not good riding boots."

"These? They're perfectly good boots."

"Not if a horse bolts. Then you need some like these." He slapped the side of his own boots, which had a thicker and taller heel.

"I've never seen boots like those."

"That is because you English do not really ride, you with your small boots. You just perch on top of the horse like a sack of grain and—"

"I'm not English; I'm a Scot," she said sharply. "Can't you tell from my accent?"

"English or Scot." He shrugged. "Is there so much difference?"

"Oh! Of course there's a difference! I—"

He threw up a hand. "I don't know if it's because you are a woman or because you are a Scot, but thus far, you've argued with everything I've said. This, I do not like."

She frowned. "As a Scot, I dislike being ordered about, and as a woman, I can't imagine that you know more about my state of well-being than I do."

His eyes lit with humor. "Fair enough. You cannot be much injured, to argue with such vigor." He stood and held out his hand. "Come. Let us see if you can stand."

She placed her hand in his. As her rescuer pulled her to her feet, one of her curls came free from her braid and fell to her shoulder.

She started to tuck it away, but his hand closed over the curl first. Slowly, he threaded her hair through his fingers, his gaze locking with hers. "Your hair is like the sunrise."

And his eyes were like the green found at the heart of the forest, among the tallest trees.

He brushed her curl behind her ear, his fingers

grazing her cheek. Her heart thudded as if she'd just run up a flight of stairs.

Cheeks hot, she repinned her hair with hands that seemed oddly unwieldy. "That's— You shouldn't touch my hair."

"Why not?"

He looked so astounded that she explained. "I don't know the rules of your country, but here men do not touch a woman's hair merely because they can."

"It is not permitted?"

"No."

He sighed regretfully. "It should be."

She didn't know what to say. A part of her—obviously still shaken from her fall—wanted to tell him that he could touch her hair if he wished. Her hair, her cheek, or any other part of her that he wished to. *Good God, what's come over me?*

"Come. I will take you to your home."

She brushed the leaves from her skirts and then stepped forward. "Ow!" She jerked her foot up from the ground.

He grasped her elbow and steadied her. "Your ankle?"

"Yes." She gingerly wiggled it, grimacing a little. "I must have sprained it, though it's only a slight sprain, for I can move it fairly well."

"I shall carry you."

"*What?* Oh no, no, no. I'm sure walking will relieve the stiffness—"

He bent, slipped her arm about his neck, and scooped her up as if she were a blade of grass.

"Mr. Roma—Romi— Oh, whatever your name is, please don't—"

He turned and strode down the path.

"Put me down!"

"*Nyet.*" He continued on his way, his long legs eating up the distance.

Lily had little choice but to hang on, uncomfortably aware of the deliciously spicy cologne that tickled her nose and made her wonder what it would be like to burrow her face against him. It was the oddest thing, to wish to be set free and—at the same time—enjoy the strength of his arms. To her surprise, she liked how he held her so securely, which was ridiculous. She didn't even know this man. "You can't just carry me off like this."

"But I have." His voice held no rancor, no sense of correcting her. Instead his tone was that of someone patiently trying to explain something. "I have carried you off, and carried off you will be."

She scowled up at him. "Look here, Mr. Romanoff-ski—"

"Call me Wulf. It is what I am called." He said the word with a faint "v" instead of a "w."

"Wulf is hardly a reassuring name."

He grinned, his teeth white in the black beard. "It is my name, reassuring or not." He shot her a glance. "What is your name, little one?"

"Lily Balfour." She hardly knew this man at all,

yet she'd just blurted out her name and was allowing him to carry her through the woods. She should be screaming for help, but instead she found herself resting her head against his shoulder as, for the first time in two days, she found herself feeling something other than sheer loneliness.

"Lily. That's a beautiful name. It suits you."

Lily's face heated and she stole a look at him from under her lashes. He was exotic, overbearing, and strong, but somehow she knew that he wouldn't harm her. Her instincts and common sense both agreed on that. "Where are you taking me?"

"To safety."

"That's a rather vague location."

He chuckled, the sound reverberating in his chest where it pressed against her side. "If you must know, I'm taking you to my new home. From there, my men and my—how do you say *babushka*?" His brow furrowed a moment before it cleared. "Ah yes, grandmother."

"Your grandmother? She's here, in the woods?"

"I brought her to see the new house I just purchased. You and I will go there and meet with my men and my grandmother. I have a carriage, so we can ride the rest of the way to your home."

I was right to trust him. No man would involve his grandmother in a ravishment.

He slanted a look her way. "You will like my grandmother."

It sounded like an order. She managed a faint smile.

"I'm sure we'll adore one another. However, you and your grandmother won't be escorting me home, but to Floors Castle. I am a guest of the Duchess of Roxburghe."

His amazing eyes locked on her, and she noted that his thick, black lashes gave him a faintly sleepy air. "I met the duchess last week and she invited us to her house party. I was not going to attend, but now I will go." His gaze flicked over her, leaving a heated path.

Her breath caught in her throat. *If the duchess has invited Wulf to the castle, then perhaps he is an eligible parti.* Suddenly, the day didn't seem so dreary. "I beg your pardon, Mr. Wulf—or whatever your name is—but who are you, exactly?"

He shrugged, his chest rubbing her side in a pleasant way. "Does it matter?"

"Yes. You mentioned your men. Are you a military leader of some sort?" That would explain his boldness and overassuredness.

"You could say that."

"Ah. Are you a corporal, then? A sergeant?"

"I am in charge." A faint note of surprise colored his voice, as if he couldn't believe that she would think anything else.

"You're in charge of what? A battalion?"

He definitely looked insulted now. "I am in charge of it all."

She blinked. "Of an entire army?"

"Yes." He hesitated, then said in a firm voice, "I shall tell you because you will know eventually since I plan on joining the duchess's party. I am not a general. I am a prince."

"A pr—" She couldn't even say the word.

"I am a prince," he repeated firmly, though he looked far from happy about it. "That is why her grace finds it acceptable that my grandmother and I attend her events. I had not thought to accept her invitation, for I do not like dances and such, and you English—"

She raised her brows.

"I'm sorry, you *Scots* are much too formal for me."

"Wait. I'm still trying to grasp that you're a prince. A real prince?"

He shrugged, his broad shoulders making his cape swing. "We have many princes in Oxenburg, for I have three brothers."

She couldn't wrap her mind around the thought of a roomful of princes who looked like the one carrying her: huge, broad shouldered, bulging with muscles and grinning lopsided smiles, their dark hair falling over their brows and into their green eyes. . . . *I fell off my horse and into a fairy tale.*

Hope washed over her and she found herself saying in a breathless tone, "If you're a prince, then you must be fabulously wealthy."

He looked down at her, a question in his eyes. "Not every prince has money."

"Some do."

"And some do not. Sadly, I am the poorest of all my brothers."

Her disappointment must have shown on her face,

for he regarded her with a narrow gaze. "You do not like this, Miss Lily Balfour?"

She sighed. "No, no, I don't."

One dark brow arched. "Why not?"

"Sadly, some of us must marry for money." Whether it was because she was being held in his arms or because she was struggling to deal with a surprising flood of regret, it felt right to tell him the truth.

"I see." He continued to carry her, his brow lowered. "And this is you, then? You must marry for money?"

"Yes."

He was silent a moment more. "But what if you fall in love?"

"I have no choice." She heard the sadness in her voice and resolutely forced herself to say in a light tone, "It's the way of the world, isn't it? But to be honest, I wouldn't be looking for a wealthy husband except that I must. Our house is entailed, and my father hasn't been very good about— Oh, it's complicated."

He didn't reply, but she could tell from his grim expression that he disliked her answer. She didn't like it much herself, for it made her sound like the veriest moneygrubbing society miss, but that's what she'd become.

She sighed and rested her cheek against his shoulder.

He looked down at her, and to her surprise, his chin came to rest on her head.

They continued on thus for a few moments, comfort seeping through her, the first since she'd left her home.

"Moya, I must tell you—"

She looked up. "My name is not Moya, but Lily."

His eyes glinted with humor. "I like Moya better."

"What does it mean?"

His gaze flickered to her hair and she grimaced. "It means 'red,' doesn't it? I hate that!"

He chuckled, the sound warm in his chest. "You dislike being called Red? Why? It is what you are. Just as what I am is a prince with no fortune." His gaze met hers. "We must accept who we are."

She was silent a moment. "You're dreadfully poor? You said you'd just bought a house."

"A cottage. It has a thatched roof and one large room, but with a good fireplace. I will make stew for you. I make good stew."

It sounded delightful; far more fun than the rides, picnics, dinner parties, and other activities the duchess had promised. "I like stew, but I'm afraid that I can't visit your cottage. It would be improper." Furthermore, she didn't dare prolong her time with such a devastatingly handsome, but poor, prince. She had to save all of her feelings so that she could fall in love with the man who would save Papa.

Wulf's brows had lowered. "But you would come to my cottage if I had a fortune, *nyet*?"

Regret flooded her and she tightened her hold about his neck. "I have no choice; I *must* marry for money. I don't know why I admitted that to you, but it is a sad fact of my life and I cannot pretend otherwise. My family is depending on me."

He seemed to consider this, some of the sternness leaving his gaze. After a moment he nodded. "It is noble that you are willing to sacrifice yourself for your family."

"Sacrifice? I was hoping it wouldn't feel so . . . oh, I don't know. It's possible that I might find someone I could care for."

"You wish to fall in love with a rich man. As my *babushka* likes to tell me, life is not always so accommodating."

"Yes, but it's possible. I've never been in love before, so I'm a blank slate. The duchess is helping me, too, and she's excellent at making just such matches. She's invited several gentlemen for me to meet—"

"All wealthy."

"Of course. She is especially hopeful of the Earl of Huntley, and so am I." Lily looked away, not wishing to see the disappointment in his gaze yet again.

Silence reigned and she savored the warmth of his arms about her. At one time, a wealthy gentleman had seemed enough. Now, she wished she could ask for a not-wealthy prince. One like this, who carried her so gently and whose eyes gleamed with humor beneath the fall of his black hair. But it was not to be.

She bit back a strong desire to explain things to him, to tell him exactly why she needed to marry a wealthy man, but she knew it wouldn't make any difference. As he'd said, he was who he was, and she was who she was. There was no way for either of them to change things, even if they wished to, so it would be better for them both if they accepted those facts and continued on.

For now, though, she had these few moments. With that thought in mind, she sighed and rested her head against his broad shoulder. *This will have to be enough.*

Five

From the Diary of the Duchess of Roxburghe
I knew I shouldn't have invited that prince from
Oxenburg, polite or no. Lily has been here but two
days and already he's orchestrated a rescue, and
the poor girl has yet to meet the Earl of Huntley.
How is Huntley to match such an entrance? Damn
that prince! If he weren't so unfashionable and ill-
kempt, I would be worried.

"Och, lassie, ye've hardly touched yer tea." Mrs.
Cairness shook her head.

"I'm sorry." Lily allowed the housekeeper to pour
her now-cold cup of tea back into the pot and refill her
cup with warmer tea.

"Drink that, miss. Ye'll feel much better."

"Thank you." Lily obediently sipped, her gaze
drifting to the sun pouring in through the windows.
She was sitting in the small salon on a settee, her legs
stretched before her, a thick blanket tucked all around.

Her ankle was already much better, now that her boot was off and a pillow rested beneath her foot.

She watched the light stream into the room. It was a cozy location, especially as the guests who'd already arrived were off playing pall-mall upon the lawn and she had most of the castle to herself. Normally, she'd enjoy the peace and quiet and might even find a sewing project to busy her hands, but instead, she found herself staring morosely out the window.

Despite the prince's plans, she didn't get the chance to see his cottage or meet his *babushka*, for they'd only walked for a few more moments in blissful silence when his men had met them on the road, a fresh horse ready. She had the impression that Wulf hadn't been any more pleased at the intrusion than she was, though he hadn't said much. He'd set her on her feet, climbed upon his horse, and then lifted her before him.

The ride back had been lovely, his arm warmly resting about her waist, his broad back protecting her from the wind as they rode out of the forest. All too soon they were at Floors Castle, and he was carrying her through the huge doors and into the foyer. All bedlam had broken loose then, for the pugs had taken exception to the prince's swinging cape, while the duchess and Lady Charlotte—called from the sitting room by the loud yapping—exclaimed in dismay and demanded that the prince immediately put Lily on the settee in the small salon.

The duchess had sent the servants scurrying as

she rapidly ordered tea, a physician, a pillow for Lily's foot, and then efficiently herded Wulf from the room.

Lily had been sorry to see him go. Indeed, she felt sadly bereft, as if she'd left something behind . . . something important. She had to shake her head at her own silliness, even as she acknowledged that the prince was the first person she'd met since her arrival at Floors Castle who'd made her feel comfortable. *But that doesn't matter. You're not here for comfort; you're here to find a husband.*

She sighed and put her teacup back on the tray. "Mrs. Cairness, I think I've had enough now. It was delicious."

"Her grace said ye are to drink it all, miss. If'n I were ye, I'd do as she says. She's a determined woman, and smart, too. If'n she tol' me t' dance, I'd dance. If'n she tol' me t' jump upon one foot and toss fairy dust, I'd do it wit'oot askin' why." The housekeeper glanced at the door and then bent lower. "Trust me, miss. The duchess ne'er suggests ye t' do somethin' wit'oot a reason."

Lily sighed as the housekeeper poured yet more tea into her cup. "I shall float away, but fine. I'll drink more tea."

"Good," came the duchess's voice from the doorway. She entered with a rustle of blue silk overlaid with pink lace, her bright blue eyes twinkling. Behind her trotted the six Roxburghe pugs, wheezing and snorting as they tried to keep up. The duchess stopped at the end of the settee, and one of the pugs jumped into Lily's lap.

She laughed and patted the little dog, who grinned, his tongue hanging out one side. "And who are you?" she asked the dog.

Lady Charlotte, who'd followed the dogs into the room, her knitting basket at her side, smiled. "That's Feenie. He's a cuddler."

Lily patted the dog. "He's certainly friendly."

The duchess sank into an empty chair opposite Lily, while Lady Charlotte followed suit, the remaining pugs dropping in various spots on the rug.

"Poor Miss Balfour!" Lady Charlotte shook her head, her lace cap flopping over her ears. "How is your ankle?"

"It's fine. It barely aches, and I feel silly for taking up the entire settee. I'm sure that if I just walked around, it would feel better immediately."

"You may walk once the doctor has seen it," the duchess said serenely. She glanced at the housekeeper. "Pray pour Miss Balfour more tea. It will flush the bad humors from her system."

Lily managed to swallow her protest as she caught the housekeeper's knowing gaze. The teacup was refilled yet again and Lily took it with a murmur of thanks.

"Mrs. Cairness, could you bring another tea tray?" her grace asked. "Lady Charlotte and I haven't had time to take tea, what with all of the other guests arriving, and then our concern when Miss Balfour went missing, and, oh dear, all manner of things."

"Yes, yer grace." The housekeeper dipped a curtsy and bustled out.

The duchess regarded Lily with a smile. "I daresay a young woman of high spirits like yourself is tired of being coddled, eh, Miss Balfour?"

"Yes, I'm not comfortable just sitting about." She eyed Lady Charlotte's knitting with a feeling akin to jealousy. Maybe Lily could send home for some cloth, or perhaps the housekeeper might have some odds and ends she'd be willing to part with. *If I had a project, even a small, simple one, it would make me feel much more at home.*

The duchess tsked. "I am so sorry you were given such an unruly mount. It is unconscionable, and I had a word with my head groom about it."

"Oh no! Truly, it was not the groom's fault, nor the horse's. I'm not a confident rider and I allowed myself to get distracted. The fault is all mine."

"It's the groom's duty to ascertain your skill and then to choose a mount within those parameters. The groom did not do so. It will not happen again."

Lily wished to protest yet more, but the duchess's sharp tone effectively closed the conversation. Lily forced a smile. She should never have gone on that ride. All it had accomplished was to get her tossed to the ground, cause a groom to receive an ill-deserved dressing-down from the duchess, and place Lily directly in the arms of an arrogantly sure-of-himself prince, whose absence was making her feel even more bereft and lonely.

Her grace picked up a particularly fat, graying pug and placed it in her lap, where it grunted happily. "I hope the prince treated you courteously."

"Of course he did." Lily was certain her face was as red as the pillow under her ankle. "He was very gentlemanly." Except for plying her with enough compliments to make her feel oddly light-headed, and carrying her with such ease that she'd almost wished he'd never reached Floors.

The duchess sniffed. "I had some reservations about inviting Prince Wulfinski to my house party, but I can do little about it now, especially since we owe him some courtesies for assisting you."

"I'm sorry my accident has caused you such distress," Lily said sharply.

The duchess didn't seem to notice Lily's irritation. "It's regrettable. And while you say the prince behaved himself, I can't help but think that his attitude in striding into the house as if he'd saved the world from an invasion—well, I won't stand for such theatrics."

Lily blinked. "But all he did was carry me into the house."

"Now, now." The duchess patted Lily's hand where it was fisted on her knee. "I'm sure you wish to speak in defense of your rescuer, but I cannot feel that his attitude was totally appropriate. Sadly, the prince isn't staying under my roof, so I have no control over his actions when he's not here. But when he *is* here, I shall expect his behavior to be exemplary."

"I'm sure it will be," Lily said stiffly. "And once again, let me assure you that the prince was everything kind."

"Yes, dear," Lady Charlotte said, her knitting needles clicking quietly while her bright gaze locked with Lily's. "Our of curiosity, what did you and the prince find to converse about?"

"He told me about his grandmother—"

"A horrid woman," Lady Charlotte interjected.

"I didn't get the opportunity to meet her. We were on our way to his cottage when his men caught up with us."

"Cottage?" The duchess smiled indulgently. "As his highness has seen Floors Castle, I'm sure his estate seems smallish to him, although I wouldn't use the term 'cottage.'"

Lily wondered how much land had come with the prince's cottage. Perhaps it consisted of several acres. "The prince said he was the po—" She caught the suddenly intent gazes of both women and she bit her lip. "I'm sorry, but that's not for me to repeat."

The duchess leaned forward, her red wig slightly askew. "Of course it is! What did he say?"

Lily wasn't sure why she felt she needed to protect the scant information she possessed about the prince. After all, she barely knew him. Furthermore, she didn't suppose he'd told her anything that wasn't easily discovered. "I don't suppose it matters. He said he was the poorest of his brothers."

"Ah! So he has no funds." Lady Charlotte's needles clacked along. "I'm not surprised. Europe is crawling with supposed princes, and not a farthing to be had between them."

The duchess sniffed. "There would be more *wealthy* princes if foreigners didn't breed like rabbits."

Lady Charlotte agreed. "They should take after the English Crown; we have only one, perhaps two heirs to the throne at a time. It makes things so simple. Otherwise, what would one do with all of them? I suppose that's why Prince Wulfinski is here; his family simply felt there were too many princes wandering about, and so they sent him off."

"Perhaps." The duchess shrugged, then glanced at the open doorway. Once she was satisfied that none of her guests were lingering in the foyer, she scooted her chair closer to Lily and said in a low tone, "My dear Miss Balfour, as we have a few moments, I should mention that your father wrote me a most interesting letter. I received it just this morning."

Lily's stomach sank. *What has Papa done?* "Papa wrote you?" *Why would he do such a thing, unless—*

"There's no reason to look upset. He merely wished to thank me for attempting to help your family out of your predicament."

Lily wished she could sink into the ground. "He told you *everything*?"

Her grace nodded.

"So tragic," Lady Charlotte said. "Lord Kirk always seemed like such a gentleman, too. Or he was before his accident. I hear he's horridly changed since then, and not just physically."

"He's a cold and calculating man," Lily said. "Poor Papa didn't have a chance."

The duchess nodded in apparent sympathy. "I've had commerce with Lord Kirk before. A land purchase, I think it was. Your father is quite right in thinking that Kirk would never give him a respite on a debt owed. The man can be inflexible."

Lady Charlotte tugged more yarn from her basket, frowning when she saw that it was tangled beneath a sleeping pug. She put out a slippered foot and nudged the dog out of the way. Its eyes opened slightly, but otherwise it gave no indication of moving. "It's good that your father explained the depth of your predicament. Her grace and I suspected it, but now we know that you must marry a wealthy man and quickly."

Face heated, Lily nodded. "I hate these circumstances."

"Nonsense," her grace said in a bracing tone. "It's unladylike to pursue a career or even obtain a decent education, so what else is left us?"

"I—I cannot imagine marrying without love, but I suppose I must."

"My dear, I've married no fewer than five times, all of them to men of great wealth, and all of my marriages have been for love. There's no reason you couldn't do the same."

Lily didn't want to marry five times. She wasn't even sure she wanted to be married once. The pug at Lily's side snuggled against her and she absently patted it. "I had no idea you'd been married so many times, your grace."

"The first four passed away of natural causes; they were much older than I." The duchess's face softened. "They were great men, all of them, although I believe Roxburghe to be my true love. At least thus far."

Lily wasn't quite sure how to answer this, so she merely nodded.

"My point is this: you can indeed have a very passionate relationship with a wealthy man. All you have to do is give yourself the *opportunity* to fall in love with the right man."

"It's a shame there aren't other opportunities available to women," Lady Charlotte said, her round face folded in thought. "I do think I would have made an excellent butcher."

Her grace turned a surprised look on her friend. "A butcher?"

"Oh yes. I saw pigs being butchered many times when I was a child."

"But you were raised at Highclere Castle. I can scarcely believe they'd allow the daughter of the house to witness such a thing."

Lady Charlotte knitted on serenely. "My father believed in the old ways. We cured our own ham, bacon—we were quite self-sufficient."

"We do the same here, but *not* in full view of the

daughter of the castle. Surely you weren't encouraged to attend such bloody events?"

"Oh no, but I went anyway. It was quite interesting. First, they— Here, let me show you." Lady Charlotte set her knitting aside and bent over to scoop up a pug. She settled it into her lap, then took a loop of yarn in one hand. "First, they'd throw a heavy rope about the pig's back feet like so. And then they'd bash him in the head with a large wooden mallet right here." She placed her finger between the pug's eyes. "And then, once they were certain he was dead, they'd slash his throat right here—"

"Goodness!" The duchess snatched the pug from Lady Charlotte's lap. "Meenie doesn't like to hear about pigs and their slaughter." The duchess hugged the dog, who yawned and then closed its eyes once again. "As I was saying, Miss Balfour, Lady Charlotte and I fully intend on helping you reach a satisfactory arrangement as soon as possible." With that, the duchess began expounding upon the benefits of marriage in a way that made Lily almost ill to her stomach.

A lump of panic grew in Lily's throat. *Surely I won't need to marry that quickly. I really only need to get engaged. Once I accept an offer, I will just inform my newly intended of Papa's dilemma, and once that obligation to Lord Kirk is paid, we can take our time getting to know each other before actually marching down the aisle. Yes. That's what we'll do.*

Lily suddenly realized that both the duchess and

Lady Charlotte were looking at her as if awaiting an answer. Not sure what they'd been saying, she nodded and murmured, "Of course."

The duchess beamed. "I think you'll find we're right. Huntley is an excellent choice."

They are very determined that I like this earl. I hope I do. She managed a smile.

"*If,* of course, he appeals to you," Lady Charlotte said kindly.

"And if I appeal to him, too," Lily said.

"Oh, we've no fear on that score." The duchess patted the pugs in her lap while she beamed at Lily. "Your biddable nature alone will recommend you to him."

"Biddable nature"? Good God.

Lady Charlotte smiled. "If only we can get him to come to the point before the Butterfly Ball. Then he could announce it right then. Oh, it would make the event so memorable."

"Charlotte, what a delightful thought!" The duchess couldn't have looked happier. "That settles it: Lily, Huntley *will* make you an offer and he *will* do it before the ball."

The duchess spoke with such firmness that Lily began to feel sorry for the unknown earl. *This is getting out of hand.* "Your grace, I can't—"

Mrs. Cairness entered carrying a tea tray.

"Ah, tea!" The duchess peered at the tray. "I'm famished."

Lily was left to wait as the housekeeper filled the teacups and handed out tea cakes. Finally, she left.

As soon as the housekeeper was gone, Lily said, "I am very grateful for your help, your grace, but what if Huntley isn't the one for me?"

"He will be, if you'll let him." The duchess sipped her tea. "He's a lovely man."

"Oh yes," Lady Charlotte added, her soft blue-gray eyes shining with enthusiasm. "So distinguished."

"Very handsome, too," the duchess added. "One of the handsomest earls I've yet to meet." The two pugs in her lap were now wide-awake and staring intently at her tea cake. "In addition, I've been grooming Huntley for you."

"We both have." Lady Charlotte licked butter off her fingers, looking like a plump fairy. "He's looking forward to meeting you."

Lily wondered if the pigs on Lady Charlotte's home farm had seen what was coming their way. She tried to look appreciative, though it took quite a bit of effort. "It was quite kind of you to mention me."

"It was my pleasure," the duchess assured her. "Huntley's been a bit of a recluse since his wife died, but—"

"Wife? Pardon me, but . . . he's a widower?"

"Oh yes. He was quite attached to his first wife and refused to enter company for several years after her death."

"But now he's back in society." Lady Charlotte dipped a spoon into a jar of marmalade and spread it over her tea cake. "But you needn't fear that he developed a new interest in that time, for he hasn't. We asked him."

"You *asked* him?"

"Of course." The duchess set down her teacup. "How else would we discover his situation? He was a bit reluctant at first to discuss his private life, but Charlotte quite won him over."

"Yes, first I told him that it was obvious that he was once again joining the ranks of the eligible, and I would hate to waste his time introducing him to every female the duchess and I know. We know quite a few, too."

"Many." The duchess chuckled. "You should have seen his face! But it did the trick, for he revealed what he was looking for in the way of a wife. And what he told us made us very hopeful for you, my dear!"

Lily looked down at her teacup. A wealthy, handsome earl looking for a wife . . . what more could she ask for? Yet in her mind's eye arose a vision of a large man, his shock of black hair framing brilliant green eyes, his dark, accented voice rumbling through her.

But that was not to be. Lily pushed the memory aside and met the gaze of her expectant hostesses. Steeling her heart, she swallowed her misgivings and firmly faced her future. "That's lovely. I look forward to meeting the earl. I'm sure we'll suit very well."

The duchess and Lady Charlotte beamed and began to discuss the various events they'd planned for the coming few weeks.

Six

From the Diary of the Duchess of Roxburghe
The stage is set, the players cast. All that's left is to
open the curtain. . . .

"Have all of the guests arrived?" The duchess was
resplendent in blue silk with cream rosettes, her red
wig adorned with an emerald pin that matched her
necklace and earrings.

Standing in the wide doorway leading to the ballroom, Charlotte looked at MacDougal.

He bowed. "Everyone on the list is here except
Lord Huntley. He hasna' arrived yet, yer grace."

Margaret frowned. "I ran into him in the hallway
after dinner and I specifically asked him to arrive early
so that I could introduce him to Miss Balfour." She
hesitated. "I wonder if I was a bit too forward when I
did so."

"You think he took offense?"

"I hope not." The duchess was silent a moment
as she regarded her other guests, who were talking

and laughing and watching the dancing, which had just begun. Finally she sighed. "I thought I detected a hint—just a *hint*—of stubbornness in his lordship's demeanor when I spoke to him about Lily."

Charlotte sighed. "Oh dear."

"He was polite, but no more. Perhaps he's sending us a not-so-subtle message, which is that he will not be manipulated."

"That quite upsets our plans."

Margaret frowned. "Our plans don't call for us to manipulate anyone. We're merely giving two people a chance to meet and, if so inclined, fall in love."

"Oh. Quite right. I don't know what I was thinking."

"I do hope he overcomes it; I cannot imagine that Miss Balfour would enjoy a stubborn man." Margaret looked around the room, her irritation seeping away as she watched the couples twirl about her dance floor. "For an opening dance, we've an excellent turnout." She sighed. "I wished to introduce our potential couple while no one was about. Now Miss Balfour will meet her earl for the first time here in the ballroom, in front of the other guests."

"At least they'll both be dressed in their finest."

"That's true. I've no doubt Huntley will outshine every man present."

"And Miss Balfour will outshine every woman. Oh, Margaret, it will be so romantic!"

"Excessively so." Margaret eyed the refreshment table. "MacDougal, put out more cake and sliced ham. I won't have it said that I scrimp on refreshments."

"Yes, yer grace." The butler stepped to one side to murmur orders to a waiting footman, then returned to his post just as a murmur arose at the door.

"It's about time," the duchess said.

The earl stood in the doorway as a footman announced him and his companion.

"Who is that with him?" Lady Charlotte asked.

"That's Miss Emma Gordon. She's a friend of Huntley's. She was bosom bows with his wife before she died."

"Oh dear, you don't think—"

"No, no. Huntley says she is like a sister, and I believe that says it all."

"Ah. So Miss Balfour need not worry."

"Hardly. She has the advantage of looks and youth, for she's at least ten years younger than Miss Gordon." The duchess glanced around the room. "Where is she?"

"She's speaking with Lady MacKenna by the punch bowl."

"Good. Wave her over, will you? Huntley's on his way to us now."

Across the ballroom, Lady MacKenna squinted toward the door. "Pardon me, Miss Balfour, but it looks as if Lady Charlotte is signaling for you to join her."

Lily instantly knew why. Her heart thudding sickly, she looked for the closest exit. *But, no. I can't run. Think about Papa.* She collected herself as well as she could, made her excuses to Lady MacKenna, then walked toward Lady Charlotte and the duchess, refusing to look at the small group gathered there. *Just stay calm.*

As she walked past a mirror, she swiftly glanced at her gown and hair. She'd made her gown, a deceptively simple affair of white lace over a deep blue silk undergown. The gown sported delicate cap sleeves and gathered beneath her breasts with a wide, white silk ribbon. The neckline was scooped and unadorned, and she wore only a simple pair of sapphire earrings that had once belonged to her mother.

She smoothed her skirt with one hand, her dance card swinging at the wrist of her elbow-length glove. The duchess let no detail go unnoticed, and the card was folded like a fan with a gold cord looped about one end. *Perhaps Huntley will ask me to dance. I'm sure the duchess would tell me that he is a superb dancer. She can find no fault in the man.*

No man could be all of the things the duchess seemed to think him—handsome, wealthy, and pleasant. Still, if the earl were simply wealthy and pleasant, Lily would be be well pleased. She reached Lady Charlotte and dipped a curtsy. "Lady Charlotte, you wished to speak wi—"

"There you are!" Her grace tucked an arm though Lily's and turned her toward a tall gentleman and a fashionably dressed woman. "Miss Balfour, this is Geoffrey MacKinton, the dashing Earl of Huntley."

Lily curtsied. "How do you do?"

The duchess beamed. "Huntley, this is my goddaughter, the lovely Miss Lily Balfour."

Lily's hand was instantly enveloped in a warm clasp, and she found herself looking up into a pair of sherry-brown eyes that gleamed with humor. He was nearly as tall as Wulf, but not nearly as broad shouldered. And his hair was neatly trimmed, unlike—

I must stop that. Huntley was handsome in a lean, aristocratic way, and that would have to do.

The earl bowed over her hand. "Miss Balfour, we finally meet. I've heard so much about you."

"And I, you." She noted the marvelous fit of his coat, which whispered of a master tailor, and the sparkling ruby that twinkled in the depths of his cravat, as well as a matching one in a ring on his finger.

"Allow me to introduce you to a dear friend of mine." He turned to the tall, elegant woman who'd been standing slightly behind him. "Miss Balfour, this is Miss Emma Gordon. I've known her for years and she is almost a sister to me."

Lily curtsied. As she rose, she exchanged smiles with Miss Gordon. The earl's friend had brown hair and fine brown eyes, and while not conventionally pretty, she possessed a humorous air that put Lily at ease.

"Miss Balfour, I hear you're from the same area of the country as my grandfather, near Cromartie. It's a lovely area."

"It's beautiful, but very cold in the winter. The ponds are ice for months on end."

"Oh, Huntley, you must tell Miss Balfour about how you tried to rescue my poor cat, Tibby, from that iced-over pond."

He laughed. "No, no. I refuse to embarrass myself."

"Then I shall tell it for you." Looking mischievous, Miss Gordon launched into a description of the earl's many attempts to rescue her cat from an icy pond, only to end up stranded himself. Huntley contributed to the merriment by making droll observations on Miss Gordon's propensity to exaggerate tales.

The duchess and Lady Charlotte stood back beaming and allowed the three to talk. Finally, the earl glanced at the orchestra. "Miss Balfour, I hate leaving you so abruptly, but I always dance at least one country dance with Emma. After that, however, I would very much enjoy a dance with you if you've any left open upon your dance card."

Lily flushed. "Of course." She slipped her dance card from her wrist and handed it to him.

He used the small pencil that dangled from the card and wrote upon it. "Thank you." He returned the card to her. "I took the liberty to claim two dances. I hope you don't mind."

From the corner of her eye, Lily saw Lady Charlotte give a hop of joy even as the duchess clapped her hands together. Cheeks hot, Lily sank into a curtsy. "I am honored, my lord."

He bowed. "Until our dance, then."

With that, he made his farewells to the duchess and Lady Charlotte and escorted Miss Emma to the dance floor.

The second he was gone, Lady Charlotte sighed. "Isn't he lovely?"

"More than lovely," the duchess declared. "Well, Lily? What do you think?"

Lily didn't know what she thought. "He seems very nice, just as you said."

"And?" Lady Charlotte urged.

"Oh, ah. He's very handsome, too."

"Yes?" Lady Charlotte waited.

"Yes."

The duchess looked disappointed. "Nice? Handsome? That's all you have to say?"

"He's—he's also very tall."

"He's *perfect*," the duchess said.

In all fairness, Lily had to nod. "He seems so, yes."

Chortling, Lady Charlotte tucked Lily's arm in hers. "There, we all agree!"

The duchess beamed, finally happy. "Charlotte, while Lily is waiting to dance with the earl, why don't you introduce her to some other guests, and see to it that her dance card is filled? She's far too pretty to be a wallflower."

"A capital idea! Nothing spurs a gentleman's interest more than a well-pursued woman." Lady Charlotte tugged Lily toward the refreshment table. "Ah, there's Lord Spencer now."

An hour later, Lily finished dancing with a young viscount who'd talked nonstop about a horse he'd just purchased. He escorted her to the refreshment table to procure her a glass of orgeat, and she escaped him by claiming that she needed to find a retiring room to pin a torn flounce.

As the viscount wandered off, Lily peeked at her dance card, glad to see that the next dance was Huntley's. *Where is he?* She stood on tiptoe and thought she saw him on the other side of the dance floor in conversation with a portly man in a striped waistcoat. She could tell from his expression that Huntley was not happy to be so entrapped. *I shall rescue him.*

She was halfway to the dance floor when a large hand encircled her wrist. Instantly, her skin heated as if she'd been immersed head to toe in warm water, and a deep shiver traced through her. *Wulfinski.*

"Ah, Miss Lily Balfour." His husky voice seemed to caress her name. "I look for you and there you are."

She took a shivery breath, far more pleased to see him than she should be. "Prince Wulfinski, I didn't expect—"

"Dance with me." His voice was as deep as the ocean.

"I would, but—"

He turned and walked into the swirling dancers, pulling her ruthlessly behind him.

Lily could either follow him or plant her feet and be yanked onto her face.

Scowling, she scrambled to keep up. "Lord Wulf— your majesty or—Lud, whatever you name is, please slow down! I cannot keep up—"

He came to an abrupt halt and looked down at her. "You cannot keep up, eh? Then I walk slower." His gaze dropped to her slippers where they peeked from beneath her skirts, a look of distaste on his face. "You cannot walk because of those shoes. Silk is for sheets, not shoes."

She blinked. "Sheets?" She couldn't imagine silk sheets. *Why, that would cost a fortune.*

"*Da.* You need leather shoes to protect your feet."

"These shoes are for dancing."

"*Nyet.* The women in my country, they would never wear such frivolous footwear."

"That is their loss. I'll wear leather shoes while walking in the woods, thank you. But these"—she extended one so that the jeweled buckle sparkled in the candlelight—"are *perfect* for dancing."

He sent them a dismissive glance. "I do not like them so much, but if you do . . ." He shrugged and then said in a gracious tone, "As you wish."

Fuming, Lily tugged her wrist free. For one second, she'd been glad to see him, her body welcoming him before she had. But now . . . now she just wanted to find Huntley and claim their dance. *This is good; the last person I need to be attracted to is a man with no fortune.* "Prince Wulfinski, I did not come to this ball to be dragged about the room and have my shoes insulted."

Surprise crossed his face. "You are upset."

"Yes, I'm upset. These shoes are *beautiful.*"

His lips twitched, but he managed to say in a grave voice, "There are many gems glittering upon them, yes."

Well, paste gems, but no one knew that but Lily. "I love these shoes."

"Hm. My mother's shoes are more——" He clipped off the word as if unwilling to finish.

His mother's shoes what? Were more useful? More utilitarian? More——

Oh. Wulf had told her that he was the poorest of the many princes in Oxenburg. *Perhaps that's all she can afford.*

Feeling as small as an ant, Lily tucked her foot back under her skirt. "I'm sure your mother's shoes are lovely, too, however they look."

He shrugged. "It matters not. She is not here for us to compare. Come. The music appeals to me." He put his hands about Lily's waist, lifted her easily, and set her down directly in front of him. Then, as if she were a marionette, he placed one of her hands upon his shoulder and grasped the other. "We dance, Moya."

"Wulf, I don't think——" But they were already moving as, with a sweeping step, he swung her into the twirling couples. To her surprise, he was sure-footed and graceful. It was easy to move with him, and he led with a deft touch that let her know what he wished her to do without her feeling manhandled.

A cacophony of feelings fluttered through her. He lacked Lord Huntley's elegance, but he more than made up for it in graceful power. His coat might not fit as well, his breeches didn't cling as was the fashion, but she found him irresistible. And judging by the glances other women kept sliding their way, she wasn't the only one.

You're doing it again. You must stop this.

She glanced up at Wulf to find him regarding her with a faint smile. "What?"

His brows rose. "We don't have—how do you say it—the little talk?"

"Small talk. Would you like to discuss the weather?"

"With you, even that discussion would hold my interest."

Her cheeks warmed. No one had ever paid her such extravagant compliments, and while they made her uncomfortable, they were rather nice to hear. "You are very gallant."

His eyes gleamed. "I am dancing with the most beautiful woman in the room. How can I be anything but gallant?"

She didn't know what to say to that. "I think we should find a safer topic to discuss, something other than me."

"Name this topic and I shall discuss with you. Perhaps you'd like to talk about how beautiful you look wearing blue? You should always wear blue, Moya. It makes your gray eyes turn a pale blue, like the early-morning sky."

"That isn't a different topic. Wulf, we—"

"Pardon me." Lord Huntley stood beside them. He locked gazes with Wulf. "I don't believe we've met."

"I am Prince Wulfinski." The prince's gaze narrowed. "You would not be an earl, would you?"

Huntley's brows rose. "Why, yes."

"Then you are Huntley."

Huntley blinked, surprised.

Lily gave a weak laugh. "The duchess must have mentioned you to the prince."

"How kind of her." Huntley bowed. "I'm afraid I haven't had the same advantage. It's a pleasure to meet you, Your Highness, but I believe this dance with Miss Balfour is mine."

"*Nyet.*" Wulf slipped an arm about Lily's waist and pulled her to his side. "This is *my* dance with Miss Balfour. I have claimed it."

Aware of the shocked glances from some of the other guests, Lily stepped out of Wulf's embrace. She could see from Huntley's tight expression that he assumed that the prince was being deliberately provocative, though that was far from the case. The prince had no idea how to comport himself. A wave of protectiveness surprised her. "Prince Wulfinski, you don't understand. Huntley claimed this dance earlier, before you arrived. He did so on here." She held up her wrist where her dance card dangled, the small pencil tied to it.

"What is that?"

"A dance card. It's a custom of our country for each woman to have one. When a man wishes to dance with her, he signs his name on the card beside that dance."

"I wish to see this dance card."

She slipped her hand from the loop and handed it to him. "It's very simple, really. I'm sorry no one mentioned it to you before."

Wulf looked at the card, distaste upon his face. "There are many names on this card."

Lily fought back a smile. "Lady Charlotte introduced me to the other guests."

Wulf looked at Huntley. "You are a friend of Lady Charlotte, too, then?"

Huntley bowed, looking less pleased than Wulf. "I am, and of Miss Balfour's godmother, too. Now if you don't mind, I must claim Miss Balfour soon or this dance will be over."

Wulf grunted and his gaze returned to the dance card. "I suppose you may have her. But first . . ." He took the pencil and put a large 'W' on every dance she had left.

"Oh dear, you can't—" Lily began.

"I claim you for these other dances," Wulf said calmly.

"You can't do that!"

"But you said it is done just so."

"Yes, but a woman cannot dance more than twice with the same man in an evening."

"Twice? Pah!" Wulf raked a hand through his hair, looking thoroughly perplexed. "You Scots and your damned rules! If you cannot dance with me more than twice, than we shall sit out the dances I have claimed and we will talk instead."

"Talk? But I—" Words left her.

He lifted his brows. "But?"

Looking into his eyes, she couldn't think of a "but" anything. His jaw was set and she suddenly knew how he felt—as if he were navigating a raging river of societal rules with nothing but a teaspoon as a rudder.

Social events often felt the same way to her. "I suppose it wouldn't hurt to talk. I could perhaps explain some of the other rules."

"Miss Balfour?" Huntley said impatiently.

Lily bit her lip. This was her first opportunity to speak to the earl alone, and she was flattered by the determined note in his voice. Yet she hated leaving Wulf to wander about the ballroom alone, stumbling over the invisible dictates of polite society.

Wulf handed the dance card back to Lily. "Very well, Huntley, you may have her. For now." Wulf bowed to Lily. "I will see you in two dances, Moya. Until then." He inclined his head and left.

The earl shook his head. "Who is this Prince Wulfinski?"

"I'm not really sure," Lily said, having trouble looking away from where he'd disappeared into the crowd. Now was *not* the time for her to be thinking about an impossible prince. Not when an available earl was standing before her, ready to sweep her into the dance.

"He's quite sure of himself, isn't he?" Huntley's voice recalled her.

"You have no idea," Lily said fervently as she put her hand into Huntley's waiting one. "Shall we, my lord?"

"Yes." He smiled down at her and led her into the dance.

His hands were light, his dancing sure and capable, his conversation polite and within the bounds of propriety. She found herself laughing easily with him, and she made him burst into laughter once as well.

She had to admit that he seemed to be everything the duchess had said.

Still, she couldn't help stealing peeks over his shoulder to see if Wulf was behaving himself; he could so easily get into trouble. And it was no use hoping that the duchess might assist him, for she obviously held no love for the foreign prince or his grandmother.

But that's not your concern, Lily told herself as she pulled her attention back to the earl. Her concern had to be for her family.

Yet something about the prince touched her heart. Perhaps it was his innocence, for while he was very much a lion of a man, he was a lamb in the ways of this society. And she, struggling to find her place in a world that left her only one option for security, understood his frustration all too well.

But perhaps it was something more. Perhaps it was also because she'd been so honest with him about her dilemma the day before. Other than the duchess and Lady Charlotte, Wulf alone knew her feelings about what life offered her. She had to give him credit, too, for he hadn't judged her harshly, but had seemed to understand her predicament, and how dire it was.

She glanced up at Huntley, who was talking about his aversion to certain country dances. If she wished to be successful in her attempt to save her father from gaol, then she had to focus on the earl and rebuff the prince. He was far too obvious about his intention to pursue her, and she had a definite weakness for his company. Dancing with him would only make her decision more difficult.

She hated to hurt the prince's feelings, but it would be better to do so now, and to do it boldly so that there could be no mistake. *But who will help Wulf follow the dictates of society, if not me?*

And yet even as she had the thought, Lily realized that it *couldn't* be her. She couldn't afford to pay so much attention to another man, especially a single one, without jeopardizing her burgeoning relationship with Huntley. *I cannot make any mistakes with this. I must save Papa and Caith Manor.*

Setting her shoulders, Lily saw to it that she was surrounded by people for the rest of the evening, even during the times Wulf had marked on her dance card. She caught sight of him once or twice at the edge of the crowd and once locked gazes with him. But she deliberately turned her back and pretended not to see him.

She could tell from his growing glower that he was well aware of her actions, and she was certain that only his pride kept him from stalking up to her, throwing her over his shoulder, and carrying her off— something he looked more than ready to do.

A short time later, she was relieved when, his face grim, the prince stalked from the ball. And Lily, pretending she didn't care, danced once more with the dashing Earl of Huntley.

Seven

From the Diary of the Duchess of Roxburghe

Ah, what a night! I'm so tired that I can barely hold my pen, but my dance was a triumph. Everyone was well amused, and I succeeded in introducing Miss Balfour to Huntley. I can tell he's intrigued and she . . . she's harder to read, I fear, but I know that she had to have been pleased for he's everything she could hope for.

The clock is now chiming three, and I can safely predict that I, and all of the guests, will sleep well past noon.

A little after seven the next morning, Lily pushed open the door to the library and peeked inside. "Ah, empty!" Smiling, she entered and, shifting a large hatbox to one side, held the door wide. "Come on," she told the fawn-colored pug who stood in the hallway looking up at her with a curious gaze. "We can't linger in the hallway or we'll be caught, for the servants are already stirring."

He took two steps toward the door and then

halted, tilting his head to one side as if asking her a silent question.

"Yes, yes. In an hour, I'll ring for a breakfast tray and I'll specifically ask if there's a bone you might have."

The pug's tail wagged harder and he pranced past her into the library.

"That was a bit too easy," she told the dog. "Just so you know, I was willing to go up to two bones."

Blissfully unaware of the criticism being heaped upon his head, the pug began sniffing the rugs. Lily used her hip to close the door, then carried the heavy hatbox to the desk and set it on the leather surface. "This will do nicely."

Humming to herself, she went to the four large windows and threw open the heavy drapes to let light stream into the room. "Much better!"

Outside, the morning dew sparkled on the green lawn, while a mist clung to the lake, growing thicker as it rolled toward the forest. "Beautiful," she murmured. She glanced at the pug, who sat at her feet, waiting patiently. "Should we open the window and let in some fresh air or is it too cold?"

Feenie sneezed.

"Yes, it's a bit stuffy in here. We can always light the fire if it gets too chilly."

The pug sneezed again.

"Exactly." Chuckling, Lily threw the windows open. Instantly, the fresh morning air flooded the room, making her feel far more awake. "Even better."

She'd only had five hours of sleep and was a bit cotton-headed because of it, but she was unused to late morning hours and, despite going to bed at two, had found herself wide-awake with the sunrise. She went to the desk and unpacked her hatbox. Inside rested a stack of wool stockings with holes in the toes or the heels, as well as a pillowcase and three linen napkins in dire need of hemming. Lily dug a small box from the bottom of the hatbox, took the pillowcase, and settled into the corner of the settee. Feenie jumped onto the settee beside her and curled into a ball to sleep.

Lily opened the box and pulled out a needle, thread, and a pincushion. Within moments, she was busy hemming the pillowcase with delicate, precise stitches. As she sewed, she relaxed, her mind wandering over the events of the last few days.

She'd danced well into the night and had enjoyed several conversations with Huntley, yet she couldn't shake the memory of Wulf's furious gaze following her about the room. She'd hated doing such a thing, but if she wanted to secure the earl's interest and perhaps fall in love with him, then she had to keep her distance from the prince.

She smoothed her stitches, noting the evenness with satisfaction. Thank goodness she'd managed to convince the housekeeper to share the mending that was usually left to a maid. Though obviously surprised by the request, Mrs. Cairness had quickly agreed once Lily had explained how much she enjoyed such duties. "Och, miss, say no more. Me Mam used to say, 'Busy hands, peaceful heart.' I'm sure we've some darnin' and hemmin' ye could do."

And so now, since she'd awakened at such an early hour, Lily was beyond delighted to settle in for a few hours of peace and quiet. As birds chirped in the bright morning air, she finished the pillowcase and smoothed it out, then folded it and rose to place it beside the hatbox. Then, she took the linen napkins and settled back into place as she prepared her needle and thread.

As she'd sewed, the house had slowly stirred to life. In the distance she heard doors opening and closing, voices calling to one another, and the jangle of silver and china as the footmen prepared the breakfast room.

She picked up the first napkin and had just inserted her needle when horse's hooves clattered up the drive. It could be anyone—a message from a neighboring estate or a valet of one of the houseguests returning from an errand. Yet she found herself staring at the open windows and wishing she had a view of the front door.

She gently moved Feenie to one side and went to the window. She had to lean out to catch sight of the rider, who was just dismounting at the front portico. And there he was, Prince Wulfinski, hatless in the morning sun, the breeze ruffling his hair and stirring his black cape as he handed the reins of his horse to a sleepy-eyed footman. Hurrying toward him was Mac-

Dougal, who was hastily smoothing his hair. Soon Lily could hear MacDougal's lilting accent mingled with the prince's deeper, foreign one.

What's the prince doing here at this time of the morning? Surely he must realize that no one will be awake at this hour, especially after such a late-night dance? Who does he wish to s—

As if he could hear her thoughts, he looked her way.

She gasped and tucked back into the window, hiding behind the thick curtains. She held her breath, and in a moment the conversation between the butler and the prince resumed. She blew out her breath and realized that Feenie was staring at her from the settee, his head cocked to one side.

She knew she had to look foolish, hiding behind the curtains. To be honest, she wasn't sure why she was doing it, except that since last night, she hadn't been able to stop thinking that perhaps—just perhaps—she hadn't been fair to Prince Wulfinski. Instead of avoiding him without a word, perhaps she should have explained how he was making things more difficult for her, and how it would be better not to see him at all, and then demand that he stop pursuing her? "Life would be easier if that big lummox would just do as I say."

Feenie jumped to his feet as if in agreement, his tail wagging wildly.

She chuckled. "You agree, do you?"

He barked and turned in a circle.

"Perhaps I'll talk to him th—"

"Good morning, Moya."

Feenie barked wildly as Lily wheeled toward the open window. Sitting astride the windowsill, one booted foot in the gravel outside, and one planted on the library rug, was the prince. He looked even more handsome up close, his green eyes twinkling gravely as he lifted a brow. "I came to see if I could speak to you." He glanced at the barking dog and frowned. "Silence."

He didn't raise his voice, but the dog instantly stopped barking and sat, his little tail wagging fiercely.

"Good dog," the prince said before he turned his attention back to Lily. "The butler informed me that he dared not deliver my request to speak with you as he was certain you were still asleep. But you look awake to me." Wulf's gaze traveled over her slowly, lingering in places it shouldn't have. "Delightfully so."

Her entire body flushed, as if he'd run a hand over her. "I've been awake for a while, but I didn't tell anyone."

"Ah." His glance swept the room, resting on her discarded sewing. "You have made a little nest for yourself here, eh? It is pleasant to find peace and quiet after all of the talking, talking." He opened and closed his hand to mimic a mouth. "I thought I would go mad last night, listening to so many words."

She chuckled. "It did get noisy."

"Too much so." He crossed his arms over his broad chest and leaned back against the window frame, the morning sun making him glow. "You did not enjoy the dance."

How had he known that? "It was quite lively."

"Killed by faint praise." His mouth curled into a heart-stopping, lopsided smile. "Do not pretend you liked it, for I saw you. You were not happy last night."

Mainly because as soon as she'd decided to distance herself from Wulf, she'd been fighting a huge case of guilt. "I had a pleasant enough time."

"I didn't," he said bluntly. "Which is why I am here this morning. We must talk, you and I." He stood as if to climb the rest of the way inside.

"No!" She glanced at the closed door. "It would be very scandalous if we were caught alone."

He growled. "These rules of yours will be the death of me. But if I must follow them in order to spend time with you, then I will. What if we open the door?"

"I suppose that would be better—"

"Then we do so." He swung his leg over the windowsill and, with that, was inside the library, his cloak fluid about him as he crossed to the door, his booted feet muffled by the rug.

The room instantly seemed smaller and Lily hurried back to the settee, scooping up Feenie as she went.

Wulf opened the door wide. "There. Now we are safe within your little book of rules."

She shot him a hard look. "It's not my book."

"It is society's, but you have decided to play by it. Except, of course, when it comes to me." He undid his cape and tossed it over a chair. "I signed your dance card last night as you instructed, but you ignored it."

"I'm sorry." And she truly was. "I just . . . I panicked."

His brows snapped down. "I would never hurt you."

"I don't fear you." No, she feared something much, much worse—herself. Clutching Feenie, Lily sank onto the settee and settled the dog in her lap.

"I don't understand."

"Neither do I. It's difficult to explain." She caught his dark gaze and sighed. "Wulf, you and I met under very romantic circumstances. I'd fallen from my horse and there you were, looking so—" She flushed.

"Thank you," he said gravely, though his eyes twinkled wickedly.

She hurried on. "Naturally such an unusual set of circumstances can create a false sense of closeness that is merely an illusion of—"

He laughed, a rueful tone in his voice. "Moya, Moya!"

She stiffened. "What's so funny?"

"You, trying to explain away the passion that flares between us. It is real, Moya, no matter what you say."

"It doesn't matter what does or doesn't flare between us. I must marry a wealthy man, and I must take this step with my whole heart."

"You are an honorable woman to protect your heart for your intended, but this path you are set upon does not suit you. Thoughts of your future bring you here, to a little nest where you can hide."

"I just wished for some quiet."

He reached over to pick up her hatbox from the desk and looked through the contents. "Woolen socks. A servant's?"

She nodded.

He ran a finger over the neatly hemmed edge of the pillowcase and then replaced the hatbox, his gaze moving to the napkins pooled by her side, her needle and thread tucked into the top fold. "You like to sew."

She nodded. "I love to sew. I'm very good at it, and it's calming."

Concern darkened his green gaze. "You shouldn't have to search for calm."

It seemed as if the prince could read her mind, which made her even more uneasy. To hide her expression, she bent to scratch Feenie's ear. "Why are you here?"

"Because it pains me to see you distressed."

Suddenly restless, she straightened. "I'm not distressed." *Not yet.* "I'm fine. Truly I am."

"Moya, do not lie to me. I can see what you are and are not." He sighed. "You don't understand how this is. All of my life, I have known that when I finally met the woman I was meant to spend my life with, I would know it in an instant." His dark green gaze locked on her. "That woman is you."

This magnificent, bold, sensual prince wished to spend the rest of his life with her? A woman he barely knew? She shook her head. "It's impossible. You don't know me well enough to wish to spend a day with me, much less a lifetime."

His brows drew down. "I do, too."

"Oh? Then what's my favorite color?"

His gaze slid to her gown. "Blue."

Blast it! "What dance is my favorite?"

"The waltz," he said without hesitation.

He must have noticed that I enjoyed dancing it last night. "When's my birthday?"

He opened his mouth, then closed it. "I don't know, but when I find out, I will never forget."

"Humph. How did I get the scar on my knee? How many sisters do I have? When's the last time I read—"

"Hold!" He took a deep breath. "I may not know the little details, but I know the important ones. You are a kind person, Moya. Very. It shows in your eyes and the way you treat others and worry about them, too. You love your family enough to make the greatest sacrifice of all—to give up your happiness for theirs. I know, too, that you are beautiful, with hair of fire, and a laugh that makes me ache with desire." He spread his hands. "What more do I need to know?"

"Wulf, that's— Oh dear." She pressed her hands to her hot cheeks, her heart galloping in an odd way. "That's very kind of you, but— No. I can't accept that."

"I am always hones—" Surprisingly, his face reddened. "I am honest when I can be."

"What does that mean?"

"Moya, what must I do to convince you that I am serious in my pursuit?"

"We haven't known one another long enough to engender the feelings you think you have."

"I do not *think* anything: I know. And it is difficult to watch you sacrifice so much. I am very tempted to fix your problems, but—" Wulf shook his head and wondered if perhaps he'd been hasty in hiding his wealth. *But I must. She must choose me on my own merits.* "*Nyet.* It cannot be."

Lily stiffened, her eyes now ablaze. "I never asked you to 'fix' my problems. This is *my* obligation and no one else's."

He eyed her uneasily. "You are ruffled like a threatened dove. I said I was *tempted* to help you, not that I was going to." If he were truthful, had he not been determined to secure her affections without the trappings of wealth, he would have done just that, and without consulting with her, either. Looking at her now, he realized that it would have been a mistake of the first order.

Her eyes were a frosty gray. "I would no more ask a stranger to assist me with such a personal matter than I'd invite the king of England to tea."

Knowing the king, the overweight sovereign was much more likely to want brandy than tea, but Wulf wisely held his tongue. "Moya, please, I did not wish to upset you. I was trying to tell you something good, something wonderful—that I am in love wi—"

"No! Don't say that!"

"But it's true!" At her set expression, Wulf blew out his breath and raked a hand through his hair. His declaration was going horribly awry and he wasn't certain why. Last night, watching Lily from across the room, he'd thought that the reason she was being so distant must be because she didn't know how he felt. He had to tell her in plain language, so that there could be no misunderstanding: he loved her and wished to marry her. It was that simple.

Or so it had seemed at the time. On the ride here, he'd even been so foolish as to imagine how she'd react to his declaration, one most women dreamed about. None of the scenarios had included her facing him with icy fury. "Moya, please—I have obviously said something wrong, but you don't understand. When I met you, it was like a thunderbolt. I just knew that—"

"That's it." She set the dog to one side and jumped to her feet, the pug watching her with an astonished gaze that mirrored Wulf's own.

She marched up to him, her eyes blazing. "I don't want to hear another word of these—these *feelings* you say you have. Never. Ever. Do you understand? I regretted ignoring you last night because I realized that you are a stranger to our ways and don't understand the implications of many things you say and do. Our rules are complicated, and I can see how they might be difficult for someone new to our country to understand. But your *preposterous* tale that you have decided that I'm the one you wish to spend your life with— No! I don't need such a distraction in my life right now. I've got enough things to worry about as it is."

He rubbed a hand over his beard, eyeing her cautiously. "So I'm never again to speak of my feelings for you?"

"Never. Not if you want me to continue to be your friend."

His brows snapped down. "I wish to be more than friends, Moya. I've said—"

She threw up a hand, stopping him in his tracks. "You don't get to decide this. I'm probably going to regret even being friends, but you've no one to guide you, and I can't just leave you alone to struggle through the duchess's house party without a mentor."

Wulf sighed. "You are a stubborn woman."

"So now you know yet another thing about me. If you want me to continue to speak to you and advise you on how to comport yourself, then you have to stop telling me this"—she waved a hand—"this story."

"It is not a story, *but,*" he said firmly before she could interrupt, "I agree to stop speaking of my feelings since they make you uncomfortable." *Damn it, I could name a dozen women who would welcome a declaration from me—two of them princesses of the realm, and all of them beauties. But not Moya. She stands here with her mouth thinned in disapproval. Damn it, why must I fall in love with such a stubborn woman?*

He'd never been put so thoroughly in his place in his life. Part of him wanted to storm away, while another part wanted to toss her over his shoulder and take her to his cottage and show her what he felt in a way she couldn't deny.

But as he looked into her eyes, he realized that her pride would defeat him at every turn. Tata Natasha was right: love was far more complicated than he'd realized. And for the first time since he'd met Lily, he realized an astonishing, frightening fact—it was distinctly possible that, no matter what he said or did, she might not accept him.

The thought sent an ice-cold shiver through his soul. He'd finally found the woman he'd dreamed of, the woman destined to be his, yet she wouldn't even let him discuss his feelings. *Bloody hell, what am I to do?*

He frowned as he considered his options. Perhaps she'd already given him an answer by offering to help him navigate their bizarre societal rules. At least then she'd continue to speak with him, and that was something . . . wasn't it? Perhaps mere talking could lead to something more, like a kiss. *A kiss would be nice.* His gaze brushed her plump bottom lip. *Very nice, indeed.*

"Are we agreed, then?" She brushed an errant curl from her cheek. "I'm sorry if my outspokenness shocks you, but it's best that we determine this right now. You distract me from my purpose in coming here to the duchess's house party, and I can't allow you to do that."

He caught the note of wistfulness in her voice and hope bloomed anew. "It is I who should be sorry. You and I are passionate people; perhaps it is only natural that we should find ourselves at cross-purposes now and again, *nyet?*" He smiled at her. "I do not wish you to stop speaking with me. Is unacceptable. I will do what I must to keep that from happening."

Her expression softened and she offered him a shy smile that sent his heart thudding in his chest. "I wouldn't like that, either."

"Finally, something we agree upon."

She chuckled. "It didn't take us long, did it?"

"Two days, but who is counting." He grinned. "But I must ask for one thing first." He captured her hand and placed a kiss to her fingers in a courtly, nonthreatening manner. "I must ask for your patience. I am not the sort of man to keep his feelings to himself, but I will try."

"Thank you." Her gaze locked with his and he became aware of the softness of her hand in his. He lifted her hand again, only this time he turned it over and pressed a kiss into her palm.

Instantly, her eyes turned smoky and her lips parted. Just as quickly, her cheeks blazed and she tugged her hand free and moved away.

It dawned on him that she hadn't asked for any restrictions on his actions, only his words. He almost grinned, but wisely hid his jubilation. *Ah, Moya, already I have found a crack in the walls you build. If you forbid me to speak, then I will seduce you with something other than words.*

Unaware that she was already bested, Lily clasped her hands behind her back and took some distancing steps. "Now that we've settled this, I can spend my time doing what I came here to do: find a husband."

"Someone like the Earl of Huntley?"

She didn't seem able to meet his gaze. "Perhaps."

"Do not deny that he is your intended target."

"Target? I'm not shooting at him."

"Yes, you are. With little cupid arrows of demure smiles and shy glances, hoping one will strike his heart so that he will wish to marry you and save your family."

"It sounds horrid when you say it like that."

"Nonsense. I honor your commitment to your family. How could I not? But this kind of love you talk about—one born of necessity—will not sustain you." His gaze locked with hers, his voice deepening. "You deserve real passion, Moya. The touch of a man who makes you tremble."

Her chin lifted. "If I marry a man I can honor and respect, the rest will come."

"Perhaps and perhaps not. Sadly, if it doesn't, you won't even know what you are missing." He moved closer to her, ready to prove his point.

Lily caught the look in his eyes and her pulse leapt in response. Before he reached her, she whirled to face the window. "It's certainly bright outside. I do hope the weather holds, for the duchess has been talking about a visit to the folly built on the island in the lake."

He stood so close behind her that she could feel his warm breath on her hair. "It is very sunny. I do not think it will rain."

"Good, for it would be sad if we didn't get to see the folly. I've heard it's beautiful."

Her thoughts were completely divorced from what she was saying. Was Wulf right? Was it possible that if she married an honorable and good man, one she respected and cared for, passion might never flare between them?

She rubbed her arms, feeling alone once more. *Never is a long time.* She didn't wish for a passionless marriage, but how did one make certain that didn't happen?

There had to be signs she could look for, clues to the ability for that passion to bloom. But would she recognize them? She knew so little about it.

She turned to look up at Wulf. He was a man of experience. Perhaps he would know. "May I ask you something?"

"You may ask me anything you wish."

"How would I know if passion were possible between myself and a man?"

A slow smile curved his mouth, his eyes warming. "Ah, that is the question. Passion is not easy for some, and too easy for others."

"That doesn't help. Is there a test of some sort?"

"A test?" He looked surprised, but then he chuckled. "I hadn't thought of them as tests, but I suppose they could be used so. For example, you might try this." He brushed his fingertips down her bared arm, moving slowly.

Goose bumps lifted, and a delicious tingle raced through her.

His long fingers locked about her wrists and he tugged her forward until her chest rested against his. "Do you feel that? The tremor that passes between us?"

She could only stare up at him and nod. Her heart stuttered in an agony of anticipation, her entire body softening.

"That, Moya, is passion. And it is a rare, rare gift."

Every word stirred her more; a wanton restlessness filled her. "Th-that seems to be a very effective test. I'll have to remember it." She tried to move away, but he held her firm.

"There is more. You should know it all."

"Oh?"

"*Da.* A kiss, Moya. If it makes your heart beat like a caged bird, then you have passion. And if not—" He slowly shook his head.

"Those—" Her voice was so husky that she cleared her throat. "Those are good tests."

"You need to perform them correctly, though, if you really wish to tell." He slid his hands up her arms to her shoulders. "We should kiss. Just as a practice."

A kiss? She blinked. "Wulf, that's not—"

"You *must* know. You are young and vibrant. A marriage without passion would be a fate worse than death. Think about it." He bent so his lips were beside her ear, his warm breath on her cheek. "Years and years, cold and alone, never touched, or worse, dreading it."

She wet her lips nervously, torn between a shiver of intimate desire and the barren picture Wulf had painted.

But if I want, I can try it right now, this moment. She closed her eyes, lifted up on her tiptoes, and pressed her mouth to his. He enveloped her, his arms slipping about her as he held her closer, his mouth moving over hers, teasing and tempting, opening her lips so that they were, finally, one.

At the touch of his tongue against hers, a flash of heat roared through her, a delicious mix of shock and desire. She couldn't get enough of him, enough of his touch, enough of the intoxicating feel of his hard muscles as they slid under her seeking fingers, enough of his hands molding her to him.

His hands slipped from her waist to her hips and then lower, to cup her bottom. She moaned against his mouth as he lifted her, rubbing her body the length of his as he plundered her mouth, thrusting his tongue between her lips in an intimate dance.

She was awash in feelings she'd never before experienced, feelings that threatened to drown her, pull her under, lose her. And she thrilled to it, feeling so alive, so—

A servant's voice called out to MacDougal, the sound splashing over Lily like a bucket of ice water. She broke the kiss, breathless and aching, her gaze flying to the door.

Wulf's gaze followed hers and he stepped away, too.

MacDougal's voice rose in the hallway. "Och, now, John, get the polish, fer the candlesticks need a bit o' work."

A servant replied, and then silence.

Lily took a deep breath. "Th-that was unwise."

"Nonsense. Knowledge is necessary."

She pressed a hand to her cheek, her fingers trembling. "You should go. Someone will find you here."

Wulf's hot gaze swept over her. "Are you sure, Moya?"

She wasn't sure of anything, except that Wulf must leave now, or she might do something that would ruin her chances of a good marriage forever. She nodded. "I'm sure."

He sent her a regretful look. "Are you certain? I can—"

"Go."

"But I—"

"Please."

His lips thinned and he looked as if he might say something more, but one look at her face and he let out his breath. "Fine." He collected his cloak and tossed it over his arm. "But only because you asked me to." He walked to the window, pausing by her to whisper. "When you next see Huntley, think about our kiss."

He put a finger under her chin and lifted her face to his, their gazes locking. For a long time, he remained thus, looking deeply into her eyes. A wild rush of thoughts flew through her: Perhaps just one more kiss— If only Papa hadn't made such a mull of things— What if she didn't feel anything at all with Huntley—

Wulf smiled and dropped his hand. "Think of me, Moya." He turned and crossed to the window. He glanced outside to make certain no one was in the courtyard, and then, with a final heated look and a swirl of black cape, he was gone.

Eight

From the Diary of the Duchess of Roxburghe
The meeting has occurred, the introductions made, first impressions accomplished, and now all that's left is to make certain our two lovely candidates spend a lot of time together . . . a *lot* of time together. Preferably *alone*.

Two days later, Lily stepped onto the wide portico where the guests milled about, talking and laughing in small groups as footmen served trays of iced lemonade. She carried her bonnet by its ribbons as she strolled to the eastern edge of the terrace, smiling at those who greeted her.

The vista was breathtaking. The late-morning sun spread a golden glow over the lawn, which raced down to the lake on one side and the river on the other. A faint wind stirred the skirts of Lily's blue walking gown, and she shivered.

The shiver brought on by a cool breeze was vastly different from one caused by being kissed by a green-eyed prince. One type made one want to run for shelter, while the other made one want to beg for more.

Despite her determination not to, she glanced about, but he was nowhere to be seen. *Yet*. Over the last two days, he'd been at every amusement planned by the duchess: the opera singer brought in from London, a battledore tournament with lavish prizes, a late-night whist party. He was an amusing companion, his blunt assessment of every event sending her into giggles when she least expected it, but his presence had greatly hampered her ability to spend time with Huntley. Fortunately, today's picnic offered a chance to remedy that.

Still, Wulf had been true to his word and no longer importuned her with outrageous declarations. But while he was on his best behavior verbally, it seemed that he never lost an opportunity to touch her. They were seemingly innocent touches—a brush of his hand over hers, his chest against her arm, his foot by hers under the dining-room table—so she could hardly protest, but each one reminded her vividly of their embrace in the library.

Before that day, the few kisses she'd shared had been shy, timid, and decidedly chaste. She now realized they'd also been passionless. But then she'd kissed Wulf, and now she knew what to look for. Now, all she had to do was entice Huntley into a kiss.

Sadly, the earl was far more polite than Wulf, who would never let a thing like propriety stand between him and the woman he wanted. If Lily wanted a kiss from Huntley, she'd have to win his confidence and then maneuver him into a private meeting. If he didn't come up to the mark and sweep her into his arms, then unladylike as it might be, she might have to kiss him. But at least then she'd have the reassurance she sought—that passion lurked between her and Huntley, too, but was just more subtle than the roaring sensuality that Wulf enjoyed sparking.

She was certain that, with time, she and Huntley would have the same passion that Wulf inspired.

The wind stirred again, and she rubbed her arms vigorously and glanced at the door. Perhaps she should run back to her room and fetch the red cloak Dahlia had lent her. Lightly lined, it was the perfect wrap for early spring. She walked toward the door, but just as she reached it, the duchess came sailing out.

Her grace was dressed in a fitted habit, an impressive riding hat pinned to her red wig, a white gauze scarf wrapped about her neck and floating behind her. She was followed by a swirl of pugs who barked madly and jumped up in the air, as if trying to entice her to pick them up.

She caught sight of Lily and brightened. "Miss Balfour, how serendipitous! I was going to seek you out and see how you were faring. I didn't get the chance to speak to you at all yesterday, although I noted that you and Huntley were paired together in the battledore contest." The duchess gave Lily an arch look. "I saw him giving you instruction in how to better use your racket."

Lily hid a grimace. It was the one time Huntley had said or done something that had irked her. She was a good player, but for some reason, before he'd even seen her play, he'd assumed she knew nothing about the game and had taken it upon himself to explain every possible swing in detail.

She'd borne it with a smile, although she'd been irked. *Which is silly, for he was just trying to be helpful.* "His lordship was very instructive."

"He seems very fond of you. He even told me that— Oh!" One of the pugs had launched itself high enough to paw one of the duchess's leather gloves. She examined the glove and frowned at the dog. "Look what you've done, Meenie! You tore it." She turned. "MacDougal!"

As if he'd been hiding inside the door, the butler instantly stepped outside. "Yes, yer grace?"

"Meenie tore my glove!"

The butler turned an eagle stare on the offending pug, who promptly threw itself on its back and pawed the air in a pathetic manner.

Lily covered her mouth in an attempt to keep from laughing.

The duchess chuckled with her, her blue eyes twinkling. "They're terrible, but just look at those angelic eyes. How can I say no?"

"It's impossible," Lily agreed. The swarm of dogs, all of them now on their feet, looked eagerly at the duchess, ready to follow her anywhere but where she ordered them. They were as fat as Christmas geese, their bellies round, their little legs splayed to hold their weight. But it was the expression on their faces that made Lily smile—they all looked upon the duchess with adoring eyes and wide grins, their tongues lolling in a variety of directions, completely and utterly in love with her.

The duchess peeled off her riding gloves. "Mac-Dougal, I have another pair in my bedchamber."

The butler bowed, took the gloves, and then handed them to a nearby footman.

The young man started to dash back into the house but Lily stopped him. "Would you mind also fetching my red cloak? It's in the wardrobe in my bedchamber."

"Yes, miss." The footman bowed and hurried off.

The duchess eyed the pugs. "When I have my new gloves, *none* of you will mar them. Do you hear me?"

The dogs didn't answer, though Lily thought that one or two of them grinned even more broadly.

MacDougal cleared his throat. "Pardon me, yer grace, but perhaps we should lock the puir bairns in the sittin' room until ye're gone. They'll wish to go wit' ye, and ye know how they like to worry Lord MacTavish's bull."

"Lud, yes. I've asked MacTavish to move the bull out of the south field, but he's ignored my requests. I thought for certain we'd lost Teenie the last time they got into that blasted bull's way." The duchess stooped and picked up the two closest pugs and handed them to MacDougal, who turned and handed them to a waiting footman to carry them off.

The duchess turned back to the pack and began collecting the remaining dogs, who—having seen the way the wind was blowing—were now dancing out of her reach. Lily was surprised when neither the footmen nor the butler offered to catch the remaining pugs, but stayed where they were, politely looking the other way as the duchess scrambled about, huffing and puffing with her efforts.

Just as Lily started to help, the duchess caught two more dogs and passed them to the butler. Once again, the pugs were carried into the house, squirming and barking as they went.

"May I help you catch the last two?" Lily asked.

"What? Oh no, dear." The duchess shoved her hat farther back on her head, her wig sliding with it. "The footmen have chased the poor things until they're quite nervous, so it's best if I collect them myself."

"Ah."

The duchess set off after the last pugs, but they had been well warned of their fate by their wiggling, barking brethren and began a series of evasive maneuvers, spinning out of reach, running between the legs of two nearby footmen, and dashing in circles around the duchess.

Her grace leapt first left and then right, trying to grab one, and then the other dog, but to no avail.

Lily bit her bottom lip to keep from giggling as one

dashed under the duchess's skirts and then out the other side, his tongue flying out the side of his mouth.

The duchess was now panting. "Roxburghe vows that chasing is good exercise for them, and so he encouraged the footmen to dash after them pell-mell, but all it's done is teach them how to escape." She glared over her shoulder at the footmen as she spoke. "There are *better* ways to exercise the dogs."

The footman closest to the duchess nodded smartly. "Yes, yer grace. Chasin' is bad fer the dogs, it is."

"Exactly." The duchess lunged forward and finally caught one of the pugs. "There!" She handed the dog to the footman and looked about for the final one. "Ah, Feenie! Come to Mama."

The final pug ran a safe distance away before turning to face the duchess, his tail spinning in a circle, his front feet splayed as he readied to hop out of the way.

The duchess took a step forward.

The dog hopped backward.

"Blast it! Hold still, you—" The duchess dove for the pug.

The dog turned and ran past the duchess, grabbing her gauze scarf as it went.

Lily reached out to help, but before the dog could get more than a foot away, MacDougal stepped on the scarf, pinning it to the ground. The dog tugged and tugged and, in doing so, allowed the butler to scoop him up.

MacDougal removed the end of the scarf from the

dog's mouth. "Feenie, ye spalpeen. Stop yer yappin'." The butler inclined his head at her grace. "Pardon me, yer grace. I'll deposit this bundle in the sitting room and return."

The duchess blew out her breath and adjusted her hat. "Thank you, MacDougal." She watched the butler leave, the little dog licking the butler's chin in an attempt to get back into the old man's favor. Fanning herself, she said in a breathless voice, "My, but that took some doing."

"Yes, it did. Are you well?"

"I'm fine. Just a bit out of breath."

As the duchess spoke, Huntley stepped out of the wide doorway and paused on the threshold, one foot on the step. Every female eye instantly locked on him, and Lily couldn't blame them.

The earl was dressed for riding in well-fitted breeches, his white-topped Hessians shining like mirrors, his coat smooth over his lithe frame. His neckcloth was snow-white and framed his square chin, complementing his handsome face.

He cut quite a dashing figure and Lily couldn't help but stand a little straighter when his gaze passed over every woman present and alighted on her. Instantly, he brightened and came her way.

The duchess couldn't have looked happier as she murmured to Lily, "That's a promising sign."

He reached them and bowed. "Your grace. Miss Balfour."

Lily curtsied, while the duchess inclined her head in a gracious manner. Her grace took in his riding clothes. "I take it that you will be riding."

"Miss Gordon and I hoped to sneak in a quick gallop this morning. We wish to stretch our riding legs a bit, something we don't get to do as often as we like." His gaze touched on Lily's blue walking gown, and his brows knit. "Miss Balfour, you're not riding?"

"I am claiming a seat in one of the carriages. I'm not the best rider, you know."

The duchess made an impatient sound. "You just need a little tutoring. Perhaps you should change into your habit and allow Huntley to show you how it's done."

Huntley hesitated, but quickly said, "I should be honored if Miss Balfour will allow me."

Lily laughed. "You would be irked, is what you'd be, for I'd slow you down and you just admitted you were longing for a gallop. Go and ride! I'll see you at the picnic. We'll both be happier for having arrived in our chosen forms of transportation."

He laughed, his sherry-brown eyes warm as he captured her hand and pressed a firm kiss to her fingers. "I look forward to seeing you there. May I hope to sit beside you?"

"You'll get there first, so pray save a seat for me."

"I'll do that." He gave her hand a squeeze, then bowed to the duchess and went to join a group of men who stood examining the horses.

The duchess's gaze followed him. "He's quite taken with you."

"He's a very nice man."

"And wealthy. *Very* wealthy. Don't forget that!" The duchess regarded Huntley with pride, as if she'd made him herself. "And so polite, too."

"Very much so." He was so polite that not once over the last two days had she been able to imagine him kissing her the way Wulf had. But then, the earl was the sort of man who respected propriety. *That's good . . . isn't it?*

The duchess beamed. "Things are going along splendidly."

Lily was saved from answering when a short, round lady with a large, white feather in her bonnet called on her grace to serve as a moderator for a disagreement she was having with an equally portly gentleman, over the merits of a mustard plaster over Persian Tonic for a cough. Excusing herself, the duchess went to answer the call of her other guests, and Lily was left to wait for her cloak and observe Huntley.

He was everything she could possibly want in a husband—a true gentleman, kind, polite, handsome, and capable of helping her family. He was the perfect candidate, and she should have been thrilled to the tips of her toes that he seemed interested in her. *I should be thankful for this opportunity.* She straightened her shoulders. *I am* thankful.

So why am I feeling so uncertain? I must throw myself into this with full enthusiasm, and yet I keep hesitating.

Lily bit her lip, her heart sinking. If she were honest, she knew why: since Wulf's visit to the library, it hadn't been the earl who'd filled her thoughts, but the prince. No matter how she tried not to, she couldn't help but compare the earl to Wulf, and for some reason she couldn't fathom, the earl seemed . . . less. *But once I know him better, I'm sure that will cease to be so.*

"Ah," the duchess said, sweeping past Lily toward the footman who'd just exited the house. "My gloves!" She drew them on as the footman delivered the cape to Lily, who murmured her thanks.

A group of maids came from the house carrying large hampers, which were strapped to the backs of the carriages. "There's the food," the duchess said with satisfaction. "If you'll pardon me, I will go and make certain that everything I requested has been brought out."

"Of course."

"I'll see you when we arrive, then. That is, I'll see you with *Huntley*." With a smile, the duchess hurried off.

Lily was left to wait as the carriages were lined up along the far side of the courtyard.

"It looks as if everyone is going, doesn't it?" came a feminine voice at Lily's side.

She turned to find Miss Gordon dressed in an elegant habit of lilac that became her brown hair and eyes. Lily smiled. "Who could say no to a picnic on a day like this?"

Miss Gordon took a deep breath of the fresh air, aglow with pleasure. "Who indeed?"

Over the last few days, Lily and Miss Gordon had had several pleasant conversations and had even partnered to win a battledore match. "A picnic doesn't offer as much exercise as battledore, but it has its merits."

Miss Gordon chuckled. "Not the way you play it, no." Her gaze flickered over Lily's clothing. "You are not riding?"

"To be honest, I don't ride very well." She threw up a hand. "Spare me your disappointment. I've already had to bear Huntley's and it was more than enough."

Miss Gordon laughed. "Was he blue as a megrim?"

"Bluer." Lily eyed Miss Gordon with interest. "You know the earl very well."

"I've known him for ages. His wife—" Miss Gordon's smile dimmed. "Sarah was my dearest friend, and poor Geoffrey was devastated when she died."

"I'm so sorry for your loss."

"Thank you. We miss her, of course, but we cannot dwell." Though her eyes were shiny with unshed tears, Miss Gordon managed a shaky laugh. "La, I've grown maudlin! And on such a beautiful day, too."

Lily slipped her arm through Miss Gordon's and gave her a hug. "I shouldn't have pried."

"Nonsense. You were asking a simple question. I'm the one who turned into a watering pot." She turned and looked at the guests. "It looks as if we're all here."

"There are so many."

"Not for one of the duchess's amusements. I've been here with three times as many guests."

"What a crowd!"

"Yes, you never see the same people, and so it's difficult to have a meaningful conversation, much less remember their names." Miss Gordon chuckled. "Huntley says my mind is too weak to retain names, although it never forgets one bit of gossip."

"My sister Dahlia says that gossip is good for the soul."

"It definitely keeps life interesting." Miss Gordon tugged on her gloves. "It will be a lovely outing."

"Yes. This seems like a merry crowd."

"Oh, the duchess never invites boring people. She says they give her the frets."

Lily laughed, looking over to where the duchess stood speaking with MacDougal. She was gesturing toward the line of carriages across the courtyard. Each one was hooked up to teams of exceptional-looking horses. "What lovely horses."

"Oh, yes. The duke is mad about horses. They say he has one for every day of the year and two for every Sunday."

"I can't imagine having the funds to feed so many."

"Nor can I. Tell me, Miss— Do you mind if I call you Lily?"

"Of course not. It would make me feel at home." Lily smiled. "I miss my sister far more than I thought I would."

"Please call me Emma, then. You have two sisters, don't you?" At Lily's surprised look, Emma said, "Your sister Rose's brilliant marriage was the talk of the *ton* for months."

"Oh? And what did they say?"

"Nothing notorious. Only that the duchess orchestrated the courtship and that your sister and Lord Sinclair are wildly and passionately in love." Emma made a humorous moue. "That's quite against fashion, you know, which makes it very fashionable in itself."

Lily laughed. "Fashion is so contrary."

Emma's gaze flickered over Lily's gown underneath her red cape. Of pale blue muslin and set with a wide, white ribbon under her breasts decorated with a small line of red rosettes, it was deceptively simple. "If you don't mind me asking, where did you purchase that gown? It's lovely."

Lily had made her gown, but it would have been gauche to admit it, so she merely said, "Someone from Caith Manor made it."

"It's not French?" Surprise lifted Emma's voice.

"Not at all. I—she got the pattern from a women's magazine and made it from there."

"I wish I had someone to make me such gowns. I'm relegated to purchasing them on Bond Street, which is well enough, but does make one's clothing seem far too much like everyone else's." Emma's gaze locked on something over Lily's shoulder. Whatever it was, it drew the attention of everyone near them. "Don't look, but Prince Wulfinski just arrived. Such a handsome man." She slanted Lily an arch look. "You know him rather well, I believe."

Lily kept her face expressionless. "Slightly." *If Emma has noticed how much attention Wulf has been paying to me, then how many others have?* With a casual shrug, Lily said, "The prince doesn't know many people yet."

"But he does have a preference." Emma's gaze turned back to Wulf. "He's escorting his grandmother. I've heard she's quite a character."

Lily turned and saw that Wulf was tying off a large black gelding to a shiny brougham that held a tiny, shriveled apple of a woman dressed all in black.

"His grandmother is the grand duchess something or other." Emma sighed. "See? I don't remember names well at all. One of my many failings."

From across the courtyard, Wulf's gaze caught Lily's. Her breath tightened and her skin prickled as if a gust from a fire had suddenly swept over her. He smiled and moved toward her, ignoring a sharp call from his grandmother, who turned a gaze as black as her gown in Lily's direction, a disapproving scowl on her face.

But Wulf paid the woman no heed as he crossed the courtyard, his narrow hips encircled by a thick leather belt, his loose, black breeches tucked into leather boots that lacked the shine of the Hessians worn by the other gentlemen. Whereas the other men wore a cravat, waistcoat, and fitted coat, he wore a white, flowing shirt and a loose coat, a tie knotted carelessly about his neck, a cape swinging from his broad shoulders.

But it was his mouth, both sensual and masculine, framed by his trim black beard, that quickened Lily's breath the most. Her hand, still tight about the ribbons of her bonnet, grew damp.

"He's very handsome, isn't he?" Emma murmured, her gaze moving appreciatively across Wulf. "Rather like a large bear."

He is certainly as strong as a bear. The first day they'd met, he'd carried her through the woods as if she'd weighed no more than a feather. And two days ago when he's kissed her, he'd actually lifted her off her feet and had held her there forever. Her gaze flickered to his arms; she was well aware of his strength. She wondered if she could fit her hands about his muscular arms. Not that she would ever try, of course, but still—

She shook her head. She had to stop thinking about "ifs" and instead think about what really *was*—her father was counting on her and she could not fail him.

And yet . . . just looking at Wulf made her wish—

She closed her eyes. *No.*

And with a hollow ache in her chest, she turned her back on the prince. "Come, Miss Gordon. Show me the horse you're to ride."

Nine

From the Diary of the Duchess of Roxburghe
I will not stand for Prince Wulfinski interfering in
the budding romance I've set on course between
Lily Balfour and the Earl of Huntley. I hope the
prince is used to failure, for he will make no gains
in this particular pursuit.

I shall make certain of that.

Emma leaned forward. "Lily, you seem upset. Is it—"

"No, no. I'm just looking to see if the duchess is
ready for us to leave."

"Where has her grace gone to— Ah! There she is,
by the carriage."

Lily couldn't help but notice that while she faced the
crowd, they were looking past her at the prince. And
who could blame them? It was difficult enough to—

"Good morning."

The deep voice poured over her like honey, and
aware that many eyes were now turned her way, she
reluctantly turned and curtsied.

Emma curtsied, too. "Your Highness, we've only met briefly, but I'm Miss Emma—"

"Gordon," he finished, bowing in her direction. "I never forget a name or"—his teeth flashed—"a pretty face."

Emma turned bright pink, and Lily suspected that the older woman might say something arch, but Wulf's attention had already returned to Lily.

He inclined his head in her direction. "I was hoping you would be here."

She colored under his gaze, her lashes dropping as she looked away. Her skin was as pale as fresh cream and decorated with a smattering of freckles across her nose—exactly eight—which he suspected would become prominent if she stayed in the sun for any length of time. His gaze flickered to her neck and lower. He frowned. "You are not riding?"

"I will be traveling by carriage."

"Do you know which one? Perhaps—"

"Miss Balfour!" the duchess called from across the courtyard. "Lady Charlotte insists that I join her in her carriage, so I will not be riding after all. Would you care to join us?" Her grace was standing with Lady Charlotte, who was wearing a ridiculously large hat with two huge feathers poking from the top, one of which was already broken.

As Lady Charlotte went to accept a hand from a footman, Lord Huntley broke from the small group of gentlemen standing nearby. He waved off the footman and assisted Lady Charlotte into the carriage.

"Miss Balfour?" the duchess asked again. "Are you coming?"

Wulf's jaw tightened. There was no mistaking the frown that flickered across the duchess's face when she looked at him.

"Sadly," Emma said in a low voice, "I don't think her grace is really *asking*."

"So it seems." Lily curtsied to Emma and Wulf. "Excuse me, but I am wanted." She left, hurrying off as if the hounds of hell were hard on her heels.

He rubbed his chin as he watched her. She was such a small thing, his Moya, her hair gleaming red-gold in the late-morning sun. She reached the carriage and, taking Huntley's hand, stepped up, her cape and gown revealing the tempting curve of her ass as she bent to take a seat. Instantly, Wulf's body was ablaze. *Oh, Moya, what you do to me—*

The sound of someone clearing her throat recalled him, and he turned back to Miss Gordon. "I'm sorry. I was lost"—he pointed to his head—"here."

"I saw exactly where you got lost," she returned in a surprisingly dry tone.

Up until now, Wulf hadn't been impressed with any of the women he'd met at the duchess's castle other than Lily. But as he looked into Miss Gordon's smiling brown eyes, he realized he'd been hasty. She didn't bat her eyes and giggle like a schoolgirl as the other women had. She had a steady, direct gaze that he rather liked. "I beg your pardon for my inattention. If you do not mind, can you tell me what we do here today, about this—what do you call it? A peeknil?"

She chuckled. "You mean 'picnic.'"

"And what is this picnic?"

"It's a luncheon served outdoors. I daresay you have something similar in your country, for I know they have them in France and Italy, and I would imagine everywhere else, too."

He shrugged. "It is cold in Oxenburg, and very wet. I do not think we have such things."

"Too bad, for it's wonderful fun. We all go to the same location—atop a hill with a view, or near a lake or something pretty. The servants pack up a luncheon and we take it to that spot and we eat."

He waited. When she merely smiled up at him, he frowned. "That's all there is to a picnic?"

"Yes. Isn't it enough?"

"Not to me. You just"—he waved a hand—"eat under the sun?"

"Oh, don't look like that. I assure you that it's very civilized and is an excellent opportunity to commune with nature."

"In my country, we do not commune with nature. We sleep out of doors when we must, when we travel or camp. But we do not visit it so."

"It's considered quite romantic."

"Not if it rains. Or if there are"—he walked his fingers up his arm—"what do you call them?"

"Ants?" She chuckled. "Yes, those can be very off-putting for a picnic. But it's something to do and the duchess *loves* having something to do. Besides, everyone is going, so why not enjoy this lovely weather?"

"I am going. I just did not fully understand what it was." He watched as Huntley leaned against the carriage, talking to Lily and Lady Charlotte while the duchess stood to one side, beaming as if they were all puppets of her making.

Miss Gordon's gaze followed his. "Please pardon me for being blunt, but you seem intrigued with Miss Balfour."

"I enjoy her company." At Miss Gordon's amused look, he grinned sheepishly. "It is no secret that I also find her attractive. You have noticed, *nyet?*"

"You have been very attentive. I mentioned that to her this morning."

"Ah. Perhaps that is why she was so determined to leave just as I arrived."

"Because of something I said? I hope not."

"She is a prickly one, is Miss Balfour. Very, very stubborn, too."

"She's lovely."

"She is exactly as I have dreamed," he said quietly.

Miss Gordon's eyes widened. "Careful, Your Highness, or someone might think you are in love."

"Perhaps I am." He crossed his arms and rocked back on his heels. "I am thinking I am more so every day."

"My! You are a refreshing change." When he

quirked a brow her way, she gave a rather brittle laugh. "Most men do not so freely admit when they are in love." Her gaze flickered to Huntley. "Some don't even know it."

"Fools. I know when I feel something, and I feel it strongly. My Tata Natasha—my grandmother— thinks I have fallen too swiftly for Miss Lily for it to be real, but she will see."

"She is wrong. Falling in love can take only a moment." Miss Gordon looked past Wulf, a sad curve touching her lips. "But it can last forever."

Wulf followed her gaze to where Huntley was saying a laughing good-bye to Lily and Lady Charlotte. *So that's how it is.* His sympathy stirred. "Men can be fools."

Emma reluctantly returned her gaze back to his. "That is not a particularly comforting thought, Your Highness."

"Please, call me Wulf."

"I would be delighted. Pray call me Emma."

"Emma, then." At her smile, he continued, "As for men and their foibles, we are not the most observant of creatures and frequently miss what is under our very noses."

"How do you know this when most men that I'm acquainted with do not?"

"My grandmother is not shy in pointing out every fault—perceived and otherwise—of everyone she meets, especially me. Perhaps it is due to self-preservation that I honestly admit to the faults that are mine."

Emma chuckled again. "However it is, your openness is a unique trait. Sadly, you are not the only one who is taken by Miss Balfour."

"You speak of Huntley," Wulf said, suddenly grim.

"Perhaps. Of course, with the duchess sponsoring her . . ." Emma shrugged. "It is a great advantage."

"So I've been told." Wulf watched as Huntley laughed at something Lily said. "They like one another." Wulf's heart felt like a weight in his chest.

Emma sighed regretfully. "Yes. I know Huntley well, and he is charmed with your Lily."

Wulf scowled. "This, I do not like."

"I'm not fond of it myself."

Damn it, it seemed as if he'd waited his entire life to meet the woman of his dreams, and now, because she was unusually stubborn and had a meddling duchess for a godmother, things were not progressing as they should. What should have been easy was difficult, and growing more so by the moment. "The duchess would prefer that I see less of Miss Lily."

"And if she has her way, I will see less and less of Huntley, too, until . . ."

"Until what?"

"Until Lily and Huntley become attached. And then engaged. And once they are engaged, there is nothing we can do about it—especially if the duchess announces it in front of everyone, which she will."

"I don't understand. Why would a public announcement make their engagement more difficult to break off?"

"It is scandalous to break off an engagement, especially for a man. Huntley is very protective of his honor. Once he's set such a course, nothing will sway him from it."

Wulf scowled. "So many rules! You are all tied up in knots with them."

"There are far too many."

Wulf rubbed his chest. He'd thought he'd made progress with Lily over the last few days, first with their kiss in the library, and then their continued conversations after that day. Though she hadn't been encouraging, neither had she been discouraging. Today, something was different. Today she was letting him know that she was moving closer to Huntley and thus further away from him.

He watched her smile at something the earl was saying. *But our kiss, Moya. How can you forget that?*

He had to find a way to turn her attention back to him, but how? How did one secure the attentions of a woman determined not to pay any attention to one? How did one— His gaze fell on his companion. "Hmmm."

Her brows lifting, Miss Emma put a hand to her cheek. "What? Do I have something on my face?"

"*Nyet.*" He slipped a hand under her elbow. "Miss Emma, we seem to be in danger of losing the attentions of those we hold dear."

"So it seems," she said wistfully.

"Then let us become partners, we two."

"In what way?"

"We will become partners in securing the interest of . . . shall we call them 'others'?"

Her eyes were bright with curiosity. "That's an interesting proposition."

"Huntley and Lily have the duchess watching out for them, so you and I will watch out for each other."

Emma's gaze slid to where Huntley and Lily conversed while the duchess beamed upon them like a fairy godmother. "It would be nice to have someone on my side for a change."

"*Da*, and I think I know a way to capture their attention."

"Oh? Pray continue, Wulf. You have my complete attention."

"Simple. By pretending to possess an interest in each other."

Emma's brows lifted. "You think they will pay more attention to us if they think we are courting?"

"It has certainly made us pay more attention to them."

"True." She pursed her lips. "A very intriguing scheme. I suppose it wouldn't hurt to have an ally."

"It is war, Miss Gordon. An all-out war."

"Then the deal is struck, Your Highness. When do we begin?"

"Now is a good time. Are either of them looking this way?"

"No, they are merely talking to one an— Oh!" Emma turned her head slightly and said in a low voice, "Huntley just gestured toward his horse, so he's facing this way."

Wulf instantly captured her hand and lifted it to his lips, smiling as he kissed her fingers. "Do you know how to simper?"

"Oh, I've always wished to be an actress. How's this?" She gave him such an odd simper that he laughed.

She joined him. "Was it that bad?"

"It was worse than bad. Is he still looking this way?"

From under her lashes, she looked toward the carriage. "He's looking directly at us."

"Excellent." Wulf stepped closer and held her hand between his own hands. "Now you must pretend you think I am handsome and funny and know many, many interesting stories."

She chuckled and sent him an arch look. "I think I like this game." She glanced under her lashes toward the carriage. "He's turned back to Lily, but his expression before he did was quite stern."

"Excellent. We will make it more so as the day progresses."

She slanted him a humorous look. "I must applaud your devious nature. I fear for your enemies."

"You are a wise woman. Lily will be at the duchess's house for less than three weeks, so I have precious little time to gain her interest."

"That shouldn't be too difficult."

"But it is. I've told her how I feel, and she refuses to accept it and has forbidden me to discuss it with her ever again."

"You told her? Just like that?"

"*Da.* Why?"

Emma hesitated. "I don't mean to intrude, but while I'm sure that your declaration was quite touching, women like to be wooed."

"Hmm. I shall think about that."

"Good." She glanced back at Huntley. "At least your beloved doesn't think of you as a sort of sibling."

Wulf winced. "Has he said so?"

"Many times. I was Huntley's late wife's best friend, almost like a sister-in-law, which was fine while she was alive. Now . . . now I see him as something far, far more, while he holds me firmly as 'sister.'" Her color high, she added, "It's difficult to change that vision once it's established."

Wulf caught sight of Huntley casting a concerned glance their way and pressed another kiss to Emma's hand. "We will change how he sees you."

She chuckled. "My dear Prince Wulfinski, if you think it might help either of our causes, please shower me with your attentions whenever you wish. I shall attempt to bear the burden with grace."

He grinned. "I shall. Soon everyone will think we are the most intimate of friends—"

"No, no," she said, suddenly flustered. "Not intimate, just close."

"'Intimate' . . . that is a bad word?"

"It implies certain liberties."

"Ah. Then with you, I will be close. With Miss Balfour, I will be intimate."

Emma's color deepened.

"What? I said it wrong?"

"Yes . . . and no." She gave an uncertain laugh. "You speak very plainly, Your Highness. I can see you're a pragmatic sort of man."

"I'm a very determined man, and I will have Lily Balfour."

Emma regarded him with fascination. "I think you could do anything you set your mind to."

"So can you. I can tell you are a woman of strength. It is in your eyes."

"Thank you, but I don't feel very strong where Huntley is concerned."

"But you *are* that strong, Miss Emma. And if you wish to win Huntley, you must remember that."

Her expression turned wistful. "I wish I believed that, but I—" Her gaze went over Wulf's shoulder.

He turned and saw that Huntley had mounted and ridden his horse to the side of Lily's carriage. He was leaning down, speaking with her, and she, her bonnet now tied under her chin in a jaunty fashion, was laughing up at something he'd said. *She isn't discouraging him a bit, the little wretch. But then, I knew she would not.* "At least they will not be riding together. Huntley is already on his horse and—" Wulf snapped his mouth closed as the duchess said something to Huntley. He seemed to argue, but after Lady Charlotte and then Lily joined in, the earl threw up a hand and—laughing—climbed down from his horse and tossed the reins to a groom standing nearby. Huntley then climbed into the carriage beside Lily and closed the door.

"Damn it!" Wulf growled.

Emma's mouth tightened. "Huntley was to ride with me. It seems that I am forgotten again."

Wulf caught the pain her voice. "Emma, if you want Huntley, then you must go get him. Just as I must go and get Lily."

"Sadly, Huntley doesn't wish me to 'go get him.' Men don't like to be pursued."

Wulf chuckled. "That is untrue."

"Perhaps that's how it is in Oxenburg, but not in Edinburgh. Besides, even if he did wish to be pursued, I wouldn't know how to go about it."

"Pah. Women pursue men all of the time, they just do it differently. They smile and send glances, drop their kerchiefs, show their ankles . . ." Wulf shrugged.

Emma's gaze grew thoughtful. "They do, don't they? Flirting is a form of pursuit, I suppose. Men flirt, too."

"Yes, heavily, like big oxen. Women flitter here and there, featherlight in their touch. Sometimes it is easy to miss their intent."

She tilted her head to one side and regarded him for a long moment. "So you think that I should pursue Huntley more openly."

"Yes. Men like to know they are wanted, just as women do."

"But . . . what if he doesn't like it? What if he tells me no?"

Wulf's lips quirked. "Ah, Emma, that is not the question to ask. The question to ask is, what if he tells you yes? What will you do then?"

Her eyes widened, but after an astonished moment, she laughed. "What indeed?" She tucked her hand in Wulf's arm and they walked toward their horses. "Come! Tell me more."

He did so, and yet he remained painfully aware of Lily now cozily tucked in the carriage beside Huntley. *One day, Lily, you will ride with me and we will both be happier.*

Ten

From the Diary of the Duchess of Roxburghe
It's always fascinating to watch new love blossom and grow, especially when one has planted those very seeds and can take credit—if one were the sort of woman to do so—for every bloom on every branch.

While the duchess and Lady Charlotte discussed the various delights packed in the baskets strapped to the backs of the carriages, Huntley and Lily carried on their own conversation about the beauty of the day and how pleasant it was to be outside.

Lily had just been about to comment on how much she liked the vista from the library windows when she heard Emma's merry laugh. Lily turned just in time to see Emma slip her arm through Wulf's as they strolled toward their horses. Wulf was being attentive, his hand over Emma's, his head bent close.

A pang twisted through Lily. Emma was gazing up at Wulf as if she owned him. *What is she doing? He belongs to me.* The thought made Lily blink. *No, that's not what I mean. He doesn't belong to anyone, least of all me, but he should take care paying attention to women lest they think it means far more than it does.*

Lily wished she could see Wulf's face, but only the back of his head and his broad shoulders were visible.

Huntley had followed her gaze and now stared at Wulf and Emma with a sharp frown, a crease between his brows. "There's something about that man I don't trust."

"You don't trust Wulf?" Lily watched as Emma hung upon Wulf's arm while gazing at him in what seemed to be an open invitation. "Frankly, I had no idea Emma was such a hardened flirt."

Huntley's jaw tightened. "She is no such thing! Emma and my wife were best friends, almost sisters, so I know her very well. If she's anything, she's naïve in the ways of the world, and I hate to see her speaking to a man like Wulfinski."

Lily frowned. The prince was a nuisance and socially inept, but he didn't deserve Huntley's dismissive tone of voice. From what Lily could see, all Wulf was doing was putting up with the inane giggles of a desperate woman. "You may rest assured, Huntley, that for all of his overbearing ways, the prince would never seduce an innocent. I simply couldn't believe such a thing."

Huntley's expression softened to indulgence. "Miss Balfour, I fancy that I know the ways of the world quite a bit better than you. Believe me, that man is not to be trusted."

One could make many criticisms of Wulf, but untrustworthy was not one of them. If anything, he was too trustworthy, too honest, and far too open with his feelings. "I must disagree. In his own way, he is quite an innocent himself."

Huntley turned a surprised gaze her way. "Surely you're jesting."

"He's not used to our ways," Lily insisted. "He's a foreigner, and a prince. I'd venture to say that he's been very protected."

Huntley's smile could only be called smug. "My dear Lily, I must give your good nature credit for that kind assessment. I'm sure the prince is charming when he wishes to be, and I'm certain he *seems* like an innocent to you, but he's not. He's a wolf in more ways than one."

"You don't know him."

"And neither do you. Pray do not be fooled by his I-don't-understand-English-and-so-I-may-say-whatever-I-wish-to ways. He uses that as an excuse to say and do some very reprehensible things, which is why I've half a mind to step down from the carriage and put a word of warning in poor Emma's ear."

Lily didn't think "poor Emma" would appreciate such heavy-handed interference. "And what will you say to her? That the prince will blurt out exactly what he thinks? That she may find his honesty refreshing and some of his comments amusing? Or that at the next ball, he may try to dance with her for every dance, regardless of propriety? Perhaps he will take her too far into his confidence and baldly admit that he has no funds?" At Huntley's surprised stare, Lily flushed, realizing that she'd revealed too much. "I will agree that Wulfinski is arrogant, but he's not the sort of man one must warn a woman about. In fact, considering Miss Gordon's age and the way she's looking at him now, perhaps the prince is the one more in need of a word of warning."

Huntley looked astounded. "Miss Balfour, I'm shocked that you'd even suggest such a thing." He shook his head, his brows creased. "You don't know Emma the way I do. There's not an avaricious bone in her body. She's been an amazingly devoted daughter. The only reason she hasn't married is because she took care of her father during his very lengthy illness, and then, immediately after, she came into our house to nurse my wife during her final days. And please don't suggest that Emma's on the lookout for a wealthy husband, for she was her father's sole heir and is very well placed. In fact, from what you've said, if anyone could be accused of being a fortune hunter, it would be the prince!"

For some reason, knowing that Miss Gordon was well-off made Lily's unease all the sharper. "I'm certain Miss Gordon's wealth is to her advantage, but it will do little to fix her interest with the prince. Wulf believes in love above all else."

"How do you know?"

Lily opened her mouth, ready to retort with a firm *He told me so*, but then realized she shouldn't admit that she'd had such a personal conversation with the prince.

To be honest, a good deal of their conversations had been out of the bounds of propriety, as she felt much more comfortable with him than with anyone else at the castle. Well, she did when he wasn't looking at her as if he'd like to gobble her up like a tea cake.

Sadly, Lily found herself far too aware of him. Even now, while in the middle of a conversation or walking to breakfast or while combing her hair, the memory of his kiss would force itself into her mind and instantly she would remember the pressure of his mouth on hers, the warmth of his hands as they cupped her so intimately.

In a husky voice she finally answered Huntley, "The prince told me—and I'm sure many other people—that in his country, even though he is a prince, he may marry for love, and that he is determined to do so."

"A prince? That's ridiculous." Huntley's gaze narrowed. "I'm surprised he's mentioned such a personal subject."

"He's an open book."

"Hmm. Well, be that as it may, I sincerely doubt he's thinking of marriage at all." Huntley's gaze returned to where Emma stood with the prince by their horses, talking and smiling. "I think the prince has very low goals and only wants that which he cannot have."

Across the courtyard, Emma said something that made Wulf laugh long and loud. A twinge of something bitter and painful made Lily clench her hands tightly about each other.

Huntley's mouth was pressed into a thin line. "I shall speak with Emma. That man will make a fool of her."

Lily had to bite back a most unladylike retort that was as instant as it was unexpected. *Good God, why am I so angry with Huntley? He is merely being cautious with the feelings of a dear friend, which does him great honor. Yet I would wager my life that Wulfinski is just as honorable as Huntley, if not more so.*

But such feelings—inexplicable even to her— would not be enough to reassure Huntley, who was scowling at Wulf as if he wished to kill him.

Wulf waved off a waiting groom and helped Emma onto her horse, lifting her without seeming effort.

Huntley muttered at this, while Lily merely watched, uncertain at the myriad of feelings rushing through her. *I've just met this man four days ago; I cannot be jealous.*

The prince adjusted one of Emma's stirrups, and though he appeared to be listening to whatever she was saying, he turned his head and—as it so often did—his gaze met Lily's.

Instantly, her heart leapt against her throat as triumph washed over her. The instant warmth in his gaze, accompanied by a satisfied curve of his lips, told her that he was pleased at finding her attention on him. She almost—*almost*—returned the smile before she caught herself.

Emma leaned down and pointed to her stirrup, and Wulf, recalled to his duties, turned his gaze from Lily and set about fixing the stirrup.

Lily was left feeling bereft. *How could he look at me in such a way while paying attention to another woman? Perhaps Huntley is right and the prince is the hardened flirt—not Emma.*

Perhaps she didn't know him as well as she thought, and she certiaintly couldn't afford to care. With a jaw that was already aching from how tightly she held it, she turned to face Huntley. "You *should* put a word of warning in Miss Gordon's ear."

"I shall. I don't trust foreigners; I never have. And just conversing with a man who isn't aware of the proprieties can cause harm to your reputation."

"I would hate to see Emma suffer." At Huntley's surprised look, Lily added, "I've spoken to her several times over the last few days."

A pleased look crossed his face. "She's very kind, isn't she?"

"Yes." *Finally, something we can agree on.*

"Everyone says so. She came and stayed during my wife's final weeks and did what she could to make us both comfortable. Then afterward, she made a point of visiting every day while I struggled for . . ." A pained smile touched his lips. "I suppose you could call it sanity. I fear I was very unfit company, but Emma was very kind, and knew that I could not bear to speak of all that had happened. She never once asked me a thing, but brought me soup and cards, and funny poems—anything she could think of—in an attempt to help me climb out of the black hole my wife's death had left me in." His gaze locked back on the prince. "Which is how I know Prince Wulfinski—if he really is a prince—is not fit to touch her shoe." Huntley's voice had risen, his face flushed.

"Oh, Wulfinski's really a prince." Nothing else could explain his arrogance.

Huntley patted her hand where it rested on her knee. "Miss Balfour, you're as much an innocent as Emma. You don't know how many pretenders there are in the world and—"

"I beg your pardon, but I'm not a fool, if that's what you're hinting at."

"No, no. You're just inexperienced in the ways of the world."

His condescending air grated on Lily's nerves. "I'm not—"

"Oh my," Lady Charlotte's soft voice interrupted them. "Margaret, I do believe that Miss Balfour and Huntley are having a disagreement."

The duchess's gaze flickered between the two of them, a displeased look on her face. "What's this? What are you two arguing about?"

"Nothing important," Huntley said before Lily could speak, his smile noticeably tight. "Miss Balfour and I were talking about Prince Wulfinski . . . *if* he is a prince."

"He's definitely a prince," the duchess said, looking none too happy. "I wrote to Roxburghe and had him make some inquiries. Both Prince Wulfinski and his grandmother are who they say they are."

Lily swallowed a very unladylike *Ha!* Instead, she said as demurely as she could, "Of course they are."

Huntley's jaw tightened, but he didn't reply.

Lady Charlotte and the duchess exchanged glances, but no one ventured another word.

The duchess finally interrupted the silence with a dry "I'm sure we're all famished. It does make for short tempers." She waved to MacDougal, who stood waiting in the center of the courtyard. At her signal, he bowed and then nodded to the coachman at the front of the line. Instantly, the coaches and carriages began to move. There was a bit of a scramble as those who'd been standing near their horses now hurried to mount up. "We'll all feel better once we've had some sustenance."

"In the meantime, it would be pleasant if we all agreed." Lady Charlotte looked from Huntley to Lily. "Of course, sometimes we have to agree separately."

The duchess looked at Lady Charlotte. "What does *that* mean?"

"I was only saying that agreeing is very pleasant, but that sometimes one cannot, and so one must agree by oneself even if one doesn't agree with others about—"

"Charlotte, please, don't say another word, I beg you."

"I was just tying to explain—"

"Yes, yes. But you were making no sense. Not even a little. So for the love of peace, leave it be."

Lily, her irritation subsided, hid a sigh. This was not the way to make her case with the earl. The duchess had gone to great lengths to help Lily and her family and she was ruining it over a conversation about the reputation of a man she barely knew.

I must remember my purpose in coming here. She slipped Huntley a look from beneath her lashes and then cleared her throat. "The earl and I agree on one thing: that Miss Gordon is a delightful woman and deserves a suitor who is as good as she is, if not more."

Huntley, who'd been sitting stiffly, gave a surprised chuckle. "I suppose we did agree on that. Miss Balfour, I don't know how we came to argue in such an odd manner. I certainly had no intention of upsetting you."

"I feel much the same. We were talking, and then out of the blue, we were arguing." She spread her hands. "Perhaps her grace is right and we're both hungry."

"Of course I'm right," the duchess said, looking pleased. "We all have little tiffs. It is very good to air out your feelings now and then, or so I tell Roxburghe when he gets upset after I've had to point out that he's wrong about something."

"Which happens far more frequently than one might imagine," Lady Charlotte said helpfully.

Lily and Huntley exchanged amused glances, and

just like that, their equanimity was restored. *Surely the fact that we can overcome an awkward moment so quickly is a good sign.* "I hope Miss Gordon will join us when we eat."

"I can't think why she shouldn't." Huntley beamed at Lily. "You are too good to think of her."

The duchess tapped a finger to her chin. "I don't know why I didn't think about it before, but Miss Gordon needs a suitor. She is a lovely woman."

Huntley's gaze jerked toward the duchess, his smile fading. "She doesn't need or want a suitor."

"All women need suitors."

Lady Charlotte nodded. "All."

"Not Emma," Huntley said firmly. "She's told me time and again that she's quite happy not being married."

"Nonsense," the duchess declared. "It is a woman's purpose in this world to be married. How else is she to find fulfillment if not as a wife and partner?"

"But—"

"Don't worry, Huntley. I shall put my mind to it right away and find her a delightful suitor who will— Oh my! Prince Wulfinski has just pulled his mount next to Miss Gordon's." The duchess regarded them over her hooked nose, her mouth pursed in thought. "Hmm. That's interesting. I wouldn't have imagined, but . . . Yes, they might do very well together." Her gaze flickered to the brougham that was now lined up with the others. "I daresay it would upset the grand duchess, though."

Lady Charlotte brightened. "It would, wouldn't it?"

Huntley threw up a hand. "Your Grace, there's really no need—"

"Huntley, please, I'm not a novice." The duchess smiled munificently at him. "Rest assured that I shall be very subtle. Miss Gordon will never know she's being nudged into the prince's arms."

Lady Charlotte nodded, her feathers flaying the air above her head. "Her grace is very delicate. Not that it matters where Miss Gordon is concerned, as she is not a youth, but a mature woman. She will be glad for some assistance in this matter, as I'm certain she doesn't wish to die old and alone, with nothing but cats and servants surrounding her."

Huntley must have seen that saying anything further would only worsen his case, so he subsided into an unhappy silence, one Lily sympathized with. *Now the duchess will begin throwing Emma and the prince together. Added to that, the two of them seem to have already found common footing of some sort. Lovely, just lovely.*

Lily folded the edge of her cape between her hands, feeling as sulky as Huntley looked. Now that Lily thought about it, Emma had been the first to note Wulf's arrival. *Had she been waiting for him?*

Lily blinked. *Good God, were Emma's pleasantries just a mask of her true purpose, which was to lure Wulf into conversation?*

The thought didn't sit well with Lily. She hated to think of such a manipulator attempting to trap Wulf.

But that's the natural way of things, Lily told herself with an inward grimace. *After all, Wulf must be in need of funds, and Emma is well-placed. Not only that, but judging from the way the two have been laughing together, it is obvious that they enjoy each other's company, so . . .*

There was nothing more to be said. Yet the sinking feeling in Lily's chest could not be ignored.

Wulf had baldly stated that he wished for true love. Would he realize that what Emma offered with her smile wasn't the deep love he claimed to be seeking, but only an answer to her own search for a husband to ease her way into old age? Someone needed to speak to the prince so that he was aware of Emma's true purpose in welcoming his attentions. Just one word, though. After that, the decision was his.

Lily hoped that at some point during the picnic, she'd be able to speak privately with the prince and share her suspicions. While she was mulling exactly what she should say, Huntley made a polite comment about the lake as the carriage rolled past. Lily, glad for the distraction, put her thoughts away and answered him with a warm enthusiasm she was far from feeling.

She'd find time for a private word with the prince later on. It was the least she could do.

Eleven

From the Diary of the Duchess of Roxburghe

Love is a funny creature. It lifts its head, peeks into one's soul, and then more often than not, not finding what it seeks, turns and scurries away. It is my intention to capture this creature just as it lifts up its ears, marking only a vague interest, and then luring it into taking up residence where it most desires to be—in the hearts of two lovers.

I do hope Huntley and Lily are ready to fall wildly, deeply, and passionately in love, for I plan on seeing to it that they do.

Two days later, a despondent Lily watched down the long length of the dinner table as Emma Gordon flirted madly with Prince Wulfinski, a sight that was becoming all too familiar. Lily had been ready since the day of the picnic to whisper into the prince's ear her gentle warning about Emma's weaknesses and desperation to wed, but no opportunity had presented itself. Something had changed the day of the picnic. Before, Wulf had sought out Lily too much. Now, he rarely did more than bow in her direction before attaching himself to Emma's side.

Fighting a very real—although childish—desire to pout, she straightened her forks. How could he forget her so quickly?

She found it all very lowering, which was silly, for she'd wished for more time with the earl, hadn't she? Since Wulf and Emma had begun their flirtation, Lily had seen quite a bit of Huntley, although their conversation seemed to always be about the other couple. Sadly, they were both so distracted by the blatant courtship that was happening under their very noses that they weren't making any progress in their own.

The whole thing was maddening, and Lily found herself in the oddest position, missing something— and someone—that she had wished gone only a few days hence. But it was true; she missed the prince's unfiltered observations and bold honesty. She missed his amused glance and the way he looked at her just so, until a breathless rush settled through her. Even more odd, over the last few days, she'd thought of a hundred little things she wished to share with him, only to have no one there to listen but Huntley, whose sense of humor was decidedly less in step with her own.

Her throat tightened and she took a sip of water as the elderly gentleman beside her began to talk to whoever would listen about the many horses he'd owned, beginning when he'd been a lad of six with a fat pony named Stepsides and continuing through the decades unabated, horse by horse. Sighing, she turned to the gentleman seated on her other side. Older than her by a score of years or more, Lord MacKeane was quite willing to engage in conversation. Though it was widely known that he had no fortune and was hoping to marry an heiress, he was more than willing to engage Lily in conversation. He was astonishingly well read, too, and was able to discuss his favorite books and authors with some interest.

Lily might have been content with that, except that Emma's laughter kept bubbling up and distracting her, each tickle of laughter an irritant, until Lily couldn't keep from glaring. *That's it. I'm going to speak to the prince this evening. If I wait much longer, he'll fall under Emma's spell and never realize that he's been made a pawn.*

She stole a glance down the table and caught Huntley also glaring at the laughing couple. *I'm not the only one who is unamused by that flirtation.* It was becoming plainer day by day that her own courtship with Huntley couldn't progress until the worrisome issue of the prince and Miss Gordon was resolved. Once Wulf was made aware of how he was being manipulated and a safe distance was once again established between him and Emma, then Huntley could relax and return to the charming man that Lily had danced with that first evening.

Thus, an hour later, Lily waited until the men

joined the women for port, and then she determinedly marched across the room to speak to the prince. Just as she rounded a settee, a clawlike hand grasped her elbow in a painful grasp.

"*You!*" hissed a heavily accented voice that dripped with ice.

Lily blinked down into the wizened face of Wulf's grandmother. *What is her title? The Grand Duchess Natasha Niko-something?* Lily pulled her elbow free and curtsied. "Your grace."

The wizened face puckered with obvious dislike. "*You* are the one." The older woman's accent put a "v" in front of "one."

"I beg your pardon? I'm the one what?"

"You are the one trying to steal my Wulf's heart."

"Oh no. You have me confused with Miss Emma Gordon. And I can understand your concern, for"—Lily leaned forward and said in a low voice—"even though Miss Gordon is a lovely woman, she's all wrong for—"

"*Nyet!*" A bony finger leveled at Lily's nose. "Do not think you can trick me. I have been watching you, my little *pretendsient!* I see these looks you give him, fool that you are! Wulfinski is a prince of Oxenburg and you are a nothing. You can *be* nothing to him."

Lily wondered if Wulf's grandmother had partaken of too much wine at dinner. The old woman had been glaring at her for several days now, but as Lily had never seen any other expression on the woman's face other than extreme irritation, she hadn't considered for a moment that the grand duchess might bear her any ill will. "Your grace, I barely know your grandson. He rarely even speaks to me." *Anymore*.

"That is what I tell him, too, that he barely knows you, but he will not listen. So *you* will listen instead, Miss Lily Balfour. And if you do not"—the grand duchess squinted, her wrinkled mouth puckered— "you will pay."

Lily's brows rose. "Pay?"

"*Da*. I will put the curse upon you and all of your family!"

A flicker of irritation made Lily's gaze narrow. "I've done nothing wrong."

"Ha! You will stop looking at my grandson in the way you have. You will not speak to him, nor even think his name."

Lily's jaw set. "I will think about him if I want." At the duchess's gasp of outrage, Lily continued, "Fortunately for you, I don't *wish* to think about him, and so I don't."

"*Lies!*" The tiny woman leaned forward and squinted at Lily. "If you do not leave him be, I will see to it that all of your goats and cows become as barren as the rocks that dot this wasted country of yours."

Lily's irritation disappeared before an urge to laugh. "I see. That would be tragic, indeed, if I had any goats or cows. But I do not."

The little woman blinked. "You have none? Not one goat? One cow?"

"No. A few horses, but that's all the livestock we own. We don't have much, you know."

"You are poorer than I thought. Not even one goat. Pah! Well, I will make *you* barren, then."

"First of all, you have the wrong woman, which I've told you already. Second, I don't believe in curses, so do as you will."

The woman's black eyes blazed. "You don't believe! Well, I'll show you that you *must* believe." The old woman held up her hands, swaying back and forth, and began to mutter in a foreign tongue that didn't sound anything like the prince's language. Her jumbled words increased in speed and turned sing-songy as her hands swirled in the air, tracing odd symbols before Lily.

People around Lily had stopped speaking and were now openly staring as the old woman's movements became more and more frenzied.

Lily cleared her throat. "Your grace, people are beginning to stare. Can we discuss this curse some other—"

"*Nyet!*" thundered a deep voice. Wulf grasped the duchess's hands and stopped her in midsymbol. "Tata, stop that!"

The old woman's eyes flew open and her mouth tightened. After a hard glare, she squenched her eyes closed and began to sing the curses again, swaying as if she were in a trance.

Wulf growled. He'd been deep in conversation

with Lord MacKinton about the best way to approach a deep fence while riding to the hunt when he'd chanced to look up just in time to see Tata Natasha attempt to place a curse on the womb of the woman he was determined to make his own. He'd left Mac-Kinton in midsentence and had leapt over a low table to halt Tata. In their language, he snapped, "Open your eyes, old woman, for I know you can hear me."

She kept them squenched closed, mumbling the rest of her curse. He released her wrists. "Fine. Make your curse. I will marry her anyway, and then where will you be?"

She scowled and opened one eye. "You would not marry a barren woman."

"I would marry this woman if she were barren a hundred times over. She is mine, Tata. Get that into your stubborn head. Nothing and no one can change that."

She opened both of her eyes and threw her hands into the air. "Pah! She is no good for you. She doesn't even have any goats."

"I don't want a woman with goats. And whatever woman I do want is my own concern—not yours."

"It is the concern of all of your family." Tata Natasha pointed at Lily and said in clear English, "Just look at her! Even without my curse, she has no meat on her bones and will bear you no sons."

Everyone's attention turned to Lily, who was every shade of pink imaginable. Wulf wished he could sweep her away, but that would only cause more talk.

Furious beyond words, he ground out, "Tata, you have said enough. We will leave now."

"Fine. I have said what I would say, which is that this one is unfit to be your wife—"

"*Unfit?*" The Duchess of Roxburghe shouldered her way through the small crowd that had collected, coming to a halt before the small duchess from Oxenburg. "How dare you speak that way about my goddaughter!"

Wulf inwardly groaned.

"I may speak as I choose," Tata said. "*You* are the real reason for this foolishness, you and your matchmaking meddling!"

"I *never* meddle."

"Ha! I've seen you do so. You are like a giant puppeteer, telling this one to talk to that one, whispering to that one to dance with this one— and everyone knows it!" Tata swept a glance up and down the thin form of the Duchess of Roxburghe. "You should be ashamed of yourself, encouraging such a nobody to think she might have a chance with a prince."

"I've never encouraged—"

"You have done nothing but tease Wulf with your pale Scottish redhead."

Lily frowned. "I'm not a red—"

"*Quiet!*" both the duchess and Tata snapped.

Tata glared at the duchess.

The duchess glared back. "This is *my* castle and I say what will or will not happen within these walls."

"This does not concern you."

"If it concerns Miss Balfour, then it concerns me. And if I wish your grandson to court Miss Balfour, then court her he will."

Tata crossed her arms over her sparse bosom. "So you admit that it is all your doing. That you have been throwing this woman at my grandson's head."

The duchess mirrored the gesture. "No, I haven't. I've never tried to promote a match between your grandson and my goddaughter. *She* is far too good for *him*."

Tata gasped, her face as crimson as the rug beneath her feet. "How *dare* you!"

Wulf slanted a glance at Lily, who was watching the two women as one might watch a pair of cobras preparing to strike. He rubbed his neck, feeling as helpless as a newborn foal. For the last two days he'd tried to stir Lily's interest by flirting with Miss Emma, but to no avail. Though he'd caught Lily's gaze upon him, not once had she said a word to him about it. *Why is this courtship so blasted hard?*

Tata leaned forward and poked the duchess's arm with a bony, gnarled finger. "Listen to me, you old harridan. My grandson is *better* than your goddaughter, and you're a——"

"Tata!" Wulf slipped an arm about Tata's waist and drew her to his side. "You've had too much wine."

"I've only had——"

"It is late and time we returned home. Your grace, I apologize for my grandmother's ill temper."

Tata opened her mouth, so he held her a bit

tighter. That worked, for she gasped but could say nothing.

"That's quite all right," the duchess said in a frosty tone. "*Some* people can't handle their wine."

He increased the pressure on Tata's waist to keep her from answering, and with a quick bow to the duchess, he turned to Lily. He met her gaze, a million words flooding his mind, all of them hot and passionate and not a one that he could say in front of a crowd.

He hoped she could read in his eyes what he couldn't say. He managed a quick incline of his head and then, holding Tata Natasha firmly by his side, he left.

Twelve

From the Diary of the Duchess of Roxburghe

I was never more insulted in all of my life. To come into *my* house and tell me what to do! I was ready to strangle that woman. Sadly, the prince bustled her away before I could have her thrown out as she deserved. He, at least, was contrite for her behavior. But she— Oh! The nerve!

It would serve her right if I decided to match her precious grandson with Lily. It's a pity the man has no funds, for I'd like nothing more than to show that old hag who knows how to control whom!

Inside the cottage, Vladimir Arsov stirred the fire and then returned the poker to the rack. Turning to the prince, he said with notable satisfaction, "The fire is stoked. The chimney draws very well."

Wulf sat at the table, sharpening a large knife on a leather strop tied to the back of a chair. "You sound surprised that my chimney functions at all. You've been listening too much to my Tata Natasha."

Arsov grinned. "I don't listen to old witches." A square man, he had a shock of thick brown hair and a horrible scar across his left cheek and shoulder from a threshing-machine accident at age sixteen that had left him near death. Though he'd recovered, he was no longer able to work in the mill as his arm could hold no weight.

Fortunately, an uncle who was a groom in the palace had brought Arsov to the stables to see if the boy could be of use there. Though young, Arsov had a commanding presence, one made more so by the scar on his face. Before long he had organized the younger grooms and stable hands into an efficient, well-oiled machine. The horses were never better taken care of; the five stables had never been so clean. The head groom was ecstatic and Arsov was given a permanent place.

Over time, Wulf heard of Arsov's efforts. When Wulf stopped by to congratulate the new groom on his accomplishments, he'd been surprised to find Arsov reading a book of Greek translations. A short conversation had revealed that Arsov's father had been a tutor to a wealthy family and had given his own sons a love of reading and a wide knowledge of the ancient languages.

Wulf had just turned fourteen, but something about this quiet, older lad had appealed to him, and on the spot he'd made Arsov his personal servant and captain of his guards. That had been almost twenty years ago, and Wulf had never regretted it.

"Old witches are stubborn." Wulf continued sharpening the knife. After a moment he said, "She tried to put a curse on Miss Balfour tonight."

"She always resorts to the old ways when she is frustrated."

"She must get used to being frustrated, for I am a grown man and will decide my own way."

Arsov grunted his agreement. "Perhaps you should have a talk with her."

"Another one? It will do no good." Wulf smoothed the blade over the leather strop. "I have asked her to come here and talk, but she will not. Perhaps that is good."

Arsov shot him a curious look. "You are angry with her."

"Angry" wasn't a strong enough word. "She interfered where she had no right."

"She often does." Arsov looked about the small cottage. "This house is well crafted."

"But not as comfortable as the manor house?"

Arsov shrugged. "There is a bed for me there and none for me here."

"You would find it too small."

"Most likely." He took the chair opposite Wulf's and slapped his stomach. "I've grown fat and lazy in your service, my prince."

"So it seems." Wulf lifted a brow at Arsov. "The chimneys in the manor house, do they smoke as much as Tata complains they do?"

"Far less than the ones in her grace's house in the

old country. It does not truly bother her, if that is your worry."

"She's an old woman. I need to remember that."

"Old and stubborn." At Wulf's surprised glance, Arsov added, "She has been very kind to me, though."

"That's a lie."

Arsov's lips twitched. The grand duchess barely countenanced Arsov, thinking he'd been offered a position he hadn't deserved. "Your grandmother says your cottage is not fit for a prince."

"It's fit for this prince." Wulf glanced around with satisfaction. "It's warm, snug, and well built. The chimney doesn't smoke, the thatched roof is now repaired, and the doors and shutters have been fixed—I am happy here, Arsov. Happier than I would be in that cold stone block of a manor house."

"Which is exactly why your grandmother hates it."

"Her feelings are many and fervent."

Arsov's brown eyes twinkled with amusement. "As you say, Your Highness. It would be difficult to find happiness if one attempted to live by the duchess's definition."

"Yes. Her idea of happiness revolves around the number of invitations one receives and how many compliments are paid to one's jewels."

"Such is the way of those who weren't born with many jewels, Your Highness. From a distance, one can come to believe that the sparkle means happiness."

Wulf looked at his Arsov thoughtfully. "You've been reading Plato again."

Arsov inclined his head. "You should read him sometime."

"I prefer Hume."

"He has much to say, too." Arsov's dark gaze rested on Wulf's face. "Pardon me, my prince, but I am confused."

"Yes?"

"You wish this woman to value you and not your money. And yet that money could remove her family's hardships."

"You *have* been listening to Tata Natasha."

"*Nyet*, or I would have used the terms 'mad' and 'ridiculous.'"

Wulf chuckled. "True."

"If this woman would choose you over her family obligations, doesn't that prove that she is not the sort of woman one should marry?"

Wulf placed the knife on the table and untied the strop from the chair. "If she comes to me as I am, without money, even though she has need of it, it will mean that she trusts that, together, we can find a way out of her difficulties."

Arsov nodded. "Then I hope that she may come to her senses." After a moment he rose and stretched. "I should return. Your Tata Natasha should be tired from her ranting and will be asleep by now."

"You can hope." Wulf tucked his knife into the sheath inside his boot. "If not, feel free to return and sleep before the fire."

"I may do that. Do you need me for anything else, my prince? I washed your shirts and placed them in your wardrobe."

"Thank you, Arsov. That will be all."

"Good evening, then." With a bow, the servant left.

When Wulf had first hired Arsov, the man hadn't known how to tie a cravat or shine boots, but Wulf hadn't cared. The man was resourceful, organized, and intelligent. And Arsov hadn't disappointed Wulf; he'd learned his duties quickly and efficiently. It had helped that Wulf was no fop and cared little for the starch of his cravats and whether his leather boots shone like mirrors. He mocked men who thought such trivialities were important.

Real men did not care about their boots, except whether they had enough heel to hook into a stirrup. Wulf rose, careful not to hit his head on the low ceiling as he went to the small desk he'd had brought from the manor house. While much of the other furniture was rustic, some of it rejected pieces from the servants' chambers, he'd needed a desk and there were no spares to be had. He'd finally selected one from among the manor's many sitting rooms, as it was small enough to fit in the limited space.

He ran his hand over the surface. It was too fine a piece for the cottage, but functional, with an assortment of drawers for storing his correspondence. He looked at an overflowing drawer and grimaced, for the morning's missives were still waiting. There was no such thing as an idle prince; travel or no, Wulf's duties followed him.

He picked up the packet and broke the seal, then picked up his pen to answer the missives within. He'd just dipped the pen into the inkwell when the faint clop-clop of a horse's hooves coming down the path made him lift his head. He replaced the pen and went to the window. Through the woods, he could see the flicker of a red cape that he knew very well. His heart lurched in his chest. He grinned and hurried out of the cottage, but it wasn't Lily who sat astride the large, plodding horse, but a pale-haired servant girl who looked as nervous as a fawn.

He swallowed his disappointment. "Yes?" he asked courteously.

"Och, ye really do live in a cottage. I thought—" She blushed. "I'm sorry, Yer Highness. I was jus' surprised, is all. I was tol' t' bring ye this." She fumbled in her cloak and then held out a missive sealed with a round button of blue wax.

Wulf took the letter, his gaze drawn to the flowing writing that sailed across the crisp foolscap. *Lily. Perhaps you have come to me after all.* He opened it and held it to one side so that the light from the cottage fell across the page.

Wulf,
   I must speak with you. Meet me in the meadow by the river tomorrow at three and I'll explain all.
                              L

His smile widened. *Finally, she calls for me.* "Tell your mistress that I'll be there, come rain or wind or the devil himself."

The girl's expression softened and she said in a pleased tone, "'Deed I will, Yer Highness."

He reached into his pocket and pulled out a coin and handed it to the servant.

She looked astonished at the bright coin. "'Tis gold!"

"So it is."

"Indeed!" She carefully slipped it into her pocket. "Thank 'ee, Yer Highness."

"You're welcome. Be careful returning. Stay on the main path." He turned the horse for her and saw her off, watching until she was well out of sight. Then he patted the letter that he'd placed in his pocket over his heart and grinned. It was a beginning.

Feeling better than he had all week, he went back into the cottage.

Thirteen

From the Diary of the Duchess of Roxburghe
Poets always compare love to roses. They both
grow, both have thorns, both are beautiful . . . and
they both require a good, thorough mulching at
least twice a year, preferably by a master gardener.
Even nature needs help now and then.

Lily turned her horse down the path, following the
other guests in their small party. There were ten in all,
and two grooms, too. The presence of the grooms had
surprised her; she'd have to find a way to deal with
them somehow.

Beside her, Lord MacKeane chatted on and on
about an Italian manuscript he'd once purchased for a
huge amount at an estate outside of Lyons. Lily could
only suppose that his story explained why he was in
such financial straits today.

She was rather glad MacKeane was more interested in reliving what was apparently a fond memory
rather than having an actual conversation, for she had

no desire to talk to him. In fact, she'd spent much of the last half hour trying to figure out a way to be rid of him and the entire riding party.

Last night Lily had realized that she could no longer hope to simply chance upon a private conversation with Wulf, even though it was becoming increasingly important that she warn him of Emma's probable purpose in paying him such close attention. After the scene between Lily, the duchess, and Wulf's grandmother, people would be watching them all, hoping for additional drama. And so Lily had done something she'd never thought to do—she'd arranged an unchaperoned assignation with a single man, a meeting that, if discovered, could ruin her reputation.

It was a large risk, but it had to be done. Though for different reasons, both she and Huntley were distracted with worry over the prince and Emma's relationship, and it was impeding their ability to think about anything else. It hadn't helped that since the day of the picnic, the duchess had tossed the two together at every juncture. Something must be done, and soon.

Lily looked up along the line of riders to where Emma rode beside Huntley, who'd apparently issued the warning he'd been dying to since the day of the picnic. The talk was not going well; Emma's color was high, and the hard, incredulous looks she was shooting his way were far from her usual calm, smiling gaze. Huntley, too, was flushed, his mouth thinned, his brows drawn. It was proof that Lily was right: Emma's refusal to give up Wulf proved beyond a doubt that the older woman had designs on the prince.

The path turned, and to the right of them lay a small hill that hid the meadow where Lily had asked Wulf to meet her. Lily peeked at the small watch pinned to the lapel of her riding habit and was relieved to see that she had twenty minutes still, plenty of time to follow the group farther down the trail, slip away unnoticed, and make her way back to the field. It would take only a few moments to express her concerns to the prince, then before anyone had time to launch a search party, she'd be back on her way to rejoin the group, claiming a lost kerchief or some such nonsense.

It was a perfect plan.

Except for the grooms.

And Lord MacKeane, who'd attached himself to her side.

Fine, maybe it isn't such a perfect plan, but I must make this work.

She cast a glance over her shoulder and met the gaze of the groom who followed the group. He touched the brim of his hat and inclined his head. She smiled and turned back as Lord MacKeane droned on and on, now describing a Dutch painting he'd once purchased for an incredible amount of money.

Lily glanced at the hill, which was covered with beautiful yellow flowers. It was a gorgeous spring day, the sun shining, the wind teasing her skirts and tugging at the scarf that tied her hat. *Hmmm. The wind . . .*

She reached in her pocket and pulled out her kerchief. While no one was looking, she let it slip into the breeze. It tumbled over the horse's haunches and was then whipped into a clearing on the opposite side of the trail. She turned to give the groom a beseeching stare.

He touched his hat and left the trail in an effort to catch the kerchief.

The second he was gone, Lily pulled up her horse, undid her small watch, and tucked it into her pocket.

It took Lord MacKeane a second to realize she was no longer by his side, and when he did so, he had to ride a little ways back down the trail to her, just as she'd hoped.

"Och, my dear Miss Balfour, what's amiss?"

"My watch is missing. It was pinned on my lapel and I just checked it, but now it's gone."

"Stay right there. I'll look for it." With that, he dismounted. "What does it look like?"

"It's very small and gold, about the size of a shilling." She frowned. "But it was probably more like a couple of minutes ago that I looked at it."

"Ah, then it will be a bit farther down the path. I will find it." He turned and led his horse away from her.

It was the perfect moment. The groom had followed her kerchief off to parts unknown, MacKeane was too far off in one direction, and the rest of the group in the other, to hear her leave. She turned her horse and headed for the hill, clearing it and riding down a gentle slope, finally safe as she rode out of sight of the rest of the group.

Smiling, Lily allowed the horse to have his head, the meadow luring her with its beauty. Her horse whickered softly in approval of the thick, green grass beneath his hooves, decorated with small bunches of bright yellow flowers. The soft sigh of the breeze and the faint rush of water as it danced down the riverbed were the only sounds, so she felt fairly certain that she hadn't yet been missed.

She undid the scarf she'd tied about her hat and let the breeze cool her ears and forehead. When she reached the middle of the field, she pulled the horse to a halt near a small, broken, ancient stone wall and decided to wait for Wulf there. But a sudden gust snatched the hat from her head, and it bounced off the horse's haunch before tumbling away. At the slap of the hat brim, the horse jumped and then set off in a wild canter.

Lily grabbed the reins and, with more determination than talent, brought the animal under control and turned it back toward the meadow. She was *not* leaving her hat in the middle of field. Her sister Rose had sent her that hat from Italy, and it was highly unlikely that Lily would ever get another of such quality.

Seeing her hat nestled among a clump of wildflowers, she pulled the horse up and looked down at it. Once she climbed off her horse, she would have no way to get back on. There was no groom to help, and the horse was too tall. Perhaps she could use the ancient wall? It looked sturdy enough.

Yes, that should do it. She guided the horse to the

wall, gathered her skirts, and slid off, smiling as her booted feet touched the stone. The horse, happy to be relieved of duty, whickered softly and then dipped its head and began to graze.

Well, that was easier than she'd expected. She threw her long riding skirts over her arm and then jumped off the wall. But as she landed, her boot slipped on the moss-covered ground and she fell backward, landing on her shoulder against the ragged stone. Pain splintered through her.

The sunshine flickered as the outline of an angel appeared. At least she thought it was an angel, for his black hair made a blue aura where he blocked out the sun. She was still trying to grasp her circumstances when the angel spoke, his deep voice rich with an accent she knew all too well. "Easy, Moya."

She took a shuddering breath and then clutched her shoulder. "I fell."

"I saw. I wish I had been close enough to catch you. Don't move. What hurts?"

"Only my shoulder." She rolled to her side to rise, but the pain made her gasp.

Wulf's face, now illuminated by the sun, was stern. "I told you not to move."

She gritted her teeth against the burn, managing to gasp out, "I'm fine. Just give me a moment."

"Let me see." He reached for her arm.

Instinctively, she jerked back, then cried aloud as a pain shot through her shoulder.

He cursed, long and low, a symphony of words she

didn't know, but understood all too well. "Let me see your shoulder," he demanded. "I must see if you've broken something."

Still clutching her arm, she leveled a hard stare at him.

"I know what I am doing," he insisted. "My men and I frequently play polo, and such injuries are not unusual."

"Polo?"

"A game with sticks and a ball that is played from the backs of horses. It's very difficult and there are many injuries."

She sighed. "I'm not going to disrobe here, in the middle of a field."

"But—"

"No. If someone saw us . . . I cannot."

"Ah, these rules of yours will kill me!" He glowered, but after a moment said in a gentle voice, "Come. I will help you up. You should not be on the damp ground. Just be cautious and hold your arm to your side."

She did as he asked, tucking her elbow close and holding it in place. He bent, and with an arm about her waist and her good shoulder pressed to his chest, he gently lifted her into his arms.

There was something to be said for a man who could carry one without the slightest bit of discomfort. She could see that coming in handy in a variety of situations.

And not only could he carry her with ease, but

while she was snuggled against his broad chest, his cologne tickled her nose in the pleasantest way. Spicy and sensual, it made her want to turn her face and burrow against him. *I've missed this. I've missed him.*

He carefully placed her on a flat stretch of the wall, then stooped to place a finger under her chin and tilted her face to his, his expression somber. "There. This is better. Not so damp."

It was better. Much. She tentatively moved her arm. The pain had lessened some, though she had no doubt that she'd have a large bruise. "I don't think it's broken."

"Poor Moya. I hope not."

For some reason, that made her laugh. "I'm not poor Moya. And I do wish you'd stop calling me that. My name is Lily."

"I like Moya." He ran his thumb over her chin, touching the bottom of her lip. "When I saw you fall—" His gaze darkened and he cupped her neck with his warm hand. "Don't scare me like that again. You are my light."

"You shouldn't say things like that." Yet she was glad he was saying it to her, and not to Emma.

The thought of Emma made her frown.

"Ah, now you are upset."

"I'm not upset."

"Yes, you are. Beautiful, and upset." His eyes twinkled. "Don't tell me you dislike hearing me say how beautiful you are; I would not believe it."

She pushed a strand of hair from her eyes, realizing how many of her pins had been lost in her fall. "I am far too mussed to be beautiful."

He chuckled and tipped her face to his. "You, Moya, are beautiful. I love how your eyes turn to silver when you are angry, the red-gold of your hair under the sun, your determined little chin, and . . ." His gaze flickered down her neck, lingering on her breasts. "All of you. Every last bit."

His gaze was like the lick of a flame, tracing a shiver across her skin. She couldn't look away, even if she wanted to—which she didn't. She wanted to lean forward and capture his lips with her own and run her hands over his broad shoulders and—

Stop it. She dropped her gaze. *Why, oh why, does he fascinate me so?* Something had changed since Wulf had kissed her in the library, and she was beginning to think that it was her. "I should return to the castle. I can ride if you'd help me onto my horse."

"With your arm injured, you might not be able to control your mount." He reached out and plucked a piece of grass from her hair.

She sighed. "I'm mussed."

"*Da.* There's a smudge of dirt on your nose, too."

Instantly, she reached for her nose, but in doing so, she unthinkingly lifted her injured arm. "Ow!" She rubbed her shoulder. "It's stiff."

His smile faded. "Moya, I—"

"Please, just help me back on my horse. I'm certain I can reach the castle."

His jaw set. "I will agree only if you allow me to examine your arm. You needn't disrobe, you know. I just wish to move it and ascertain the extent of your injuries."

She sighed. She didn't want him to "examine" anything, but the firm line of his jaw told her that she had no choice. She nodded. "Fine."

Wulf slipped a hand under her elbow and placed another on her shoulder. "This will only take a moment." He slowly rotated her arm. As soon as she winced, he stopped. "Where did that hurt?"

She placed her hand on the spot she'd landed. "It feels like a bruise."

"No sharp pain?"

She shook her head. "It just hurts all over, not any one place in particular."

"Hmm." He finished rotating her arm and then sat back on his haunches. "I think you're right; it doesn't seem to be broken. But you can't ride back to the castle. Your arm is weak and there is little you could do if the horse bolts. So I will lead the horse for you."

She glanced around the clearing and realized that her horse was the only one in sight. "You didn't ride."

"My cottage is just on the other side of the river, so I walked." He stood and held out his hand. "Come. Let's see if you can move now."

She stood but staggered when her heel came down on a rock. Instantly, Wulf slipped an arm about her waist to steady her. His voice was muffled against her hair as he said, "Lean against me."

She didn't need to lean against anyone now that her heel was back on firm ground, but he was conveniently close, and it took so very little to rest there. *And why not?* she asked herself. *We will never be alone again to enjoy such a thing.* She closed her eyes, savoring Wulf's strong arm gently tucked about her waist. For such a large, powerful man, his touch was amazingly gentle.

She snuggled closer as he pressed a kiss to her forehead, his breath warm on her skin.

I shouldn't encourage this, but it just seems so natural. Besides, perhaps this cherished feeling wasn't because of Wulf. Perhaps there was something innately comforting about the weight of a man's arm—any man's arm. *I could get used to this.*

She suddenly realized that the silence between her and Wulf had changed. Gone was the peacefulness of the moment, and in its place was a simmer of heat. Her skin prickled as if he were touching her far more intimately than he was, and her mind flickered back to the kiss they'd shared in the library. She'd dreamed of that kiss ever since.

The breeze strengthened and her skirts slapped playfully against his riding boots and brushed the flowered grass at their feet. The sunshine warmed her shoulder, though it didn't match the coziness from the one pressed against Wulf's chest.

It was so peaceful, so . . . right. *But this can't be right. I can't let it be right.*

Yet she didn't move. Instead, she allowed the simmer of attraction grow, as palpable as the sunlight that warmed their shoulders.

Lily lifted her face to his. His gaze caressed her as he brushed a strand of hair from her cheek, his fingers warm on her skin. She was locked into place, unable to look away. His dark lashes cast his green eyes into shadow, making her think of the moss at the bottom of a stream. The warmth of his hand on her cheek made her breathless, and her skin tingled with awareness. *I should stop this, but I can't.*

Instead, she yearned to lean forward . . . toward him . . . into him. . . .

Fourteen

From the Diary of the Duchess of Roxburghe
Though many consider me a great matchmaker, I must admit that there are circumstances even I cannot overcome. Fortunately, thus far I've been able to offset those circumstances with those two weapons of good fortune: luck and timing.

Woe betide the relationship not blessed with either.

Lily lifted her lips to Wulf's. The gentle, sweet touch set off a wild, uncontrollable flash of desire that roared through her, sweeping away every thought, every hesitation, every wish to resist either his desires or hers. She wanted this man so badly that her hands shook, and her heart thundered so loudly that she was certain he could hear it.

As if he could read her wanton thoughts, Wulf deepened the kiss, his tongue sliding over her lips, teasing them apart. She opened to him, welcoming the onslaught of heated passion, pressing herself against him, refusing to let anything come between her and this man.

Murmuring her name, he slipped a hand behind her head, sinking his fingers into her hair. His touch was demanding and urgent, stirring her passion yet more. His kiss changed and he teased and taunted. As with the kiss in the library, he taught her as she went, and she found herself a desperately eager student, panting and aching.

Sensing her need, he cupped her face between his hands and kissed her wildly. Lily moaned as he captured her and devoured her as he plundered her mouth with his.

Suddenly kissing wasn't enough. She unthinkingly went to slip an arm about his neck, but the pain from her shoulder made her break the kiss with a gasp.

Instantly Wulf paused. He was flushed, his eyes bright, his breath as quick as hers. "Did I hurt you?"

"No, no. I forgot about my arm and reached for you." She pressed a hand to her heart where it fluttered against her chest. "I think my heart would fly away if it could escape."

He chuckled softly. "It seems all of our kisses are destined to be interrupted. But one day . . ." He rested his forehead to hers. "One day we will kiss until there are no more kisses to be had."

What would that be like? she wondered, almost unable to breathe at the thought. *Hours and hours of kisses. I think I would go mad. Deliciously and decadently mad.*

She yearned for that madness, especially as her life now seemed so focused on sacrifice and control.

Wulf slid his hand along the line of her jaw until he cupped the side of her neck, his skin warm against hers. "Ah, Moya, your eyes call to me," he whispered. "They say the things your lips will not."

His thumb brushed her bottom lip and her body instantly tingled.

She longed for his touch with an intensity she'd never before felt, yet still she hesitated. Nothing good would come from this. Pleasure, yes, but later she would face certain heartache, and the loss of everything her family held dear.

She couldn't give in.

His gaze locked with hers, and reading her expression, he closed his eyes, his hands in fists as he growled to himself under his breath.

Finally, he opened his eyes again. "Why do you always fight me?"

"Because I must. My path is set and it doesn't lead to you."

"No?" His thumb brushed the sensitive spot behind her ear, which sent tremors racing through her. "Are you certain? Why shouldn't it lead to me?"

"You know why." She met his gaze steadily, though it cost her. "And yes, I'm certain. Very."

He sighed. "What am I to do with you, Moya?"

"Nothing. Nothing at all."

"That is not acceptable." He tugged her closer, careful of her injured arm as he rested his forehead against hers once more. "Moya, I came as you asked. What did you wish to talk to me about?"

His green eyes were so close that she could see the golden swirls that made them shimmer, his breath warm as it brushed over her lips. "There are things I—" Her breath caught as he trailed his fingers down her neck to where her cape was tied at her throat. "Wulf, don't."

"I'm listening, Moya. Continue."

"I—I can't. Not while you're— Wulf, stop. This isn't talking."

"You want talk?" He cupped her face and bent to nuzzle her neck, sending shivers dancing over her. "I will talk, then, and you will listen. I want to cover you in kisses from head to toe, discovering . . . each . . . secret." He punctuated each word with a featherlight kiss on her neck.

She gasped and closed her eyes. "Yes," she whispered, a deep ache settling between her thighs in the most wanton way. "Tell me more."

He slid his hands over her, down her back to her bottom, cupping her through her riding habit. "One day, Moya, we will kiss and there will not be so much clothing between us."

"Just silk?" she asked breathlessly.

He chuckled. "You like silk, do you? I will have sheets made of it. Gowns and night rails. Chemises and petticoats. You will never wear anything but silk."

Each word added to the cocoon of growing heat that surrounded her. She gripped his lapel with her good hand and turned her mouth toward his as he captured her lips with his own, his tongue plundering her mouth with deliberate intent.

Finally, unable to catch her breath, Lily broke the kiss and rested her head against his shoulder, panting wildly. She felt as if she'd been running downhill, reckless and out of control, her knees shaking like jelly. Her entire body was aquiver, her heart thudding hard against her breastbone. But more disturbing was the way she yearned for his touch. *One more kiss,* her mind tempted. *Just one more kiss.*

But, no, she tried to tell herself. *His kisses make me want more. So, so much more.*

She pressed a hand to her temple. She'd asked to meet him to warn him about Emma—not to be seduced. *It's so easy to lose myself when I'm near him. He overtakes me so quickly.*

She flattened her hand against his chest, feeling his heart thud hard against her palm. When he bent to kiss her once more, she shook her head. "Wulf, please—no more. This is madness."

"But most pleasurable." He traced the line of her cheek with his fingertips. "Would that I could go so mad every moment of every day. I would kiss you here." He touched her lips. "And here." He slid his hand to the base of her throat. "And all the way to here." Gaze locked with hers, he cupped her breast, his thumb resting lightly on her nipple.

The heat from his palm soaked through the material. She wanted to lean toward him, to press herself more firmly against his hand, to—

"*No!* I—I can't." She swung on her heel and left the circle of his arms to stand several feet away, her breathing so rapid that her knees trembled.

Good God, what was she doing? She had so much to gain—and so much to lose. She pressed a hand to her eyes. *I must think about Papa. Where he will be if I don't—*

"Moya?"

Wulf was watching her, his head tilted to one side. "It was just a kiss. There is nothing wrong with that."

"True, but . . . Blast it, Wulf, I didn't ask you here for this."

"Ah? Why did you ask me here, then?" He untied his cravat, which had been carelessly knotted about his neck.

She blinked. "What are you doing?"

"Fixing a sling so that you may ride more easily." He unwound his cravat and shook it out.

She couldn't help but stare at his exposed neck, tanned and muscled, framed by his black coat. *He has muscles everywhere. I wonder what he'd look like without clothes.* She flushed and looked away.

He smoothed out the long cloth. "Hold up your arm, Moya. Hold it steady so that we do not hurt it worse while I'm tying the knots."

She did as he asked, wincing only once when she lifted it too high. He swiftly fixed the sling, his fingers brushing the back of her neck as he knotted it, sending tremors through her yet again. When he finished, she relaxed her arm into it.

"Better?"

She nodded. "Much."

"Good. It is not as well done as if you'd sewn one, but it will have to do." He adjusted it where the muslin bundled at her wrist. "Did you finish all of the socks I saw in your basket?"

"Yes. And I've begun a larger project—a ball gown of pink sarcenet. Mrs. Cairness had the material tucked away and it's just enough for one gown."

"A ball gown? You can sew such a complex thing?"

She gestured to her habit. "I made this. In fact, I make most of my own gowns."

He examined her riding habit, his brows lifting, flattering appreciation in his gaze. "You have great talent, Moya. But then I'm not surprised. If you wish to do something, you will find a way to do it. I know this about you."

"Thank you." She tried to keep from staring at the base of his throat, exposed by the loss of his cravat, his heartbeat visible. A wild, untamed part of her yearned to lift up on her tiptoes and taste that spot of skin. *I would only have to—*

"Moya, if you keep looking at me like that . . ."

Her face heated. "I'm sorry. I was just—" She threw up a hand. "Wulf, I invited you here because I need to speak to you about a serious matter." She wet her lips, trying to find the right words. "I don't know how much time we have before I'm discovered missing and the duchess sends someone to find me, so I must say this now. It's about Miss Gordon."

"Ah!" His eyelids were half-closed, so she couldn't

read his expression. "Yes," he said, his tone almost dulcet. "Emma—Miss Gordon is a very interesting woman."

Lily's heart contracted. *Interesting? What does that mean?* "You should know that she's actively looking for a husband."

"Actively?"

"She wishes to marry soon. She's w—" Lily almost said "wealthy," but stopped herself just in time. "Miss Gordon is at a juncture in her life when she thinks such an alliance would be valuable."

"So she seeks marriage. You know this for a certainty?"

"Yes, Huntley believes it, too. He's worried for her, although I'm not. I know you are an honorable man."

"But he has his doubts."

"I can't speak for the earl. Wulf, you are not used to our ways and I don't want you to get caught in something you don't expect."

He shrugged. "I've nothing to worry about—"

She caught his arm. "Wulf, please. In our country, one social misstep could lead to a marriage you don't want. You must take care never to be alone with her."

"I'm alone with you right now."

"That's different," she lied. "We're in a field in broad daylight, and—and I've an injury, too. Besides, I will be on my way back to the castle before anyone knows you are here."

His grin was as instant as it was wicked. "So many protections, and yet still I kissed you."

Lily had to fight an oddly pleased smile. "You are incorrigible."

"At times. Do not worry about Miss Gordon. She is a friend, yes. But I have many friends."

Lily almost relaxed until he added in a thoughtful tone, "Still, I can see where you might feel some concern, for she is delightful woman. Very intelligent, too."

To her horror, Lily realized that somehow both of her hands had turned into fists as if she were ready to pummel someone.

Wulf was looking at her with raised brows as if waiting for an answer, so she pasted a polite smile on her face. "Oh yes. She's quite pleasant." And she was, too. Lily liked Emma—or had until she and Wulf had begun their friendship.

"*Da*, she has a delightful sense of humor, too. And her eyes are very fine, don't you think? She will make someone a fine wife one day, just not me."

"Do not be so certain about that. Wulf, you don't know the ways of society, so you must have a care. Our rules are—"

"Far too plentiful. I will have a care, but do not worry about Emma. She is a pleasant companion and has become my friend. Besides, if I cannot be with you . . ." He shrugged. "She will do to pass the time."

"Surely there are other guests whose company you might enjoy. Perhaps Lord MacPhearson? Or Mr. Daniels?"

"MacPhearson has decided that because I do not have a Scottish accent, I must be deaf, and so he yells everything he says. I dislike that."

"So would I. What about Mr. Daniels? He seems very nice."

"He is well enough, I suppose, but I enjoy Miss Gordon's company better. She entertains me very much and I like speaking with her."

Lily frowned, suddenly cross. *So Wulf thinks Miss Gordon a paragon, does he? Lovely. Just lovely.* When Lily had imagined this meeting, things had gone much differently. Wulf had been much struck by Lily's sincere warning, admitted that he secretly found Miss Gordon's company wearing, and then declared that he'd no longer so much as look in the woman's direction.

But instead . . . Lily sighed. Perhaps she was being unreasonable. After all, she was spending as much time with Huntley as she could, so she could hardly expect such a passionate man as Wulf to spend all of his time alone.

Suddenly, her heart ached far worse than her shoulder.

Concern instantly darkened his gaze. "Something is wrong. Is it your shoulder?"

She moved away, looking toward her grazing horse. "I will have the duchess's physician look at my shoulder, although I suspect that all he'll suggest is ice."

Wulf's brows lowered. "I don't trust your Scottish

doctors. You should let me send Arsov to you. He is very good with injuries."

"Arsov?"

"Yes, my valet. He is very skilled at healing."

"Thank you, but I'm sure the duchess's physician will be knowledgeable enough to tend to a simple bruised shoulder. Now, I must get back. Would you please help me onto my horse?"

As depressing as it was, it was time she returned to her position as a proper guest of the duchess and the potential future wife of the Earl of Huntley. The thought sank her low spirits even lower.

She caught Wulf's gaze and realized that he looked none too pleased, either. She managed a smile. "I've been remiss; I haven't even thanked you for coming to my rescue. It was very kind of you."

He waved a hand. "It was nothing."

"No, you were very patient."

The sparkle in his eyes made her heart ache. "I was, wasn't I? Don't worry, Moya. I know how it is when the pride is involved. My brothers all have more than their fair share."

"You, however, have only a moderate amount."

He sent her an amused smiled. "Do not expect me to admit to more."

She really should mount up and leave and yet . . . She tilted her head to one side and regarded him, admiring how the sunlight warmed his skin to gold. "You are close to your brothers. I can hear your affection for them in your voice."

"Very, especially Alexi. He is next to me in age, and the most fierce, too."

"My youngest sister can be warriorlike, too. Dahlia is shorter than either Rose or me, but Father says she makes up for it in character."

"You are close to her?"

"To both of my sisters, although Rose is gone now. She married a few months ago and is in Italy on her honeymoon."

Wulf caught the sad downturn of Lily's lips. God, but he loved her mouth. Full and soft, it begged for kisses. He cleared his throat. "You miss this Rose."

"Every day. She and I managed the household together. Papa is useless when it comes to practical things, as evidenced by this debt that has us in such a quandary."

Wulf had to bite back a sharp comment. It wasn't fair that a father would so burden his own children by not taking care of the most basic of necessities, that of providing a roof over their heads. What sort of a man would risk the safety and comfort of his own children? The thought made Wulf's blood boil. He wanted nothing more than to take all of Lily's problems onto his own shoulders, to take care of her, to cherish her . . . but he couldn't do that without making it difficult for them both to discern whether she came to him out of gratitude or love.

He didn't wish to purchase her affections, but wanted with every ounce of his soul to win them. Yet the self-control it took not to sweep in and fix every problem in her life tried him mightily. "Moya, do not look so sad. You will find a way to help your family. I *know* it."

She sent him a grateful look. "I hope so. I don't know what I'll do if Huntley doesn't come up to the mark and I—" She flushed. "I'm sorry. I always tell you things I shouldn't."

"Because you know I won't think poorly of you. Royal princes marry for many reasons other than love: sometimes they do so to combine powerful houses, sometimes to form an alliance or confirm a treaty, and sometimes to add gold to the coffers of an ailing kingdom."

"That must be horrible."

"It could be; I have seen my cousins wed for such reasons, some of them not well. Fortunately, my father is a romantic and made certain his sons would be free to choose our own brides."

"You are very fortunate. I wish I—" She stopped and then shook her head, absently rubbing her shoulder where the sling had been knotted.

"Is it too tight?"

"No. Just a little uncomfortable." She sighed. "There are times I wish things were different."

"What things?"

"It doesn't matter. My wishes are just that— wishes. But my responsibilities are everything."

"You cannot deny your own feelings. It is impossible, try as you will." Wulf reached out and captured her hand and tugged her closer. "How do you feel about Huntley?"

"He is a very nice man," she said stubbornly.

Wulf met her gaze steadily and realized that she wasn't going to give an inch. *Damn it, why must you resist me at every turn?* It was maddening; he didn't think he'd ever met a prouder woman in all of his life. "Nice, eh? That is all?"

"What more should there be?"

"Ah, Moya, so much more." Wulf pressed a kiss to her fingers, satisfied when her lips parted from her quickened breath. "Huntley seems very predictable. The sort of man who would eat the same thing for breakfast every morning."

"Is that so bad?"

"You tell me. Is that what you want? A man of no excitement, a man so predictable that he doesn't even need to be in the room for you to know what he is doing and why?"

For a long moment, their gazes locked. Her heart sinking, Lily tugged her hand free. "There are worse things than being predictable. If Huntley and I wed, I will cherish him as a good wife should. There's nothing more to be said." She turned away, found her hat, and settled it firmly on her head. "We must head back or the duchess will be worried."

His dark green gaze swept over her. "If I had my way, I'd toss you over your horse and take you to my cottage."

"Where you'd ravish me and ruin my chances of capturing a wealthy husband? No thank you," she said pertly, though her skin prickled with goose bumps.

He tugged her to him and kissed her, a hard, purposeful kiss that stopped her thoughts. Her body was instantly afire as his large, warm hand cupped her breast, his thumb flicking over her nipple. She arched against him, no longer in control, trembling with new wants and needs as she was swept into his embrace, his kiss, into *him*.

"Your kisses are wine," he said in his chocolate-rich voice. "Wine and madness, and I crave them more with each one. You are like food to my soul, and I cannot get enough of your sweetness, your touch."

God help her, she knew exactly what he meant. He was the same to her, as necessary as air, and just as—

"Lily!" A feminine voice came from across the field. "Where are you?"

Lily whirled out of Wulf's embrace. "It's Emma!"

Fifteen

From the Diary of the Duchess of Roxburghe
Once again, Miss Balfour has gone missing. I'm
beginning to think it's a bad habit.

Wulf gave a low curse, his disappointment so sharp
that it was an almost-physical ache.

Emma cantered across the field. Once she reached
them, she pulled up her horse and quickly dismounted, genuine concern on her face. "Lily, what
happened to your arm?"

"My hat blew off and I used that small wall to dis-
mount. Unfortunately there's moss and it's quite slick,
and when I fell, I hit my shoulder."

Guilt flooded Lily for her uncharitable thoughts
about Emma. *What if she really cares for Wulf? What
then? I'm being so selfish for not wishing him to find a
good match while I'm so ruthlessly pursuing one of my
own. I know this and yet I can't help but feel that Emma
isn't the right woman for Wulf.*

It all was so confusing. Lily fought back a desire to

sit down in the middle of the field and refuse to ever get up. "Once the duchess learns I've gotten another injury from riding, she'll never let me near the stable again."

"You'll know her grace's thoughts soon enough, for once she discovered that you'd disappeared from the party, she was determined to find you herself. She is out riding with some of the others—oh, there they are now."

The duchess cantered into view, Huntley and two footmen trailing behind her.

Emma pursed her lips. "Lily, perhaps it would be better if we say that I arrived before the prince did. Just for propriety's sake."

Wulf nodded. "It is well with me. I do not wish to make Moya's life difficult."

Emma's brow lowered. "Moya?"

"It's what he calls me," Lily said, the ache in her arm and her disgruntled feelings dampening her temper further. "It means 'red,' and I dislike it excessively."

Wulf sent her an amused look. "I never said 'Moya' meant 'red.'"

"Oh. What does it mean, then?"

His smile was mysterious. "I will gather your horse." He went to fetch the grazing animal.

The duchess drew up her horse, her gaze instantly locked on Lily's makeshift sling. "Miss Balfour, have you been unseated yet again?"

Huntley and the two footmen joined the duchess. The earl's face was creased with concern.

"She's holding her arm!" Huntley dismounted, handing his reins to a footman. "My dear Miss Balfour, you're injured. What happened?"

"It's a silly thing, but the wind snatched my hat, so I dismounted to fetch it and slipped on a mossy rock. I'm fine, though. Only bruised."

"I'm glad you didn't suffer a worse injury," the duchess said. "Miss Gordon, I didn't expect to see you here."

Emma curtsied. "I couldn't stay in the castle while everyone was looking for Miss Balfour; I had to help find her."

"You are too good," Huntley said sincerely.

Emma gave him a smile that didn't quite reach her eyes. "It was the least I could do."

The duchess's eagle gaze locked on Wulf. "And how did you come to be here, Your Highness?"

"Miss Emma's calls brought me. I was walking along the river, trying to decide when would be the best time to visit you, your grace, when I heard her shout out for assistance."

The duchess's finely arched brows rose. "Why would you wish to visit me?"

"To apologize for my grandmother's behavior last night. It was rude beyond belief."

"*You* have nothing to apologize for," the duchess said sharply. "Your grandmother, on the other hand, does."

Emma hurried to inject, "Miss Balfour and I were glad that the prince was close enough to help."

Lily murmured her agreement.

The duchess didn't look as if she believed a word, but Huntley managed a stiff bow. "Wulfinski, thank you for being so quick to answer Emma's call for assistance."

The prince bowed and Huntley turned to Emma. "How did you know Miss Balfour would be here?"

Emma hesitated.

"The flowers," Lily said. "I came to see the flowers in the field. Emma said that she'd noticed them earlier when we rode through, so she was certain this was where I'd left the path."

"Yes." Emma nodded. "I guessed that once she'd wandered off the trail, that she couldn't find her way back."

The duchess tsked. "Miss Balfour, we should return to the castle so that my physician can take a look at your injury."

"It's just a bruise."

"Perhaps." The duchess turned to one of her footmen. "Ride ahead and have the doctor attend us there as soon as he can."

The footman dipped his head and then wheeled his horse and hied across the field. Meanwhile, Wulf stepped past Huntley and helped Lily onto her horse, lifting her easily into the saddle. Her gaze clung to his for a long moment.

"Miss Balfour." The duchess pulled her horse beside Lily's, though not before she shot a dampening look at the prince. "We will take the forest path since it's smoother. We will ride slowly, for jostling might harm your shoulder more."

"Yes, your grace."

Wulf remained beside Lily's horse as she arranged her skirts. "I'll walk beside Miss Balfour in case she gets tizzy."

"It's not 'tizzy,' but 'dizzy.'" Huntley chuckled, climbing onto his mount and bringing it beside Lily's. "You need not bother, Wulfinski. I will ride beside her."

Wulf caught the plea in Lily's gaze. Swallowing the bitter lump that had suddenly appeared in his throat, he nodded. "Fine." He stepped back from her horse. "I'll visit tomorrow and see how you fare."

With a final glance at Wulf, she turned her horse and went with Huntley. The duchess let the two of them ride out of hearing range before she turned to Wulf. "In more ways than one, it's fortuitous that you were here. I wished to have a private word with you. I must inform you that, after that little scene last night, your grandmother is no longer welcome at Floors Castle."

"I don't blame your grace. I will tell her when I return home."

"There is no need. I wrote her a letter this afternoon, although I daresay you left before she received it." The duchess arched a brow. "Sadly, this will make our little house party untenable for you, too. I'm sure you won't wish to attend now that your grandmother no longer can."

"I'm not—"

"No, no. I perfectly understand. I wouldn't expect you to do anything less."

Wulf's jaw tightened. "I see."

"I'm sure you do." The duchess turned to Emma. "Miss Gordon, shall we?"

"No, thank you." Emma's eyes sparkled with outrage. "I wish to have a word with the prince before I return."

"Alone?"

"Surely one of the footmen can stay for a few moments? I will catch up with the party soon."

The duchess didn't look pleased, but she nodded. "Fine. Keep a footman with you, well within sight. I'll not have it said that my house parties are devoid of the proprieties."

"Yes, your grace."

The duchess inclined her head to Wulf. "Your Highness." She turned her horse and cantered across the field to catch up with the others.

The footman touched his hat and then walked his horse several steps away, just out of earshot.

Emma wheeled to face Wulf, her face flushed. "Why didn't you argue with the duchess? She is being unfair!"

"She has a plan for Lily and I am an obstacle. I can't fault her for wishing to be rid of me." He gave a wry smile. "I can't blame her grace for being angry with Tata, either. Her behavior was beyond the acceptable. Tata and the duchess are both strong-willed women, so they are bound to clash. What is ironic is that they have the same objective: to keep me from Lily."

Emma sent him a curious glance. "You don't seem very despondent at being banned."

"I've no intention of allowing either to tell me what I can or cannot do."

"You've either discovered the secret to happiness, or you're simply mad."

"I am mad—madly in love. And that, Emma, is happiness. I cannot leave Lily be."

"So I noticed," Emma said drily. When he lifted his brows, she said, "I saw you kissing her."

To his surprise, his face heated. *Good God, I am no youth, to be embarrassed by a kiss.* "I did not see you arriving."

"Do tell," she said. "If I had not come when I did, the duchess might have found you. This is for the best. I think we've allayed everyone's suspicions but her grace's. Huntley, at least, is reassured of Lily's innocence. As for the kiss"—Emma twinkled at him—"it gives me hope that perhaps her heart will not become entwined with Huntley's, no matter how hard he tries."

Wulf smiled. "She does not love him, if that is what you fear."

"She said as much?"

"And more."

Emma sighed in relief. "That's something, at least."

"For now. Come. I will help you mount. It's time for you to return home, my friend." He went to her side, placed his hands about her waist and lightly tossed her into the saddle. As she settled in, his smile broadened. "In all of the excitement, I forgot to tell you that Lily asked to meet me here to warn me about a dangerous woman."

"Oh?"

"Yes, you."

Emma chuckled. "Odd. Huntley spent all morning warning me about *you*."

"Then our plan is working. How are things with Huntley?"

"Oh, as well as can be expected."

His gaze narrowed. "You did tell him you find him attractive, did you not?"

"Not precisely." Her color could not be higher. "When it came to telling him how I feel . . . Oh, Wulf, I couldn't do it."

"Emma, you must. You wish him to see you differently, and so you must *be* different."

"I tried! I truly did, but I couldn't find the words, and he looked so impatient."

Wulf grasped her hand. "Try again. If Lily and Huntley become engaged, we'll wish with all of our hearts that we were bolder, not more timid."

Emma's shoulders sank. "You are right; I will try again. Meanwhile, I wish you luck in convincing the duchess to put you back on her guest list."

"Thank you." He released her hand and stepped back from her horse. "I hope to see you at the castle soon. Meanwhile, with Lily injured and thus laid up for a day or two, Huntley may be free of her presence, at least for a bit. You won't wish to miss such an opportunity."

Emma brightened. "I hadn't thought of that. I will do what I can. Good luck, Wulf." With a smile, she cantered from the field, the footman falling in behind her.

Sixteen

From the Diary of the Duchess of Roxburghe

Though I've tried to put it from my mind, I cannot stop thinking about how that *woman* dared suggest that I was attempting to fix her grandson's interest on Miss Balfour. What a ludicrous thought! As those who know me will attest, I do not get involved in the lives of those around me. Let them find their own happiness, I say. I merely provide the opportunity through my hospitality.

That said, my opinion of the prince has grown since he assisted Lily when she was injured, although not enough for me to wish him to have free access to my home. I have to wonder just why he was in that field to begin with. His story, while chivalrous, didn't ring quite true.

Something is afoot. But what?

The next day, Lily sat on the settee by the fireplace in her bedchamber. It had been a long day and a half, though she couldn't remember much of yesterday afternoon since the physician had insisted on giving her a draught of some sort. The bitter liquid had done nothing for her shoulder, but it had put her to sleep. And sleep she had—for the rest of that day and most of this one. When she'd awoken well after noon, she'd found herself sore and starving and cross as a bear.

Her mood only became worse when, among the notes and cards brought on her lunch tray, she didn't find one from Wulf. It was silly to expect anything, but she hadn't been able to stop thinking about him since she'd awakened. It was the fault of the laudanum, of course, for it had left her feeling hollow and filled with lingering bits of dreams, most of them ending with her in Wulf's heated embrace.

She moved restlessly and wished for the hundredth time that it had been Huntley who'd kissed her and not the prince. Then she'd have dreamed of Huntley . . . wouldn't she?

She sighed and closed her eyes, struggling through the lingering fog. Bits and pieces of the dreams flickered through her mind, of her and the prince waltzing through the field of yellow flowers while the sun warmed the world about them into a golden haze. He'd smiled at her, bold and beautiful as he lifted her to her horse, though first he'd held her and kissed her and—well, much more than that.

She scowled and kicked at the cover entangled about her legs, wincing as she moved her shoulder. The hours and hours of sleep had done nothing to help—it was stiff and sore. *It would have been much better if I'd been awake and had moved it.*

She pushed the cards on her tray to one side, frowning. *He didn't even send a note, asking how I fared. At least Huntley has been attentive.* It seemed that every few hours there was some message from him. *Which is good, as he's the man I wish to fall in love with.*

Yet she couldn't help but wonder where Wulf might be. Was he in the castle? Or at home in his cottage? Though her dreams were broken and vague, she vividly remembered the day before. She remembered the feel of his strong arms as he carried her through the field. The scent of his cologne when her cheek rested against his coat. The way his thick lashes shadowed his green eyes. The taste of his mouth on hers and how his hands had—

Lily shivered. *Stop thinking about that!* She shouldn't have kissed him to begin with. She'd hoped that the embrace would quench her yearning, but all it had done was set ablaze a new fire, one that was far more difficult to control. His touch was so—

Stop thinking about Wulf! Think about Huntley. Calm. Logical. Always-correct Huntley. Instantly, her heart slowed, her face felt cooler. *That's better. So, what do I like about the earl? He's kind and thoughtful. He's handsome, and tall, and . . .* She waited. Nothing came. *There have to be more things I like about him.* She picked up one of the notes he'd left. *He has excellent handwriting.*

She grimaced and threw the note onto the table. Good God, that was beyond sad. Besides his fortune, there had to be a thousand things that she liked about him. It was just that her mind was still lingering on Wulf's kisses, and that was her undoing.

She absently picked up the small bouquet of flowers that Huntley had sent. It was lovely, of roses and two white lilies. *Wulf doesn't seem like the type to send flowers or—* She caught herself and moaned. *Forget him! He says that he wishes to be with me, but what does that really mean? What can it mean? He knows I must marry a wealthy man.*

She bit her lip. To Wulf's credit, her bald pronouncement hadn't chased him away. He'd even seemed sympathetic to her plight, which she hadn't expected. He'd made no secret of his feelings for her. But . . . what sort of feelings? Could she trust a man who claimed to have fallen in love with her at first sight?

She pulled a pillow from the settee and placed it on her lap, threading the gold fringe through her fingers. "If he truly cares, then I could be in an unbearable dilemma. But perhaps he just means that he wants me physically." That would be less complicated, but—to be honest—disappointing.

But why? Why would that bother me? She punched the pillow. "Blast it, why am I even thinking about this? He's—"

A soft knock sounded at the door. Lily called out a greeting, and Freya, the maid assigned to her by the housekeeper, entered the bedchamber. A talkative girl, she had two missing teeth and a surprisingly positive outlook on life.

The maid peered around the room as she placed a tea tray before Lily. "Och, there's no one here. I though' I heard ye speakin' to some'at."

Lily tossed the pillow to the other end of the settee and gave the maid an embarrassed smile. "I was just thinking aloud."

"I do the same meself." The maid left the room and came back in carrying a stack of towels and a small vase of flowers. She placed the towels and the vase on a dresser and went to shut the door.

As she started to close it, she looked down and frowned.

A pug marched into the room, stood and looked around, then gave a huge sneeze.

"Och, Meenie, wha' are ye doin' here? The duchess will no' be pleased." Freya shook her head and held the door wider. "Oot wit' ye, ye muddy creature!"

The dog merely sniffed the air, wagging its tail as it looked around.

Freya stomped her foot. "I said oot wit' ye!"

But the dog had already caught sight of Lily's tray and was trotting her way.

"The blasted pugs!" the maid muttered. "I'll call a footman to come an' get 'er, miss."

"Oh, no. She seems quite harmless." Lily watched as the dog came to sniff the side of the tray. She patted the settee beside her. The dog gave a ferocious wag of her tail, and then jumped up and curled beside her. "Such a wee, pretty dog!"

"If'n ye'll excuse me language, miss, she's a wee pain in the arse, is wha' she is." Freya shut the door with a thump. "I left her in the kitchens wit' the others who are a-gettin' their baths today, but she must have followed me."

"You bathe them in the kitchen?" Lily asked as she selected a tea cake.

"The pantry, actually. MacDougal has special tables brought in fra' the barn fer the dog washin', which we do once't a week."

"I'm surprised MacDougal doesn't just wash them in the barn."

"Wha'? Her grace's puir, wee, delicate bairns, oot in the barn where they might take cold?" The maid snorted. "They only go to the barn if they've been bad an' they need lockin' up to keep them from harm's way. There's a special room fer them tha' is more like an inn than else."

"Fancy, eh?" Lily sipped her tea.

"Och, 'tis better than me own room in the attic. Each o' the dogs has a bed wit' their names, and little silver bowls, too, as if they was—" Freya caught herself and grimaced. "I'm sorry to go on an' on aboot the dogs, fer they're guid creatures, as dogs go. But her grace does spoil 'em."

Lily patted Meenie's soft head. The dog was lying

still, as if sleeping, but Lily could tell by the way the dog watched the tray that she was just waiting to steal some tea cakes when Lily turned her head.

"I'll draw yer bath, miss." As the maid went to collect the towels, Lily caught sight of the flowers in the vase. They were bright yellow and remarkably similar to the ones in the field. "Freya, these flowers . . . where did they come from?"

"I dinna know, miss, fer they was already on the table in the hall when I came in."

"Then . . . they were not for me?"

"There's no note, so mayhap one o' the upstairs maids put them on the table to brighten up the hallway. Since no one would see them there, I brought them here fer ye to enjoy."

"Thank you. That was very kind."

"Ye're welcome, miss." Freya went into the dressing room, and the sound of the bathwater came from the doorway. After a moment, she came out to collect the towels. "Yer talkin' to yerself made me think o' Lady Charlotte. She does tha' all o' the time. Mutters aboot this an' tha'. It used to bother me, until I realized tha' she dinna even know she's doin' it."

"Neither did I, I fear. I don't normally talk aloud to myself, but I'm still half-drugged from the doctor's potion." To be honest, Lily was also a bit lonely. At home she usually had her sisters to talk to, but now she was relegated to discussing her life with a pillow. It would have been a lowering thought, but at just that moment, Meenie grunted and plopped her chin on

Lily's knee and looked at her with an imploring black gaze. Chuckling, Lily patted her.

"Her grace's doctor do like to use the laudanum." The maid glanced back into the dressing room. "Yer bath is almost ready, miss. I'll bet a good soakin' afore dinner will feel good."

"Lud, yes. It'll help this shoulder more than anything."

The maid moved the tray out of the way, placing it on a high dresser and Lily rose and went to the tub. Meenie sighed sadly, got up, and hopped off the settee.

Freya helped Lily out of her dressing gown and then assisted Lily onto the small stool that was perched beside the tub. The dog trotted along with them and sat down by the door to watch as Lily sank gratefully into the water. She slid down to her chin as the heat soaked though her, the scent of lavender tickling her nose and easing her muscle aches. "Ah. That's just lovely."

"There's verrah little tha' hot water willna cure. There's soap on the washcloth on the edge o' the tub, miss." The maid left Lily and began to straighten up the room, moving back and forth across the open doorway. When she stopped by the tray of letters, she called out, "Yer flowers are beautiful, miss."

"They're from the Earl of Huntley."

"He's a fine gentleman. Everyone is sad ye were injured, miss. There's been verrah little talk of else in the drawin' room."

"How tedious for them! The sooner I'm out of the sickroom, the better." Lily picked up a washcloth and began to carefully wash her shoulder where a bruise had formed.

It was no wonder she was feeling a bit maudlin, waking from such a deep sleep and then sitting alone in her bedchamber. She needed company, talk, the warmth of a meal shared with others. It would be good to join the duchess's guests tonight.

Meanwhile, there was less than two weeks left of the house party. The time had come to secure Huntley's interest and make certain that such a union would make them both, if not happy, at least satisfied. *That's enough for a good, solid marriage. Surely I could be content with that.*

Meenie peeked over the edge of the tub, her back feet on the stool, and Lily laughed in surprise. The dog panted happily, her tongue hanging out one side as she looked at the water with interest.

"You'd best have a care or you'll slip and fall in," Lily told the dog. "I don't think you'd like that."

Ignoring Lily's warning, the dog put her paws on the tub edge, leaned over, and began to drink the bathwater.

"Och, no!" Rushing into the dressing room, Freya scooped up the dog and tucked it under her arm. "I'm sorry, miss. I tol' ye they were a wee bit spoiled." But even as the maid spoke, she gave the dog an affectionate rub on the head.

Lily laughed and continued her bath while Freya settled Meenie on a towel in the corner. After Lily washed her hair, she allowed Freya to assist her out. Together they selected a gown for the evening, and the maid combed Lily's hair before the fire so that it would dry.

Hours later, Lily was dressed and ready for her first public appearance since her accident. She looked forward to rejoining the others. Now, if only she could keep her thoughts on the Earl of Huntley rather than a mysterious green-eyed prince. *I must,* she told herself as she smoothed the Indian silk shawl Freya had just draped across Lily's arm. *Time is slipping by and I must make the hard decisions now, before they are too difficult to make.* "Freya, can you hand me my fan?"

"Yes, miss." Freya handed Lily a small, hand-painted fan with an ivory handle. "Ye look as pretty as a picture, ye do."

"Thank you." Before she drew on her long gloves, Lily paused to give Meenie a final pat.

"Are ye ready, miss?"

"As ready as I shall ever be."

Freya opened the door and Lily, clutching her determination to her as tightly as she could, swept through it.

Upon joining the other guests in the sitting room as they gathered to wait for dinner, Lily was instantly surrounded by well-wishers and inundated with solicitous remarks.

She was a bit relieved when Huntley arrived and, with a firm air of command, escorted her through the swarm and established her on a settee, fetching her a glass of water and pulling up a chair so close that his knees brushed hers. The other guests noticed, and several times Lily caught people exchanging significant glances.

She should have been glad for such specific attentions—and was, truly, but somehow it made her feel awkward and she was glad when Emma joined them.

Emma smiled. "I can see that you're feeling better."

"Much, although I'm embarrassed to be the center of so much attention."

"It can be wearing, can't it, having to tell each person that you're quite well, which they'd see if they'd just look at you?"

"Yes, it is, though everyone is being very kind." Lily glanced at Huntley, who'd been distracted by the comments of a young lord who was quizzing him on the arrangement of his neckcloth.

Huntley's quite fashionable. That's not something I wished for in a husband, but it could be considered an asset. She'd certainly never seen Wulf wear anything like the intricately tied cravat and blazing ruby that the earl was sporting. The prince never spent such time with his clothing, yet he still managed to seem elegant, as if he'd been born to fit the fashion rather than fashion having been made to fit him.

Lily forced herself to smile at Huntley, who left off

his conversation to lean forward almost eagerly. "Miss Balfour—Lily, are you getting tired? Should I procure you a glass of Madeira?"

"No, thank you. I'm merely bruised and a bit sore."

"I'm glad you were not seriously injured." He glanced around and, seeing that only Emma was within earshot, added, "I was going to invite you for a walk tomorrow, for the duchess has nothing planned as of yet, and I thought it might be a good time to see her gardens. I hear they are quite phenomenal."

"I'd love to."

He smiled warmly and she was touched by his enthusiasm. *See? Being married to him wouldn't be a trial at all. I've been allowing my imagination to run away with me when—*

Emma stood, her movement so jerky that Lily and Huntley looked at her in surprise.

She flushed when she met Lily's gaze. "I'm sorry, but I cannot— I mean, I think I—" She took a shaky breath. "Lady Charlotte wishes to speak to me, so if you'll excuse me, I'll just—"

Huntley caught Emma's hand and held it between his. "Emma, please, whatever's wrong? You look ill."

"No, no," Emma said, untangling her hand. "I'm famished, that's all. It's getting late and I haven't eaten since noon."

The earl looked surprised. "Should I fetch you some refreshment and—"

"No, no. I'll be fine." Emma had composed herself

and appeared almost normal, though her cheeks were still faintly pink. "I was just feeling a bit dizzy is all. I'm better now."

Huntley smiled beguilingly. "Then stay a few more minutes. Please?"

She bit her lip, and after a moment sank back into her seat. "I suppose I can see Lady Charlotte after dinner."

"Of course you can," Huntley said, concern in his brown eyes. "You may speak to her during our whist game. You must play, for I intend on winning back some of the coins you stole from me." He told Lily, "Emma and I played billiards this afternoon and she won every game."

"Ah," Lily said, feeling as if she'd somehow missed something. "I have been warned."

"I was just on a lucky streak today." Emma smoothed her gown, bright spots of color in her cheeks. "The duchess has grand plans for us the day after tomorrow. She wishes us all to visit the folly built on the island in the middle of the lake. We're to take boats and paddle over, and then spend the day exploring."

"There'll be a luncheon, too," Huntley added.

"That will be lovely." Lily liked follies, and she'd seen several beautiful ones. Follies were quite the rage. Ornate buildings built to seem like ancient ruins, usually constructed to resemble fallen Greek or Roman temples, they were strategically placed to surprise and delight visitors strolling about one's property.

"This one is supposedly very elaborate," Emma said. "Her grace showed us the architect renderings last night, and I'm excited to see it, for it's extensive. There is a half-fallen temple, surrounded by carefully overgrown vines and, farther into the woods, two huge columns lying upon their sides to look as if an even bigger temple of some sort had fallen long ago—"

"*Ionic* columns," Huntley inserted.

Emma looked pleased. "Yes, they were! I should have known you'd appreciate that detail."

He shrugged. "I've been a student of architecture for the longest time." A half smile touched his mouth. "But then, you know that."

"It's a pity you've never designed something. I've often said you should."

He laughed. "You think I could do anything."

"You can. You've only to try and I'm certain you could do it."

"Ah, Emma, you are always encouraging me to try new things. You are the sister I always wished to have."

Emma's smile disappeared, a stricken look in her eyes.

Huntley didn't seem to notice. Instead, he smiled at Lily. "I hope you'll let me be your guide when we visit the folly. It would please the duchess, for she suggested it. It would please me, too."

Self-conscious, Lily glanced under her lashes at Emma, who was now looking with a fixed expression across the room, seemingly detached from the conversation. But Lily was certain she knew what Emma's expression meant. *Emma cares for him. Good God, how did I miss that?*

But then Emma caught Lily's gaze and smiled, as calm and serene as ever, and Lily wondered if she'd imagined the expression in the older woman's eyes. *Perhaps Emma was reacting to something else?*

"Lily, if you don't wish to go for a walk tomorrow, we could find another amusement." Huntley leaned closer, his smile fading. "If it's is too much, then—"

"No, no. A walk would be just the thing."

"Excellent. We will go after breakfast. It won't be as entertaining as the folly will be, though, will it, Emma?"

"No, indeed. The duchess says it's historically accurate."

"It will be magnificent." Huntley began to expound upon Greek architecture, obviously a subject near to his heart.

"Huntley," Emma finally said, breaking into his detailed description of a temple he'd seen when on the Continent in his youth, "the butler just informed her grace that dinner is served."

People were starting to move toward the doorways. As the three of them followed the other guests, Lily scanned the crowd.

"Looking for Prince Wulfinski?" Emma's voice was low so that Huntley couldn't hear.

Lily's cheeks heated. "I wished to thank him, of course."

"You won't see him here. The duchess has forbidden him to attend any more of her functions."

Lily stiffened. "Why would she do such a thing?"

"She says that it would be awkward to have him here when his grandmother is not allowed. She told him yesterday after your accident."

Lily's hands tightened into fists. *How dare the duchess do such a thing? Why, I might never see him again—* Her heart sank. *But that would be for the best, wouldn't it?* She stole a glance at Huntley and her heart tightened, aching as if she'd bruised it and not her shoulder.

Before she could sort through her turmoil to frame a reply, MacDougal and a footman opened the wide doors to the dining room and the procession in to dinner began.

Seventeen

From the Diary of the Duchess of Roxburghe
Tomorrow we visit the folly. While I am not fond of them, Roxburghe says that nothing inspires him more than a Greek ruin. I can only hope that my guests will feel the same. I must admit it *is* a rather romantic spot. I wonder if certain guests will be inspired by it? I certainly hope that Huntley and Miss Balfour are, although the decision is, of course, entirely their own.

The next night, as the guests were all retiring to their rooms, Lily paused at the bottom of the grand staircase and listened to the rain beat furiously against the tall windows that lined the foyer. The glass panes were swirled with wetness, the air so moist she could almost taste it. The stormy weather matched her mood.

She and Huntley had taken their walk after breakfast, and she'd tried to find out more about him, hoping to build their relationship into a real friendship. She'd asked him about his childhood, and his favorite horses, how long he'd held his title—oh, a number of topics all designed to help her get to know the earl better. But although he'd been forthcoming, the answers had all left her feeling vaguely dissatisfied.

The entire walk had proven futile, and she felt no closer to Huntley now than before the walk. In fact, she'd been relieved when the rain had moved in and they'd had to hurry back to the house. She'd excused herself on the pretext of changing her damp gown and hadn't joined the others until they'd gathered for dinner.

Huntley had searched her out then, and although flattered, she'd spent the entire time wondering why she didn't feel as close to him as she did to Wulf. Right from the beginning, she'd found herself sharing personal thoughts and desires with Wulf that she hadn't shared with anyone else. She didn't know why that was, but she wished she could re-create it with Huntley.

Alas, that goal appeared much more difficult to achieve than she'd thought. Sighing, she turned and climbed the stairs to her bedchamber, murmuring good-night to the other guests who passed her.

Longing for bed, she opened the door just as a brown dog flashed by, scampering into the bedchamber before she stopped and grinned up at Lily. "Meenie, what are you doing here?"

Freya looked up from where she was running a bed warmer between the sheets. "Och, no!" She left the pan and came rushing over to capture the pug.

Meenie gave a sharp bark and dashed around the maid, and the chase was on. Freya was thin and wiry and quick on her feet, but the pug could get in places that even the maid could not. Lily tried to help, but Meenie ran between her feet and, scampering madly, dashed pell-mell under the bed.

"Och, tha' dog." Freya pushed her mobcap back onto her head and plopped her fists on her hips. "There's no gettin' her oot from under there wit'oot help. I'll fetch some o' the footmen and we'll catch her."

"If the duchess doesn't mind, she can stay here. I'd like the company." Lily felt especially lonely tonight, feeling Wulf's absence all the more after her failed conversation with Huntley.

Freya's gaze softened. "I must warn ye tha' they sometimes snore, and loudly, too."

"So does my sister, but I'm used to having her in my room."

The maid chuckled. "Verrah weel, then. So long as MacDougal knows where the dogs are a'sleepin', 'tis well with her grace."

"She doesn't wish them to sleep in the same place each night?"

"Wha' her grace wishes fer her dogs and wha' she gets fra' them are two different things. She had beds made fer the lot o' them, all lined up in her bedchamber, but no' a one will use them. So they're allowed to sleep where they wish. Ye can ring me if'n Meenie gets too noisy fer ye."

"Thank you."

Freya helped Lily undress and slip into her night-gown, then combed and braided her hair. The maid removed the bed warmer from the now-toasty sheets, helped Lily between the covers, stirred the fire, blew out the candles, and bade her a cheerful good-night before closing the door. Nothing was left but the sound of the rain pit-patting against the windows.

A few moments later, there was a scrambling noise as Meenie clawed her way out from her hiding spot. She found the step stool to the bed, climbed onto the thick coverlet, made her way to Lily's feet, walked three times in a circle, and then settled with a sigh into the impression she'd made.

It was rather comforting having the dog there. But though the bed was warm, the dog was cozy, and the house had grown silent, Lily was too fraught with her thoughts to sleep and lay awake staring at the ceiling. Why had the duchess banned Wulf? It hardly seemed fair; how could he be responsible for his grandmother's behavior?

Lily sighed. *And why, oh why, do I care so much about seeing him?*

After a half hour of useless fretting, she turned onto her other side, tugging the heavy sheets and blankets closer. The dog grunted, but didn't awake. Lily tucked her toes under its warm body and sighed at the softness of the sheets. She was completely spoiled, living here with such luxuries and a personal maid.

Things at Caith Manor were far simpler. She had Cook, of course, and a manservant who'd served as butler and groom for longer than she could remember. Both servants were elderly, and Lily tried to lighten their loads as often as she could. Other than those two, they hired a lady to come from the village once a week to help with the laundry, while Lily and Dahlia did most of the cleaning, dusting on Thursday and polishing silver every Friday. Linens were washed and repaired on Saturdays, while floors were scrubbed each Monday. This difficult work used to be done by a small army of servants, but that was long ago, before Father had spent their funds on his greenhouses and horticultural experiments.

Lily flopped onto her back, noting that the rain had finally stopped.

The dog snuffled awake and, after giving a disgusted grunt, got up, turned in a few circles, then plopped back into the same place on the heavy coverlet. Within seconds, it was once again sleeping.

Lily listened absently to the dog's snores, her mind locked on her predicament. *Surely, if I try, I can be happy with a man as kind as Huntley.* He truly was a good person; but why didn't he make her feel breathless the way Wulf did? And why didn't his smile give her a fluttery feeling? Was she wrong in wishing for more than simple, calm affection? To hope that he'd actually come to care for her and—

Plink!

Meenie grunted in her sleep as Lily looked toward the window. *That sounded like a pebble.*

Plink! Plink! Plink!

Meenie jumped to her feet, a low growl in her throat.

"Hush," Lily said softly. She threw back the covers and slipped from the bed, her feet hitting the hard, cold floor. She shivered and rubbed her arms beneath the thin night rail and tiptoed to the window. She'd just reached it when— *SMACK!* Something hit the window with a decided crack.

Meenie, who'd walked to the edge of the bed, hopped back to the middle with a yelp.

"Some brave protector, eh?" Lily pushed back the curtains and threw open the shutters. A pebble rolled to the floor as the shutter swung open, and she could now see where a spiderweb of cracks surrounded a small hole in the glass.

From outside came a low string of foreign curses uttered by a familiar deep voice.

Her heart thudding, Lily peered out. The bright moon shone upon the courtyard below, making the wet flagstones look like a shimmery pool. And right in the center of it stood the prince, a flowing, black cloak flung back from his shoulders, his booted feet planted firmly on the flagstones while his loose white shirt hung open at the neck. His arm was cocked back as if to throw another pebble, but at the sight of her, he dropped the rock and cupped his mouth. "Moya, open your window."

His voice was low, but Lily still held her breath and listened for the sounds of other shutters being thrown back . . . but nothing happened.

She breathed a sigh of relief. *If the duchess realizes the prince is outside in the courtyard at this time of night, she'll call for her footmen to remove him.* A flicker of anger at the unfairness stiffened Lily's resolve. He wasn't like the rest of them, trained in how to move through the complicated circles of their society, and it was frustrating to watch the duchess and others judge him for it.

Well, she wasn't so closed-minded. There was something appealing about his sheer enthusiasm and lack of care for the rules. *He is caring and passionate, as his culture and heart dictate. What's wrong with that?* It was a relief to realize that what she felt for him was pure sympathy and nothing else.

Lily unlatched the window and pushed it open. Instantly a swirl of damp night air grabbed it. She gripped it tighter and leaned out, shivering.

"Why are you here?" she whispered as loudly as she dared. She glanced to either side and was glad to see that all the other windows were tightly closed and shuttered.

Even from two stories up, she saw him smile. "I would talk to you. Alone. This is the only way I could think to do it."

It was a highly improper answer, as was her instant reaction, a flush of warmth that made the air seem even colder. "You shouldn't be here."

His smile dimmed. "I am here, and that is enough."

"Come back in the morning and I—" She frowned. "How did you know this was my window?"

He shrugged. "When I wish to know something, I know it."

"You bribed one of the servants."

"Perhaps. Or perhaps I have been watching your window and have seen you. Come down and speak to me. There are things we must discuss."

"No. Come back tomorrow." She leaned farther out the window and whispered a bit louder, "The duchess has arranged a visit to the folly on the island, but not until noon or later. Call for me in the morning at eight; no one but the servants will be up that early."

"The duchess's butler will just say you are not available." The wind pressed his shirt against his broad chest. "That is what he said this morning when I came to call. He did not even pretend to find out if you wished to see me."

So he had visited her after all. "No one told me."

"I came more than once." His brow lowered. "I left you a card and flowers, too. Did you not get them?"

She turned to look at the vase on her dresser, the wind making her hug herself. *I knew it!* Her irritation with the duchess grew full score.

Yet deep in her heart, Lily wondered if perhaps she was to blame for her grace's machinations. Lily had asked the duchess to assist her in securing a good marriage; had her grace sensed Lily's hesitations about Huntley and noted her equally inappropriate attraction to Wulf? Perhaps the duchess thought it necessary to keep Lily and Wulf apart. "I'm so sorry you've been banished."

"Do not fear, Moya." Wulf grinned. "I'm too resourceful to be so easily thwarted. Even by you."

Lily had to fight an answering smile. It was tempting to think of slipping downstairs to see him, but the thought of getting caught stopped her. Such a scandal would ruin any chance of ever getting a good marriage. Still, she *wanted* to talk to Wulf, to discuss why the duchess had banished him.

Lily sighed. "Emma told me that you'd been denied an invitation to the duchess's events, but not that you weren't allowed to visit at all."

"Emma must not know, then. She has been a good friend to us. If she knew, she would have said so."

So Wulf still considered Emma a "good friend"? An odd flicker of irritation traced through Lily. "Come back tomorrow," she said, suddenly cross. "If you can't speak to me, at least you can talk to your 'good friend' Emma."

"I came to see you, Moya. Not Emma."

Her irritation didn't subside. "You've seen me, *and* you've broken my window, which I'll have to explain in some way."

"I just wanted your attention. I'm sorry about breaking the glass; I tried to call out to you, but you were sleeping very hard."

She hadn't been sleeping at all. She'd been thinking about him, blast it all. The wind must have kept his voice from carrying. "Wulf, you must go now. This is madness."

She'd leaned out as she spoke, lowering her voice

to keep anyone else from hearing her. From where he stood below, Wulf noticed that the damp wind had caused the delicate fabric of her night rail to cling to her rounded bosom in an interesting fashion, her nipples peaked and eager. His cock stiffened at the sight and he had to force his gaze back to her face. "I *must* see you." If he did not, he would explode in flames.

She hesitated. "I'll send a note to your cottage. We will arrange a meeting."

"Moya, I—"

"No. Wait for my note." With that, she refastened the window and softly closed the shutters.

Wulf stared up at the window, his jaw tightening. After two days of trying to visit her, he'd been beyond happy to see her leaning out the window. But now, staring at the empty spot where she'd just been, he wanted more. Much more, damn it.

This was the duchess's fault. She was actively curtailing his access to Lily, and because of the old woman's devious nature, she was succeeding. It was obvious from Lily's expression that she hadn't received either his notes or the flowers, so the duchess's servants were in on the scheme as well, which was daunting. He could fight an old woman, but not an old woman and an army of eyes and ears, all willing to do her bidding.

His hands curled into fists. He'd wager his last ruble that Huntley's missives had been delivered, and that he'd been encouraged to spend time with her, damn the man. Things were at an even worse impasse than Wulf had realized.

He eyed Lily's window with renewed determination. He could not wait for tomorrow to make his case; she'd be off spending more time with Huntley. He had to see her now. He scanned the front of the castle and noted a trellis two windows over. He could climb that and then use the ledge beneath the windows to reach her room. Lily had closed the shutters almost immediately, so he didn't think she'd taken the time to latch the window. *Good. That will help.*

He glanced about. The silent courtyard was empty; no lights shone in any rooms. This would be risky, yes, but necessary, too.

Now, if only the vines were strong enough to hold his weight. There was only one way to find out. He undid his cloak and tossed it into the shrubs and then rolled up his sleeves. . . .

Eighteen

From the Diary of the Duchess of Roxburghe

Love is like a flower. It needs a certain amount of sunlight, the right mixture of soil, and a gentle but firm hand with the watering can. Too much or little of any, and the flower will wither and die on the vine.

Such is the care I give my guests who show the bud of a promise of love. . . .

Lily climbed back into her bed, tucking her toes under the warm spot made by the pug. Meenie snorted in her sleep, but didn't awaken, thank goodness.

The nerve of that man, to throw stones at her window. Did he think she was a misty-eyed chit who'd swoon at every romantic gesture? She was far too sensible.

Still . . . he'd made the effort to visit her, even though the duchess had banned him. That was nice. And it wasn't the milquetoast niceness that Huntley exuded, but a different, warmer, far more seductive nice. Wulf had taken chances trying to see her. And chances were the one thing she couldn't see Huntley taking.

A faint smile tickled her lips and she turned toward the window and wondered if she'd perhaps been a little abrupt? He'd just wished to see her. What was wrong with that? It was rather charming, in fact. And she'd been anything but kind about it. She'd even been a wee bit rude.

She sighed. What was it about Wulf that made her emotions swirl between irritation and fascination?

Perhaps her irritation came from the way he made her feel . . . naked, somehow. Exposed. As if he could see far more of her than she wished him to.

She listened to the silence, expecting to hear his horse riding away, but no sound came. *He must have ridden over the lawn. Such would be the way of an up-to-mischief prince.*

She smiled a little. If she were honest, it was flattering to be shown such attention. But a little uncomfortable, too, which was perfectly understandable considering—

The shutters flew open, a blast of wind swirling the curtains. *Blast it, I didn't latch the window.*

Meenie jumped to her feet, barked once, then ran to the far side of the bed.

"It's just the window." Lily threw back the covers.

The dog growled and hopped in place, her gaze locked on the window.

"Oh, hush. There's nothing to be scared of." Lily

scooted off the bed, shivering as her feet hit the cold floor. She'd taken several steps toward the open window when a man's boot appeared, followed by a large, muscular leg encased in military-style breeches.

Lily froze in place. *He wouldn't dare.*

Meenie growled and ran forward to the front of the bed, then back to the farthest edge.

How could *he?* Her heart surged against her chest.

Wulf's arm and then his shoulder and face appeared as he straddled the windowsill.

He smiled, his gaze flickering over her, making her intensely aware of her lack of a robe. "Good evening, Moya. I'm sorry to importune you, but I was not finished speaking."

She crossed her arms over her chest, more to cover herself than anything else. "Leave."

Meenie hopped in place, growling louder.

"Oh ho," Wulf said. "You have company."

"She's one of her grace's pugs."

"Hmm." His gaze returned to Lily and flickered over her night rail. "That is lovely. I thought you might wear something less—" He gestured. "How do you say . . . laced?"

"Lacy." Her robe was hanging over the end of the bed and she snatched it up and drew it on, her cheeks afire. She'd made this night rail herself and was well aware of the thinness of the fabric. She managed to say in what she hoped was a cool tone, "Did you expect to find me dressed in wool?"

He chuckled. "You are fire and ice, Moya, so with

you, one never knows. I breathlessly await to see which I hold in my arms."

She ached to believe him, but . . . no. They were alone, for heaven's sake, and she was in her night rail and robe, and he was—*delicious*.

The thought sprung unbidden to her mind and she pressed her hands to her cheeks. "There will be no holding, Wulf. This is highly inappropriate, and if someone discovers you here— I can't allow that. You must go."

"I have not yet arrived." He swung his other leg into the room. "But you are right that I should not be seen. I should close the window so no one knows."

"That's not what I mean—"

But he was already closing and latching the window. He sent her a humorous glance over his shoulder. "You shouldn't leave your windows unlatched, Moya. It's not safe."

"How did you manage that climb? The walls are too smooth."

"I have many talents."

She had no doubt about that.

Wulf started to walk toward her.

Meenie bounded across the bed in two huge hops. She stood at the edge and growled, teeth gleaming.

Wulf chuckled and walked past Lily to the dog. He picked her up with one hand and held her even with his face. "Enough, little one. I mean you no harm."

The pug started to growl, but Wulf scratched her

ear and her growls stopped. "Ah, you cannot resist a soft touch."

The pug's tail began to twirl. A few more scratches and Meenie, her tail wagging so fast that Lily could no longer see it, tried to lick Wulf's nose. He laughed and placed the dog on the floor. Tail still wagging, the pug sniffed Wulf's leg and then happily trotted off to curl into a ball on the settee.

Traitor, Lily thought.

"Now I see why you did not latch the window. You have a guard dog."

"She's more of a foot warmer." Lily was tautly aware of him, of the fluid movement of his walk as he approached her, of the power he wore without thinking.

She tugged her robe a bit closer. "Well, Wulf? What do you want? Because if you've come for—for kisses, then I shall have to disappoint you."

"That would be lovely, but, no, Moya." He held out his hands, splayed wide. "I merely came to speak with you."

She felt a flicker of disappointment. *Good God, I am more lost than I thought.* "Say what you wish then, and leave. And make it quick."

His brow darkened. "The duchess has made it very clear that she intends you for Huntley."

"Which is what I want, too." Or what she should want. Lily's chest tightened as if a weight pressed upon it. She'd never been one to blindly conform to anything. Perhaps her lack of reaction to Huntley was simply her refusal to do as everyone expected.

If that was so, then the best way to move forward was to embrace her path. And who better to declare herself to than the one person who tempted her less-disciplined self from that path? "Wulf, you know my circumstances."

His expression grew somber. "It is your circumstances that I wish to speak to you about. Moya, you have set upon marriage as your only answer, but you cannot sell yourself in such a way. There must be other avenues you have not yet explored."

"I've looked for other answers and there are none."

"If you wished to, you would find another path."

"Do you think I would throw myself upon the marriage altar just to amuse myself? There's nothing else I can do."

"Can you not speak to the holder of this debt? Tell him your situation?"

"There is only one thing that the man who holds our debt would accept in exchange for it, and that is marriage to my sister."

Wulf's expression darkened. "Who is this man?"

"An older neighbor who wants a young wife to give him children."

"If he just wished for a young wife, then he could have asked for you." Wulf rubbed his chin. "So it is not just a wife he wishes for, but your sister. He cares for her."

"He couldn't care for her, or he wouldn't have

demanded the repayment of the loan. She stands to lose her home and will be devastated. Besides, he's so much older than Dahlia and he's grumpy and sarcastic. He's never said a nice thing to anyone, and he's just wretched. He would make *her* wretched. I couldn't allow it."

"Hmm. And Dahlia? What does she think of this match?"

"She's a very generous soul. She would marry him instantly, without thinking it through, only to regret it later. I can't have that."

"So instead, you offer yourself as a sacrifice and will marry into a loveless union."

"It won't be loveless."

"Oh, Moya. You lie." He moved closer, the faint scent of his cologne wrapping about her and making her knees quiver.

She had to fight the urge to lean toward him. With just one step, she would be in his arms. She had to gulp some air before she could speak. "I am not lying."

"You do not know that you are lying, but you are. You will not love Huntley." Wulf drew a finger across her cheek, leaving a trail of heat. "Do you know how I know?"

An intelligent woman wouldn't ask. An intelligent woman would demand he leave her bedchamber. A *really* intelligent woman would turn and run from the room, praying to forget the feeling his touch was causing.

Lily raised her gaze to his and asked in a breathless voice, "How do you know?"

He bent closer, his deep voice brushing her ear. "From the taste of your kisses, Moya. No woman who cares for another man could kiss me in such a way."

She shivered and he straightened, his gaze caressing her as surely if he'd used his hands.

Lily gathered her wits. "No. You are wrong," she said stubbornly. "I will love my husband." *Even if it kills me.*

"You will try, I do not doubt that. But love cannot be ordered about like your little dog, brought to heel with a few pats and the promise of some scraps from the table. Love happens where you least expect, like a strike of lightning."

"I refuse to accept that; I will plan things so that it succeeds."

His shook his head. "You stubborn, stubborn woman. Why will you not listen to me?"

"Because I have no reason to. Besides, why do you think you know more about love than me? Have you ever been in love? I mean *really* in love?"

"Once."

The way his deep voice caressed the word made her gaze jerk to his, and something bright and bitter coursed through her. Whoever had won his love, Lily had no doubt that it was returned. How could it not be?

"I hope you were very happy." Her words sounded hollow to her own ears.

He lifted her thick braid from her shoulder and caressed it. "We are not yet happy, Moya, but we will be one day. I promise you that."

She stared up at him, comprehension dawning. "You mean me."

He slipped her braid through his fingers. "I have loved you since the day I first saw you."

"Stop." Lily stepped away, pulling her braid free. "This is not love."

"I know what it is," he said stubbornly.

She gave a shaky laugh. "Love doesn't happen like this. It grows slowly. What you feel is a far more simple emotion: desire."

"No. It is love."

He was like a huge mountain, calm and immovable.

"Have you been in love so many times that you know it so quickly?"

"No. I've never been in love before because I didn't know you. But desire? That I have tasted many, many times."

"How many?" It was a foolish question, but she couldn't help it.

His gaze grew guarded. "When I was young, I followed my desires as all young men do."

She wet her lips. "So would you say . . . ten times?" *Good God, why am I asking?*

"Much more." He caught sight of her face and added a hasty "Perhaps."

"How many more?"

"It does not matter. What matters is that I know that what I feel for you is much more than mere desire."

She realized that her hands had somehow curled into fists. She could not deny that there was an attraction between her and the prince, but that was all. There was nothing to grow love upon. He might think that their lust—which was stronger than anything she'd ever imagined—was more, but she knew better. She could feel the tug that flowed between them, the whisper of desire that made her breasts swell and her heart flutter, the ache that made her restless. She wanted him, desired him, *lusted* for him. And he lusted for her.

And that was all they had. All they would ever have. All too soon, it would be gone. They would part and these few moments would be all they had left. She stepped forward, closing the space between them, her chest lightly brushing his. Instantly he sucked in his breath, his eyes gleaming. He was so close that she was enveloped in the heat of his body.

"We're standing far too close," she managed to say, her voice husky even to her own ears.

"I will not touch you unless you wish me to, but, oh, what you do to me."

Because this is lust. She placed her hand on his chest. His heart thudded against her fingertips, her heart answering it beat for beat.

He slipped an arm about her waist, the weight of it as familiar as if he'd done it a million times before.

"I long for more, Moya. With you, I always long for more."

Oh, how she longed, too. And then, not knowing when or how, *she* was touching *him*, sliding her hands up his chest, her fingers brushing the fine lawn of his shirt.

Wulf moaned her name and bent, his hands tightening about her waist as he lifted her from her feet and pressed her to him. The feel of her soft breasts against his chest captivated him, and already stiff and aching, he captured her mouth with his.

She melted to him, twining her arms about his neck, gasping when his hands slid to cup her behind. His hands curled about her, the feel of her fanning his passion even higher.

Then somehow they were on her bed as he thrust his tongue between her lips, teasing soft gasps and moans from her. She grasped his shirt and pulled him closer, writhing to get impossibly closer. While he kissed her, his hands never stopped, tugging open her robe, pushing aside the neckline of her night rail. He trailed kisses over her neck, to the delicate hollows of her shoulders. She pressed against him and he slid a hand to her breast. She moaned and he gently swirled his palm over her, her nipple tightening.

Encouraged, he pushed her gown aside, gazing down at her exposed breasts. They were small, the nipples rosy and pink. He'd never seen more beautiful breasts and he bent to kiss each one, flicking his tongue over her nipples until she arched against him.

Wulf's body ached with the need for more. As he took her nipple into his mouth and laved it with his tongue, he slid a hand over her hip, her thigh, down to the bottom of her filmy skirt. Her legs parted, her hands roaming up over his shoulder to rake through his hair. Wulf slid his hand from the inside of her ankle to her knee, the warm silk of her skin beneath his fingers.

She gasped against his mouth and, as his hand slid upward, opened for him, her kisses growing more frantic. God, he was aflame, his cock rigid with need. But this moment wasn't about him. He had to show her that they belonged to one another, that she belonged to him. He trailed his fingers over her inner thigh to her most secret center.

Her eyes flew open as he drew his fingers across her mound. "Wulf," she gasped, and grasped his wrist.

It took every ounce of strength he possessed, but he froze, his breath tight in his chest. "Moya," he whispered. *"Please."*

Her silver gaze locked with his, and then slowly, ever so slowly, she released his wrist.

Nineteen

From the Diary of the Duchess of Roxburghe
Love, the grandest passion of all, is dangerous, desperate, and delicious.

Ohhh, that's quite good, if I say so myself. I shall have Lady Charlotte embroider it upon some pillows and scatter them about the sitting room. Perhaps they will inspire someone.

At Lily's capitulation, Wulf kissed her deeply as he trailed his fingers over her once again. She gasped and willingly opened for him, and he stroked her yet again, then again, each time increasing the pressure. Each touch made her writhe and moan, her hands grasping his shirt, his coat, tugging and pulling as, slick with want, she pressed against his fingers.

He kissed her lips, her chin, the delicate line of her jaw to her ear. In his native tongue, he murmured his love into her ear, told her how beautiful he found her, begged her to love him, too.

She grasped his shoulders, gasped and arched, her

eyes closing as waves of pleasure washed though her. Though it took every bit of strength he had, Wulf subdued his own desires, unable to look away from the beauty of her raw reaction. *God, she is magnificent. I would capture this moment and hold it forever.*

But like all pleasure, it was over too soon. She collapsed against the sheets, a faint sheen of perspiration on her brow, her breathing ragged. After a moment, she covered her eyes, her body still shivering under his fingers. He carefully slid his hand back down her leg, returning her skirts to a more modest position before he gathered her close, his chin resting on her head, her cheek pressed to his chest.

Slowly Lily's breathing returned to normal. She finally took one last, shuddering sigh, then dropped her hands from her face, moving away from him as she did so.

Wulf lifted up on one elbow so he could see her better. "I knew from the moment I saw you that you are a passionate woman. I was not wrong."

"I never thought—" She shook her head wordlessly.

He smiled and ran a finger along her long braid. It was curved across her pillow, long strands of strawberry-blond hair now free from the constricting ribbon and curling across the sheets like the froth of a wave.

Her liquid-silver gaze found his. "I didn't know that lust could be so keen, so wild."

Her words made him frown. "That wasn't just lust, Moya. Lust will give you pleasure, true, but it doesn't . . ." He struggled to find the words. "It doesn't keep you warm after."

"I don't understand."

"It leaves the second your passions are released. Love *never* leaves—even when you are spent and tired and wish only to sleep." He took her hand and pressed it to his chest. "Do you feel that, Moya? With each beat, I think of you. I want you. I dream of you. I—"

She rolled away, scooting off the bed so quickly that he was left looking at the spot where she'd just been.

He sighed. "You still do not understand."

She adjusted her gown and belted her robe tightly. "I won't hear any more talk about love, Wulf. You cannot love me. It's impossible."

He sat on the edge of the bed, his heart growing heavier with each word. "Oh, Moya, you frustrate me."

"And you frustrate *me*." She crossed her arms over her chest and whirled away, pacing a short distance and then coming back. "I can't keep fanning this fire between us and still continue to develop my feelings for Huntley."

"Then don't see Huntley."

"Wulf, please try to understand. The earl is a good man. A kind man. Someone who will be just and honorable to his wife and family." She gestured, an almost hopeless quality to it. "He's exhibited all of those qualities and more."

"But you do not love him."

"It takes time to love someone. Here is where you and I differ. You think love is one moment, one grand feeling. But while I want that grand feeling, I want more, too. I want someone who will be there for me not just when the sun is shining and the flowers are in bloom, but someone who will fight at my side through the dark days."

He grabbed her hand and tugged her to him until she stood between his legs. He took her face between his hands and looked into her eyes. "I am that man. Give me that chance."

Her thick lashes slid down and she grasped his wrists and pulled his hands from her face. "No. We have passion, I'll admit that. I lust for you every time I see you."

"That is part of true love: to want someone, to dream of tasting their lips, of touching their—"

"*No!*" She broke away again, moving well out of reach. "You must stop this. You *must*." Her eyes pooled with tears. "You will seduce me, and I will let you, for I have no strength over myself where you are concerned, and all that I work for, all I must do, will be lost! My *family* will suffer, Wulf. I cannot allow that to happen. Do you understand?"

He felt as if the weight of the world had just dropped upon his shoulders. He'd thought that if he could just show her how rich the passion between them was, how full and joyous, that she'd realize how precious and rare the connection that joined them was.

Instead she saw that connection as a chain, one that had to be broken. "I do not wish you to betray your family, Moya. I would never ask that."

"Then what *do* you ask?"

"For your trust. Trust that together, we can solve these problems, find a way to help your family. Together we can—"

"No. Not together. I am alone in this, Wulf. I know what I must do. I may not feel the things for Huntley that I feel for you, but I will. I will make it so."

Wulf raked a hand through his hair, his chest so tight that it felt as if someone had put a metal band about it. His plan had been flawed; she had no experience, nothing to hold as a comparison to her reaction to him. "You think that if you work hard enough, you will grow to desire Huntley as you desire me, but you are wrong, Lily. What we have is very rare. I will not stop pursuing you. I will not stop touching you and reminding you that you long for me—"

"You must!" Her cry roused the sleeping pug, who jumped off the settee and came to stare up at her.

She scooped the dog up, hugging it forlornly, her lips trembling as she tried to hold back tears.

The sight wrenched his heart and Wulf wondered how he'd made so many errors. He'd only wished to show her happiness, yet he'd somehow managed to do the opposite.

She rubbed her cheek against the dog's head before she said in a tremulous voice, "The duchess is right; it would be better if we did not see one another again."

Wulf gritted his teeth. He'd bared his soul to this woman, had shown her the miracle that flared between them, and she wanted none of it. There was nothing more to be said.

For now. "Fine. You wish me gone, so I will go. But I can't promise I will not try to see you again. I cannot keep such a promise."

"You will only make it more difficult for us both. I'm trying to fix things and you—" A sob broke from her and she pressed her face to the dog and turned away.

He closed his eyes. He could stand anything except seeing her cry. "I cannot do as you wish. I cannot."

There was a long silence before she gave the dog a final hug and then put it back on the floor. She then crossed to the nightstand for a handkerchief to dry her eyes. "I *hate* not having a choice for my life, but I don't."

He sighed and came to her. Her lips were still swollen from his kisses, one cheek red from where his beard had brushed her, her thick lashes spiked from her tears. She'd never been so beautiful, nor he more enslaved. "Is this what you really want, Moya? Huntley as a husband?"

She hesitated, then nodded firmly. "I must, Wulf."

But he'd seen her hesitation, and hope flooded him. *Perhaps all is not lost. There is doubt there now; that is new.* "You think he will ask you to marry him?"

"I don't know. He's been quite nice and he seeks me out. He is grateful that I've been kind to Emma, I think. She is like a sister to him."

"So I've been told." Wulf sighed. "I cannot believe that I am about to do this."

"Do what?"

"Help you with Huntley."

"You . . . you would do that?"

"You give me no choice. If you wish Huntley to feel so strongly for you as to offer for your hand, he must see you as something more than 'nice.' You must be special."

"How do I do that?"

He looked at her, her long, reddish-blond hair coming loose from its braid, her eyes large and mysterious in the low light. She was already special, and it irked him to his core that she didn't know it and Huntley was too stupid to see it. But she must be shown the futility of her plan to wed Huntley and then fall in love. Which meant that Lily needed to see more of Huntley . . . and more of him, too.

She is right; she needs choices. I can at least give her that. "I can show you how to gain Huntley's attention. You do not know how men think, how to drive their passions, but as a man, I do."

"Wulf, I don't know . . ."

"Oh? As things stand, will Huntley make a declaration in less than the two weeks you have left here?"

"I don't know. He's never really—" She bit her lip.

"I hoped that if we continued to talk that it would just happen."

"*Nyet*. I do not know much about Huntley, but he does not seem the sort of man to do anything on impulse."

"He's not. He's very careful."

"So I thought. He will not put himself into a marriage without great thought. If you wish him to declare himself in such a short time, then you will have to appeal to both his reason and his passions."

Lily paused. "You're right. I don't know how to bring him to the mark. Though I've spoken with him every day, I can't tell if he prefers me or if he's merely being nice." Her gaze grazed Wulf's face and then shifted away. "It's not the way it is between you and me."

"No lust, eh?" *And there will never be, if I can help it.* "Men look for certain things in women. Some look for peacefulness, some for laughter, some for intelligence, some for wide hips to bring forth many babies. What does Huntley look for?"

"I don't know. We've never had that conversation."

"And you won't. Men do not announce these things to the women they think to court for fear of fakery."

Her brows locked. "What do you look for?"

"Just you, and no one else. But you know that."

Her cheeks stained pink. "You make no sense."

"One day you will see that I do. Meanwhile, I will help you. I will win Huntley's confidence and he will tell me what he wishes in a wife. I will then tell you.

You can become that woman if you wish, or you can choose not to. It will be up to you."

He could see from the way her lips pursed that she was tempted to accept his offer. He prayed that she would take it. If they were working together, he and Lily, then she'd have to speak with him, have to meet with him. Right now, he'd trade his right arm for such a circumstance.

"Why would you do this for me?"

"I do not give this favor freely."

Her gaze narrowed. "Oh?"

"If you ever find yourself with Huntley and know that you cannot continue with your plan to marry him, then you will come to me."

"And then?"

"You will marry me and become my wife."

She looked bemused. "And live in your cottage in the woods?"

"It is my home."

A smile touched her lips. "One day, I wish to see your cottage. I—" She caught herself and pressed her lips together. "Very well, Wulf, I accept, but I won't change my mind about Huntley. I can't."

"We will see. Sometimes what we think we want is not what we expect when we finally get it." He crossed to her and captured her hand and pressed a kiss to her fingers. "We are agreed, then, you and I?"

She nodded. "How will you gain access to Huntley since the duchess has forbidden you to visit?"

"That will be my first hurdle, but I will overcome

it." He gave her hand a gentle squeeze before he released it. "Now, I must go. Good night, Moya." He captured her gaze as he leaned forward and pressed his lips to her forehead.

She stood still, and then, with a sigh, turned away.

But it was a sad sigh. He would take that and stay hopeful. He turned and went to the window and unlatched it. As he pushed back the curtains, he caught sight of the pug standing at his feet, looking at him with adoring black eyes, her tail twirling.

Wulf chuckled. "I cannot take you with me, little one. Not this time." He picked up the dog, tickled its chin, and then handed it to Lily.

She held it in both arms, resting her cheek on its head.

He straddled the windowsill. "Starting tomorrow, I will extend my friendship to Huntley, earn his trust, and discover what he wishes in a wife. Miss Gordon knows him well, too. I will see what I can learn from her, too. Whatever hints I find, I will give to you."

"Thank you. That's very generous of you."

"You're welcome," he replied grimly. It would turn his mouth sour to help her win a man who couldn't look at her as she was now, sleepy eyed and mussed, and realize how beautiful she was, inside and out. But that was a truth she had to find out herself. "Just remember your promise, Moya: if you change your mind, you will come to me."

She nodded, and with her sad gaze haunting him,

he climbed out the window and down the vine to his horse. He mounted and, just as he turned for home, he heard her window close softly and he realized that she'd watched him leave.

Feeling more hopeful than he had in days, he turned and rode for home.

Twenty

From the Diary of the Duchess of Roxburghe
Contrary to what others have said, I am not a proud
woman. I am generous, too, often to a fault. But
like Queen Elizabeth, Cleopatra, and all other great
women, a good apology is never wasted on me. I
enjoy every one.

Lady Charlotte's hands froze in mid-knit, her needles
stilled. "*Who* did you say has come calling?"

"Och, it has surprised us all, it has," MacDougal
said. "But the grand duchess and the prince arrived
no' five minutes ago. I put them in the green salon and
came here to tell ye."

"Oh dear." Charlotte glanced at Margaret, who
had stiffened by the window.

"That Gypsy is no longer welcome in my house,"
she said coldly.

The butler gulped. "Aye, yer grace."

She threw up a dismissive hand. "Tell them we're
not here."

MacDougal looked miserable, his face red as he shuffled from one foot to the other. He looked pleadingly at Lady Charlotte.

Poor man. "There's more?" she asked gently.

"It's jus' . . ." He looked anxiously at the duchess before he turned back to Lady Charlotte and said, "I hesitate to say anythin', me lady, but knowin' how the grand duchess earned her banishment, 'tis tha' verrah thing which makes me—all of us, to be honest—hesitate to send her off." He bent low and whispered, "We dinna wish to be cursed."

"Oh, for the love of—" The duchess stomped across the room, picking up Randolph as she went. The gray-nosed pug grunted happily as she dropped into a chair across from Lady Charlotte and settled him in her lap. "I won't have such nonsense at Floors Castle, MacDougal. We will not run our household based on silly superstition."

"Verrah weel, yer grace." MacDougal was ramrod straight, though he looked as miserable as could be. He knew the duchess, though, had served with her longer than any other servant, and he knew she was close to losing her temper.

Charlotte resumed knitting, though her gaze was on Margaret. "I don't believe in curses, but—"

"I should hope not!" Margaret rubbed Randolph's ear and was rewarded when the dog drooled a bit on her skirt. "Such foolishness."

"However," Charlotte added carefully, casting a covert glance at MacDougal, "I do think it would be to our advantage to heed the servants' fears. We really don't wish them to be falling all over themselves with worry, thinking every normal toothache has been caused by some sort of Gypsy-muttering."

The duchess's expression grew stiff and she turned her blazing gaze on MacDougal. "There are those who seriously believe that the grand duchess can place curses?"

The butler tugged at his neckcloth. "No' me, yer grace. But there are others who might think jus' tha'." At her muffled exclamation, he hurried to add, "But 'tis jus' one or two. However, I do think tha' Lady Charlotte has the right o' it: if'n we send the grand duchess off wit'out seein' ye, she is like to be verrah mad. And if she *can* put a curse on someone, an' they dinna have a talisman to ward it off, then——"

"Ha! I dare her to try!" Margaret's blue eyes were icy cold. "Curses and talismans—good God, what nonsense!" Her lips thinned. "I vow that my patience with this woman has about reached its end. I'd rather die than receive that woman again."

Charlotte slipped a glance at the butler and almost tsked aloud. The poor man was caught in the jaws of a horrid dilemma—facing a Gypsy's curse or the wrath of his mistress. "Margaret, you're quite right not to allow that wretched woman entrance. I'm sure she's come to apologize, and I've no wish to hear her grovel, not even for a moment——"

"Apologize?" The duchess sat up straighter. "Do you think that's why she's come?"

"Why else would she be here?"

"Oh. She *does* owe me an apology, of course. Several, in fact." Margaret cocked a brow at MacDougal. "Did she mention her purpose in coming?"

"No, yer grace."

"Humph. Does she look sorry? Or a bit guilty?"

"No, yer grace. She just looks angry. I'm no' certain, but from the way she was glarin' at her puir grandson, I believe he may have made her attend ye here."

Charlotte considered this. "Perhaps the prince has demanded that she apologize."

The duchess absently patted her pug. "Which would make it all the more delightful. However it is, the fact that she doesn't want to be here has made me wish to prolong her visit." Margaret inclined her head at the butler. "Bring them in."

He bowed and then sent a look of blinding thanks to Lady Charlotte before he hurried out of the room, a lift to his step.

Charlotte bent over to tug a ball of yarn free from her basket and then settled back into her seat. "Margaret, I must say that it's very kind of you to see the grand duchess after her indiscretion."

"Well, you were right. If I don't see her, the servants would be next to useless, for they'd be too busy blaming every broken lace and dropped tray on some supposed curse." Margaret rubbed Randolph's ears. "Silliness, but there you have it."

"It's still very kind of you to see her after her actions. Of course, the question now is whether or not you will allow them to attend the rest of our house-party events."

Margaret pursed her lips. "If the grand duchess apologizes . . ." She shrugged. "Why not? Besides, I think our Miss Gordon has an interest in the prince."

"Oh?" Charlotte cocked an interested gaze on her friend. "And you would favor that match?"

"Of course. Miss Gordon is a close friend of Huntley's, and if she's busy with the prince, it will leave Lily more time to cast her spell over the earl."

Lady Charlotte smiled. "I vow, you are positively devious."

Margaret looked gratified. "Thank you, Charlotte. I do try."

"And you succeed, too." Charlotte's needles clacked softly. "If you could bring about two matches at one house party—oh my! Your name will be legend among the hostesses of the *ton*."

The door opened and MacDougal appeared, announcing in a respectful tone the Grand Duchess Nikolaevna and Prince Wulfinski.

Meenie gave a joyous bark and ran forward to dance about the prince's feet.

The prince chuckled and bent to scratch the dog's ears. "Ah, Meenie. You miss me, eh?"

Margaret watched, surprise clear on her face. *What's wrong with Meenie? It's as if she recognizes him.* "Meenie!" she called. "Come!"

The prince gave the dog a final pat and then

reclaimed his grandmother's arm, and they walked toward Charlotte and Margaret. The prince was so tall and his grandmother so short that they made one think of a powerful giant assisting a bent, gnarled elf.

Charlotte watched them closely. MacDougal had been right; the grand duchess's face was tight with rage and she sent her grandson dagger glance after dagger glance as they approached. The prince didn't seem perturbed, accepting her glares with an amused look.

As their guests reached the sitting area, Charlotte put aside her knitting, and she and Margaret stood to welcome them.

"Your grace," the grand duchess muttered. "Lady Charlotte." The old woman bobbed a barely there curtsy, her mouth twisted into a scowl.

"Good morning." Her grandson made his bow, murmuring something under his breath to his grandmother as he straightened.

She sent him a bitter look, but then she set her shoulders and said sullenly, "I have come to say I am—" She looked at her grandson, who lifted a brow.

She grimaced and turned back. "I was wrong and I am s—" She scowled as if the word had cut her tongue. "I am s—" She threw up her hands and rattled off a spate of words in her native tongue.

The prince answered in English, "Tata Natasha, you were wrong and you know it."

"Wrong isn't what I'd—"

"You gave your word."

She waved a hand. "Fine! Fine! I will do it. I said I would, and I will." She faced Margaret again. "I'm sorry for casting magic indoors at your castle. I lost my temper, thinking Miss Balfour was making eyes at Wulfinski."

Margaret managed a magnificent smile that she was certain would scald her reluctant guest. "I accept your apology."

Lady Charlotte added, "I'm sure we were all a bit out of sorts that evening and said things we didn't mean."

Margaret's smile slipped, but she managed to catch it before it completely disappeared. *She hadn't said one blasted thing that she hadn't meant.*

The grand duchess sniffed. "Perhaps. I should not have attempted a curse indoors—"

"Tata, you should not cast curses on anyone," her grandson corrected. "*Ever.*"

She folded her lips into a straight line.

He crossed his arms. "Need I remind you of my promise if you do not make things right with her grace?"

"Oh, I remember! You're a heartless boy, you are, to threaten to send me home locked in a trunk. Pah! You are my grandson! You shouldn't speak to me like that."

"You left me no choice."

"Well, I've apologized, but I still think the same of Miss Balfour as I ever did. You are a prince and she is a nobody, a Scottish wench with no looks or property or title—"

"I beg your pardon," Margaret said icily, "but Miss Balfour is my goddaughter and is quite well born, too. She was gently raised and is every inch a lady. Furthermore, you are grossly mistaken if you think Miss Balfour has *any* interest in your grandson. She is on the brink of a very suitable proposal from the—Well, it doesn't matter who, but you will soon see that she never has been, and never will be, interested in your grandson. Although if she were"—Margaret's voice snapped like a whip—"then I would *personally* see to it that the prince and Miss Balfour were together, regardless of your opinions."

Charlotte stole a glance at the prince, who was smiling, a faintly satisfied look in his eyes.

He caught her gaze and smiled more broadly, a twinkle in his green eyes that she couldn't help but like. Though not sure why he was so pleased, Charlotte found herself smiling back.

"How dare you, you-you-you—" sputtered the grand duchess, her hands curling and uncurling as if longing for a weapon. "I shall—"

"I think that's enough of an apology." Wulf took his grandmother's arm and cocked a brow at her.

She clamped her lips closed, her face puckered with fury.

He bowed deeply to Margaret. "Your grace has been most gracious."

"Thank you," Margaret said, though she seemed

mollified. She sent a smug look at the grand duchess, then smiled and turned to the prince. "My dear Prince Wulfinski, I hope you *and* your grandmother will join us this afternoon. All of my guests, including Miss Balfour, will be visiting the folly on the island. We'll be leaving in a few hours if the weather holds."

"I would be most pleased to join you. Unfortunately, my grandmother will be sleeping as she needs a nap."

"Pah, I do not need a nap! I'm—"

"Tata, enough." He didn't raise his voice, but it was so icy that even Margaret's eyes widened.

Chastened, his grandmother merely muttered under her breath.

With a final bow, Wulf tucked his grandmother's arm in his and walked her to the door, Meenie trotting after them. As they reached the door, the prince looked at the small dog and said one word in his native tongue. To Charlotte's surprise, Meenie instantly sat, her tail wagging as hard as it could.

The prince gave the dog an approving look and escorted his grandmother out the door, MacDougal closing it behind them.

Margaret collected the pugs that had overtaken her chair and sank down. "Well! That was the most ungracious apology I've ever enjoyed." Her eyes sparkled with humor. "But I did enjoy it."

Charlotte watched as Meenie stared at the closed door, her expression despondent. The dog whined and then barked. "The prince has a way with animals."

Margaret followed Charlotte's gaze. "Meenie, come!"

The little dog didn't even glance their way, but kept her gaze locked on the closed door.

"That's odd," Margaret said.

"She likes the prince." Charlotte took her own seat and settled her knitting in her lap. "And I believe . . . no, I'm certain that I like him, too."

Margaret looked surprised. "Do you?"

"Yes. He seems very resourceful. I like that in a man."

"He certainly brought his grandmother to heel." Margaret chuckled. "Send her home in a trunk! No wonder she was cowed."

"You don't think he'd really do that, do you?"

"No, it was the threat of being sent home that brought her here. Mark my words, we'll see more of that woman, and she'll do what she can to keep Miss Balfour from Wulfinski." A smile played about Margaret's mouth. "You may think me petty, but it would almost be worth the trouble to put them together just to irk her grace."

Charlotte set her needles back into motion. "My dear Margaret, I can think of nothing that would amuse us more. Should we?"

"It's tempting . . . but then there's Huntley, and he seems quite taken with our Lily. If I thought him suitable for another, I just might . . ." The duchess pursed her lips and stared without seeing across the room.

Charlotte knew better than to interrupt when that

faraway look settled in Margaret's eyes, so she tugged her basket closer and continued to knit. As soon as the duchess had everything settled in her mind, she'd share her thoughts.

All Charlotte knew was that whatever mischief Margaret was brewing, they would all be the better for it.

Twenty-one

From the Diary of the Duchess of Roxburghe
It had better not rain. That's all I have to say about it.

At one o'clock, the guests—all wrapped in shawls and coats against the overcast, rather threatening skies—rode by horse and carriage to the lake, then were punted across the gray water by enthusiastic footmen. The duchess had decided to chance the trip to the folly, declaring that in Scotland gray skies were far more normal than the beautiful blue ones they'd enjoyed over the last week.

Lily rode across the lake in a boat with three young ladies who'd apparently known each other since childhood, judging by their whispers and giggles. Ignoring them, she enjoyed the beauty of the setting and tried to calm her emotions, which were still in turmoil from Wulf's late-night visit. How had she so forgotten her sense of propriety to allow that to happen? But that was how it was: whenever Wulf was about, she forgot many things she shouldn't do.

The memory of her wanton behavior made her cheeks heat with a breathless excitement. She'd never thought about the physical aspect of a marriage before. It was assumed that a wife would do what was necessary; enjoyment was never a part of it. But last night, Wulf had shown her true physical pleasure.

If Huntley and I marry, will I feel the same way? She couldn't imagine even kissing Huntley, much less anything else.

She'd never known such passion was possible, but, oh, how her body had come to life under Wulf's touch. Even now, she yearned to feel that bliss again.

But that was not to be. *Never.*

Still, she couldn't regret it had happened. Her only regret was that her enthusiastic response had given the prince the last thing he needed—encouragement.

The man was impossible, demanding and unrelenting. *And sensual and handsome and*— No. She should be thinking about one thing only: Wulf had agreed to help her win Huntley.

She reached out to trail her fingers in the cold water. *Of course, Wulf first has to win his way back onto the duchess's guest list. That will be quite a feat, if it's even possible.*

"Ye'd best hold on, misses. We're aboot to land." The footman pushed the boat onto the island's shore with a thud. Once the boat was grounded, he placed the pole back into its lock, then hopped off to help the guests climb out onto the hard-packed beach.

Lily's three companions hurried away, looking for

other members of their party. Left alone, Lily gathered her cloak and walked to where more boats were pulling onto the shore.

From where he was helping Miss Gordon from their boat, Huntley called to Lily, "Miss Balfour—Lily! Hold a moment, please!"

He was obviously happy to see her, and grateful for his enthusiasm, she returned his smile. *There, this isn't going to be so hard, is it?*

Once Emma was safely on the shore, Huntley strode toward Lily. She watched him approach, aware of the envious glances of several other ladies. He was handsome and dressed as usual in the top of fashion, although today, because of the nature of their outing, he wore a long multi-caped coat, sturdier boots, and a simpler neckcloth.

He reached her side. "I was hoping we'd be in the same boat, but you'd already left by the time Emma came downstairs. I'd promised her that I'd wait, but she had a broken lace on her boot and had to redo the entire thing."

"Had I known, I would have waited for you."

"No matter. We're here now." He took Lily's arm and began to lead her up the low-sloped bank.

"Should we wait for Miss Gordon?"

He glanced over his shoulder. "Emma's already talking to someone—Mrs. Simpson, I believe. You know Emma; she'd rather one didn't bother her too much. She's very independent."

Lily sent him a side glance. Was that dismissal

in his voice? She rather liked Emma's independent nature. Or she did when Emma wasn't using it to flirt with Wulf.

Keeping up an easy flow of small talk, Huntley escorted Lily to a rise from which they could watch the other boats arriving. As she'd expected, none of the boats carried a large, black-haired prince with a devilish smile.

"Ah, there's the duchess now." Huntley nodded toward the final boat. "I spoke to Lady Charlotte earlier, and she said we're to wander down the main pathway and then on to the folly. The servants came hours ago and put up a tent and brought a sumptuous tea for this afternoon."

"Good, for I'm famished." Even under gray skies, it was a beautiful island, and it seemed that every blade of grass had been artfully planted. She caught glimpses of several statues here and there in the woods, some standing and some tilted as if disturbed by an earthquake or another natural disaster. Twined over it all ran ropes of flowers and vines.

"It's lovely, isn't it?" Huntley said.

"It's amazing. Do many people prepare such elaborate follies?"

"Some, though I know of none who've made use of an entire island. One part of Vauxhall Gardens in London is similarly plotted, although they've added water features."

"I've never been to London."

"No?" He smiled. "Perhaps one day we will be there together. You'll enjoy it."

"I'm sure I will. My sister Rose loved her season there."

"Ah, yes, she's Lady Sinclair now, isn't she?"

Lily slanted a glance at the earl, wondering at the repressive note in his voice. "Yes, she is." For some reason she felt the need to add, "She and her new husband are deeply in love and are very happy together."

"Oh, I and everyone else heard all about it. Not to say anything untoward, but your sister and Sinclair were not very circumspect."

"They were very much in love."

He shook his head. "There are only two kinds of love stories—those that are well-bred and those that are not. One you will read about in lending-shop novels and features bloodstained knights as unlikely heroes who make public announcements in the most vulgar manner, while the other occurs properly in the drawing rooms of England's best houses and are conducted as all private affairs should be—in private."

She managed a smile, though she was certain Wulf would disagree. *But perhaps Huntley is right about one thing: not all love stories have knights—or princes—who slay dragons and kiss the princess senseless until she can no more think than breathe. Not real love stories, anyway.*

"I've often thought that— Oh, there's the duchess. It appears that she is telling everyone to continue on to the folly, for she's gesturing toward the path and shooing people along. Shall we lead the way?" He pointed to the path to their left. "Lady Charlotte said they placed servants along the pathway with umbrellas, in case the rain comes."

Lily took his arm. They'd only gone a few steps when a low branch hit his hat and sent it tumbling. He gave a low exclamation as he collected it. "Look at it! There's mud on the brim." He pulled out a handkerchief and carefully wiped off the mud, frowning as mightily as she'd ever seen him.

He looked so serious that Lily had to bite her lip to keep from grinning. "Do you need another handkerchief?"

"What I really need is some water and a stiff brush. I'll have my man take care of it when we return." Huntley tucked the hat under his arm and offered her his elbow again. "Shall we?"

As they walked, Lily glanced at the earl, noting his calm expression. She'd never seen Wulf calm. He was too energetic, too vibrant. He couldn't speak without revealing his passionate nature, and she wondered what he would say to Huntley's observations about love and courtship.

A stiff breeze made Lily tug her cloak tighter. "It feels as if the weather's turning. I hope we find one of the servants who is handing out umbrellas before it rains."

He patted her hand. "We will."

For some reason, the same certainty that Wulf wore so easily was an irritant when employed in Huntley's stiff fashion. She mentally shook herself and forced a smile. "If it rains before we find an umbrella, we'll just take shelter somewhere."

He looked at her approvingly. "I told Emma this morning that one of the things I like best about you is your pragmatic nature. I knew you were such a woman the first time I met you."

She wondered uneasily how one looked "pragmatic." "Huntley, I'm just curious, but . . ." She turned to face him. "What do you think about romantic gestures?"

His brows rose. "What sort of romantic gestures?"

"Oh, you know . . . climbing into a window or up a trellis or—"

"Hold. How is climbing up a trellis or into a window 'romantic'?"

"Well . . . if you did it because you wished to speak to someone and there was no other way, then it could be romantic."

"Hardly. That sort of behavior is exactly what I was talking about. I can't imagine how anyone would find it romantic to be forced to witness such foolhardy, crass behavior."

"Crass?"

"Yes, crass." He caught her expression and he laughed softly. "Oh, I see. You read such a scene in a book, didn't you, and thought it excessively romantic? I'm sure it is—on paper. But in real life, would you really applaud someone for being so careless with your good name? I think not."

"It sounds as if I'm not the only person who is pragmatic in nature."

He chuckled. "That is quite a compliment. My wife used to—" His laughter faded, his sherry-brown eyes darkening.

Lily put her hand on his arm. "I'm sorry. It's still a fresh wound."

"It shouldn't be, as she died more than two years ago." He shook his head. "She would not have wished me to hide away and grow old alone, so I— Good God, just listen to me." He chuckled ruefully. "Here I am, walking through a beautiful woods with an even more beautiful companion, and I'm being about as much fun as a dead horse."

"I'm sure it was an extremely difficult time for you."

He looked down at her with a warm smile. "You are very generous, Lily."

"I would think less of you for not caring."

He squeezed her hand, and they turned the corner and found themselves facing three divergent paths.

"We face an intriguing choice, Lily. Which shall we choose?"

She was about to suggest that they take the shortest pathway to tea when Wulf's deep rumble interrupted her reply.

"Ah, Huntley! There you are."

He stood on the path behind them, Emma on his arm. Wulf was dressed in buff breeches tucked into black boots, his deep blue coat open and his cravat carelessly knotted about his strong throat. His black hair fell over his forehead and framed his striking eyes.

"What a surprise," Huntley said, looking far from pleased to see Emma's hand resting on the prince's arm. "Your Highness, I didn't expect to see you here."

"The duchess re-invited me." Wulf's gaze locked with Lily's, a smile curving his mouth. "I had to row myself over, as I was late arriving, but I did so and now here I am."

"How fortunate for us all," Huntley said. "Emma, I thought you were walking with Mrs. Simpson?"

"She stopped to wait on Lady MacInnis, and the prince was coming this way, so I joined him." Emma leaned against Wulf's arm and smiled up at him. "Shall we continue on? It might rain on us if we linger."

"Yes," Lily agreed. "I'm famished as well, and I hear that a lovely tea awaits."

"Then we go." Wulf started toward the wider path to the left, Emma with him.

Lily started to follow, but Huntley didn't move. As her arm was tucked into his, she stopped as well.

Wulf looked back, frowning. "Do you not come?"

Huntley smiled. "You may take that path. Lily and I will take this other and meet you at the tent for tea."

Emma's brow creased. "The duchess said to keep to the widest path."

Huntley's smile dimmed. "We're on an island. I'm certain that all of these paths eventually converge."

Lily half expected Wulf to argue, but he merely

shrugged his broad shoulders. "Do as you wish. I must find this tea. I have not had lunch and I hear there will be apple and peach tarts."

Lily's stomach rumbled at the mention of food.

Huntley didn't notice, for he was already tugging her to the far path. Unable to say more without stepping on the earl's pride, she went with him, aware of Wulf's gaze as they disappeared in the forest.

The Roxburghe folly had been designed to look like a half-collapsed Grecian temple, complete with a crumbling portico, large fallen columns, and an ornate mural half hidden by vines. Trees surrounded the small clearing, where a large tent had been raised to protect the guests from inclement weather.

Underneath the tent was a repast of hard cheeses, scones, tea cakes, cold duck, crusty bread, roasted beef, an assortment of jams and jellies, bowls of pears and apples, a platter of grapes, and an assortment of the promised tarts. A small table held eight kinds of tea, all in decorative pots, while footmen carried trays of chilled champagne across the lawn for the more adventurous.

Ladies and gentlemen ate and talked, laughed and mingled, while a three-piece ensemble played off to one side, flooding the area with soft music.

Emma, oblivious to it all, looked at the threatening skies. "Where can they be?"

"Walking. While you fetched your scone, I asked one of the footmen about the path Huntley chose. It goes to the other side of the island and ends at a small cove on the lake. They will have to turn and walk back if they wish to join us for tea."

"Oh no!"

He frowned. "Why are you so worried? A little rain will not hurt them."

"You don't understand." She glanced around and then leaned forward to say in a low, urgent voice, "If anyone realizes they are alone and in the woods together, it could cause a scandal."

"If someone mentions it, we will just say that we saw them near the temple. It is a large area, and there are many places they could be with perfect propriety."

Emma didn't look convinced. "I wish you had demanded that they come with us."

"I didn't know that the path Huntley chose to take wouldn't end up here. Besides, I didn't wish to antagonize him."

Emma's brows rose. "That is a change of tune."

"I wish to win Huntley's confidence."

"Why?"

"Because I wish to, that is why." Wulf regarded Emma over the edge of his champagne glass. "You may help me with that."

"I?" Her gaze narrowed. She put her empty plate on a small table. "Why this sudden urge to befriend Huntley?"

Wulf took a drink of the champagne. "Did you take my advice and tell Huntley how you feel?"

Emma's cheeks stained pink. "No."

"A pity. Meanwhile, I told Lily that I loved her and have since I first saw her."

"What did she say?"

He finished the champagne and placed it on the table beside her plate. "It was as you said; I frightened her."

"I thought that's how she would react. You are either very brave or very foolhardy; I can't decide which."

"I am in love. And at least now Lily knows I am here and that I will wait for her. She also made me a bargain."

"Oh?"

"Yes. I am to help her in her quest to gain Huntley's interest."

Emma, who'd just taken a sip of tea, choked.

Wulf looked at her in concern.

Coughing, she pressed a hand to her throat, finally catching her breath. "Wulf, you cannot help Lily win Huntley! That's madness."

"It *is* madness. But I have thought of this and it is for the best."

"How? Why?"

"Because if she is with Huntley enough, then one of two things will happen. Either they will grow tired of one another and realize they do not belong together, or—" He didn't seem to be able to finish the sentence.

She scowled. "Or they will fall in love and we'll both be lost."

"If that happens, then they were not meant for us, and we must let them go."

Emma's eyes darkened and she was silent a moment, staring into her teacup. Finally she sighed. "You may be right."

"Sadly, I am."

She set her cup onto the saucer with a clip. "But don't expect me to help you. Huntley is entranced already, and you said yourself that Lily is determined to wed him for his fortune. I *won't* help them."

"Emma, they must come to us on their own or it will not matter."

"Speak for yourself! I would take Huntley any way I could get him."

"Oh? You wish to be an unloved wife? Even Huntley's unloved wife?"

She looked away. After a long moment she sighed. "No."

"Then we must make them choose, Emma. And they must choose us. It is a devil's bargain, but it is all we have. And if it will win Moya for me, and Huntley for you, then it is worth the risk."

Emma stared across the lawn with unseeing eyes.

"Well? Will you help me by answering some questions about Huntley? Or shall I ask another of his friends?"

She sent him a cross look. "What do you wish to know?"

"I must get closer to him, get him to talk to me

as a friend. But he dislikes me. I don't think it is just because of Moya, though that is part of it."

"He thinks you're too flamboyant. He dislikes people who garner attention. All of his friends are gent—" She caught herself and flushed. "I mean—"

Wulf chuckled. "Do not apologize. I know what you mean and I am not offended. I have no wish to be a 'gentleman.'" He crossed his arms and rocked back on his heels as he considered her words. "So he dislikes people who garner attention. That is good information. Very good. I can use it."

"Fine." Her voice was rather irritated as her gaze scanned the tent and surrounding grounds. "They're still not here."

He checked his watch again. "I will go and find them. If anyone asks where we are, say that you think we are inside the folly."

"Very well. But you'd better hurry, for it's beginning to rain."

Twenty-two

From the Diary of the Duchess of Roxburghe
I'm quickly coming to the conclusion that Nature is best observed at a distance.

Lily stared at the small cove at the end of their path. "This didn't take us to the folly at all!"

The earl stood beside her, a chagrined expression on his face. "Apparently not."

She swallowed a sharp retort. Twice in the last twenty minutes she'd suggested that the path was heading in the wrong direction, but Huntley wouldn't hear of it. Oh no, they must press on, he'd said. They couldn't turn back now, he'd said. He couldn't possibly be wrong, he'd said.

Lily wanted nothing more than to smack the man. She turned and marched back to the path, her stomach growling with hunger, her temper just as thin.

"Lily, wait!" Huntley hurried after her, his voice coming closer. "Where are you going?"

"I'm going to follow the path back to where it

intersected with the wide path and then follow it to the folly, which is what we should have done to begin with." She passed through some trees, walking faster.

"Lily—Miss Balfour—wait! I'll come with you." He caught up, his boots crunching on the path. "I'm sorry if I misjudged the direction. I assure you that it was an innocent mistake."

She was sure it was an innocent mistake, but there was no excuse for the way the earl had dismissed every suggestion and opinion she'd had.

"Lily, please!" He grasped her arm and pulled her to a stop.

She closed her eyes and took a calming breath. *I can't afford to take offense at every little thing. Think of Papa. Think of Dahlia.*

"Lily?"

She opened her eyes and found the earl looking at her with such genuine contrition in his sherry-colored eyes that her irritation fizzled like a snuffed candle. He was just doing what he thought was best. *He's always doing what he thinks is best. Somehow, that annoys me worse than someone trying to do his worst.* She shook her head. "I'm sorry. I'm being dreadfully ill-tempered, and I don't mean to be. I'm just famished."

"I'm sorry I led you astray." He grimaced. "I let my dislike of the prince prod me into making a hasty decision. I just don't like how he's always flirting with Emma. And then there are times he looks at you as if— But that's still no excuse." The earl took her hand and tucked it into the crook of his arm. "Come, we'll walk as quickly as we can."

They walked in silence for most of the way. Lily couldn't imagine being in such a silent state with Wulf. For one, the man had never met a silence he didn't wish to fill. If he didn't fill it with words, then he filled it with kisses. The kind that made her heart race and her—

Her stomach growled and she placed her hand over it, glancing at Huntley, who was looking off into the forest, a polite expression on his face.

Her face heated, more embarrassed by Huntley's reaction than her own. What had promised to be a lovely day was now tense and uncomfortable; it couldn't possibly get any worse.

But she was wrong. It started with a plop here and there. *Rain.* She tugged the hood of her cloak over her head as, without a word, they picked up their pace. Soon, the rain fell in a gentle shower all around.

Moments later, they rounded a bend and a deep voice met them. "Ah, there you are."

Wulf was leaning against a tree, his arms crossed over his broad chest. He looked handsome and calm, an amused glint in his eyes.

Huntley inclined his head. "Wulfinski."

The prince shoved himself from the tree and delivered a proper bow. "Huntley. Miss Balfour."

"It's raining and I wish to get Miss Balfour to shelter." Huntley settled his hat so that the brim shadowed his eyes. "How far away is the folly?"

"Ten minutes, but you're just two minutes from the boats. It would make sense to head straight there and return to the castle. Once this rain begins in earnest, everyone will leave. The boats will have to make several trips to fetch all of her grace's guests and I fear that the last batch or so will be very wet before they reach the opposite shore."

The rain increased, striking now with more force, bending leaves and tapping across Lily's hood. "He's right, Huntley. Let's return to the castle. We will eat once we get there."

Huntley frowned. "Where's Emma?"

"She's at the folly with the other guests." Wulf glanced at the sky. "The duchess was just ordering the servants to pack up the food when I left."

"I'm not leaving without Emma," Huntley said firmly.

Wulf shrugged as if Emma were the last thing on his mind.

Huntley's face grew sterner.

Lily hid a groan. "Huntley, please, Wulf is right. With the rain coming, the duchess will send everyone home. Emma will be here soon enough."

"She'll have to come here," Wulf said. "The tent's not large enough to offer shelter for all of the guests."

"It doesn't matter. I'm going to find Emma." The earl held out a hand for Lily. "Shall we?"

She managed a tight smile and said to Wulf, "I

should—" Her gaze locked on his hand, which had just slid into his coat pocket. He pulled it out and there was a linen napkin. Smiling, he unwrapped it and revealed a flaky tart.

Her stomach rumbled and she pressed a hand to it.

Wulf's eyes gleamed with humor. "Peach."

Huntley frowned. "Peach? What are—"

Lily whirled on him. "I'm going with the prince."

"No," the earl snapped.

Lily raised her brows.

Huntley flushed, but after a brief hesitation said, "You may if you wish, of course, but—"

"I do wish." God, she could almost smell that peach tart. "Huntley, go. Emma will be waiting."

Huntley couldn't have looked more disapproving, but the patter of the rain seemed to make up his mind. "I'll see you both back at the castle." He bowed stiffly and stalked off.

The second he was gone, Lily held out her hand. "The tart, Wulf."

"When we get to the boat." He took her hand and tugged her down the path to the shore.

"No. I want it *now*." Her stomach growled again.

He chuckled and handed her the rebundled tart.

She eagerly unwrapped it from the thick linen napkin. "There's two!"

"You may have them both."

The scent of warm cinnamon and peach assailed her. She tugged her hood so that it hung well over her face and she could eat the tart without the rain softening the lovely crust. She'd already devoured one before they reached the shore.

Forced to wrap up the remaining tart before climbing into the punt, she barely noticed that Wulf had waved off the footman and had taken the pole himself.

As soon as she was seated, he planted the pole and pushed the punt out into the lake, the rain pattering softly all around.

She took the opportunity to unwrap the second tart. Her thick cloak soaked in the rain, but as long as she had her tart, she couldn't care less.

"It's good, hmm?" Wulf was watching her with a satisfied gleam in his eyes as he navigated the punt across the lake.

"It's heavenly." She finished the final flaky bit, wiping her fingers on the napkin before she tucked it into the pocket of her cloak. "I don't imagine you were carrying peach tarts in your pocket for any reason other than to tempt me."

"I knew you would be hungry."

"I was. I was famished, in fact."

"I don't blame you. You walked quite a long time." Wulf wiped the rain from his eyes with his sleeve and raked a hand through his wet hair, revealing the strong lines of his face. Her gaze roamed over him, touching on his broad shoulders and chest, and finally coming to rest on his hands. Instantly she was hit with a memory of the night before, and a tremor raced through her.

"Are you cold?"

"A little." She tugged her cloak more tightly about her. "As delicious as they were, it was very underhanded of you to lure me into your boat with peach tarts."

"I'm surprised that you find it surprising. I've been very clear, Moya. I will stop at nothing until I can call you my own." His jaw firmed. "Even if it means letting you spend more time with Huntley, which I do not like, but I promised, so I will do so."

Lily had just spent several hours with the earl, and right now she felt that to be enough. Yet other than his stubbornness in choosing the wrong path, she could find no fault with his behavior. He was a bit pompous and too concerned with being right, and he hadn't listened to a single one of her suggestions, but he *had* recognized his shortcomings and apologized.

Still, she'd spent two hours with him—alone, too. But because of her temper and his pride in refusing to admit he was lost, they hadn't spent their time well at all.

From under her lashes, she watched Wulf as he confidently guided them across the lake. "How did you get the duchess to put you back on her guest list?"

"I asked my grandmother to apologize to her."

"And she did?"

"With a little persuasion, yes."

"This 'persuasion' didn't involve holding a pistol to her head, did it?"

He laughed. "No, that was not necessary. But I did tell her that if she did not fix what she'd broken, then she would be returning to Oxenburg on the next ship to live with my parents. She does not like my father, so after thinking it through, she decided that she was ready to apologize after all."

"My, you are a miracle worker."

His gaze touched hers. "I am motivated, Moya. I moved that mountain for us, and I will move more. I will move however many I must."

If only her problems were so easily solved as his. They reached the dock and Wulf secured the pole and threw the rope to one of the footmen who waited. As soon as they climbed out of the punt, a footman hopped into their boat to return to the island, where the other guests could be seen gathering on the shore.

Wulf took the umbrella from the footman who held it over Lily's head and sent the man to have his horse brought to the front door.

The prince held the umbrella over them as he slipped a possessive arm around her waist. "Come, Moya. We cannot wait here or you will be wet through and through."

"I fear it's too late to worry about that." They walked back to the castle and she was aware of the strength of the arm around her. Although her cloak was growing heavy with rain, she walked slowly, aware that as soon as she was indoors, they'd go their separate ways.

She never felt sad to see the earl go. And while she could easily see him holding an umbrella for her, walking her to the door, or even punting her across the lake, she couldn't imagine that she'd feel the way she did when Wulf did those things.

They reached the portico that protected the front doorway of the castle just as Wulf's horse was brought from the stable. The door opened and MacDougal appeared, ready to take the umbrella and her wet cloak. They were surrounded by servants.

Wulf took her hand and pressed a kiss to her fingers. "Until tomorrow evening, my dear."

"Tomorrow evening?"

"Why, yes. For dinner. The duchess said there would be dancing, too."

Lily could barely contain her smile.

He gave her hand a squeeze, and then he turned and went to his horse.

Wet from head to foot and cold through and through, Lily stood under the portico, the rain tinning across the roof as she watched Wulf ride out of the courtyard.

And then, her heart filled with a hundred unanswerable questions, she turned and went inside.

Twenty-three

From the Diary of the Duchess of Roxburghe
The trip to the Roxburghe folly was lovely. Everyone enjoyed it . . . until it began to rain. I had no
idea rain could collapse a tent in such a way. Sadly,
the majority of the water landed upon the unsus-
pecting heads of poor Lady MacInnis and Miss
Gordon, neither of whom could walk, their skirts
and shoes were so filled with water.

The next morning Wulf strode up the winding road to
his large manor house, the air especially brisk since his
overcoat was still draped over a bench to dry in front
of the fire at his cottage. Fortunately the walk to see
Tata Natasha had warmed him and he was no longer
chilled.

As he arrived, a servant threw open the door and
then stood at attention as Wulf entered the foyer. Blue
Chinese-silk paper featuring exotic birds cavorting
among flowers adorned the foyer walls, while large
windows—reflected several times over in a series of

ornate, gold-framed mirrors—gave the impression of splintered light. Wulf rather liked the patterned marble floor and the curving staircase that swept up in a grand arc, but he had no use for the gilt furnishings his grandmother loved to tuck into every corner.

A servant took Wulf's hat and gloves. "Welcome home, Your Highness."

"Thank you. I'm only here for a few moments. Arsov is to bring my horse around at ten."

"Very good, Your Highness."

Wulf reached into his pocket and withdrew some missives. "These need to be delivered to my father as soon as possible."

"Yes, Your Highness. The messenger he sent is still resting, but is to begin his journey home later tonight."

"Make it so. Where is my—"

A set of wide, ornate doors opened in a dramatic burst. Framed by the doors and dressed in a black gown and black lace, Tata Natasha pointed a trembling finger at him. "*You!*"

"Yes, it is I. How are you this morning?"

"I am dying for all that you know!"

He looked her up and down. "Actually, you look quite charming today. Is that a new gown?"

She sniffed and crossed her arms over her thin chest. "No one invited you here."

"Need I remind you that I own this house and everything in it?"

Her chin lifted, her black eyes sparkling. "You may own it, but you do not live here, nor are you welcome."

"I'm banished, eh?" He bent to kiss her withered cheek, and though she batted at him, reminding him of a fluffed-up cat, it was halfhearted and he knew she was pleased he'd come to visit. "I have a horse being brought around. If you don't wish me here, I could just lea—"

"Come." She turned and walked into the sitting room.

Smiling, he followed. The furnishings were sumptuous and had cost him more than he liked to remember. The walls were covered in red silk, the windows flanked by red curtains tied with large, gold tassels, and red-and-gold-striped pillows were tossed onto a bevy of red settees and fat, gold chairs. The entire place looked as if a Chinese silk merchant had dumped all of his wares into this one room and then run away. Wulf stifled a sigh. It was his own fault, as he'd left the furnishing of his new house to Tata—well, all of it with the exception of the master suite. Wulf had asked Arsov to oversee that task, which had irked Tata no end. But thanks to Arsov, the master suite, a monstrous room indeed, was done in a masculine but elegant style.

Sadly, the rest of the house was all Tata, who had filled it with the most expensive and gaudy furnishings and decorations she could find. He started to walk toward the fire but found his way blocked by not one, but four small red cushioned ottomans. "This room looks like a brothel."

"What?" Tata's voice crackled.

He raised his voice. "I said, 'This room is beautiful.'"

She sniffed, although he could tell she was pleased. "It is well."

She gestured to a settee, but he shook his head. "I've only a minute. I'm to ride this morning with some of the duchess's guests."

Her lips thinned and she perched on the settee and scowled. "You ride with Miss Balfour."

"No, with several gentlemen, including the Earl of Huntley."

"Huntley? Why would you ride with him?"

"Perhaps I am on a secret mission."

"And perhaps you have been drinking, though it is not yet ten in the morning."

He chuckled and leaned against the fireplace.

She gathered her black shawl closer. "What do you want, that you come so early?"

"What? I cannot visit my favorite grandmother without a reason?"

"No," she said baldly.

"Tata Natasha, don't look so bitter. You cannot still be angry with me for making you apologize to the duchess."

"I will be angry with you until the day I die."

"It is a waste of time and energy, Tata. But if you wish to be angry . . ." He shrugged.

She scowled, but after a moment said, "Have you had breakfast?"

"Arsov brought me breakfast hours ago. I came to send a missive to my father."

"Couldn't Arsov have done that for you?"

"Yes, if he'd been available, but he's here caring for the horses. My only regret about the cottage is the lack of a proper stable. I can only keep one horse there at a time."

"Do not complain to me. I warned you of the consequences of living beneath your rank."

"Pah. According to you, men of my rank should attend endless dances and balls, speak pretty words that have no meaning, and devote themselves to mindless pleasures. I am not such a man."

Her mouth puckered as if she'd sucked a lemon. "You have come to torment me."

"*Nyet.* I came to ask if you'd like an escort to the dinner and dance at the duchess's tomorrow evening. Do you go?"

She muttered something under her breath.

"The Duchess of Roxburghe is not an ill-mannered witch," he chided.

"You don't know her the way I do. You are too trusting, like a babe in the woods." Tata's gaze narrowed. "Miss Balfour will be there, I suppose?"

"I can only hope." He'd slept little last night, thinking of Lily. She'd looked bedraggled and forlorn when he'd left her after the rain. *That is good. Maybe she wished you to stay but did not dare ask.*

Tata's expression softened. "Wulf, I worry for you."

"Why?"

"You are not yourself."

"I'm in love, Tata. That is the grandest adventure of all."

Tata didn't smile. "I don't wish to see you hurt. You have been spoiled, Wulf. Everything you wanted—horses, pistols, women—they have all been given to you. Now, you face the reality of a woman who may not be for you."

"She will be mine. I won't accept anything else."

Tata's brow furrowed. "There are no guarantees in love. If this Lily does not do as you hope, and if she marries Huntley as the duchess wishes her to . . . what then? What will you do?"

Wulf's chest tightened. *Then a part of me will never live again.* He curled his hands into fists. "I will go home and help Father."

"And marry as he wishes you to?"

"No. I will never marry. If I do not have Lily, then I will have no one."

"Never?"

"Never."

Tata's shoulders slumped. She sighed deeply and stared down at her bejeweled hands clasped in her lap. Finally she grumbled, "If that is how it is, then I suppose you must have your Lily."

Her words surprised him so much that he laughed. "I never thought to hear you say such a thing."

"I have no choice. You have the madness."

"Of the worst kind." He came to sit before her, pulling up one of the silk-covered ottomans so that he was directly before her. "Tata, I do not know how this will end; it's possible—" He took a breath. "It's possible that I will not win Lily."

"You admit that now, eh?"

"I must. At first I thought that all I had to do was love her enough, but her circumstances are complicated, as are mine. It was a naïve way of thinking."

Tata nodded. "You are growing, my Wulf."

"I have grown up, Tata. Now, I am just facing reality and I find it painful. Lily's time here is short and I must return home soon, too. My father sent for me."

"Why? Your brothers, they are well?"

"Everyone is healthy. The treaty with Luxemburg is in danger. I know the Luxemburg ambassador very well, as we went to school together in France. Father hopes I may be able to help with the negotiations."

"I see. So what will you do about your Lily?"

"I will fight."

Tata patted his hand. "Good for you. If she is worth winning, you will do it."

Outside a horse neighed and through the window, Wulf watched as Arsov brought his horse to the front steps. "I must go." He pressed a kiss to Tata's fingers and offered a faint smile. "When we return to Oxenburg I will be a prince of work, but today I am a prince of leisure. As I will not be back until tomorrow, shall I come ride with you in your carriage to the duchess's for dinner?"

"Yes." Her hand tightened on his and she looked at him beseechingly. "Be careful, Wulf."

"I'm always careful, Tata."

"With everything but your heart."

He laughed, gave her a hug, and then left, but her words followed him. She was right. He hadn't been careful with his heart, and now it was lost, held tightly in the hands of a woman with silver eyes and reddish-gold hair. But though he might face a loss of the worst kind, he could not be sorry.

Lily awoke late as the clock chimed ten. She eyed the clock with one open eye, then rolled over and stretched before she tossed back the covers and arose. Yawning, she padded to the bellpull and tugged it.

The morning sun teased her through a crack between the curtains. Lily shoved the curtains aside, washing the room in pale morning light. Still yawning, she leaned against the windowsill and looked out at the beautiful view. A heavy mist had settled over the lake, following the River Tweed as it meandered through the fields around Floors Castle, making it seem as if she were floating above the clouds.

Feeling a draft of cool air, she caught sight of the small hole made by the prince's tossed rock. She touched the small circle and then traced the surrounding cracks that spiderwebbed around it.

She'd hoped to see Wulf at dinner last night, but he hadn't appeared. Neither had several other guests—including Huntley—who had claimed exhaustion from the day at the folly and had opted to have a tray brought to their bedchamber instead of dressing and joining the others at dinner.

A horse neighed and she looked down. Below in the courtyard, several male guests appeared, all dressed for riding. Huntley was among them. Dressed in buff riding breeches, his dark blue coat hugging his slender shoulders, his gold-tasseled Hessians catching the morning light, he looked elegant and polished and far more handsome than the other men. *Why can't I fall in love with him?*

But no answer came.

The sound of a horse cantering up the drive made her turn to see Wulf arriving. He, too, was dressed for riding, but his dress was more that of a Cossack soldier. His coat was wide at the shoulders, his breeches narrow at the waist but flared from there. His black boots had thick tops, but none of the shine or tassels displayed on the others. But the way he rode captured her attention, lithe and sure, as if he were an extension of the horse rather than a rider perched upon it.

The prince entered the courtyard, dismounted, and joined the group waiting for their horses to be brought from the stables. Instantly the others gathered to look at his horse. She imagined they were quizzing him about the magnificent animal.

As she watched, Wulf casually detached himself from the other riders and approached Huntley, who'd held back from the group. She could tell from the set of Huntley's shoulders that he wasn't happy to speak to the prince, but Wulf persisted. After several moments, something he said made Huntley laugh, and the stiff set of his shoulders disappeared.

The other horses were brought and the men mounted, Huntley falling in with Wulf. As they left the courtyard, Wulf turned and looked up at her window, the morning sun limning his face with gold.

Lily's heart thudded. *He is doing as he promised.* She lifted her hand. He dipped his head a barely perceptible amount and then was gone.

She rested her forehead against the cool glass. *Perhaps Wulf will give me the key I need to bring Huntley up to the mark.* Yet a growing part of her hoped that he wouldn't.

A soft knock sounded on the door and Freya entered carrying a tray, Meenie on her heels. "I found the puir bairn sleeping ootside o' yer door."

Lily watched the little dog sniff eagerly about the room.

Freya brought the tray to Lily. "Ye've a letter, miss. It just arrived."

Lily recognized her father's handwriting and tucked the missive in her pocket to read later. "Thank you."

"Ye're welcome." The maid went about her morning duties, stoking the fire and setting out a gown for Lily to wear, pausing only to watch Meenie sniffing an invisible trail. "Tha' dog looks to be searchin' fer somethin'. Mayhap she left one o' the bones Cook gave the dogs yesterday. I'll look under yer bed while ye're at breakfast to make sure it's no' tha', miss."

Lily thanked her but knew it wasn't a bone that Meenie was looking for, but a tall, broad-shouldered prince. She scooped up the dog and hugged her, whispering in her ear, "If you wish to see the prince, then you should wait for him in the foyer."

Perhaps she should wait along with Meenie. She should find out whatever information he'd culled, after all. But she knew that wasn't the reason she wished to see him. She wished to see him because—well, she liked him. There was nothing wrong with that, was there?

She rubbed her cheek against the dog's soft fur. She liked Wulf and found him attractive, but she was not going to allow that to take control again. *If I focus on just liking him as a friend, perhaps the rest will go away.*

"Yer wash water is ready, miss, and I've laid out a blue mornin' gown. I'll help ye dress when ye're ready."

Lily sighed and put Meenie back on the floor. An hour later, she was dressed, her hair neatly pinned, and on her way downstairs. Freya took Meenie with her toward the kitchen, while Lily made her way to the breakfast room. Glad to find it empty, she poured herself a cup of tea and opened Papa's letter.

She knew as soon as she spread out the much-crossed sheet that something was wrong. Father's handwriting was never good on the best of days, and when he was agitated, it was even worse. In addition, to save the cost of sending an extra page, he'd gone back and written between the lines, and she could barely decipher it. But decipher it she did, and she read with growing alarm. Dahlia had decided that she could no longer allow Lily to sacrifice herself and was determined to go to Lord Kirk and offer herself to settle the debt. Papa had stopped her for the moment, but he wasn't certain what he would do the next time she decided on such a rash move.

Lily closed her eyes, her hand so tight about the letter that it crinkled. *Dahlia, just give me a bit longer. Another week and Huntley and I will be settled and Papa will be saved and—* A noise made her look around.

Emma stood just inside the breakfast-room door, a concerned expression on her face. "I'm sorry to interrupt." Her gaze flickered to the letter and then to Lily's face. "If you're busy, I'll come back another time."

"No, no!" Lily folded the letter and returned it to her pocket. "I was just—it's a letter from my father. It was some unexpected news, but nothing too concerning. Please, come and join me."

Emma entered, took a plate from the buffet, filled it, and then sat next to Lily.

A footman arrived with trays of food to replenish the warmers, the scent of bacon and scones lifting through the air. Emma poured herself a cup of tea. As soon as the footman left, she turned to Lily. "I'm sorry you received distressing news. Is there anything I can do?"

"It's nothing, really." Lily smiled as Emma poured more tea into her cup. "I didn't see you at dinner last night. I wanted to ask Prince Wulfinski or Huntley if you were well, but neither of them came to dinner, either."

Emma's hand quavered and tea splashed onto the table. She put down the pot, her cheeks bright red. "I'm sorry. I'm dreadfully clumsy this morning."

A footman appeared with a cloth and wiped up the spilled tea and refilled Emma's cup. Then, with a bow, he left.

"I have mornings like that, too," Lily said. "I hope you didn't miss dinner because you were feeling ill from being in the rain? The duchess said several of her guests caught a putrid throat from getting wet."

"No, I didn't, although if getting wet caused a putrid throat, then I'd have one. I was under the tent when it collapsed."

Lily gasped. "No! I'd heard that it had folded, but not that anyone was underneath."

"It was horrid." Emma shivered. "I thought I would drown. Another lady and I were standing at the worst possible place, too, while the duchess was yelling at the footmen and Lady Charlotte was calling for a towel and—" Emma blew out her breath. "If Huntley hadn't arrived just then and taken charge, I don't know what we would have done."

"He is the sort to take charge. I'm glad he was there. He's fond of you."

Emma's smile didn't reach her eyes. She glanced at the footmen to make certain they were out of hearing, then she leaned forward and said in a low voice, "After Huntley untangled me from the tent, he *carried* me to the boat."

She sounded so scandalized that Lily had to

chuckle. She couldn't count the times Wulf had carried her, sometimes for no reason at all.

Emma shook her head in astonishment. "Of course, I don't know what I would have done if he hadn't, for my skirts were so water-soaked it would have been impossible to walk."

"Huntley is very chivalrous."

"Oh, so much so. I was worried that it might hurt his back, but he never said a word. Fortunately, when we docked, Prince Wulfinski met us. He'd ridden there from the castle to make certain that everyone had returned safely. And so"—Emma's face flooded with soft color—"so *he* lifted me onto his horse and brought me to the castle, and then carried me inside. I think he found it easier to lift me than Huntley, for Wulf wasn't even breathing hard."

So Wulf hadn't gone straight home yesterday as she'd thought. For some reason, Lily felt slightly betrayed. Aware of Emma's gaze on her, Lily managed a smile. "Goodness. You certainly had an exciting afternoon." Much more exciting than Lily's, which consisted of getting lost, being bribed by a tart, and little more.

Emma put down her fork. "Lily, do you mind if I ask you a question? It is very personal, but"—Emma bit her lip, her color high—"I don't know who else to ask."

"Not at all. What is it?"

Emma leaned forward and asked in a breathless tone, "Have you ever been kissed?"

Lily blinked.

"And not like a sister," Emma added. "But—*really* kissed."

Lily set her cup on the saucer so hard that it clacked. In her mind's eye, she could see it all—Emma wet and bedraggled, tucked before Wulf on his horse as he tenderly wrapped her in his arms and then bent and touched his lips to her— *"No."*

Emma drew back. "Lily—Miss Balfour, I'm sorry if I've offended you—"

"No, no. I was just—" Lily took a deep breath. "I was thinking about something else." *You shouldn't be surprised,* her pragmatic side stated coolly. *You've refused him and even pressed him to help you secure the affections of another man, so what do you expect? You had to know that eventually he would kiss another woman. And soon he'll fall in love and marry and have children and—*

Emma's hand closed over hers. "Lily, please forget I said anything. I didn't mean to upset you."

"No, no, you didn't. I was thinking about a kiss I once received that . . . Never mind. We're talking about your kiss. What did you want to know?"

"I just wanted to know how you . . . reacted." Emma's face couldn't be any redder. "I didn't know what to do, and I'm not sure I responded as well as I should have."

Though her heart ached with jealousy, Lily patted Emma's hand. "If you were honest in your response, then I'm sure that this man was perfectly happy with your reaction."

"I hope so. I'll be better prepared to deal with the next kiss." Emma pressed a hand to her cheek. "*If* he does so again. He may not, although—" Emma glanced toward the open door and then said in near whisper, "It was heavenly. I was quite breathless afterward." A blissful smile trembled on her lips.

Lily nodded, her throat oddly tight. "A kiss is a lovely way to begin a courtship."

"A courtship!" Emma's gaze grew starry and then she gave a shaky laugh. "I never thought that he would ever—" She shook her head. "I'm dizzy even thinking about it."

There was a commotion in the front hallway, the sound of men laughing, Huntley's and Wulf's voices among them. Boots thudded through the marble entryway and mingled with the barking of the Roxburghe pugs. At Emma's startled look, Lily explained, "Some of the men went out riding this morning, but I'm surprised they're back so soon."

But Emma wasn't listening. Her gaze was fixed over Lily's shoulder, her lips parted, her eyes filled with such longing that Lily's throat closed.

Without knowing how or why, Lily knew what she'd see when she turned. Wulf stood in the hallway, laughing at something Huntley had just said, looking dark and dangerous and far too handsome not to make every woman fall in love with him, whether he meant to or not.

As if he could feel Lily's gaze, he turned her way and gave her a mock salute, his green gaze twinkling, before he turned back to continue his conversation with Huntley.

Lily turned back around, feeling hollow, as if something necessary had been stolen from her. "Emma, this kiss—"

"I shouldn't have mentioned it." Emma's attention was now focused firmly on her breakfast plate, her face so red that she looked as if she'd been slapped. "It was very indiscreet of me to even mention it. Please, let's talk about something else." Before Lily could respond, Emma launched into observations about the weather and the day's events, and speculations about whether tomorrow's dinner party would include a waltz, and rumors that she'd heard about the coming Butterfly Ball, which would be on their final night at the duchess's.

Lily listened with but half an ear, aching at the light that warmed Emma's brown eyes. *Oh, Wulf, what have you done?*

Twenty-four

From the Diary of the Duchess of Roxburghe

Charlotte has come up with the most delightful ideas for the Butterfly Ball. Since we're having it outdoors in the gardens, we will release hundreds of butterflies just as the orchestra strikes up the first dance. The butterflies will waft through the air, delicate and lovely, and cause such a stir! In addition, we will dress the Roxburghe pugs in little butterfly costumes, which will add an air of gaiety.

Surely Mrs. Cairness will know a good seamstress who can make six costumes in short order.

When all is said and done, the ball will be one that our guests will never forget.

The next morning, the duchess peered into the small breakfast room. "Ah! I was hoping you'd be here."

Lady Charlotte looked up from *The Morning Post*, her spectacles perched on the end of her nose. Even with the spectacles, she was still holding the paper at arm's length, but on seeing the duchess, Charlotte folded the paper and set it aside. "Good morning, Margaret. You're up early."

"The pugs arose at six for some reason, and there was no sleeping after that." Margaret stood to one side to let the pugs enter before she shut the door. "But I'm glad they awoke me, for I've work to do of a *most* important nature today."

"Oh?"

"Yes, we've things to do for the ball, for Miss Balfour, and Huntley, and—oh, so many items that must be dealt with, and in a scant two days." Margaret took the chair beside Charlotte and poured herself some tea as the pugs found comfy spots on the rug before the fire. "I spoke to a gentleman this morning who says he can orchestrate the surprise we've planned for our Butterfly Ball."

Lady Charlotte hopped in her chair. "I *knew* it could be done!"

"He knows of a butterfly arboretum that will sell him a large number of butterflies. It is such a good idea, Charlotte—quite brilliant! This will make my ball the most talked-about event for months to come."

"I do hope that—"

A soft knock sounded on the door and MacDougal entered. "I beg yer pardon, yer grace, but Miss Balfour has asked fer a word wit' ye."

"This early?"

"Aye, yer grace. If ye dinna mind me sayin', but she seems a mite distressed. Somethin' is wrong, yer grace."

"Oh, dear. Please bring her here."

"Yes, do." Lady Charlotte picked up her knitting basket. "We'll have a lovely coze over some tea. Mrs. Cairness just brought a tray."

MacDougal bowed and went to fetch the young lady. The small breakfast room was not widely known to the guests who visited Floors Castle. Tucked away, it was a private room where the family had their meals when they wished for something more intimate than the large, formal dining room.

MacDougal made his way to where Miss Balfour stood in the foyer, staring out the window to the court-yard beyond. Something about the curve of the young lady's mouth was tragic, as if the weight of the world sat upon her shoulders. MacDougal liked her grace's young guest who, according to Mrs. Cairness, had voluntarily darned the stockings and fixed torn flounces and ripped seams of nigh half of the staff with such tiny, perfect stitches that the housekeeper was in raptures.

The butler cleared his throat. "Miss Balfour?"

She turned from the window and he noticed faint circles under her eyes. "Yes, MacDougal?"

"Her grace will see ye now."

"Thank you. You were very kind to find her for me."

"Och, 'twas my pleasure, miss." He gestured to the small hallway and then led the way.

Lily followed. She felt as if she were moving in a fog this morning, her mind unable to function. Last night, sleep had been impossible. Every time she'd closed her eyes, Emma's expression as she'd looked at Wulf had flashed through Lily's mind. She'd known that Emma and Wulf had been spending a lot of time together, but . . . love?

Yet she could not mistake the glow in Emma's eyes, nor ignore the question the other woman had asked about a kiss. Emma was obviously deeply in love, and not with Huntley as Lily had once thought.

Lily couldn't imagine that Wulf's emotions were similarly engaged—at least, not yet. But it had brought home one icy reality: once she was out of Wulf's life, he would move on and eventually fall in love with another woman. Somehow Lily had managed not to think of that before this morning, but she could no longer avoid it.

And why not Emma? Lily asked herself for the thousandth time. *She's kind and very, very nice. Plus she possesses a fortune, which would surely be to Wulf's advantage. It would be a good match for both of them.* Yet Lily's heart still ached.

Her restless night had made one thing clear: after only two and a half weeks, she was perilously close to caring for Wulf. She had to move forward quickly with her plan to secure Huntley's proposal, before it was too late.

But she wasn't entirely certain how to proceed. How did one encourage a suitor to come up to the mark without seeming—well, desperate? Especially when you were desperate? It was a delicate matter.

And so, as the sun rose, Lily realized that she needed the duchess's help.

The butler paused before a small door partially hidden by a large palm. He knocked once, which caused a cacophony of barking. A greeting was called out and he opened the door.

Instantly, Lily was surrounded by sniffing pugs and wagging tails. She bent to pat the closest ones.

"Miss Balfour," MacDougal announced, standing to one side as she straightened and walked inside. He waited for the dogs to follow her back into the room before he closed the door.

"Lily, how lovely to see you this morning." The duchess patted the seat of the chair beside her. "Come and sit. Would you like some tea?"

"No, thank you." Lily sank into the chair, her stomach as knotted as the skein of yarn beside Lady Charlotte's feet.

Lady Charlotte's knitting clicked along. "How lovely of you to visit. The other guests all seem to be abed."

Lily watched as the dogs took spots upon the floor as if they'd been assigned to them, panting happily. *If only life were so simple for the rest of us.* "Your grace, Lady Charlotte, thank you for seeing me." She took a deep breath, feeling lower than the rug beneath her slippers. "I've come to ask your advice."

The duchess's blue eyes brightened. "We are always willing to offer advice."

"Oh yes," Lady Charlotte agreed. "Whether you wish it or not."

Lady Margaret frowned. "Speak for yourself, Charlotte. I *never* give unsolicited advice."

Lily had to smile. "I am asking for advice now, and I feel quite awkward about it. I don't really know how to begin this. . . . I recently received news from my father that my sister is on the verge of going to Lord Kirk in an effort to sway him from collecting the debt. I fear that, in return, Kirk will demand her hand in marriage, and I cannot allow to happen."

"Oh dear, things have come to a head, haven't they?" the duchess said.

"That does sound dire." Lady Charlotte adjusted her lace mobcap. "Although I don't really think Lord Kirk would ever wish to—"

"Charlotte, Lord Kirk is not the issue." The duchess patted Lily's hand where it rested on the arm of her chair. "Preventing Dahlia from making a connection she might regret is the issue."

Lily nodded gratefully. "And so I must ask your help in securing Lord Huntley's proposal. I—I think he's interested in me—"

"Obviously so," her grace said.

"But I don't know how to get him to . . ." Lily gestured.

"Ah yes. That is a tricky point in every courtship." The duchess's shrewd blue eyes locked on Lily. "You're sure of your feelings for him, then? You won't regret this marriage?"

"No. To be honest, there are fewer and fewer reasons not to marry him. It's time I finally admitted that."

The duchess's brow knit. "That's an interesting way to put it, that you've 'fewer and fewer reasons not to marry him.' What about 'more and more reasons *to* marry him'?"

"I mean no disrespect to the earl. He's been most kind, and while we're very different in a number of ways, I think we'll suit well enough."

Lady Charlotte tsked. "My dear, marriage can last for years and years. It requires far more than a mere 'I think' and 'well enough.'"

The duchess sipped her tea, her gaze never leaving Lily's face. "To be honest, I rather thought your enthusiasm for the match to be waning over the last two weeks."

Lily looked down at her hands, clasped in her lap. She'd put off the inevitable by allowing herself to explore the attraction she'd felt for the prince. At first it had been a delaying tactic, but now . . . now she had to admit that she cared for him.

Her heart thudded hollowly. *I do care for him. And I have to stop pretending otherwise. But sadly, it doesn't change things; I still must see to my family's welfare.*

Her gaze grew blurry as tears filled her eyes. *I may never feel passionate about the earl, but I will be the best wife possible and will try to make him happy.*

The glowing look in Emma's eyes still haunted her. *Wulf deserves a love like that.*

Lily realized that the duchess and Lady Charlotte

were both watching her, and she blinked back her tears. "What do I do now? What do I do to bring Huntley to point?"

Lady Charlotte put down her knitting needles. "Huntley? Are you sure you wouldn't rather—"

"Charlotte," her grace said, "allow me to assist Lily in this. I believe I know what she needs."

Lady Charlotte resumed her knitting. "Of course, Margaret. You always know what's best in these cases."

Her grace turned to Lily. "I know for a fact that the earl is on the verge of making an offer."

Lily's heart sank. "You . . . you know this?"

"Yes. He told me last night when I ran into him on the terrace." Her grace smiled. "I think he was embarrassed to be caught outdoors after he'd pled a headache as an excuse from dinner. However, he told me that I had been right in suggesting that the time had come for him to find a wife, and that he was ready to do so. In fact, he specifically said that he hoped to leave Floors Castle an engaged man."

Lady Charlotte nodded, her cap flapping over one of her eyes. "Margaret was most excited by that pronouncement." She pushed the cap back. "We both were."

A lump seemed to have lodged in Lily's throat. So Huntley would soon propose. That was good, for all of her troubles would be over. *Except one. How on earth am I to fill this hole in my heart?* She smoothed her skirt over her knees, her palms suddenly damp. "I'm glad to hear that, of course. What should I do, then?"

"Just wait," the duchess said with an ease Lily was far from feeling. "Let Huntley pick the time and place. The ball is the day after tomorrow. Perhaps he will propose before then so that he can make the announcement at the ball."

"Unless he wishes to make his proposal *at* the ball," Lady Charlotte said, "to take advantage of the romantic nature of the event."

"That's possible," her grace admitted. "Lily, what sort of overtures has he made to you?"

"He says that he enjoys spending time with me, and that he finds me very pleasant and interesting . . . and pragmatic."

Both ladies looked a bit taken aback by that last one.

Then Lady Charlotte said encouragingly, "That seems quite significant."

Her grace added, "Especially when you consider how reserved he can be."

"Yes, he's very, *very* reserved," Lady Charlotte added. "Even a bit cold." When Lily looked surprised, Lady Charlotte hurried to add, "But I'm certain he'd be passionate with the right lady."

"Someone he might love, for instance," the duchess said with an arch air.

Lily gave a brittle laugh. "Love has nothing to do with this match."

The duchess and Lady Charlotte exchanged glances.

Lily's cheeks heated and she cursed her unguarded tongue. "I'm sorry. What I meant to say is that I'm sure that once we're married and spend more time together, I'll grow to love him as dearly as he deserves."

"I'm certain that you'd try." The duchess smiled brightly. "Now, not another word about this. You sit back and let Huntley do the rest."

"Yes, your grace. Thank you for your reassurances. I was afraid this would be much more difficult than it seems to be, but—" Lily tried to calm her thoughts. "I can't thank you and Lady Charlotte enough."

"Nonsense. We enjoy seeing people happy."

Lady Charlotte nodded. "It's what we live for."

The duchess stood and walked Lily to the door. "Rest easy, my child. We've two more evenings until the grand ball. Tonight is dinner followed by a small dance, and we've scheduled a quiet evening tomorrow so that we may all rest up for the next night's merriment. By the night of the Roxburghe Butterfly Ball, your problems will be resolved."

"That will be a relief. Thank you so much. You've been everything kind."

"I'm your godmother, my dear. It's the least I can do. Now, why don't you take a walk about the garden? You're looking a bit pale, no doubt because you're in a knot of excitement awaiting Huntley's proposal."

"A walk would be lovely. Thank you." Lily gave the duchess a polite curtsy, murmured her good-bye, and let herself out of the breakfast room.

The duchess listened to Lily's footsteps fading away before she returned to her seat.

Charlotte shook out some more yarn. "That was interesting."

"Very." Margaret picked up her teacup. "Our hopeful bride doesn't seem the least bit bride-like in her excitement."

"No. She seemed resigned, as if she were being consigned to some punishment and not a joyful marriage."

"When I first met Lily, she was quite willing to marry Huntley and fall in love. Judging by her demeanor this morning, I must wonder if perhaps the opposite has occurred: she's fallen in love, but sadly now must marry."

Charlotte blinked. "In love? With Huntley."

Margaret frowned. "Charlotte, do pay attention. Why would Lily be sad if she thought she was going to marry the man she loved?"

"Ah. So she's fallen in love with someone other than Huntley." Lady Charlotte frowned. "That's most unfortunate since Huntley said he's on the verge of asking for her hand. He will be so disappointed if she refuses him."

"Actually, he told me that he'd planned on asking *someone* to marry. Now I wonder if . . . Hmmm. Interesting."

Lady Charlotte's knitting needles paused. "What's interesting?"

"Something Huntley said . . . I shall have to speak with him again, just to be certain. All I really know for certain is that Lily is not in love with Huntley, but someone else."

"Prince Wulfinski?"

"I can think of no other man brash enough to woo a lady right out from under the nose of a wealthy earl." Margaret cupped her hands about her teacup. *It's just possible that that Gypsy might have been right.*

"Oh dear. Margaret, it seems to me that everything is in quite a muddle."

"Not yet, my dear. Not yet." Margaret set her cup back in its saucer. "But we've work to do. As I've told you before, matchmaking is not for the weak-willed."

Twenty-five

From the Diary of the Duchess of Roxburghe

Tonight we have planned some dancing after dinner to whet the appetite of those who will be attending our splendid Butterfly Ball on Saturday. The orchestra, needing to practice for the ball, agreed to give us their services for this night, so it will be quite festive.

I hope some of the gentlemen take advantage of this opportunity. *All* of it.

When Wulf and his grandmother arrived at the castle, both the duchess and Tata Natasha were surprisingly cordial as they greeted one another. Tata even went so far as to say in a grudging voice that she liked the duchess's feathered headdress.

Tata was also amazingly calm while they all gathered in a salon before dinner, sitting quietly as if thinking about something important. When Wulf asked what she was pondering, she'd merely admonished him to better spend his time by talking with all of the pretty women in the room. And she didn't once use the terms "pale" or "pasty-faced."

Then at dinner, for once Wulf was seated close enough to Lily to hear her. Huntley still had the place of honor at her elbow, which made Wulf's heart burn, but he refused to let it show.

He'd chosen this path; he would see it through. He'd spent another morning in the man's company and had garnered some tidbits that might assist Lily in securing the earl's interest. It would be like drinking poison of his own making, but he would pass this information on to her as he'd promised. *She must pick me of her own volition. She* must.

Wulf toyed with his food, absently answering the queries of the lady who'd been placed to his left. Time was slipping through his fingers like sand. He needed more time alone with Lily, to make his case one last time. But how? She'd been clear that she had no desire to make their parting more difficult.

Perhaps he could use the information he'd collected about Huntley to lure her into a meeting. *That might work.* After dinner was over and the guests had repaired to the small ballroom for dancing, he installed Tata on a settee with the other dowagers. By the time he reached the dance floor, Lily had already joined the set. "Damn it," he muttered.

Left with nothing to do, he caught sight of Huntley standing by the refreshment table. *I can gather yet more information to tempt her to spend time with me.*

He made his way to the earl's side. "Good evening."

Huntley, who'd been much warmer to Wulf since he'd given Emma a ride to the manor house after their journey to the folly, smiled in greeting. "Wulfinski, how are you this evening?"

"Wishing there was some vodka to be had."

Huntley grimaced. "Nasty business, that. I had it only once and it made me sick for days."

Wulf grinned. "Your stomach is weak."

"Or just too civilized for the disgusting stuff."

"Like milk? I can ask for some to be sent, if you'd like."

Huntley chuckled. "No, thank you, but if you happen to know where I could get some good scotch, I'd be forever in your debt."

Wulf caught the attention of a footman and sent the man looking for a glass.

"Thank you." Huntley looked at Wulf curiously. "That was quite kind of you."

Wulf shrugged. "I dislike seeing a fellow man go without." He moved a bit so that he could see the dance floor. Lily was dancing with Lord Stewart, an older man who was so tightly laced into his waistcoat that it looked as if it might pop open at any moment. Wulf shook his head. "I do not like these country dances of yours."

Huntley sent him a surprised look. "You don't dance these in Oxenburg?"

"No. We have our own country dances, but nothing so boring." Wulf shrugged. "We do not do this endless circling and barely touching of the hands. I like a dance where you can hold a woman, feel her."

Huntley's lips twitched. "I suppose the waltz did come from your area of the world."

"*That* is a dance worth dancing. You can hold your partner in your arms, and not just wave at her from the other side of a line."

Huntley crossed his arms and leaned against the wall, a smug expression on his face. "I suppose if you cannot think of another way to get your, er, partner in your arms, then a waltz is good enough."

Wulf frowned. "You think I cannot get a 'partner' in my arms? I assure you that I can."

"That rather depends upon the partner, doesn't it?" Huntley's gaze was on the dance floor, no doubt following Lily as she went down the set with her wheezing partner. "Some partners are more worth the effort than others."

Wulf glowered. He didn't like the way this man watched Lily, as if he alone had the right to enjoy her company.

Remember your purpose. Wulf eyed the earl with a sour gaze. "The duchess says you have been married before."

The earl shot him a hard look. "Though it is no concern of yours, my wife died."

"Ah. That is very bad." Wulf watched Huntley's expression. "You loved her, this wife. It shows in your face."

"Why are you asking me this?"

"In Oxenburg, when men ride together, they are as brothers. We have shared much this week."

"We are not so open here in Scotland."

"So I've noticed. It is silly how men here do not speak of anything but horses and drink. I said so to Miss Emma just this morning."

Huntley looked at Wulf. "And what did she say?"

Wulf shrugged. "Like you, she is held by conventions."

"Conventions are a good thing."

"They are a prison."

Huntley laughed softly. "Only to those who don't appreciate their value . . . and know when to set them aside."

Aha. This might be of use. "You sometimes set your conventions aside? This I do not believe."

The earl continued to look amused. "Oh, I do. But only for a very, *very* good reason."

Like a beauty with hair of red-gold and eyes the silver of a lake? Wulf fought the urge to grab the earl by his overstarched cravat and pummel him. *Damn it, Moya, the things I do for you.*

Scowling, Wulf turned to watch the dancers and realized that Emma was also in the set. "When did Miss Gordon join? I did not see her before."

"She's been there all along. I'm surprised you didn't notice."

When Lily was in the room, Wulf's attention went always with her. "I was too busy wondering if Miss Balfour's partner might pop out of his stays."

Huntley grinned. "He's getting very red in the face. He'll have an apoplexy if he doesn't take care."

Wulf grunted his agreement. *What things will Moya wish to know about this man?* Perhaps just the normal things a woman always wanted to know: what sort of woman did Huntley prefer, rounded or thin, brunette or blond, and such. *Better to ask the important question and get it out of the way.* "So, you intend to remarry soon?"

Huntley stiffened. "That's a very personal comment."

"Am I wrong to ask such a thing? You are here, therefore you are seeking a wife."

Huntley looked far from pleased, but after a moment he shrugged. "You're not wrong, but I will ask that you say nothing more about this. I haven't told anyone yet—well, except for one person, and I already regret that—and I wish it to be a surprise."

"So you have decided."

"Yes."

Wulf rubbed his chest where a weight seemed pressed upon it. "You have not yet asked her, then?"

"Not yet—and she may say no." Huntley's brow lowered. "One never knows with women."

Wulf's jaw tightened until it ached. "If I wished a woman to marry me, I would not stop asking her until she said yes."

"Such behavior would be frowned upon here. I will ask her, and I will respect her answer. I hope, of course, that she will say yes, but . . ." Huntley's eyes shadowed. "She's so difficult to read, so unlike any other woman I've known, always surprising me when I least expect it."

"The women in my country expect more than a few words. They would demand proof that you wished to marry them."

"What sort of proof?"

Wulf shrugged. "Gifts of jewelry, furs, and gold. A show of strength is appreciated, too. When my father wooed my mother, he brought her ten stallions and fought her three older brothers for the right to call her his own. He was stabbed seven times, but he did not let it stop him. They wed the very next day."

Huntley gave a surprised laugh. "You really are a barbarian, aren't you?"

"At least I'm no silver-laced, soft-stomached Englishman who cannot even drink vodka."

Huntley's smile faded. "I'm not English. I'm a Scot."

I could easily start a fight now; I can see the anger in his eyes. But it would make Lily unhappy, so I will hold my temper. "Which is why I find you bearable. Besides, I've seen you ride and I respect how you handle a horse."

The anger in Huntley's eyes faded. "Thank you. You're quite competent, too."

They watched the dancers in silence for a long moment. "She is not a very good dancer, is she? Always having to count. Never letting a man lead her as she should." Wulf shook his head.

"Miss Gordon is a excellent dancer," Huntley returned, an edge to his voice. "I've danced with her numerous times and—"

"No, no. You mistake. I speak of Miss Lily."

"Ah, her. Yes, she is a bit awkward. She stepped on my feet twice the last time we danced, and she does try to lead. Emma allows her partner to lead, as is proper."

"Ah! The dance is finished and now they play a waltz. Good evening, Huntley." Wulf bowed and went to claim Lily. Though another man might already have claimed the dance, Wulf didn't care.

Lily lifted her dance card to see who was listed next. She'd promised a dance to Lord Kitteringer, but was it this one or the one after—

A strong arm slipped about her waist and she was propelled toward the dance floor. She knew that powerful arm, knew the spicy, faint scent of the cologne that came from the black coat that filled her sight as she was swept into the dance.

No man so large should be such an excellent dancer. "Wulf, I'm promised to—"

"*Nyet.* You dance with me. You may dance with whoever else you wish after this."

"But I—"

"I spoke with Huntley. I have news for you."

She was silent, savoring the feel of his large hand engulfing hers, the warmth of his other hand where it rested on her waist. If she closed her eyes and leaned forward, her cheek would brush his coat and—

She realized how silly she must look and she pulled away. "You mentioned Huntley?" She hoped Wulf didn't notice how husky her voice had become.

"You do not need to know anything more about him."

She tilted her head back so she could see Wulf's expression. His green eyes burned as if a fire raged behind them; his mouth was set in the grimmest of lines. Her heart fluttered. "Wulf, what—"

"He will ask you to marry him. He has decided."

Lily stumbled, almost causing them to collide with another couple.

With a curse, Wulf guided her back into the dance, his hand tightening over hers. "You do not dance so well, Moya. Even Huntley spoke of it."

She stiffened. "I dance perfectly well. I was just surprised." Which was untrue, for the duchess had already told her as much. But hearing the words from Wulf had sent such a sharp stab of pain through her that it had felt like a nail. *The final one in my coffin.* She tried to shake the thought, but it returned. *After I marry Huntley, it is over. My fate is sealed.*

The desire to burrow into Wulf's broad chest was almost unbearable, and to her chagrin, tears threatened. It took all of her force of mind to be able to say, "Thank you for finding that out for me."

"Just now, while we watched you dance, he told me

he was ready to make a proposal." Wulf's gaze locked with hers. Then he whispered, "Moya, are you certain?"

She thought of Dahlia, married to curmudgeonly Lord Kirk, and of her father, how he'd wither and die in gaol, and of her own life, how adrift she'd be without her family and Caith Manor. It took every ounce of her strength, but she managed to say, "Yes."

A swell of disappointment filled her, bitter and ugly. Her eyes filled up with tears, and suddenly being in Wulf's arms made her situation all the more unbearable.

Unable to hold her tears at bay another second, she broke from his embrace, gathered her skirts and ran, leaving Wulf standing alone in the middle of the dance floor. Though she felt the looks and heard the whispers rustling through the ballroom, she ignored them as she escaped into the cool evening air, her tears already falling.

Twenty-six

From the Diary of the Duchess of Roxburghe
There comes a time in every courtship where expectations must be defined, and we have reached that stage in Miss Balfour's case. Fortunately Charlotte and I are here to oversee that process, and we are, to be honest, quite good at it.

Lily pressed her forehead to the cool marble and looked up at the clear sky overhead. She'd left the ballroom half an hour ago and had found sanctuary in one of the small courtyard alcoves that held statuary. There, hidden from sight by a plump brace of cupids, she'd wept until she could weep no more.

Her tears had finally subsided, her breathing slowly returning to normal. But she could do nothing about her swollen eyes, red nose, and broken heart.

Eventually she'd have to go back inside and face everyone, but for now, she wished to do nothing more than stand with her forehead pressed to the cool marble statue. When the last guest carriage had left and the lights went out in the castle, she'd slip up to her room.

She closed her eyes, tears threatening to well yet again. *What a mess I've made of everything, falling in love with the wrong man.*

And what a fool she'd been, too, to think she could control love. Wulf had warned her, but she hadn't listened. *Oh, Wulf, if only I had understood what you were saying. But I didn't, and now—*

A hand closed about her wrist. Lily gasped and jerked away, only to find herself facing Wulf's grandmother.

"Are you through with . . ." The old woman drew lines down her face.

"Yes." Lily found her handkerchief and wiped away her tears, her face afire. "I'm sorry I left your grandson standing on the dance floor."

"It is no matter. No doubt he deserved it." The old woman moved closer, her black skirts rustling. "I told everyone who would listen that the turtle soup at dinner did not agree with you."

"Oh. Thank you."

"It was a poor excuse for soup. There was so little turtle that it could have been water, for all the flavor it had."

"It was thin. Your grace, thank you for your assistance. It was just— I didn't mean to—"

"Here." The old woman grasped Lily's hand and pressed something into her palm.

Lily opened her hand and found a small pouch

tied with an oddly knotted ribbon that held some tiny dried flowers and a little stick figure held together with thread. "What's this?"

"It's a . . ." The old woman scowled. "How do you say? It's not-for-love potion."

"A . . . I'm sorry, but did you say a 'not-for-love potion'?"

"Yes, yes. Can you not hear?"

"I'm sorry. I just—" Lily took a deep breath. "How does it work?"

"Simple. I will explain. First, you must know that it can be used only once."

"Only once."

"*Da*, for one person. But who needs more, eh?"

"Yes, but . . . I don't understand. What do you mean by 'not-for-love'?"

"It is to forget. To erase the"—the old woman swirled her hand about her head—"so you don't have to keep thinking."

"Ah. It erases your memory."

"Memory, yes. Of one you love. Then, you can continue with your life and not be sad. That is good, *nyet*?"

Lily looked at the small bag. If she didn't remember Wulf, she could move into her new life as Huntley's wife without the weight of a broken heart. But . . . forget Wulf? Could she really?

She closed her hand around the pouch, the scent of nutmeg and cinnamon and pine wafting through her fingers. "It smells like a sachet."

The old woman bristled with disapproval. "How would *you* know how a not-for-love potion should smell? Have you seen one before?"

"No, but—"

"Then do not question my magic!"

"I'm sorry. I just don't understand. Why are you giving me this?"

"Because you must marry this Huntley, but my foolish grandson has made you fall in love with him."

"He didn't—"

"Pah! I have eyes. I see things. I am no fool."

Lily pressed her hand to her hot cheek. "If you can see it, then so can everyone else."

"No one who matters."

Lily sighed. "I didn't mean to do it."

"No one ever does. But it will pain you to leave him. Use the pouch to make a tea. Drink it, and you will remember nothing of my grandson."

"Make a tea? With this?"

The old woman muttered under her breath. "You know how to make tea, foolish girl? Steep the pouch in hot water, the longer, the better."

"With this stick figure attached?"

"*Da*, with the figure attached. You are making this difficult!"

"I just want to do it right." Not that she'd actually use it. She didn't believe in magic . . . but the pain in her heart was so overwhelming. She looked at the bag. "Once you drink it, the forgetfulness will last forever?"

"Forever. You will remember the person, but feel nothing."

"You won't remember the love."

"You remember, but you will feel nothing, like a distant memory. Good, *nyet*?"

"Yes."

"And so it works. But you can cast the spell only once, so use it wisely." The old woman glanced over her shoulder and then turned back. "I must go now. My grandson will be out soon to get into the carriage, and I do not wish him to see me talking to you. He does not like the old magics, the young fool. Youth never believe in the old."

"But—"

"There he is. I go."

Sure enough, Wulf's large form was framed in the glow from the foyer.

Lily quickly moved so that he couldn't see her. "Thank you for the potion, your grace."

"Use it. Make this go away, for my grandson's sake as well as yours."

"You worry about him, too."

The old woman's expression softened. "His life has been one of privilege and he's never had to accept a *nyet*. Now he will have to do so, and in a matter of the heart. It will take a long, long time for him to recover, but that is part of life."

Lily thought about Emma's luminous gaze. "Don't worry. He will meet someone else and forget me soon enough."

"Pah! You don't know love if you think that." The old woman's shrewd gaze narrowed. "But you *don't* know much about love, do you? It is new to you, too."

"Very new," Lily said, and her heart ached at the words.

"So you say, but I see something else in your eyes." The old woman's expression softened. "You are like a lamb facing the slaughter. Your fate before you, and no idea how to accept it. You should—"

"Tata!" Wulf's deep voice rumbled from the terrace doors.

"Make the tea." The old woman's black gaze rested thoughtfully on Lily. "Do you know what 'moya' means in our language?"

"It means 'red.'"

"Foolish girl. It means 'mine.'"

"But . . . he's called me that since we first met."

"He's met you many times before. In his dreams."

Dreams? "I'm sorry, but I don't—"

"I must go before he comes for me and finds you." The old woman turned away. "Just remember," she called over her shoulder, "you can use the potion only once, and for only one person. And that, you must decide." Then she was gone.

Peering around the statue, Lily watched the prince escort his grandmother to their carriage and assist her into the seat, spreading a blanket over her knees before he climbed in, his broad shoulders filling the carriage doorway before he disappeared inside.

"Mine"? How have you seen me in your dreams?

And your grandmother said that you won't forget me for a long, long time. How am I to pursue a life with Huntley if I know you are suffering?

The footman closed the carriage door as the groom climbed into the seat. Then the coach swept down the drive, past Lily and her hiding place, and disappeared into the night.

Twenty-seven

From the Diary of the Duchess of Roxburghe

This morning after breakfast, I told Huntley that it was time he stopped fiddling with people's feelings and declared himself forthwith. He was quite surprised by my brazenness, but by the time I finished explaining how his hesitation must seem to the one he cared about, he was in agreement.

Or I think he was. He's difficult to decipher. So little emotion.

Still, I suppose I shouldn't blame him for his caution. Neither marriage nor death should be entered into lightly.

The next morning, dressed in a pelisse of gray merino trimmed with green ribbons over a walking gown of dusky blue wool, Lily sat on the low stone wall that edged the fields around Floors Castle. Since breakfast she'd been avoiding the other guests, although Wulf's grandmother had done her job well. Most of those Lily had met seemed to genuinely believe that her abrupt departure had to do with the turtle soup, which was quite fine with her.

Tomorrow, she'd face them all at the Butterfly Ball, and then . . . and then, it would be time to accept Huntley's proposal.

She pressed her fingertips to the sides of her forehead, which pounded steadily. *How can I walk away from the feelings I have for Wulf? Even more, how can I leave him knowing that I'm causing him pain?* That last question had kept her up most of the night.

She couldn't bear to think of Wulf in agony over anything, especially her. But what would Papa do if Kirk demanded the payment or, heaven forbid, went to the constable? *I cannot win.* Someone *is going to pay for my decisions. How can I—*

"Miss Balfour, there you are." Huntley stood on the other side of the stone wall, dressed as if ready for a ride in Hyde Park, his horse behind him.

She scrambled to her feet, her heart pounding sickly. "Lord Huntley. What a surprise to see you here."

"I'm sorry if I startled you. I dismounted by the apple tree near the lake when I saw you and thought I should take advantage of the opportunity to speak with you alone." His eyes twinkled. "I'm lucky your hair shows up so nicely against a gray stone wall."

"Ah. Was that what gave me away?"

"Yes. A flame against the gray."

She didn't know what to say to that. In fact, she didn't know what to say at all. She was painfully aware that he was going to ask her to marry him, and she wished she could keep him from doing so. *If only I'd already taken the potion, because then I wouldn't mind.*

"Miss Balfour—Lily, I must admit something. . . . I was out here looking for you."

She gulped. *Here it comes. Please, no, not yet. I'm not ready and—*

"I need some advice."

She blinked. "Advice?

"Yes. There aren't many people I trust as much as you." His calm brown gaze met hers. "You're a very special woman, Lily. I feel closer to you than almost anyone."

Good God! How could she turn his mind away from proposing? In a quick, breathless voice she said, "Thank you, but surely there are others you know better. Emma, for example, or even Prince Wulfinski. I've noticed that the two of you have been quite close of late—"

"This is something far too personal to share with the prince. As for Emma . . ." He shook his head. "There is only you, Lily. May I speak frankly?"

No. She didn't wish him to speak at all. But she was at a loss to stop him.

He looped the horse's reins about a shrub, then took off his hat and leaned across the wall. "Lily, have you ever been in love?"

"Love? I—no. I mean, yes, but not—" *Oh, God, I'm making such a mull of this!*

"I mean *really* in love, until you couldn't tell if you

were up or down, waking in the middle of the night, your mind on fire, thinking about the one woman you want to spend your life with." He laughed shakily. "I sound like every sort of fool, don't I?"

Good God, he feels that way about me? I had no idea. "Huntley, that's . . . Love is admirable in all forms."

"Oh? Even when it's not returned?" he asked softly.

She gulped. *He knows. How did he find out?*

"It's a damnable situation, isn't it?" he said, giving a short laugh. "Here I am, wildly in love with someone, while that someone isn't wildly in love with me. A wise man would leave well enough alone, but I cannot. I must know. I must speak. I—" He rubbed a hand over his face. "So tomorrow night, I will offer my heart."

Tomorrow night?

"I'm going to throw all caution to the wind and— and I'm going to propose. Do you know what that means, Lily?" His gaze burned into hers.

She flushed. "It means . . . that you'll soon be wed?"

"I hope so. I don't know if I could face being told no. I'm not given to taking chances; you know that about me. That's why I wished to speak with you first."

Ohhhhh. He wants an assurance that he won't be embarrassed, and that I'll say yes. It was hardly a romantic gesture, yet she had to appreciate his honesty. "You're cautious."

"I have always been so. Something the duchess said to me this morning made me realize that I was waiting for the perfect moment. Her grace says there is no such thing, and that I should take the leap now, while my heart is behind it, and trust that all will end well. And so tomorrow night at the ball, I will propose."

She gulped. "And you'll do this in front of everyone?"

"Yes. No. I mean, I don't know. I want it to be memorable, a moment to treasure, yet such a public display seems distasteful." His gaze locked with hers. "What would you think of such a public declaration? Would you find it romantic or awkward?"

Her stomach was so tied in knots that she felt ill. "I—I wouldn't wish to be made a part of such a public display."

He brightened. "I knew it!"

She smoothed her skirts with damp palms. "However you do it, I—I'm sure it will be a night to remember."

"I hope so. I am working out the details now." He smiled. "Of course, you'll hear all about them tomorrow."

Her heart thudded sickly. She wanted to run away as fast as she could, to jump into a river and swim far away, but she heard herself say in a quiet voice, "I'm sure it will be spectacular, and"—she swallowed so she could speak—"I'm certain you will not be refused."

He pushed himself from the wall and captured her hand. "Thank you for hearing me out."

She gave his hand a weak squeeze. "You're welcome."

"I'm nervous about this, but talking to you has been reassuring. Thank you." He pulled his horse to.

"I should return. I've things to do before tomorrow night. Are you coming back to the house?"

"In a while. I want to enjoy the sunshine some more."

"Very well." He swung up into the saddle and touched the brim of his hat. "Until later."

She nodded and watched him canter toward the stable.

For the longest time, she stood perfectly still and stared at the path his horse had made in the long grass. The wind teased her hair and tugged at her skirts, but she didn't move.

Finally, she began to walk back toward the castle. Slowly at first, then faster and faster, until, as she reached the edge of the lawn, she hiked up her skirt and ran.

Twenty-eight

From the Diary of the Duchess of Roxburghe
So many threads, some of my own weaving, some not; all ready to come together and make a masterpiece. Now, to make certain all of the ends are neatly knotted . . .

The full moon shone overhead, illuminating the clearing in the woods. It was well after midnight and here she was, staring at the prince's small cottage for the first time. With a thick thatched roof, golden light shining from every window, and a curl of smoke puffing gently from the chimney, it looked as if it belonged in a book of fairy tales.

She swallowed hard. This was her last night as a free woman. Once she agreed to marry Huntley, he would become her focus, her husband, her everything. And Wulf . . . she would have to forget him. Forever.

She untied a small basket from her saddle. Inside was a loaf of fresh bread from Cook and some jams that Mrs. Cairness had given her for helping to make butterfly costumes for the pugs. And tucked into a corner was the potion Wulf's grandmother had given her. *I only hope it will work.*

After her discussion with Huntley she'd thought briefly about making the tea for herself, but as soon as she held the sachet in her hand, she knew who should get the potion: Wulf. If she knew he wasn't suffering, then she could face her own future with some peace of mind. He should never hurt because of her. *Never.*

So she'd waited until well after dark, then had dressed in her favorite gown of heavy cream silk with a wide gold sash, held beneath her breasts with a bronze Celtic-knot pin, and put on a pearl-and-gold necklace that had been her mother's. She was ridiculously overdressed, but this was her one and only chance to say good-bye. If the potion worked, Wulf wouldn't remember their love and it would only exist in her own memory.

Her lips quivered and she pressed her hand against them.

You are only making this harder. Go in, make him the tea, say your good-byes, and then leave. She tugged her red cloak closer, hoping the ride hadn't marred her gown, and found a low branch to which to tie up the horse.

That done, she picked up the basket and walked down a newly laid stone pathway that led to a rounded, green door. The door hung from an obviously new facing, and the shutters had shiny new hinges. The smell of fresh thatch soaked the air, too.

She paused at the door and took a deep breath. Tomorrow night, once Huntley proposed and she accepted, anything with Wulf would be over. *Forever.* Tears prickled her eyes.

She wasn't just here to say good-bye, but to show him how she felt. Wulf wanted her, and she knew that in coming here to his cottage alone, she wanted more than a farewell kiss. Just once, before she sold herself as a wife, she wanted to taste pure passion. The memory would have to keep her soul warm for the years to come. And Wulf was the only man to have ever awakened her passion.

Every time he touched her or just *looked* at her, her heart leapt, her skin prickled with awareness, and her entire body softened as if ready to melt into his arms. And things had only gotten worse since the night he'd visited her bedchamber. She still had dreams about him there, in her bed, his hands touching her—

Heat rose through her. After tomorrow, she'd be in no position to answer her own desires again, devoting herself to Huntley. But tonight she was still Lily Balfour, free to do whatever she wanted. And she wanted to feel Wulf, to touch him, to *be* with him. It was madness. It was crazed. Though she shook at the boldness of her actions, she had no desire for anything else.

She knocked on the door.

There was no answer.

She wet her lips and knocked harder. *Where is he? Why doesn't he—*

"*Moya.*" The deep whisper came from so close that she could feel his breath.

Mine. A shiver went through her as she turned to face him.

Wulf stood behind her, his cloak tossed over his shoulders, the neck of his shirt open over the strong column of his throat. "You have found my home."

"Yes." She had come to throw herself into his arms. She wished to become a woman in his bed and no other's.

"Come. Let me show you my home." To her surprise, he bent and lifted her in his arms, engulfing her in his warmth. Within seconds he was through the door. He kicked it closed and carried her to the fire, which bathed the room in the flicker of old gold, casting the room in intriguing dark shadows.

Wulf set her on her feet, the floor uneven under her boots.

She moved away and set the basket on a nearby table. "I—I brought you some fresh bread and tea and—"

"You didn't come here for a picnic."

She moistened her lips. "No."

His eyes gleamed. "I have wanted you here since the first moment I saw you." His hands were warm against her throat as he undid her cape and then tossed it aside, the heavy red material pooling onto the floor. Then he slid his hands down her arms. "I hope you have come not just to my cottage, but to my bed?"

How does he know? Her eyes locked with his, and she stepped out of one shoe and then the other.

His chest rose and fell rapidly. "Moya, I drink of your madness."

That's exactly what it was—hot and sinful and delicious madness. Lily untied the wide ribbon that gathered her gown beneath her breasts and let it flutter to the floor.

Wulf's gaze darkened.

Emboldened, Lily reached for the tie that gathered her gown at her neck. With a few tugs it came loose, and she pulled it down her shoulders to drop to the floor, the cream silk pooling at her feet. Beneath her chemise her nipples peaked, already yearning for his touch. Without hesitating, she removed her shift.

It was the boldest thing she'd ever done, and the most scandalous, yet she felt no embarrassment. Her bare skin prickling from the heated gaze of the man who watched her every move, all she could think about was how she longed for him to touch her.

His gaze caressed her curves, his hands fisted at his sides, his breath seemingly caught in his chest.

Lily was suddenly awash with a sense of power. He wanted her just as much as she wanted him, but he was not the one who controlled what would happen in this room. *She* was. The knowledge thrilled her to the bottom of her bare feet.

The fire crackled cozily, and it was easy to believe that in this moment, no one else existed. She felt safe and protected from life's expectations and fetters.

She stepped forward and placed a hand on his chest.

Wulf inhaled swiftly, as if her touch had burned him.

Suddenly uncertain, she started to remove her hand, but he captured it and held it in place, sliding it up to rest over his heart. She felt his blood pounding through his veins, the urgency of his breath warming them both.

"You are still dressed," she said huskily.

It was as if her words freed him from a spell. One moment, he was standing still beneath her fingertips, and the next he was undressing with a haste that made her laugh softly.

When he was naked before her, Lily couldn't look away. The firelight bathed his body in molten gold, highlighting the curve of each muscle. But it was the sight of his hardened cock that made her breath catch. *He is so beautiful.*

Wulf tugged her to him, sending thoughts tumbling. Her heart pounded in her throat as she peeked up at him through her lashes. His face was serious, and more intent than she'd ever seen it.

When his green gaze locked with hers, her breath caught. Though he didn't say a word, she heard his thoughts, felt his desire, knew he wanted her just as badly as she wanted him. She twined her arms about his neck, her breasts pressed against his chest as she lifted on her toes and touched her lips to his.

Instantly, his strong arms slipped about her as his

mouth claimed hers with a demanding passion that sent the last thought from her head. All she could do was feel him, taste him, surrender to him, as he lifted her in his arms and carried her to the large bed in the shadows.

He placed her on it and then slipped in beside her, his warm skin on hers, his cock heating a path up her thigh. He stroked her as he'd done before, but this time he only teased, drawing his hand through her thighs and making her gasp and squirm. As he did so, her hands traveled over his broad shoulders, up his muscular arms, over his chest, reveling in the crisp hair that slid under her fingertips. Every touch fanned her yearning, making her gasp his name as she moved restlessly beneath him.

He bent to lave her nipples with his tongue, the hot wetness making her arch against him. She slid her hands through his hair and held him there, pressing her breast into his mouth as he sent waves of fire through her veins.

Finally, she could stand no more. She slipped her hand between them and wrapped her fingers about his cock. Wulf gasped, his arms tightening about her.

She slid her hand up and down his length, marveling at the silken hardness, each touch making him groan in delicious agony.

Finally, gasping, he grasped her wrist. *"Please."*

She needed no more encouragement, for her body ached for him, her thighs already slick with her own desire. "Yes."

He rolled to his elbow and placed his thigh between her legs, opening her for him. Then as naturally as water slips through a streambed, he entered her.

The fullness caught her unaware, and she stiffened. He pressed a little harder, murmuring how beautiful she was, telling her how she drove him mad, whispering secrets that made her writhe against him, desperate for more. He began to move, lifting her knees as he did so. Suddenly he filled her fully and a cry of pain escaped her.

He captured her cry with a heated kiss, moving against her, his hands never ceasing. He cupped her breasts, her waist, her bottom, pleasuring her as he kissed her wildly. He rocked against her, filling her and then withdrawing, making her yearn for his fullness with each stroke.

Lily forgot the pain as she met him thrust for thrust. Finally, their passions meeting, they rode the madness until they cried out, then collapsed in each other's arms.

Twenty-nine

From the Diary of the Duchess of Roxburghe
Many people feel that words are easier than deeds.
In general, I would hold this to be true until one
tries to find the *right* words. At those times, deeds
can seem quite easy.

It was a long time before Lily could breathe. Why
hadn't anyone told her that lovemaking would feel so
heavenly? So enthralling? So *perfect*?

She let out her breath in a contented sigh. Her body
hummed with joy, her heart sang with an overpowering sense of freedom, as if she could do anything she
wished.

Wulf murmured something deep in his chest,
sleepy and satisfied as he spooned her against him, his
skin toasty warm. She was wrapped head to foot in
sensual male, his arm deliciously heavy over her waist
as he pulled her closer, his breath against her neck.

It was wonderful, and she rested within his arms

for a long time before she finally opened her eyes to look around the cottage. *I must soak this all in, experience it all fully.* She suddenly felt as greedy for the details of his life as she'd been for his body a short time ago.

Though the cottage had a dirt floor, it was freshly strewn with rushes. The fireplace blazed with nary a hint of smoke, the windows were firmly shuttered against the night, and the furnishings were well crafted and suited to their surroundings, except for his desk, an ornate secretary that wouldn't have been out of place in the duchess's sitting room. Made of beautiful dark wood, it seemed out of place compared to the other plain, serviceable pieces.

"That's an unusual desk," she said.

"Hmm?" he rumbled sleepily.

She turned toward him. "Is it mahogany?"

He opened one eye. "Is this how you greet your love?"

She sniffed. "I just asked a question."

He smiled and, with a sigh, raised up on his elbow, resting his chin on her shoulder to see the desk. "Perhaps. My grandmother was insistent that I have at least one piece of furniture that befits my station."

"Where does she stay?"

"In the manor house on the hill."

"Ah. Is she a guest of the owner?"

"You could say that." He nuzzled her neck, sending delicious chills through her.

"She spoke to me yesterday and brought me some tea. She said it was a potion."

"Tata has many potions."

"Do they work?"

"Always."

Her gaze found the basket on the small table. "I brought her tea with me."

He sighed. "Moya, you should be too exhausted to speak, enthralled by my prowess." He nipped her ear, making her giggle. "Perhaps I haven't yet completed my duties? Perhaps you wish for more of me? I cannot blame you—"

She had to laugh, and her throat tightened when he answered with a pleased grin. *How I will miss this. And you. For the rest of my life.*

"Ah, Moya, you are so beautiful," he whispered. "So utterly beautiful." He slid his hands up her arms to capture them over her head as he rolled over her again, his knee parting her thighs. His cock, hard once more, pressed against her womanhood, and she immediately lifted her hips to his.

He gasped, his breath warm on her ear as he kissed her neck.

Her body was aflame, and all thoughts of leaving scattered before it. She moaned and shifted against him.

"Yes, my little love," he whispered. "Show me what you want."

With a deep moan she wrapped her legs about his hips, opening to him yet again.

And together, they lost themselves once more in the wonder.

"Moya?" The deep voice came from far, far away.

Fighting her way up from sleep, Lily struggled to open her heavy lids but to no avail. Her body seemed inexorably melded between the soft bed and the large, luxuriously warm body that curled around her.

"Moya, you must wake." Wulf kissed her ear. "The sun will soon rise, and we must get you back to the castle."

She finally opened her eyes, frowning at him. "I don't want to go back."

"Nor do I wish you to, my love." Wulf smoothed her hair from her cheek, his hand gentle, his expression serious. "I knew you would come to me."

"I didn't," she replied truthfully.

"Ah, but I have always known that you belong with me." He trailed his fingers over her cheek. "Come. Rise. We will go to the duchess and tell her that we will marry. She may announce our betrothal at her ball and—"

"Wulf, no." Lily pushed herself upright, tugging the sheet with her. "That's not why I came here."

His smile slipped. "Then why?"

She wished with all her heart that she didn't have to tell him the truth. "I came to say good-bye."

His gaze darkened. "Good-bye?"

"Please, don't make this more difficult than it is. I can't marry you. You know that."

A hard look flashed over his face. "Still you will sell yourself for money."

She stiffened and he instantly looked guilty. "Moya, I'm sorry. I didn't mean that."

She turned and scooted to the edge of the bed.

"Moya, please don't—" He captured her hand and placed a kiss to her palm. "I was angry. I love you, Moya. I would spend my life with you. It's agony to hear you say you will wed another. I—I cannot bear it."

His voice carried so much pain, and her bruised heart answered it. "Wulf, I have no other choices."

"You always have choices. And you would not be alone. I would be with you, and we would face this together."

"I can't. Huntley will ask me to marry him this evening, and I will say . . . I will say . . ." The word stuck in her throat.

He sat up. "But what of you, Moya? What do *you* want?"

"It's not that simple. You know that."

"Then you will tell Huntley yes." His words were so heavy, it sounded as if his tongue could barely hold them.

"I have no choice—"

"You do, damn it!" He threw back the blankets and yanked her to him. "You cannot sacrifice your happiness for your family. Are they here, sacrificing their happiness for you?"

"My sister has been trying to do just that. My father wrote and warned me."

He groaned and pulled her into his lap, his arms engulfing her as he whispered, "Moya, what of *us*?"

What of *them*? Her gaze caressed every magnificent inch of him. As hard as it was, she said, "There cannot be an *us*. Tonight was my final good-bye to you, and to my freedom."

Wulf's jaw tightened. "Huntley will expect you in his bed."

"Yes, and I will do my duty—"

"*No!*" Wulf growled. "I will not allow it, I cannot—" His voice broke. "Lily, don't."

Her heart breaking, she slipped her arms about him as tears filled her eyes. "I love you so much," she whispered. "But I have no choice."

He was silent, but then he cupped her face and turned it to his. "You will do as you must—but you will think of *me*."

She *would* think about him. They both knew it. Suddenly, she couldn't imagine being with another man. Couldn't picture Huntley trying to kiss her. Couldn't imagine him reaching for her.

Her entire body rebelled at the thought. She wanted more of Wulf—of his warm skin beneath her fingertips, of the delicious feeling of the weight of his legs twined with hers, of his strong heart beating beneath her ear. She *wanted* desperately, completely, with every part of her. She was enslaved, bound to him by her passion.

She slipped her arms about his neck, holding him close, naked skin to naked skin. She stroked his hair, murmuring words of love, willing him to forget their circumstances, to forget the agony the day ahead would bring. These last few moments were all they'd have.

He turned toward her and pulled her back into the bed, sliding her beneath him with one strong tug of his arm. They made love again, each touch, each stroke fueled by desperation. It was not a gentle joining, but a flood of heated passion that left Lily breathless and weeping.

Wulf held her close, murmuring soft words into her ear, the only one she understood—"moya," mine—repeated over and over. She pressed her cheek to his shoulder and wrapped herself about him.

A short time later, Wulf finally fell asleep. Lily waited until the gentle gleam of the sunrise told her that her time was at an end. With a face wet with tears, she slipped from between the sheets and gathered her clothes.

Wulf awoke slowly, a smile curving his lips. *Moya.* He reached for her, but his hand fell upon cool sheets.

She was gone.

He sat upright. Her clothes, once scattered over his cottage, were gone, while his had been placed neatly over the end of the bed. *And that is it. We are done.* He was filled with so many emotions that he couldn't breathe.

She'd come to him as he'd dreamed, and she'd given him the precious gift of her maidenhead. She'd even admitted that she loved him. *But not enough*, he thought bitterly.

He pushed himself from the bed and walked to the fireplace. His cozy cottage was achingly empty. The fire burned and yet gave off no warmth, the rug beneath his feet seemed coarse and cold, the light flickering from the candles seemed chilled and impersonal.

He wanted to break something, to throw something, to kick over the furniture and yell at the top of his voice.

As he stood there, debating which avenue of destruction to use first, his gaze fell on his desk. There, sitting in solitary splendor, was a single mug of tea weighing down a note.

Bloody hell—the damned Scots and their tea. He shoved the mug aside and reached for the note.

Drink the tea.

He turned it over, but that was it. No declarations of love, or remorse, or anything else. Just *Drink the tea.*

With a roar, he sent the mug flying, the tea splattering the wall as the mug crashed against it, as broken and splintered as his heart.

Thirty

From the Diary of the Duchess of Roxburghe
Today is the day! The Roxburghe Butterfly Ball
will change the lives of many, and the fortunes of a
favored few. Oh, how I love a good ball.

Hours later, Wulf was awakened by the creak of a
carriage on the drive leading to the cottage, and the
sound of Arsov's voice raised in argument with Tata
Natasha. *Good God, not my grandmother.* The last
thing he wished to do was speak with her.

But the voices were getting closer and he had no
choice. Sighing, he rose, wincing as his head protested
the movement. A bottle brushed his foot as he staggered to the washbowl and dunked his head.

He'd just buttoned his breeches when a brisk rap
sounded on the cottage door. He grabbed a clean shirt
out of the wardrobe and tugged it over his head. "I'm
coming," he called as the sharp rap came again.

"Then come faster," she snapped loudly. "I'm an
old woman and cannot stand forever in the doorway."

He shook his head as he opened the door. Tata Natasha swept in, her black gown sweeping the floor, as she surveyed the room. "Why did it take you so long to come to the door?"

"I was sleeping."

"At this time of the day?"

"I have nothing better to do." He sank onto the bench before the fire and looked about blearily for his stockings and boots.

"Pah." She eyed his hair. "You must get ready. We have that harridan's ball to attend. You said you'd accompany me."

"I'm not going."

Tata's brows rose. "*Da,* you are. The duchess is sending her carriage for us."

"We have a carriage."

"Hers is better." Tata's shrewd gaze flickered about the room. "What is this?" She picked up something from the rug. "It's a hairpin." She looked from the hairpin to the mussed bed, then she spun to face him. "So, *she* was here. That is why you look as if a carriage ran over you."

Wulf scowled.

"Well? Answer me."

"I'm not telling you a damn thing." He plucked the hairpin from Tata's fingers and placed it on the mantel, his chest aching as if someone had kicked it. "Why are you here?"

"I came to see why you're not ready for this ball." Her gaze flickered over the rest of the cottage. "Why is that mug on the floor?"

"I dropped it. Tata, did you come to look in my corners?"

"*Nyet*. I brought you this. It is a letter from your father." She pulled the letter from a pocket, handing it to him.

"Thank you." He rubbed his head where an ache was making it difficult to even decipher the writing on the envelope. He broke the seal and opened the missive, struggling to absorb the contents. Finally, he put it down. "I am to return home as soon as possible. The treaty has—" He frowned. "What are you doing?"

His grandmother was standing as still as a statue by the table, something in her hands. He put down the letter. "What is it?"

She turned, and he saw that in her hands was a piece of the mug Lily had left him. Tata sniffed it. "So the Balfour woman fixed you this."

"How do you know?"

"I know. On the night of the dance, I gave her a pouch of this tea."

"Why would you do that?"

"It was a test. I told her it was a not-for-love potion."

"A *what*?"

"Whoever drinks it will forget their true love."

He looked at the broken mug and his ache grew. "She wishes me to forget her."

"*Da*. I didn't expect her to use it for you, but for herself."

He gave a bitter laugh. "She does not love me, Tata. And now, she does not wish me to love her."

Tata scowled. "You don't understand. When I saw her, she'd been weeping, realizing that she and you could never be."

"She was sad?"

"Very. Her cries touched my heart. I thought she'd drink this to free her to marry Huntley."

Slowly, Wulf sat up straighter. "She'd have no regrets."

Tata nodded. "None. Her life would be simple, fulfilling if not blindingly happy. But instead, she gave it to you."

"But . . . why wouldn't she want me to remember that I love her?"

"Think, Wulf." Tata waited expectantly, and when he continued to frown, she threw up her hands. "Men! After all the women you've been with, do you not understand how we think? A woman wants the love of only one man, Wulf."

"But I—"

"And that one man is the one that she loves." She threw him an exasperated look. "Lily left the tea for you so that your life would be better—she left it because she didn't wish you to suffer."

He looked at the broken mug, then said slowly, "She sacrificed her chance for happiness for mine."

"Aye." Tata frowned for a long moment, then sighed. "It's as I've said all along; she is a woman worth keeping."

His jaw tightened. "She wishes no part of me. She said as much."

"Since when have you listened to what people say to you? Now is not the time to become obedient. If you want this woman, then do what you do best—demand that she be yours. She has shown her love. What more do you need?"

He stared at his grandmother, then he suddenly leapt from his chair, picked her up, and kissed her cheek.

"Oh! Put me down, you ruffian!"

Laughing, he twirled her once, twice, then set her on her feet.

She staggered to one side, but he caught her and set her in a chair, chuckling. "I'm sorry to make you dizzy, but you've given me hope. I've been so caught up in my loss that I stopped thinking. You are right—I cannot just let her go."

Tata glared up at him. "Finally, some sense!"

"Yes. So now, you must leave. I'm going to bathe. I have a ball to attend tonight."

"Good." She stood, holding on to the arm of the chair as she tested her balance. Reassured when the room didn't move under her feet, she released it and made her way to the door. "I'll send in Arsov. I suppose he knows how to heat water."

"Tata?"

She looked back.

He grinned. "Thank you for helping me and my Lily."

Her expression softened. "I have watched you

through all of this, and I was impressed with your constancy. Perhaps she will be the making of you, this Scottish thistle."

"And if she will not have me?"

Tata's black eyes twinkled. "Pah. You are my grandson and a prince, the son of a princess and a king. How can she tell you no?"

"You would think she could not, but she does." He stroked his chin thoughtfully. "But while she can deny me with words, her kisses say only yes."

"Then ask her with kisses." Tata turned back to the door. "Now hurry, or we'll be late."

Lily looked at herself in the mirror as she tugged her gloves above her elbows. Her soft-gold gown made her hair seem redder than ever. Freya, who was helping three other ladies get ready for the ball, too, had returned in time to use an iron to set delicate curls about her ears. "I look well enough for a countess-to-be," she told the mirror, but the words were so hollow that she had to turn away.

She couldn't stay here alone and keep thinking. The time for that was through; now was the time for doing.

Lifting her chin, Lily left her room. She was walking down the steps behind some other guests when she saw Huntley standing at the bottom of the stairs, his back to her.

Instantly, Lily's feet faltered. *He is waiting for me,*

and now he will ask me to marry him, and I will say—
Her brain froze. *I will say yes*, she thought, continuing down the stairs. *If I can.*

As she drew closer, she saw that the earl was talking to Emma, who looked quite pretty in a pink gown set with tiny, white silk flowers. Huntley caught sight of Lily and whispered something to Emma, who glanced up and gave her a quick, warm smile before turning to join the other guests as they walked to the dining room.

So Huntley has told Emma of his plans. It wasn't surprising, for the two were close. Lily realized that her hands had turned into fists, and she uncurled them. *Smile. I must pretend this is all I want, all I've hoped for, that he is the man I—*

I can't.

The words sounded through her as clearly as the ring of a bell. She caught her breath. *I can't.*

And there, standing on the third step of the grand staircase, Lily realized that she could never, *would* never, marry without love.

She deserved better, and so did Wulf, and Huntley— all of them.

"Miss Balfour?" Huntley's voice broke into her thoughts.

Lily blinked, and with a short laugh, she descended the final few steps. "I'm glad to see you, for we must talk."

He brightened. "Yes, we must." He glanced around. "Come. We can use the blue sitting room. We'll keep the door open for propriety's sake." He led the way, talking with far more animation than she'd ever seen. "Here we are! The candles are lit, so the duchess must plan to open it during the ball."

Lily tried to compose her thoughts as he chatted on, mentioning the fabulous decorations he'd seen through the ballroom doors as the footmen carried in a bowl of punch, and how many candles were blazing in the hallway.

"Her grace certainly knows how to entertain." He chuckled, but then caught her gaze. His smile died. "My dear Lily, what's wrong?"

"I—I must speak to you about what you said yesterday morning."

"Ah, about the proposal." He reached over to grab her hands with his. "Lily, Lily, I'm so *happy*."

"I— That's lovely, but—"

His hands tightened over hers, a blissful expression in his eyes. "Love is amazing, isn't it? I've never felt anything so—"

"Huntley, *no*. I'm sorry, this is quite overpowering and while I appreciate your openness, I must say something and— Oh dear, this is so difficult. Love never comes with just one look. At least, not that I'm aware of, although some people say that it can. I've never—"

"Only one look?" He laughed, the sound surprisingly joyous. "I've looked once, twice, a thousand times, but I never *saw*. Now I see, and now I know the truth. I can no longer deny it. Lily, I had to tell you first."

"No, please don't. I'm not—"

"I must tell someone, and you're the one." He held her hands between his. "Lily, I asked Emma to marry me and she said yes!"

Lily blinked, speechless.

He laughed and wagged a finger at her. "Aha! You're surprised, aren't you? Emma was quite wrong then, for she said she was certain you suspected. She said that you caught her gazing at me at breakfast one morning and that you had to know."

She thought back to that day. *Good God—Huntley was in that hallway, too, but I only saw Wulf. I only saw Wulf, while Emma only saw Huntley.* "Goodness, it never dawned on me that— I mean, that's wonderful for you both! I thought— How could I have—"

"I am deliriously happy! I'm too enthralled to keep it to myself, yet I must because her family must be told before we announce it. My dear Emma was adamant that we tell you immediately, though. I wish I could shout it from the rooftops." Huntley went on and on, giving details about his proposal, how he'd been so nervous that his voice had been shaking, and more. Meanwhile, Lily watched him, bemused.

For three weeks now she'd thought of nothing but obtaining a proposal from him. But now that he'd proposed to someone else, all she felt was a deep, profound relief. She was happy for Huntley and Emma, though. They were so similar that they were a perfect match.

Huntley shook his head dazedly. "All this time,

I thought I cared for Emma like a sister, or a friend. I thought she was kind to me only because of her friendship with Sarah. We were both so wrong. I—I think Sarah would approve."

"If she loved you both as you say, she would want whatever makes you happiest."

He brightened, his gaze warm. "Thank you. I do believe she would. Now, I must think of what would make Emma happy."

He was so happy, so thrilled, and so obviously in love. She wanted that for herself, wanted it so badly that her throat tightened. Suddenly, Lily didn't want to be here. She only wanted to get out of this room and find Wulf.

But . . . what about Papa?

Her knees weakened and she sank into a chair. *Now I have no plan. Either Papa will go to gaol, or Dahlia will marry Lord Kirk and be miserable.*

What can I do? Wulf and I could live in the cottage, but where would Dahlia and Papa stay? I must find a way to pay back that debt. But how?

Her gaze absently dropped to her gown, a silk confection adorned with rosettes and satin ribbons—a gown she'd made herself. *I've always wanted to open a modiste's shop, but it takes time to grow a clientele. Unless . . .*

Her gaze went to Huntley's impeccable neckcloth, then she thought of the duchess's penchant for the latest fashions. *If the duchess and such fashion plates as Huntley assisted me, I could find a clientele quickly and*

*perhaps talk Lord Kirk into accepting payments. We'd
have to give up Caith Manor but—*

A million thoughts thrummed through her and she
pressed a hand to her thundering heart. *I can do this*,
she told herself with awe. *I can really do this!*

"Lily? Are you well?" Huntley's brows were lowered. "You look pale." He dropped to his knee and
took her hand between his own. "Are you crying?
Yes, there are tears in your eyes. Please don't! Whatever is wrong, don't despair. Look at me: a week ago
I thought I would never love again, yet here I am, so
deeply in love that I—"

Foreign curses flew through the air, and in the flash
of an eye Wulf appeared, his face thunder-dark as he
grasped Huntley's arm, lifted the man to his feet, and
punched him.

Wulf couldn't think, couldn't hear, couldn't breathe.
Huntley was on his knees before Lily, in the middle
of an obvious declaration. *She is mine, damn it! Mine
and no one else's!* Then suddenly Huntley was lying
on the floor.

Through his red haze, Wulf was vaguely aware of
Lily talking to him as she leaned over Huntley. Wulf
could see her tantalizing lips moving, could see the
anger in her gaze, but he could hear nothing but the
roar of his own blood. She was *his*, by God. How
could she not know that? How could she—

A pug ran into the room, butterfly wings strapped
to its round body. It paused to sniff Huntley, its curli-

cue tail spinning in happiness. Another two joined the first, all strapped with fantastic butterfly wings as they began snuffing Huntley's hair and eyes, one of them licking his ear. Behind them came a cackling sound as three women swept into the room, all talking at once.

A hand fell upon Wulf's arm, and he turned to find his grandmother beside him as the Duchess of Roxburghe and Lady Charlotte swept past them to the unconscious man, the butler hard upon their heels.

"MacDougal," her grace said over her shoulder, her sharp voice penetrating the fog that surrounded Wulf. "Have poor Huntley carried to the settee. He's going to have the devil of a swollen jaw when he awakes."

Lady Charlotte nodded. "It's already swelling. We'll need some ice, too."

"Aye, yer ladyship." The butler went to the door and called for some footmen.

Her grace helped Lily to her feet. Two footmen arrived and, stepping around the winged pugs, carried Huntley to the settee, while another was dispatched to fetch the doctor.

Tata Natasha looked with interest at Huntley's swollen jaw. "A well-placed facer," she said in their native tongue. "Well done, although it would have been better to punch him in the stomach. It wouldn't leave such a visible mark. Now Huntley will engender sympathy."

"I didn't take the time to plan things," Wulf growled. "It just happened when I saw him with Lily.

It was an outrage! The man had no right to put her in such a position."

"What position?"

"He was importuning her. I saw him. He was on his knee before her, pleading, and she was weeping into a handkerchief, obviously distressed. I could not allow—"

"Wulf," Lily snapped.

He turned and found her glaring at him. Every line in her body told him that she was furious. Swallowing, he said in a cautious voice, "Yes, my love?"

Her face bloomed with color. "I'm not your love. And you have no right to react toward anyone for me. I'm not—we're not— Oh, blast you, this isn't your affair!"

"But he was—"

"No, he wasn't." Lily sent Wulf an exasperated glance. "You're mistaken."

"I know what I saw," Wulf insisted. "He was on his knee and holding your hand."

"Wait." The duchess's blue eyes were bright as she fixed them on Lily. "Lord Huntley was on his knee?"

"Yes, but it was not what you think."

The duchess laughed, the sound surprisingly young and husky. "How do you know what I think, young lady?"

Lily flushed. "I just know that while it may have looked as if he were making me an offer, he wasn't."

Tata Natasha leaned forward, her black eyes on Lily. "So why was he on his knee?"

"Because he'd just told me—" Lily paused and

looked at the unconscious man. "He was confiding something that he did not wish to be widely known yet."

"I heard him say that he is in love with you!" Wulf said.

"No, you *didn't*." The look Lily sent him was half annoyance and half an appeal.

Wulf paused. Now that he had time to consider everything, he had to admit that Lily didn't look like a woman who'd just received a much-longed-for offer of marriage. She looked upset, yes. In fact, as he looked at her now, he noted the faint circles under her eyes and the downturn of her lips. She'd had neither when she'd been with him this morning.

Wulf raked a hand through his hair. "So Huntley didn't mention love?"

"He did, but——" Lily grimaced. "I can't say more."

"Interesting." The duchess sat in a chair across from their indisposed guest. "I suppose I shouldn't admit this, for Lord Huntley hasn't confided everything in me, but lately, I thought I sensed a certain level of interest from him in Miss Gordon, rather than Miss Balfour." The duchess looked at Lily. "Not that I see how someone could do that, for you're by far more vivacious and infinitely more beautiful."

Lily's cheeks heated. "Thank you, but we really should see to the earl. I don't suppose anyone has any hartshorn? I could bathe Huntley's forehead while we wait for the doctor."

Lady Charlotte, who'd been hovering in the background, brightened. "I have some in my room. I'll send someone to fetch it." She bustled off, three of the butterfly pugs following her. The oldest pug rose to follow his mates, but after staring about the room uncertainly, he began snuffing the carpet in circles, making his way to Wulf's feet. The pug looked up at him with milky eyes, wagged his tail, then plumped down in a contented ball.

Tata Natasha touched it with her foot. "Why no wings on this one?"

"He eats them," the duchess said as Lady Charlotte returned. Her grace eyed the prince. "Randolph seems to favor you, Your Highness."

"So does Meenie," Lily said. "She barked when he climbed into my window, but as soon as he spoke to her, she became his devoted sl—" She caught Lady Charlotte's surprised look and blushed.

"Just so," the duchess said in a dry tone. She turned to Wulf. "So you thought Huntley was trying to force his affections on Miss Balfour."

"Yes. And I do not believe this story about Miss Gordon. She is very nice, but who would look at her when Lily is about?"

The duchess chuckled at his obvious outrage. "People are very odd in their predilections. But Huntley has known Miss Gordon for years, and they've become very close since his wife died. He thought they were just friends, but she had other ideas. After I saw the two of them together, I began to suspect that she harbored feelings for him that went deeper than mere friendship." The duchess leaned back in her chair. "But now we have a dilemma. My guests were gathering for the small dinner I was having before the ball, and you, Miss Balfour, left the door open."

Lily flushed. "We didn't wish to break with propriety."

"Very proper of you, although you should have thought about how it would look when God knows how many people might walk past the door and see Huntley on his knees before you."

Tata Natasha nodded. "Very bad. People will talk."

"Exactly," the duchess said. "If I do not leave this room with at least one engaged couple, then Huntley's plans to marry Miss Emma might well be for naught."

Lily blinked. "How so?"

"Huntley was not going to announce his engagement yet, was he? You said he wished it to be kept secret for now."

"He wants to speak to her family before making an announcement."

"Quite proper of him, for Miss Gordon's uncle is a high stickler indeed, more priggish even than the earl, if you can believe it. If Miss Gordon's uncle hears rumors that Huntley was attempting to attach himself to you a mere week before he comes to them to request her hand for marriage, then it is quite possible that he would withhold his approval." The duchess regarded the unconscious man. "Sadly, I don't believe either Huntley or Miss Gordon would marry if they couldn't gain her family's complete support."

Lily pressed a hand to her forehead. "Oh no."

"So the next time you leave the door open for propriety's sake," the duchess said drily, "do not stage a play. For now it seems that we are in a fix." She arched her brow at Wulf. "Well? Do you have something more constructive to add to this mess than a fist? Or are you all brawn and no brains?"

Something about the way the duchess was looking at Wulf made him pause. *What is it that you wish me to say?* He considered her words and then said thoughtfully, "As you said, we must have an engagement."

The duchess beamed. "Exactly."

"Then if Moya will accept me, she and I could announce our engagement tonight and people might think they were mistaken and saw me proposing to Moya instead of Huntley."

The duchess's eyes gleamed appreciatively. "An excellent idea."

"There is one problem, though. I have asked Moya to marry me. I have told her I love her, too."

"Many times," Tata offered.

"Many, many times. But still she refuses me."

"Does she, indeed? So you are not the problem, then." The duchess's gaze now fixed on Lily. "So, Lily, why do you not wish to marry this man? Is it his lack of income? The fact that he has no polish? The way he dresses like a groom?"

Lily met Wulf's gaze, and to her surprise, she saw the duchess's questions reflected there.

I did that to him, she realized. *I caused him to doubt me. To doubt us. I never meant for that to happen.*

She stood, forgetting everything but Wulf. "It's not any of those things. Huntley was only comforting me because I'd just realized that I was making a mistake in marrying for anything other than love." She took one of Wulf's hands in hers. "I've been fighting loving you since the day we met—but I can't fight what is meant to be."

His hand tightened over hers, his eyes gleaming warmly. "We *are* meant to be, Moya. Forever."

She smiled. "You know my family's circumstances and why I was pursuing Huntley, and, yes, it was for all of the wrong reasons. But it wouldn't have worked for either of us. Even before he told me about his intentions toward Emma, I'd already realized that if I couldn't be with you, then life wasn't worth living. I love you and—"

He caught her to him and held her so tightly she couldn't breathe, but she didn't care. She held him just as hard, and it was as if she could feel the love pouring from him through her.

"Oh, Moya, I have longed to hear you say that," he whispered. "Dreamed of it."

"Pah!" Wulf's grandmother said. "It is as if we aren't even here. So rude."

"I know," the duchess agreed. "And while it's certainly touching, it doesn't help us with our problem."

"I don't understand," Lady Charlotte said. "Miss Balfour, excuse me for intruding on your embrace with the prince, but does this mean that you will marry him? Or will not? I'm so confused."

Her face red, Lily pulled away from Wulf, although he didn't allow her to go far. "I've discovered a better answer to my problems. It's not perfect, but it could solve my family's difficulties." She looked up at him. "Wulf, I wish to open a modiste's shop. I sew all of my own gowns, and women are forever asking me where I got them. If I opened a shop on Bond Street, and you and Dahlia and Papa helped, we could make a success of it. It will be difficult at first, but if I am good enough, I can make it work."

"Is this what you want, Moya? To own a dress shop?"

She nodded. "I love to sew. I always have."

"Then you shall do so. You want to make dresses, you will make dresses. You want to make hats, you can make hats. You want to raise goats, then we will have more goats than anyone else in Oxenburg."

Her smile slipped. "But I would have to have a shop in Bond Street. I couldn't sell gowns in Oxenburg—"

"Pah!" Wulf's grandmother said. "Why not? All of Europe comes to Oxenburg for our lace and embroidered silks. Why would they not then also come to Oxenburg to buy gowns?"

Lily opened and then closed her mouth. "I don't know. I just never thought— Lace and embroidered silks? Wulf, is this true?"

He nodded. "Lady Charlotte can tell you, for she is wearing some now."

Lady Charlotte touched her lace collar. "Oh yes. It's

very expensive, but worth every penny. I bought a yard of it and it cost me dearly, but the detail is exquisite."

"It is settled, then. You shall have a shop in Oxenburg." When Lily didn't respond, he added, "If you want one on Bond Street, too, I shall buy you one there, as well."

"But . . . Wulf, you can't buy me a shop."

"Pah!" Wulf's grandmother said. "I cannot believe she thinks a prince cannot afford to pay for his own wife! If Wulf says he will buy you a shop, he will. Two might be excessive, but"—the grand duchess shrugged—"the funds are his to do with as he wishes."

"Funds? But . . ." Lily looked up at Wulf. "You have 'funds'?"

He hesitated. "Lily, my love, there is something I must tell you."

"But . . . you said you were poor."

"Ha!" his grandmother said. "A poor prince!"

"There are poor princes all over Europe," the duchess pointed out.

"Not in Oxenburg." His grandmother looked at Wulf. "Tell her. There should be no secrets."

Wulf sighed. "Lily, I never said I was poor. I said I was poorer than my brothers, which is true."

Lily pulled away. "You live in a *cottage*."

"For years, women have pursued me—or rather, my bank accounts. I did not wish anyone to marry me for money, so I came here where I am unknown and bought the cottage—"

"And the manse on the hill," his grandmother added. "It is a lovely house. Better than this one."

The duchess stiffened. "I beg your pardon?"

Lily's attention never left Wulf. "And so your brothers . . ."

"They are very wealthy. Very, very wealthy."

"That is true," his grandmother said. "Meanwhile Wulf has only four houses and one hunting lodge. His brothers all have many more."

"See?" Wulf said, a twinkle in his green eyes. "I am a very *modest* prince."

"You—how dare you tell me—and when I was so honest with you!"

"Moya, I am sorry. I didn't mean to trick you, but I had to know that you'd come to me for one reason only: that you loved me."

She frowned, wanting to be angry, but her sense of fairness poked her firmly between the shoulder blades. "I suppose I didn't really give you much choice, after I announced I had to marry a man of wealth."

"You had no choice. Or you didn't believe you did. But from the moment I saw you, I knew you were the one for me. And now, you will marry me and we will deal with these problems together, you and I."

"Together."

"Forever. For richer or poorer, in sickness and in health." He placed a finger under her chin and lifted her face to his. "Moya, I am yours no matter the circumstances."

Her lips quivered. "You haven't yet asked me."

He tugged her close. "I will ask you when we are alone. I know ways to make you say yes."

The duchess cleared her throat. "I believe that's close enough." She stood. "If it were me, I'd marry him just to spite him."

"I'm willing." Wulf grinned down at Lily. "But if you wish to be asked, then ask I shall. Lily, my love, will you marry me so that I may shower you from head to foot with gifts, hang upon your every word with breathless attention, smother you with kisses from head to toe, and—"

"—make a fool of yourself," his grandmother added. "For the love of God, answer the man so that we may leave this room and eat. I starve."

"I'm hungry, too," Lady Charlotte said.

Lily had to laugh. "Yes, then. Yes, I will marry you. And we'll talk about my modiste's shop at another time, for I very much wish to have one."

"Good! That is done." The duchess walked toward the door. "And we now have our marriage to announce. If anyone saw Huntley and Miss Emma before, they will think they mistook their eyes and that it was really the prince."

"They are both quite tall," Lady Charlotte said helpfully.

"Very true. Dinner must be ready by now and I— Oh, we forgot Huntley. Someone call Miss Gordon. I'm sure he'd be glad to see her face on waking."

"Most assuredly," Lily murmured, tucking her hand into the crook of Wulf's arm. "You really are a *wealthy* prince?"

"I have enough."

"*Four* houses?"

"Five. Tata forgot one. And the hunting lodge. I will show them to you." He led Lily to the dining hall. "Now, tell me more about these gowns you wish to make. I am the poorest of my brothers, after all, and if we could open enough modiste shops, we could overcome their wealth, which would be most delicious revenge for all of the teasing I've endured over the years. . . ."

Epilogue

From the Diary of the Duchess of Roxburghe
I will never again include insects as decorations.
While the release of the butterflies into the gardens
at the onset of the ball caused the collective gasp
of delight I'd envisioned, the creatures quickly lost
their appeal. Who knew butterflies like to *cling*?
And cling they did, to gowns and hair and glasses
of orgeat. They landed in plates of cake, and one
poor thing even caught on fire from straying too
close to a candle and then chased Lady Lansd-
owne about a gardenia bush before thankfully
expiring.

But the worst part of the evening was, sadly,
my beloved pugs. Although they were adorably
dressed as butterflies—thanks, I later learned, to
Miss Balfour's skillful needle—they had no com-
punction in seeing the masses of butterflies as some
sort of game, which involved snapping at the near-
est insect and eating it. And so they scrambled
about, trying to eat all of the butterflies they could,

while dressed like butterflies themselves. The entire scene had a macabre, cannibalistic feel to it. . . .

Early in the wee hours of the morning, Lady Charlotte had just settled her nightcap upon her head when a knock came at her door. Recognizing the duchess's brisk rap, she hopped from bed and hurried to the door.

The duchess swept into the room, a vision in her deep blue dressing gown, belted with a white sash, her red wig still pinned atop her head. "Ah, I was afraid you'd be abed."

Charlotte kept herself from glancing longingly at her bed. "No, no. I was just sitting by the fire. Would you like to join me?"

Margaret took a chair by the fireplace and Charlotte did the same. "My mind was too full to sleep."

"It was quite an eventful evening," Charlotte agreed.

"The poor pugs are quite worn-out."

"And full. They must have eaten twenty or thirty butterflies apiece."

Margaret shuddered. "Please do not remind me."

"I'm sorry I mentioned it." Lady Charlotte plopped her feet on a low stool that faced the fire, smiling when the duchess followed suit. "At least Miss Balfour's engagement to the prince drew the proper response. Everyone was quite aflutter over it."

"Aflutter?" Margaret threw up a hand. "*Must* you keep bringing up those damned butterflies?"

"I'm sorry," Charlotte said meekly. While the butterflies hadn't elevated the ball to the fairy tale–like event they'd wished, she'd been quite fascinated with the entire thing. *Such beautiful creatures and yet so dangerous. Who would have thought?*

"About the prince and Miss Balfour." The duchess sighed, a note of contentment in her tone. "Such a lovely announcement. No one could doubt they were deeply in love."

Charlotte smiled at the satisfaction in Margaret's voice. "So they are." It had been a lovely moment, hopefully one that the guests would remember more vividly than the butterfly debacle. "Everyone is talking about how you did it yet again, bringing about a magnificent match under your roof."

Margaret sighed happily. "I know. It would have been nice if we could have announced Huntley and Miss Gordon's good news, too, but they refused."

"The world will know soon enough." Charlotte wiggled her toes at the crackling fire. A moment later she said, "I hope you don't mind if I ask a question. One that's been vexing me for quite some time."

"Yes?"

"It's about Lord Kirk, who made that horrid loan with Lily's father."

Margaret's smile grew sly. "Ah, yes. Lord Kirk."

"He's one of your godsons." The duchess had too many godchildren to count, but as Charlotte wrote most of the duchess's correspondence, she knew them all, perhaps better than the duchess.

"Kirk's one of the first children I agreed to be a godmother to," Margaret said thoughtfully. "His mother was a very dear friend of mine. It's a pity he was injured. His life has not been happy."

Lord Kirk had once been a startlingly handsome man, but a horrid accident had left him scarred and reclusive. The man rarely ventured out, so it had been a surprise to see his carriage in the duchess's drive several months ago. "He is quite abrupt."

"He has no manners at all," Margaret agreed. "We'll have to work on that. If we're given the chance, of course."

"Margaret, you're up to something. It's a bit odd that Kirk should visit you, and then, shortly thereafter, Miss Balfour should arrive in desperate need of funds because of Lord Kirk's sudden actions."

"Odd?" Margaret's smile was that of the cat with the cream. "I would call it fortuitous."

"It did bring us Lily. But then tonight you told Lily that you planned on asking her youngest sister, Dahlia, to join us for the Christmas Ball. I saw that list yesterday, Margaret, and you've added Lord Kirk to it, too."

"I owe him a favor." Margaret yawned and stretched. "A very special favor."

"Does it involve Dahlia Balfour?"

"Perhaps." Margaret sighed happily and wiggled her toes before the fire as well. "We've much to do before the Christmas Ball, but it may be our biggest triumph yet."

Charlotte wanted to ask more questions, but then thought better of it. Perhaps in time Margaret would reveal her plans. And if not, it would at least be entertaining to watch them unfold. "Very well, Margaret. Then I shall look forward to the Christmas Ball."

"We all will, my dear. We all will."

Turn the page for a sneak peek at the next
delightful novel in *New York Times*
bestselling author KAREN HAWKINS's
Duchess Diaries series

*How to Entice
an Enchantress*

Available October 2013 from Pocket Books

One

From the Diary of the Duchess of Roxburghe
Ah, the burdens of fame! I am now known through-
out the length and breadth of Scotland (and, indeed,
most reaches of the kingdom) as the most talented
of all matchmakers, a veritable Queen of Hearts. It
is a burden that goes against every principle of my
character, for intruding upon the private lives of others is anathema to me. And yet, because of my vastly
successful entertainments and my uncanny ability
to spot potential matches between the most unlikely
people, I'm credited for assisting a number of
unmarried men and women make brilliant matches.

And so now, whenever I so much as mention
having a house party or a dance, I am positively
inundated with hints, suggestions, and pleas for invitations.

Those who know me realize the truth, of course,
which is that I never get involved in the affairs of others. Still, once in a great, great while, I am moved
to reach past my natural reserve and, with the most
delicate of touches, assist nature. But only with very,
very few, and very, very special cases. In fact, one

such case—the most challenging I've ever faced—is even now awaiting me in the blue salon. . . .

The Duchess of Roxburghe sailed down the stairs, her red wig firmly pinned upon her head. Her morning gown of pale blue silk swished as her pugs bounded after her, two of them trying to catch the fluttering ribbons of the tie at her waist.

There were six pugs in all—Feenie, Meenie, Teenie, Weenie, Beenie, and Randolph. Randolph was the oldest pug by several years. Graying and usually dignified, of late he'd refused to scramble down the steps after the younger pugs, but stood at the top step, looking so forlorn that her grace had assigned a footman to carry the pudgy pug.

Her butler, MacDougal, who even now stood at the bottom of the staircase watching the footman carry the pug, thought the measure extreme. Judging by the relative ease with which Randolph could bound up and down stairs when tempted with a tidbit, MacDougal thought her grace was being played the fool. Not that he would ever suggest such a thing aloud. He'd been with the duchess far too long not to know that while it was perfectly fine to allude to her grace's pugs being stubborn, unmannerly, and unruly, they were never to be accused of trickery or sloth.

Her grace reached the bottom step and the footman, Angus, stooped to place Randolph with the other pugs panting at her feet. "That's a good boy," cooed her grace.

"Thank ye." A proud expression bloomed on Angus's freckled face.

MacDougal locked a stern gaze on the young footman. "Her grace was talkin' to the dog, ye blatherin' fool."

Angus flushed. "Och, I'm sorry, yer grace."

"I was getting to you next," she said graciously. "You did a fine job carrying Randolph."

Angus couldn't have looked more pleased. "Thank ye, yer grace!" He sent a superior look to the butler, who scowled back so fiercely that the footman's grin disappeared.

Satisfied that he had quelled the upstart, MacDougal turned to the duchess and offered a pleasant smile. "Yer grace, yer guest is in the blue salon, as ye requested, but we dinna ken where Lady Charlotte might be."

"Perhaps she fell asleep in a corner somewhere. She's gotten very bad about that since she's taken to reading novels at all times of the night."

MacDougal nodded thoughtfully. "Verrah good, yer grace. I'll send someone to look upon every settee in the castle." He cast his eye toward the hapless Angus. "Off wit' ye, and dinna miss a single settee until ye find Lady Charlotte."

"Aye, sir!" Angus hurried off.

Her grace glanced at the doors leading to the blue salon. "I hope you made our guest comfortable."

"Aye, yer grace, we did wha' we could, but—" The butler sighed. "'Tis no' me place to say naught o' yer visitors, but this one is a bit—" He scrunched his nose, searching for the word. Finally, his brow cleared. "*Abrupt.*"

"You mean rude," she said in a dry tone.

"I would ne'er say such a thing aboot one o' yer guests, yer grace."

"I would. 'Tis a well-known fact that Lord Kirk is rude and growls at everyone in sight. He has beastly manners."

"Tha' might well be understandable considerin'—"

The butler glanced about the empty hallway before he tapped his cheek.

"Because of his scars."

"Jus' so, yer grace. 'Tis a horrid sight. He's a handsome man except fer tha', which makes it all the worse. He limps, too, so he may well be missin' a limb fer all we know. If I had all o' those problems—scars and limps and wha' no'—I might be a bit rude meself."

"I'd hope not," the duchess said impatiently. "There's no excuse for bad manners."

"Verrah true, yer grace. I dinna suppose he's here fer yer help findin' a match? Tha' might be a tall order."

"Of course that's why he's here. He's my godson, and Lady Charlotte and I are quite aware of the challenge he presents. His mother—God rest her soul—was a dear, dear friend." She looked at the doors and straightened her shoulders. "And now, to begin. Please send Charlotte as soon as you find her." Much like a general marching into battle, the duchess crossed to the blue salon, the pugs waddling after her.

As soon as the door closed behind her, Margaret eyed her guest. Tall and broad shouldered, Lord Kirk stood by the wide windows that overlooked the front lawn. The bright morning sunlight bathed his skin with gold. His dark brown hair was longer than fashion dictated and curled over his collar, a streak of gray at his temple. In profile, he was starkly beautiful but bold, a statue of a Greek god of the sea.

At the rustle of her skirts, his expression tightened and, with a lingering look at the sun-splashed lawn, he turned.

Though she knew what to expect, she had to fight the urge to exclaim in dismay. One side of his face was scarred by a thick, horrid slash that separated his eyebrow halfway across, skipped over one eye, and then slashed down his cheek, touching the corner of his mouth and ending on his chin. It had been a clean cut, but whoever had stitched it together had done so with such crudeness that it made her heart ache.

Had he been in the hands of an accomplished surgeon, Margaret had little doubt that his scar, though still long, would not be so puckered or drawn. But Kirk had been at sea when he'd obtained his injury and thus was left to whatever "doctor" was available aboard the ship.

He inclined his head now, barely bowing, the stiffness of his gesture emphasized by the thick, gold-handled cane he held in one hand.

Margaret realized with an inward grimace that she'd been staring and silently castigated herself. The pugs danced about her feet as she swept forward. "Lord Kirk, how are you?"

"I'm as well as one can be when carrying a scar that causes even society's most stalwart hostess to gasp in horror."

"I might have stared, but I'm certain I didn't gasp," she returned firmly. "I cannot see your scar without wishing I could have put my own physician to it. His stitching is superb."

Kirk's smile was more of a sneer. "I assure you that I am quite used to stares."

"Yes, well, it was rude of me and few people have cause to call me such." She gestured to the chairs before the fireplace. "Shall we?" The pugs followed as she made her way to the seats.

Elderly Randolph paused by Lord Kirk to give his shoes a friendly sniff. The man didn't spare the dog a glance, but brushed past him, completely ignoring the poor creature.

Margaret had to fight a flare of temper. Randolph had done nothing to deserve such a snub. The man was beyond rude. *What have I gotten myself into?*

Kirk limped to the chair she'd indicated by the fire. She noted how he leaned heavily upon his cane as he walked, moving as if one leg would not bend properly. He didn't wait for her to be seated, but sank into his chair, wincing visibly.

She sighed in exasperation and took her seat. "Your leg must pain you in this cold weather."

He cast her a sour look, making the lines upon his face even more pronounced. "A brilliant assumption. Will you next note that my eyes are brown and that I favor my left hand?"

That did it. "Alasdair, stop being a prig."

He flushed, but after a short silence, he burst into a deep laugh that surprised her. "I haven't heard that name or that tone since my mother died."

He looked so much younger when he laughed that Margaret's heart softened instantly. "Your mother would never have stood for you acting in such a manner. Now come. What brings you?"

Kirk leaned the cane to one side. "I came to you for help and I can see that, because of my blasted temper, I've somehow managed to raise your hackles. Ironically, that is why I need your assistance." He gave a sour smile. "Your grace, as you've noticed, I'm not very good at the niceties. Since my wife died seven years ago, I've lived alone and I rarely mingle with society. I fear that's ruined what few graces I once possessed."

"So I see. I can only be glad that your mother is not alive to find out. She would have you by the ear for letting all of her hard work disappear."

His eyes gleamed with humor. "So she would have." His voice, a deep, rich baritone, warmed. "She wasn't afraid to let her opinion be known."

"Far from it. I always admired her for that."

"She admired you, too, which is why she named you my godmother."

"You were one of my first." Margaret sighed regretfully. "I cannot help but think that if your mother were still with us, you wouldn't need me to assist you in your current predicament."

"Ah yes. My predicament." His expression darkened. "When I came to you some months ago, we spoke of a—"

The door flew open and Lady Charlotte flew into the room, a book tucked under her arm and one hand on her mobcap, which sat askew, the lace flapping over her ear. The pugs began barking hysterically as they ran toward the door.

"Hush," Charlotte scolded.

The pugs lowered their barking to an occasional woof, and wagged their tails instead.

She paused to pat one or two before she hurried to where Margaret sat. "Lud, Margaret, I had just reached the page where Rosaline kisses Lord Kestrel when a footman practically dragged me into the foyer and— Oh! Lord Kirk!" On catching sight of his face, she blinked, but recovered quickly and curtsied. "I'm sorry, but I didn't see you there."

Kirk inclined his head as if he were a king, but made no move to stand and welcome Lady Charlotte.

Margaret had to fight the urge to reach out one of her slippered feet and kick him in the shin for his lack of manners. "Lord Kirk, you remember Lady Charlotte?"

"Of course."

"How do you do?" Charlotte came forward, her hand outstretched in greeting.

Still not rising, he shook it politely enough, but when Charlotte took a seat near Margaret, he frowned.

Margaret waved her hand. "Pray continue, Lord Kirk."

"No, thank you," he replied in a curt tone. "I don't wish my personal matters to be discussed in public."

Charlotte, tucking her book away, smiled sweetly, her soft blue-gray eyes fixed on him. "Oh, but I already know your personal matters. *All* of them."

"Lady Charlotte is my confidante," Margaret added. "Very little happens at Floors Castle without her assistance."

Kirk's mouth thinned, but after a moment of inner struggle, he gave an impatient sigh. "Fine. I don't suppose it makes any difference at this point. Your grace, several months ago you offered to assist me in fixing my interest with Miss Dahlia Balfour in exchange for a favor that I found most distasteful."

"That of pressing her father, Sir Balfour, to repay a loan you'd so generously made him. I remember."

"Exactly. I had no need for that money and I would have gladly made it a gift, but for reasons you never explained, you felt it in the best interest of everyone concerned that I press for repayment, which I did."

"Your actions sent Lily Balfour running to me, her godmother, looking for assistance. And with happy results, too."

"*Very* happy," Lady Charlotte said. "The happiest of all." In case Kirk didn't understand, she leaned forward and whispered, "Marriage."

An impatient look crossed his face. "Are you saying

that because I pressed for repayment of that loan, Lily Balfour attempted to contract an eligible marriage?"

"She didn't 'attempt' to contract an eligible marriage; she did so. A *most* eligible marriage, in fact. She's blissful."

Kirk's lips thinned. "While the outcome might have been happy for Miss Lily, it was less so for me."

Margaret arched a brow. "Oh? Sir Balfour hasn't repaid you?"

"Yes, he has, but my issue is not with the funds, but with Miss Dahlia's opinion. Because I pressed her father for the payment of that loan, Miss Dahlia now thinks I'm the lowest, vilest, most reprehensible man to walk the earth."

Margaret tried to look surprised, but must have failed, for Kirk's brows lowered to the bridge of his nose. "You knew she'd be angry with me."

"I didn't *know*. I merely *suspected*."

"And yet you still asked me to pursue that route, even though you knew my feelings for Miss Dahlia."

"Oh!" Lady Charlotte clapped her hands together. "You have feelings for Miss Dahlia. How lovely!"

"No, it's not lovely," Kirk snapped. "Dahlia Balfour sees me as no more than an older, decrepit neighbor who rudely pressed her father for the repayment of a loan that sent her sister off to sell herself in marriage!"

Charlotte's smile faded. "Oh. That does sound quite villainous."

Margaret tried to rally. "Kirk, I'm sure Miss Dahlia was a bit put out, but she'll come around."

"No, your grace. She's more than 'put out.' She's furious."

"Nonsense. It's been several months since the incident; surely she's softened some."

"You don't know Dahlia if you think she will soften her feelings toward anyone she believes has insulted her family."

Margaret waved aside his words. "Surely she knows that Sir Balfour was at fault for asking for that loan to begin with."

Charlotte nodded. "*And* for pretending that he wanted the funds to do something for his daughters, as he told you when he first borrowed the sum."

"That was a lie," Margaret continued, "for he spent it on expanding his greenhouses and in buying roses, which he breeds."

"It doesn't matter what he did with the funds," Kirk said firmly. "Dahlia's protective of her family, right or wrong. And now she believes that I selfishly demanded those funds and, apparently, sent her sister running off to contract a marriage."

Margaret sighed. "So you think the harm is irreparable?"

"She won't speak to me, won't answer my letters, won't even look in my direction when we meet. It's as if I'm dead to her."

"Oh dear." Charlotte looked at Margaret. "This may be more difficult than we imagined."

Margaret thought the same thing, but she wasn't about to give up before she'd even begun. "Lord Kirk, whatever ill Miss Dahlia thinks of you for your involvement with the loan I can rectify when she comes to visit by simply telling her the truth—that you pressed for the loan at my request."

"You can't tell her that, for then she'll want to know why I agreed, and you cannot admit that it was because I wished your help in securing her affections. We are stuck, your grace. We cannot admit the truth."

"Oh dear," Charlotte said again. "I hadn't thought of that."

Neither had Margaret. "We'll think of something, so never fear. Let me put my mind to it. Meanwhile, there are other issues to be addressed."

Kirk rubbed his temple and Margaret noticed how long and beautiful his hands were, like those of an artist or a violinist. It was odd to see such a thing on such a gruff man.

He dropped his hand with a sigh. "Your grace, this was a mistake. I came to you because I—" He scowled. "To be blunt, I'm desperate. I've lived a solitary life since my wife died and I'm not fit company for someone as lively as Dahlia."

"You're a widower?" Charlotte asked.

"My wife died on our return from India seven years ago."

Charlotte clicked her tongue in sympathy. "Did she die from a spider bite? There are over twenty types of spiders in India."

Margaret looked at Charlotte. "How do you know that?"

"There was an article in the paper. I read it just yesterday."

"No." Kirk's voice crackled with impatience. "My wife and I were sailing back from India when a fire broke out on the ship. We didn't realize it, but in addition to our luggage, the ship was carrying kegs of gunpowder."

"Goodness! How dangerous."

"I found out later that the captain had hidden the kegs on board to make additional money."

Charlotte shook her head. "That must have been devastating."

"You have no idea."

Margaret's heart tightened at the bleakness in Kirk's voice. "Lord Kirk and the surviving crew were left adrift for several weeks before another ship found them."

"Lord Kirk, I'm so sorry," Charlotte said.

"It is history," he said shortly. "After the accident, I tried to rejoin society, but without Lyla, it was useless, empty. Because of my injuries, I wasn't able to enjoy dances and such and"—he took a deep breath—"people were not kind. They disliked looking across the dinner table at my scar and I can't blame them; I've no wish to see it myself. And so I left society and buried myself in my house and books, never dreaming that one day I'd meet Miss Dahlia Balfour."

"And things changed," Margaret said.

"Yes. The Balfours have been my neighbors since before I wed Lyla, but I'd never really had much commerce with them. The girls are all six or seven younger than I am, and after I married, I rarely saw them. One day, I went to pick up some books I'd ordered and I met Dahlia coming out of the store. I knew her, of course, for our carriages passed each other upon occasion, but she saw the books and her eyes lit up." He shook his head in wonderment. "We started talking about books we liked and which authors we enjoyed and— I can't describe it, but we stood there in the street, for *two hours*, quoting poetry and discussing stories we'd read—" He turned to Margaret with a bemused look. "It was as if, in opening a book together, we discovered ourselves between the pages."

Margaret nodded. *Goodness, he is head over heels. I wonder if he realizes how much. . . .*

"Oh my," Charlotte said in a breathless voice. "How *romantic*."

Kirk frowned. "I wouldn't call it 'romantic.' Dahlia

and I have a lot in common, true. We both like to read, we love poetry, and we enjoy the same music, too."

"Surely you didn't play music there in the street, too?"

"At that chance meeting, I invited Dahlia to feel free to borrow whatever books she might wish to. I have an extensive collection, you know, and she was in heaven when she saw my library. She began to visit me every week or so after that and we'd talk about whatever book she'd read. Once while she was there, I convinced her to play the pianoforte I had brought from France as a wedding present for Lyla. Dahlia's amazingly talented." He nodded, almost to himself. "She will make a suitable bride."

"'Suitable'?" Margaret said, almost stuttering over the word. "Is that all you can say?"

Kirk flushed. "Yes."

There was a stubborn note to his voice that said far more than he was able or willing to. "I see," Margaret said, and rather thought that she did. "Kirk, before we continue, I must be plain. While I will do what I can to assist you in making a case for Miss Dahlia, you must make an effort as well."

"I must make an effort? To do what?"

"Whatever I say." She tapped her chin with a finger, her gaze never wavering. "Fortunately, you have a lot of potential."

Lady Charlotte tilted her head to one side, regarding him from head to toe. "Potential, but *unrealized* potential."

While Kirk did not adhere to fashion in any way— his brown coat and trousers were at least a decade old in style—he was very neatly dressed, his neckcloth knotted about his throat, the ends tucked into his waistcoat, his boots firmly placed upon the ground. There was a solidness about him that a woman could appreciate. *An older woman, yes, but perhaps not a younger one. No, if he wishes to woo Dahlia Balfour, he will have to gain some polish.* "We must get him a tailor."

"New clothes, definitely," Charlotte murmured. "And boots."

"And someone to teach him to tie a neckcloth properly."

"Oh yes." Charlotte reached down and picked up a pug that was sitting at her feet and plopped him in her lap. "Lord Kirk, I don't suppose you can dance?"

"Dance? With this?" He gestured toward his knee. "No, dammit."

Lady Charlotte tsked. "Such language."

"He'll have to work on that, too," Margaret said thoughtfully, her mind racing as she made a mental list. "And his address, for he's rude as a——"

"That's enough." Kirk grasped his cane and stood. "Forget this. I did not come here to be insulted."

"No, you came to be transformed into a man worthy of a beautiful woman, one you clearly believe is out of your reach." Margaret waited until her words had sunk in. "She's lovely."

"Yes."

"And lively as well, I take it."

"Very much so."

"And intelligent——"

"She's everything, damn you! And she's far too good for me. What the hell was I thinking to come here? I should have admitted the truth—that she's not for me—and just been done with it, but oh no. I *hoped.*" He laughed bitterly and began to limp toward the door, his knuckles white about the cane.

Charlotte exchanged a surprised glance with Margaret.

"Lord Kirk," Margaret called. "Please. Just one question and then you may go. For your mother's sake."

He was almost to the door, but at her words, he paused and then turned. "Yes?"

"You're twenty-nine years of age?"

He nodded once.

"That's all?" Charlotte exclaimed. "I would have thought—" She caught his dark gaze and flushed. "I mean, twenty-nine is a lovely, *lovely* age."

"No, it's not a lovely age." Margaret stood and walked toward him. "It's the age of a man who should be settled and married."

His eyes blazed with anger. "I'm finished with this conversation. It was a mistake. I'm sorry I wasted your time." His scowl grew blacker with each word, the scar making him look particularly sinister. He started to turn back to the door.

"Since you don't wish to win Miss Balfour's regard, then you won't mind if I turn her attention elsewhere?"

He stiffened in place. "*You* will turn her attention elsewhere?"

He really had the most amazingly beautiful eyes, sherry brown and thickly fringed. Looking at them made her think of his mother and the memory stiffened Margaret's resolve. "We'll need two months of your time."

"Two months? For what?"

"It'll take that long to teach you the basics of seduction."

His face bloomed red. "Seduction?"

"Or courtship, whichever you wish to call it."

"It will also take that long to order your new wardrobe," Charlotte added. "That coat—" She shook her head.

Kirk regarded his coat. "What's wrong with my coat?"

Charlotte looked as if she might giggle, though she wisely refrained. "It's out of fashion and ill fits you. Worsted is a horrid material for a coat, and your cravat is a mere knot, rather than a properly tied arrangement."

"I'm surprised you allowed me to enter your presence."

"You're a friend of her grace's," Lady Charlotte pointed out fairly. "I had no choice."

Lord Kirk's lips thinned. "Is there anything else I must change?"

Margaret tapped a finger on her chin and looked him over. "Your hair."

"My hair? What's wrong with my hair?"

"It's far too long for current fashion. It's a bit aging."

"I am my age, madam. I cannot change that."

"You look thirty and seven, perhaps even forty."

He started to turn back to the door once more, but as he did so, Margaret added, "Leave if you wish, but know this: Miss Balfour has already accepted an invitation to my Christmas Ball. She will attend my house party for the three weeks beforehand, and she will not leave unattached."

"You don't know that."

"But I do. I shall see to it that she receives at least one offer, if not more. It's the least I can do."

"You would work against me?"

"While I genuinely wish you to succeed in your endeavors, I cannot ignore that Miss Dahlia is also one of my godchildren."

"Her grace has so many," Lady Charlotte added.

"But only a few who warrant my attention. Miss Dahlia is one of them. She believes—as was the truth when I asked her—that I invited her to my house party for the express purpose of assisting her in making a fortuitous match."

He fixed an incredulous gaze on Margaret. "She specifically stated that?"

"Yes. At the time, as I thought you were serious about wishing to win her, I committed myself to that end. I cannot rescind my offer merely because you are getting cold feet."

"I'm not getting cold feet. I am simply questioning the intelligence of this idea. I cannot transform into something I'm not."

"Something you're not? What's that? A gentleman? Your mother would weep to hear such an admission."

His jaw tightened. "As much as I loved her, my mother is dead."

"But you're not, and you're responsible for living up to your potential. The invitation has been issued; Dahlia Balfour will leave this house attached to someone. Whether that someone is you or not is entirely your—and her—decision."

The white lines around his mouth told Margaret how furious her words had made him, but he did not leave. Indeed, he stood rooted to the floor as if every word she'd uttered had nailed him in place. *That's promising.*

Margaret turned away, leaving him to collect himself as well as he could. "Then we are understood, Lord Kirk. You will put yourself in my hands for the next two months and by the time Miss Dahlia Balfour arrives, you will be ready to meet her, a new—and vastly improved—man."

There was a long silence and then he snapped out, "Fine. I will admit that I need some polish. I'll return home and make arrangements to spend those two months here, but beware, for I will not be turned into a fop!"

"Oh no," Charlotte said. "We could never hope for that in two months. Just a gentleman of address. That will have to do."

Kirk didn't seem much impressed with this, either, and with a stiff and abrupt farewell, he left.

As soon as the door closed behind him, Margaret returned to her seat and dropped into it, her gown fluttering about her. "Good God, but that was ridiculously difficult!"

Charlotte nodded. "He looked as if he could breathe fire."

"He's furious, there's no doubt, but he asked for my help and now he will take it." Margaret stretched her feet before her and plopped them on a small footstool. Feenie rose and jumped into her lap.

"Do you think Kirk can learn what he must in such a short time?"

"He has to or the fairy tale will be quite offset."

"I hate an offset fairy tale."

"Don't we all? Fortunately, we have a secret weapon."

Charlotte's eyes brightened. "We do?" She waited. When the silence merely grew, she sighed. "You're not going to tell me what it is."

"In due time, Charlotte. In due time."

Charlotte reached to remove her book from where she'd tucked it away and began to search for her place. "Fine. Whatever your weapon might be, I can only hope it will tame our Beast before Beauty arrives."

"So do I, Charlotte. So do I."